CALCULATED IN DEATH

CALCULATED IN DEATH

J. D. ROBB

ISIS
LARGE PRINT
Oxford

First published in Great Britain 2013
by
Piatkus Books
an imprint of Little, Brown Book Group

Published in Large Print 2014 by ISIS Publishing Ltd.,
7 Centremead, Osney Mead, Oxford OX2 0ES
by arrangement with
Little, Brown Book Group
an Hachette UK Company

CIP data is available for this title from the British Library

ISBN 978–0–7531–9236–8 (hb)
ISBN 978–0–7531–9237–5 (pb)

Printed and bound in Great Britain by
T. J. International Ltd., Padstow, Cornwall

Poverty wants much; but avarice, everything.
PUBLILIUS SYRUS

Money without honour is a disease.
BALZAC

CHAPTER
ONE

A killer wind hurled bitter November air, toothy little knives to gnaw at the bones. She'd forgotten her gloves, but that was just as well as she'd have ruined yet another overpriced pair once she'd sealed up.

For now, Lieutenant Eve Dallas stuck her frozen hands in the warm pockets of her coat and looked down at death.

The woman lay at the bottom of the short stairway leading down to what appeared to be a lower-level apartment. From the angle of the head, Eve didn't need the medical examiner to tell her the neck was broken.

Eve judged her as middle forties. Not wearing a coat, Eve mused, though the vicious wind wouldn't trouble her now. Dressed for business — suit jacket, turtleneck, pants, good boots with low heels. Probably fashionable, but Eve would leave that call to her partner when Detective Peabody arrived on scene.

No jewelry, at least not visible. Not even a wrist unit.

No handbag, no briefcase or file bag.

No litter, no graffiti in the stairwell. Nothing but the body, slumped against the wall.

At length she turned to the uniformed officer who'd responded to the 911. "What's the story?"

"The call came in at two-twelve. My partner and I were only two blocks away, hitting a twenty-four/seven. We arrived at two-fourteen. The owner of the unit, Bradley Whitestone, and an Alva Moonie were on the sidewalk. Whitestone stated they hadn't entered the unit, which is being rehabbed — and is unoccupied. They found the body when he brought Moonie to see the apartment."

"At two in the morning."

"Yes, sir. They stated they'd been out this evening, dinner, then a bar. They'd had a few, Lieutenant."

"Okay."

"My partner has them in the car."

"I'll talk to them later."

"We determined the victim was deceased. No ID on her. No bag, no jewelry, no coat. Pretty clear her neck's broken. Visually, there's some other marks on her — bruised cheek, split lip. Looks like a mugging gone south. But . . ." The uniform flushed slightly. "It doesn't feel like it."

Interested, Eve gave a go-ahead nod. "Because?"

"It sure wasn't a snatch and run, figuring the coat. That takes a little time. And if she fell or got pushed down the stairs, why is she over against the side there instead of at the bottom of the steps? Out of sight from the sidewalk. It feels more like a dump. Sir."

"Are you angling for a slot in Homicide, Officer Turney?"

"No disrespect intended, Lieutenant."

"None taken. She could've taken a bad fall down the steps, landed wrong, broke her neck. Mugger goes down after her, hauls her over out of sight, takes the coat, and the rest."

"Yes, sir."

"It doesn't feel like it. But we need more than how it feels. Stand by, Officer. Detective Peabody's en route." As she spoke, Eve opened her field kit, took out her Seal-It.

She coated her hands, her boots as she surveyed the area.

This sector of New York's East Side held quiet — at least at this hour. Most apartment windows and storefronts were dark, businesses closed, even the bars. There would be some after-hours establishments still rolling, but not close enough for witnesses.

They'd do a canvass, but odds were slim someone would pop out who'd seen what happened here. Add in the bitter cold, as 2060 seemed determined to go out clinging with its icy fingers, most people would be tucked up inside, in the warm.

Just as she'd been, curled up against Roarke, before the call.

That's what you get for being a cop, she thought, or in Roarke's case, for marrying one.

Sealed, she went down the stairs, studied the door to the unit first, then moved in to crouch beside the body.

Yeah, middle forties, light brown hair clipped back from her face. A little bruising on the right cheekbone, some dried blood on the split lip. Both ears pierced, so if she'd been wearing earrings, the killer had taken the time to remove them rather than rip them off.

Lifting the hand, Eve noted abraded flesh on the heel. Like a rug burn, she mused before she pressed the right thumb to her ID pad.

Dickenson, Marta, she read. Mixed-race female, age forty-six. Married Dickenson, Denzel, two offspring, and an Upper East Side address. Employed Brewer, Kyle, and Martini, an accounting firm with an office eight blocks away.

As she took out her gauges, her short brown hair fluttered in the wind. She hadn't thought to yank on a hat. Her eyes, nearly the same gilded brown as her hair, remained cool and flat. She didn't think about the husband, the kids, the friends, the family — not yet. She thought of the body, the position, the area, the time of death — twenty-two-fifty.

What were you doing, Marta, blocks from work, from home on a frigid November night?

She shined her light over the pants, noted traces of blue fiber on the black cloth. Carefully, she tweezed off two, bagged them, marked the pants for the sweepers.

She heard Peabody's voice over her head, and the uniform's answer. Eve straightened. Her leather coat billowed at the hem around her long, lean frame as she turned to watch Peabody — or what she could see of her partner — clomp down the steps.

Peabody had thought of a hat, had remembered her gloves. The pink — Jesus pink — ski hat with its sassy little pom-pom covered her dark hair and the top of her face right down to the eyes. A multicolored scarf wound around and around just above the plum-colored puffy

4

coat. The hat matched the pink cowboy boots Eve had begun to suspect Peabody wore even in bed.

"How can you walk with all that on?"

"I hiked to the subway, then from the subway, but I stayed warm. Jeez." One quick gleam of sympathy flicked across Peabody's face. "She doesn't even have a coat."

"She's not complaining. Marta Dickenson," Eve began, and gave Peabody the salients.

"It's a ways from her office and her place. Maybe she was walking from one to the other, but why wouldn't she take the subway, especially on a night like this?"

"That's a question. This unit's being rehabbed. It's empty. That's handy, isn't it? The way she's in the corner there? She shouldn't have been spotted until morning."

"Why would a mugger care when?"

"That's another question. Following that would be, if he did, how'd he know this unit's unoccupied?"

"Lives in the area?" Peabody suggested. "Is part of the rehab crew?"

"Maybe. I want a look inside, but we'll talk to the nine-one-one callers first. Go ahead and notify the ME."

"The sweepers?"

"Not yet."

Eve climbed the stairs, walked to the black-and-white. Even as she signaled to the cop inside, a man pushed out of the back.

"Are you in charge?" Words tumbled over each other in a rush of nerves.

"Lieutenant Dallas. Mr. Whitestone?"

"Yes, I —"

"You notified the police."

"Yes. Yes, as soon as we found the — her. She was . . . we were —"

"You own this unit?"

"Yes." A sharply attractive man in his early thirties, he took a long breath, expelling it in a chilly fog. When he spoke again, his voice leveled, his words slowed. "Actually, my partners and I own the building. There are eight units — third and fourth floors." His gaze tracked up. No hat for him either, Eve mused, but a wool topcoat in city black and a black-and-red-striped scarf.

"I own the lower unit outright," he continued. "We're rehabbing so we can move our business here, first and second floors."

"Which is what? Your business?"

"We're financial consultants. The WIN Group. Whitestone, Ingersol, and Newton. W-I-N."

"Got it."

"I'll live in the downstairs unit, or that was the plan. I don't —"

"Why don't you run me through your evening," Eve suggested.

"Brad?"

"Stay in the car where it's warm, Alva."

"I can't sit anymore." The woman who slid out was blonde and sleek and tucked into some kind of animal fur and thigh-high leather boots with high skinny heels. She hooked her arm through Whitestone's arm.

6

They looked like a set, Eve thought. Both pretty, well-dressed, and showing signs of shock.

"Lieutenant Dallas." Alva held out a hand. "You don't remember me?"

"No."

"We met for five seconds at the Big Apple Gala last spring. I'm one of the committee chairs. Doesn't matter," she said with a shake of her head as the wind streamed through her yard of hair. "This is horrible. That poor woman. They even took her coat. I don't know why that bothers me so much, but it seems cruel."

"Did either of you touch the body?"

"No." Whitestone took over. "We had dinner, then we went for drinks. At the Key Club, just a couple blocks down. I was telling Alva what we've been doing here, and she was interested, so we walked over so I could give her a tour. My place is nearly done, so . . . I was getting out my key, about to plug in the code when Alva screamed. I didn't even see her, Lieutenant, the woman. I didn't even see her, not until Alva screamed."

"She was back in the corner," Alva said. "At first, even when I screamed I thought she was a sidewalk sleeper. I didn't realize . . . then I did. We did."

She leaned into Whitestone when he put an arm around her waist. "We didn't touch her," Whitestone said. "I stepped over, closer, but I could see . . . I could tell she was dead."

"Brad wanted me to go inside, where it's warm, but I couldn't. I couldn't wait inside knowing she was out here, in the cold. The police came so fast."

"Mr. Whitestone, I'm going to want a list of your partners, and of the people working on the building."

"Of course."

"If you'd give that and your contact information to my partner, you can go home. We'll be in touch."

"We can go?" Alva asked her.

"For now. I'd like your permission to go inside the unit, the building."

"Sure. Anything you need. I have keys and codes," he began.

"I've got a master. If there's any trouble, I'll let you know."

"Lieutenant?" Alva called her again as Eve turned to go. "When I met you, before, I thought what you did was glamorous. In a way. Like the Icove case, and how it's going to be a major vid. It seemed exciting. But it's not." Alva's gaze swept back toward the stairs. "It's hard and it's sad."

"It's the job," Eve said simply, and walked back toward the steps. "We'll wait to canvass until morning," she told Officer Turney. "Nobody's going to tell us much if we wake them up at this hour. The building's vacant, not just the unit. See that the wits get where they need to go. What's your house, Turney?"

"We're out of the one-three-six."

"And your CO?"

"Sergeant Gonzales, sir."

"If you want in on the canvass, I'll clear it with your CO. Be here at oh-seven-thirty."

"Yes, sir!" She all but snapped a salute.

Mildly amused, Eve walked down the stairs, cleared the locks and codes, and entered the lower unit.

"Lights on full," she ordered, pleased when they flashed on.

The living area — she assumed as it wasn't yet furnished — provided a generous space. The walls — what was painted — glowed like freshly toasted bread, and the floors — what wasn't covered with tarps — gleamed in a rich dark finish. Materials, supplies, all stacked neatly in corners, provided evidence of ongoing work.

Tidy, and efficient, probably down to the final details.

So why was one tarp bunched, unlike the others, exposing a wide area of that gleaming floor?

"Like someone slipped on it, or wrestled on it," she said as she walked over, let her recorder scan the width, the length before she bent to straighten it.

"Lots of paint splatters, but . . ."

She crouched, took out her flashlight and shined it over the tarp. "That sure looks like blood to me. Just a few drops."

She opened her kit, took a small sample before marking the spot for the sweepers.

She moved away, into a wide galley-style kitchen, more gleaming and glowing under protective tarps and seals.

By the time she'd done the first pass-through — master bedroom and bath, second bedroom or office and bath — Peabody came in.

"I started runs on the wits," Peabody began. "The woman's loaded. Not Roarke loaded, but she can afford that coat and those really mag boots."

"Yeah, it showed."

"He's doing just fine, too. Second-generation money, but he's earning his own. He's got a D&D, but it's ten years back. Her deal is speeding. She's got a shitload of speeding tickets, mostly to and from her place in the Hamptons."

"You know how it is when you want to get to the Hamptons. What do you see, Peabody?"

"Really good work, attention to detail, money well spent, and deep enough pockets to be able to spend it on really good work and attention to detail. And . . ." Unwinding a couple feet of her mile of scarf, Peabody stepped over to Eve's marker. "What might be blood on this tarp."

"The tarp was bunched up, like a rug when you take a skid on it. All the others are laid out fairly smoothly."

"Accidents happen in construction. Blood gets spilled. But."

"Yeah, but. Blood on a tarp and a body outside the door. Her lip's split, and there's dried blood on it. Not a lot of blood, so somebody might not even notice any dripped on the tarp, especially when the tarp bunched up."

"They brought her in here?" Forehead furrowed, Peabody looked back at the door. "I didn't see any signs of forced entry, but I'll check again."

"They didn't force it. Maybe picked it, but that takes time. More likely they had the code, or a damn good reader."

"Putting all that into the mix, it's not a simple mugging gone bad."

"No. He's not smart. The killer. If he's strong enough to break her neck, why smack her? She's got a bruise on the right cheek and that split lip."

"Punched her. Left jab."

"I don't think a punch, that's really stupid. Backhand. A guy only slaps a woman if he wants to humiliate her. He punches if he's pissed, drunk, or doesn't give a shit about blood and damage. He backhands when he wants to hurt, and intimidate. Plus it looked like a backhand — knuckles on bone."

She'd been hit in the face enough to recognize the signs.

"Smart and controlled enough not to punch, not to beat on her," Eve said, "but not smart enough to leave the area clean. Not smart enough just to take the tarp with him. She's got what looks like a rug burn on the heel of her right hand, and blue fibers on her pants, maybe carpet from a vehicle."

"You think somebody grabbed her, forced her into a vehicle."

"Possible. You have to get her here, to this empty unit, do what you do. He's smart enough to take her valuables, including the coat, to play the bad mugging card. But he left her boots. Good boots, looked fairly new. If you're a mugger who'd take the time to drag off the coat, why leave her boots?"

"If he brought her in here, he wanted privacy," Peabody pointed out. "And time. It doesn't look like rape. Why get her dressed again?"

"She was going to or coming from work."

"From," Peabody confirmed. "When I ran her I got an alert. Her husband contacted the police. She didn't come home. Working late, but didn't come home. She spoke to him via 'link as she was leaving the office — according to the alert — and that was shortly after twenty-two hundred."

"That's a lot of data for an alert, especially one on a woman who's a few hours late getting home."

"I thought so, too, so I ran him. Denzel Dickenson, Esquire. He's Judge Gennifer Yung's baby brother."

"That would do it." Eve blew out a breath. "This just got sticky."

"Yeah, I got that."

"Call in the sweepers, Peabody, and flag it priority. No point in not covering all asses when dealing with the judge's dead sister-in-law."

She pushed a hand through her hair, recalculated. She'd intended to go by the victim's office building, retracing the likely route, getting a feel for the area. Then backtracking before continuing to the victim's residence, gauging the ground, figuring the timing, the direction. But now —"

"The husband's been pacing the floor for hours by now. Let's go give him the bad news."

"I hate this part," Peabody murmured.

"When you don't, it's time to find another line of work."

The Dickensons rated one of the four penthouse condos with roof garden atop one of the Upper East Side's dignified buildings. All elegant gray stone and glass, it rose and rounded above a neighborhood where nannies and dog walkers ruled the sidewalks and parks.

Night security required clearance, which equaled, to Eve, a pain in the ass.

"Dallas, Lieutenant Eve, and Peabody, Detective Delia." She held her badge up to the security screen. "We need to speak with Denzel Dickenson. Penthouse B."

Please state the nature of your business, the butter-smooth computerized voice intoned.

"That would come under the heading of none of yours. Scan the badges and authorize access."

I'm sorry, Penthouse B is secured for the night. Access to the building and any unit therein requires clearance from the manager, an authorized tenant, or notification of emergency status.

"Listen to me, you half-ass, chip-brained dipshit, this is official police business. Scan the badges and clear access. Otherwise I'll have warrants issued immediately for the arrest of the building manager, the head of security, and the owners on the charge of obstruction of justice. And you'll be in a junk pile by dawn."

Inappropriate language is in violation of —

"Inappropriate language? Oh, I've got plenty more inappropriate language for you. Peabody, contact APA Cher Reo and begin processing warrants for all appropriate parties. Let's see how they like getting dragged out of bed at this hour, cuffed, and transported to Central because this computerized tin god refuses access to police officers."

"All over that, Lieutenant."

Please submit your badges for scan, and place your palm on the palm plate for verification.

Eve held up her badge with one hand, slapped her other on the palm plate. "Clear the locks. Now."

Identification is verified. Access granted.

Eve shoved through the door, strode across the black marble lobby floor to the glossy white elevator doors flanked by two man-sized urns exploding with red spiky flowers.

Please wait here until Mr. and/or Mrs. Dickenson is notified of your arrival.

"Can it, compu-jerk." She walked straight into the elevator, Peabody scurrying after her. "Penthouse B," she ordered. "Give me any shit, I swear to God I'll stun your motherboard."

As the elevator began its smooth climb, Peabody let out a sigh of pleasure. "That was fun."

"I hate getting dicked around by electronics."

"Well, actually you're getting dicked around by the programmer."

"You're right." Eve's eyes narrowed. "You're fucking-A right. Make a note to do a search and scan. I want to find out who programmed that officious bastard."

"That could be even more fun." Peabody's cheerful smile faded when the elevator stopped. "This won't be."

They walked to Penthouse B. More security, Eve noted, and damn good at that. Palm plate, peep, camera. She pressed the buzzer to alert the system.

Hi!

14

A kid, Eve thought, momentarily confused.

We're the Dickensons. Voices changed — male, female, young girl, young boy as they sounded off roll call. *Denzel, Marta, Annabelle, Zack.* Then a dog barked.

And that's Cody, the boy's voice continued. *Who are you?*

"Ah . . ." At a loss, Eve held up her badge to the camera.

She watched the red line scan. A beat later a more traditional computerized voice answered.

Identification scanned and verified. One moment please.

It took hardly more than that before Eve saw the security light blink from red to green.

The man who wrenched open the door wore navy sweatpants with a gray sweatshirt and well-worn running shoes. His close-cropped hair showed a hint of curl above a dark, exhausted face. His eyes, the color of bitter chocolate, widened for one heartbeat, then filled with fear. Before Eve could speak, grief buried even the fear.

"No. No. No." He went straight down to his knees, clutching at his belly as if she'd kicked it.

Peabody immediately lowered to him. "Mr. Dickenson."

"No," he repeated as a dog the size of a Shetland pony trotted in. The dog looked at Eve. Eve considered her stunner. But the dog only whined and bellied over to Dickenson.

"Mr. Dickenson," Peabody all but crooned. "Let me help you up. Let me help you to a chair."

"Marta. No. I know who you are. I know you. Dallas. Murder cop. No."

Because pity outweighed her distrust of a giant dog, Eve crouched down. "Mr. Dickenson, we need to talk."

"Don't say it. Don't." He lifted his head, looked desperately into Eve's eyes. "Please don't say it."

"I'm sorry."

He wept. Wrapping his arms around the dog, swaying and rocking on his knees, he wept.

It had to be said. Even when it was known, it had to be said, for the record, and Eve knew, for the man.

"Mr. Dickenson, I regret to inform you your wife was killed. We're very sorry for your loss."

"Marta. Marta. Marta." He said it like a chant, like a prayer.

"Can we call someone for you?" Peabody asked gently. "Your sister? A neighbor?"

"How? How?"

"Let's go sit down," Eve told him, and offered her hand.

He stared at it, then put his, trembling, into it. He was a tall man, well-built. It took both of them to pull him to his feet where he swayed like a drunk.

"I can't . . . What?"

"We're going to go sit down." As she spoke, Peabody guided him into a spacious living area full of color, of comfort and the clutter of family with kids and a monster dog. "I'm going to get you some water, all right?" Peabody continued. "Do you want me to contact your sister?"

"Genny? Yes. Genny."

"All right. Sit right here."

He eased down, and the dog immediately planted its massive paws on his legs, laid its enormous head in his lap. As Peabody went off to find the kitchen, Dickenson turned to Eve. Tears continued to stream out of his eyes but they'd cleared of the initial shock.

"Marta. Where's Marta?"

"She's with the medical examiner." She saw Dickenson jerk, but pushed on. "He'll take care of her. We'll take care of her. I know this is difficult, Mr. Dickenson, but I have to ask you some questions."

"Tell me how. You have to tell me what happened. She didn't come home. Why didn't she come home?"

"That's what we need to find out. When was your last contact with your wife?"

"We spoke at about ten. She was working late, and she called as she was leaving the office. I said, get a car, Marta, get the car service, and she called me a worrywart, but I didn't want her walking to the subway or trying to hail a cab. It's so cold tonight."

"Did she arrange for a car service?"

"No. She just laughed. She said the walk to the subway would do her good. She'd been chained to her computer most of the day, and she — she — she wanted to lose five pounds. Oh my God. Oh God. What happened? Was there an accident? No," he said with a shake of his head. "Murder cop. You're Homicide. Somebody killed Marta. Somebody killed my wife, my Marta. Why? Why?"

"Do you know of anyone who'd want to harm her?"

"No. Absolutely not. No one. No. She doesn't have an enemy in the world."

Peabody came back in with a glass of water. "Your sister and her husband are on their way."

"Thank you. Was it a mugging? I don't understand. If someone had wanted her bag, her jewelry, she'd have given it to them. We made a promise to each other when we decided to stay in the city. We wouldn't take stupid chances. We have children." The hand holding the water began to shake again. "The children. What am I going to tell our kids? How can I tell our kids?"

"Are your children home?" Eve asked him.

"Yes, of course. They're sleeping. They'll expect her to be here when they get up for school. She's always here when they get up for school."

"Mr. Dickenson, I have to ask. Were there any problems in your marriage?"

"No. I'm a lawyer. My sister's a criminal court judge. I know you have to look at me. So look," he said with eyes welling again. "Look. Get it done. But tell me what happened to my wife. You tell me what happened to Marta."

Fast, Eve knew. Fast and brief. "Her body was found shortly after two this morning at the base of an exterior stairway of a building approximately eight blocks from her office. Her neck was broken."

His breath came out, tore, sucked back again. "She wouldn't have walked that far, not at night, not alone. And she didn't fall or you wouldn't be here. Was she — was she raped?"

18

"There was no indication of sexual assault from the initial examination. Mr. Dickenson, did you attempt to contact your wife between your last call and our arrival here?"

"I've been calling her 'link every few minutes. I started around ten-thirty, I think, but she didn't answer. She'd never have let me worry like this, all this time. I knew . . . I need a minute." He got shakily to his feet. "I need a minute," he repeated and rushed out of the room.

The dog looked after him, then walked cautiously to Peabody, lifted a paw to her knee.

"Sometimes it's worse than others," Peabody murmured, and gave the dog what comfort she could.

CHAPTER
TWO

Eve shoved to her feet, took a turn around the room as much to release tension as get a more solid feel for the Dickenson household.

Framed photos scattered around — family shots for the most part showing the victim in much happier days with her husband, with the kids. Other shots of the kids — a girl of serious beauty still on the innocent side of puberty and a boy with an infectious cuteness that matched the voice on security.

Art tended toward landscapes, waterscapes, all in soft, pretty colors. The kind of art people could actually understand, Eve mused. Nothing splashy or pompous, not in the art, not in the furnishings. They'd gone for comfort and what Eve supposed was kid-friendly. Maybe dog-friendly. Family-friendly.

But there was serious money here. The real estate alone spoke of it in quiet, discreet tones.

The fireplace — shown in one of the photos with Christmas stockings and kids and the big red flowers people decided they had to have at Christmas — still simmered. Real fireplace with real wood. He'd kept the home fires burning, Eve thought with another stab of pity that she reminded herself did neither victim or survivor any good.

"Big space," Eve said idly.

"Two kids and a dog this size? They need it."

"Yeah. No house in the 'burbs, so they made one in the city. He's a corporate lawyer, right?" She remembered from the quick run she'd done.

"Yeah, full partner. Grimes, Dickenson, Harley, and Schmidt."

"Why do law firms actually sound like law firms? What's his deal?"

Peabody balanced her PPC and the dog's massive head. "Specializes in estate planning, tax law. Money stuff."

"Like our wit. Interesting. See if there's a connection between Dickenson and his firm and Whitestone and his."

"Dickenson's firm has two floors in . . . Roarke's building — his headquarters."

"More juicy real estate."

"No cross on him and the wit, but they might have some clients who overlap."

"I just bet they do." She paused at the sound of the front door opening, turned.

Judge Gennifer Yung rushed in. Her stride hitched when she saw Eve, and for a moment — just a moment — her body seemed to sag. Then her shoulders straightened, her face went blank. She crossed to Eve in front of a slight-bodied man of Asian descent.

"Lieutenant."

"Judge Yung. I'm sorry for your loss."

"Thank you. My brother?"

"He needed a minute."

Judge Yung nodded. "Daniel, this is Lieutenant Dallas, and Detective Peabody. My husband, Doctor Yung."

"The children," Dr. Yung said. "Do they know?"

"They're sleeping. I don't believe they know anything's wrong."

The dog had already deserted Peabody, tail slapping like a whip as he wiggled around the judge and her husband.

"All right, Cody, good boy. Sit down. Sit."

A striking woman with brown skin smooth, dark eyes prominent, a reputation for the fierce and fearless on the bench, Judge Yung laid a hand on Cody's head, stroked. Stroked.

"I'm going to speak with Denzel. I know you have questions, and I know time is always at a premium, but I'm going to take a few moments with —" She broke off when Denzel came out, his face ravaged.

"Genny. Oh God, Genny. Marta."

"I know. Honey, I know." She went to him, wrapped her arms around him.

"Someone broke her neck."

"What?" The judge pulled back, took her brother's face in her hands. "*What?*"

"They said her neck . . . Why didn't I make her take the car service? Why didn't I call them and make her take it?"

"Ssh now. Ssh. Come with me. We're going to go in the other room for a while. Just lean on me, baby. Daniel."

"Yes, of course." Yung turned to Eve. "Would you like some coffee?"

She thought she could kill for some, but didn't want to take the time. "We're fine. Were you home when your brother-in-law contacted your wife?"

"Yes. It was about midnight, and he was frantic by then. Marta wasn't answering her 'link and was nearly two hours late. He'd already contacted night security, and they had her logged out about ten, I believe. He'd called the police, but as you know there's little done when a person is, seemingly, late coming home. So he called his sister for help."

"I take it, as far as you know, Mrs. Dickenson wasn't in the habit of being late."

"Absolutely not. That is, not without letting Denzel know. She wouldn't worry him that way, any more than he would worry her. We knew something was wrong, but I never . . . Not this."

"How well did you know Mrs. Dickenson?"

"Excuse me, can we sit? This is very hard. I feel . . ." He lowered into a chair. "I feel not altogether myself."

"Can I get you some water, Doctor Yung?"

He gave Peabody a quiet smile. "No, but thank you. You asked how well I knew Marta," he said, turning back to Eve. "Very well. We're family, and for Genny and Denzel — and Marta — family is everything. My wife and her brother have always been close. The children." He glanced toward a curve of stairs. "I'm worried about the children. They're so young to face something like this, and so much of their innocence ends tonight."

He closed his eyes a moment.

"You'll want to know what their marriage — Marta and Denzel's — was like. I've been married to a lawyer — and a judge — for thirty-six years," he added, then with a long sigh, folded his hands. "I know it's something you must pursue. I'll tell you they loved each other, very much. They had a good life, a happy family. Did they sometimes disagree, even fight? Of course. But they worked together, suited each other, made each other whole, if you understand. Sometimes you're very lucky with the choices you make, the people who come into your life. They were very lucky."

"Do you know of anyone who'd want to harm her, or to harm Denzel by causing her harm?"

"I don't." He shook his head. "I honestly can't imagine it. They're both happy and successful in their work, have a good circle of friends."

"Lawyers make enemies," Eve pointed out.

"As do judges. I understand that very well. But Denzel deals with estate law, primarily, tax laws, finances. He doesn't litigate, doesn't handle criminal law or family law — the sort of thing that can incite passions. He's a numbers man."

"And Marta was an accountant."

"They spoke the same language," he said with the ghost of a smile.

"Shared clients?"

"Yes, from time to time." He rose as Dickenson came back in.

"Genny's making coffee. She . . . she asked if you'd go back and speak with her for a minute, Lieutenant."

24

"All right." Eve glanced at Peabody, got a subtle nod.

"Mr. Dickenson, if I could ask you a few more questions," Peabody began as Eve walked out.

Eve passed through another living space. More bright and comfortable furniture, this time focused around a whopping-ass entertainment screen. Shelves held more photos, various trophies, lidded boxes.

It opened into a large dining area with a dark-finished table holding a big blue vase of white flowers. And that opened into the kitchen. More dark wood in the cabinetry, a soft gray for the counters, and a window niche with padded benches flanking a table where she imagined the family usually had their meals.

Pretty little pots, the same blue as the vase, lined another window and held what Eve vaguely recognized as herbs.

Judge Yung stood at a center island arranging thick blue mugs on a tray.

"He'll never get over it, my brother. They met in college, and that was that. I didn't approve, not at first. I wanted him to finish law school, pass the bar, get established before he entered into a serious relationship."

She opened a cupboard, took out a creamer.

"I'm ten years older than Denzel, and I've always looked after him. Whether he wanted me to or not." She smiled a little. The attempt only highlighted her red-rimmed eyes. "But it didn't take long for Marta to win me over. I loved her very much. My little sister."

Those red-rimmed eyes filled before she turned away, opened a glossy white refrigerator, took out a container of cream. Composed herself.

"They waited to have children, focused on their marriage, their careers, and when they had children, focused on them. They opted not to be professional parents. They both love their work, and so they're fulfilled in that area, and devote their non-work time to each other and the family. That's an enviable balance. Denzel will never find that balance again."

She placed the filled creamer on the tray, added a matching bowl heaped with cubes of sugar.

"I'm telling you this for a reason," she continued when Eve held her silence. "I know you have to look at my brother. The spouse is always the first suspect. I'll give you a list of their friends, the neighbors, their coworkers and supervisors. The nanny, the cleaning people. Everyone you need or want to interview."

"I appreciate that. We're going to need the 'link he used to contact her, and we'll want a look at the other electronics, other communications. It would speed things up if we had permission to search the residence, any vehicles as well as his office."

"He'll give it. He'll do whatever you ask him to do. But to keep it absolutely clean, I can't arrange for the warrant. I'll have another judge issue and sign on. It shouldn't come from me. I only ask that you conduct your search when the children aren't here. I'm going to have Denzel bring them to my home for the day."

"That's no problem."

"Tell me what you know."

"I can't give you specific details at this time. You know that, and I'm sorry. I can only tell you it appears as though she was mugged, and it went south. I assume she'd have carried a handbag, maybe a briefcase."

"Both. Most likely, both. A brown leather shoulder strap-style briefcase with silver trim. Denzel gave it to her when she was promoted about five years ago. Her wedding ring, she always wore it. A white gold band etched with hearts. And the wrist unit Daniel and I gave her for her fortieth birthday. They're both insured. We can get you photographs and descriptions."

"That would help."

"You'll want their financial information. They each have individual accounts, but most of their assets are held jointly. We'll give you all that information. You know Denzel didn't hurt Marta."

"Judge —"

"You have to do the job, you have to be thorough, and eliminate him as quickly as possible. But you know. You're smart, you're cagey, and I think, very intuitive. I don't have to ask you to do your best for Marta, because you will."

When her voice wavered, she stopped a moment, pressed her fingers to her eyes and took several long breaths.

"Not long ago," she began, "I joked to Daniel, sometimes in our position we need to make light of the risks for the people we love who worry. I joked that if any of the scum I'd sent over followed through on their death threats, he was to make sure you headed the investigation into my death. Get me Eve Dallas, I told him. And I'm telling you, if you hadn't caught Marta's case, I'd have used every string I have to pull to have you put on as primary. I want you and Detective Peabody to find who did this, who killed a lovely woman, who took her from my brother, from her children. From us. Oh God."

She broke for a moment, shuddering as she covered her face with her hands. "Oh God. I have to do what's next, do what's next, and keep doing it until it's done. That's all."

She lowered her hands, visibly pulled herself in. "If Morris isn't handling her . . . her body, as he usually does with yours, please arrange that. Will you?"

"Yes. I'll take care of it."

"Then she has the best taking care of her. That's all I can ask for now."

"Do you know what coat she was wearing?"

"Coat?"

"She wasn't wearing a coat. Considering the temperature —"

"Good God." Yung took a breath, rubbed at her temple. "On a day like this, she'd have worn her long gray wool — gray with black sleeves, black buttons. And a scarf. She always wore a scarf, and has quite a collection. I'm not sure even if I went through what's here I'd know. Denzel may remember."

"We'll ask him about that detail later."

"I need to see to my brother now. The children . . ." She paused, drew in a harsh breath. "The children will be up soon."

"We'll give you your privacy."

"Thank you. I'll get you everything you need as quickly as possible. If you need more, contact me."

When they stepped outside into the murky dawn, Peabody pressed her fingers to her eyes as Judge Yung had done. "That was pretty much as bad as it gets."

"It'll get worse when the kids wake up." Eve handed Peabody the evidence bag holding the 'link Denzel had given them. "I'm going to drop you off at Central. Contact McNab and tell him to get his skinny ass in. I want him to process that 'link."

As she spoke, she pulled open the car door, got behind the wheel. "I requested Harpo — self-proclaimed queen of hair and fiber — to process the fibers on the vic's pants. I'll follow up on that. Yung's arranging for a search warrant — residence, vehicles, offices. Get Detectives Carmichael and Santiago on that as soon as it comes through, but they're to make sure the family's not there. They're going to the judge's place."

She pulled out, made the turn for downtown. "I want Uniform Carmichael to pick a team for a canvass. He'll meet Officer Turney at the scene at oh-seven-thirty, so get on that. Contact Sergeant Gonzales at the one-three-six, tell him I requested Turney for the duty."

"You want the first on scene?"

"I want Turney. She's got good instincts. There's a little Peabody in there."

"Yeah?" Peabody puffed up, then immediately pouted. "Is she —"

"Don't even *think* about asking if she's got a smaller ass, prettier face, tougher chops or whatever you're thinking. Just get it done."

"I wasn't thinking about her ass," Peabody muttered. "But now I am."

"I want EDD on the electronics, and as soon as we get the insurance information I want a sweep on the items she was wearing — wedding ring, wrist unit. The coat. We'll talk to the husband later, see if he remembers the earrings, and the scarf Yung claims she'd have worn. He couldn't take any more on this first pass. Start a run on the work places. Look for anything that links them, and links either or both to Whitestone's company. There's got to be something there. If this was a random kill, I'm a monkey's cousin."

"Uncle."

"What?"

"It's a monkey's uncle, and before you ask, no, I don't know why because, really, on the evolutionary train, cousin's about right."

"What the hell do I care?"

"I'm just saying."

Eve spared Peabody a glance as she turned to cut across town. The blocks went smooth and fast — too early for pedestrians to swarm the sidewalks and crosswalks, too late for the Rapid Cabs packed with club hoppers and partygoers.

She avoided Times Square where the hoppers and goers never gave in or up, then zipped by a maxibus filled with sleepy commuters either coming on or going off shift.

"Somebody grabbed her, and had to make the grab close to her office. Or they waited in a cab then just cruised up for the grab. They took her to that empty apartment because they knew it was empty. Either they had the codes or they're damn good at B&E. Knocked her around a little."

"You think a righty, and a backhand."

"Yeah, it reads that way to me. A backhand across the cheekbone's going to hurt a lot, knock her down, scare the living shit out of her. Too much bruising for just a slap, not enough for a solid punch."

She brought the victim's face back into her head. "Probably more than one hit. We'll see if Morris tells us she was stunned or tranq'd, but I'm betting no. They wanted to make it look like a mugging. If they'd stunned or drugged her, they'd open themselves to a closer look. Manhandle her into a vehicle, take her to the apartment where they'd have privacy."

"For what? Say this is payback on Yung, it's a pretty circular route. Yeah, they're close, but you'd go closer — Yung herself, her husband, one of her kids or grandkids. She's got two daughters, in case you wondered. One grandkid from each."

"It's not payback." Eve had circled that through her mind, poked holes through it. Eliminated it. "They'd have messed her up a lot more, made a statement for payback. And yeah, gone closer than a sister-in-law. Maybe to pressure the husband for something, but if you can grab her, you can probably grab him. And it's more pressure if she's alive. Information maybe. On a client. She'd know a lot of money secrets, tax shit, account data. They knew she was working late, so they've been watching her or they have a route inside — or they *are* inside her firm."

She pulled up at Central. "I'm going to see Morris. As soon as her offices open, we'll talk to her supervisor, her coworkers. I want her client list, her current files. Same for the husband."

"Follow the money."

"It's always an interesting route. Beat it."

"Beating it."

Eve drove away, glanced at the time, then used her in-dash 'link to contact Roarke. Maybe it was dawn, but she knew damn well he'd been up at least a solid hour, and had probably already bought a minor solar system.

"Lieutenant."

And there he was, filling her dash screen, those staggering blue eyes alert in a face created on a day God had felt particularly generous. As that mane of silky black hair was tied back, she recognized work mode.

"I figured I should let you know I won't be back."

"I assumed as much." His native Ireland cruised through the words, like music. "Eat something."

"I think I'll wait until after this trip to the morgue. Their Vending seriously blows."

"It's bad. I can see it."

"Murder's never good, but this one wasn't particularly messy. But . . . mother of two, with a husband I broke into pieces at notification. Well-heeled Upper East Side family, both of them with careers in finance, living in a penthouse condo. But without the flash, you know? Homey, pictures of the kids everywhere. And she was Judge Yung's sister-in-law."

"Judge Yung?"

"Criminal. One of the best I know." She could let the pity come, just a little with him. "You couldn't swim through the love and grief in that place. It just kept flooding the air."

"It's difficult being the one who has no choice but to open the gates to the flood."

"It's part of the job, but like Peabody said, sometimes it's worse than others. This was worse. Yung's going to make it as easy as possible for me, search warrants, full disclosure, full access."

"And yet."

"And yet the mother of two who helped build what looks like a really happy home is still dead. So, anyway. What do you know about Brewer, Kyle, and Martini?"

"Ah . . . Corporate accounting primarily, or serving those who have as much money as a corporation."

"Not yours?"

"No, but I'd take a good look at them if I decided to make a change in that area. They have a steady, straightforward reputation. Victim or husband?"

"Victim. Husband's a lawyer with Grimes, Dickenson, Harley, and Schmidt. He's Dickenson. Estate law and financial junk's his deal."

"I don't know them, but I can see what I can find out."

"Shouldn't be hard. Their offices are in your headquarters building."

"That does make it simple."

"If you have time. It never hurts to have somebody who knows that money crap on board. One more. The

WIN Group — investments, money managers, like that."

"Nothing rings, but again, it's easy enough to get information. How do they play in?"

"Bradley Whitestone — the *W* — found the body outside his being-renovated apartment early this morning when he brought a woman by he obviously hoped to bang. We met her, she says, at some gala. Alva Moonie."

"Of the New York Moonies — old money, old pedigree. Shipping, as in building ships and using them to transport cargo and people on cruises. I don't know her personally, but can tell you she was known as a wild child who lived for parties, extensive travel, shopping, drink, drugs, sex until a few years ago."

"She looked like money," Eve recalled. "She didn't look wild."

"I believe she designs or helps design the decor on the cruise ships, and does some nonprofit work these days. Is she a suspect?"

"About as far down the list as you can get at this point, but you never know."

"You do," he corrected. "Or you find out. How did she die, your mother of two?"

"Somebody broke her neck. Unless Morris tells me different," she added as she pulled up to the morgue. "I'm going to go talk to him. I'll see you tonight."

"Eat something," he repeated.

"Yeah, yeah." But she grinned at him before she broke transmission.

Sometimes you got lucky, she thought remembering Daniel Yung's words. She'd hit the mega-jackpot with Roarke, a man who understood her and loved her anyway.

And sometimes, she thought as she walked into the long white tunnel of the morgue, luck ran out as it had for Marta and Denzel Dickenson.

Too early for change-of-shift she decided as her footsteps echoed. People were either dealing with the death toll the city hauled in during the night, or doing paperwork in offices, or things she didn't particularly want to think about with body parts in labs.

She paused at Vending, rejected even the idea of what passed for coffee at this particular establishment. She ordered a tube of Pepsi instead, and chugged some caffeine into her system as she headed for Morris's area.

If he hadn't been notified and come in, she'd contact him with Yung's request.

But she heard the music — weeping sax, tearful bass, as she pushed through the double doors.

He had Marta Dickenson on the slab, had opened her with a Y-cut and delicately lifted out her heart to weigh it.

He glanced over at Eve, his dark eyes large behind his micro-goggles.

"Our day began when hers ended."

"She was putting in overtime at the office. Her day didn't end very well."

"She has children. I checked for rape, no sign of sexual assault, but signs she's borne at least one child."

"Two."

He nodded as he worked. He wore chocolate brown under his protective cape, a perfectly cut suit with a cream-colored shirt. He'd braided his hair, left it in one, long, complicated black tail down his back.

"I was going to pull you in if you weren't on her."

"I took the night shift this week. Restless." But he glanced up again. "Any particular reason you'd want me on her?"

"She's Judge Yung's sister-in-law."

"Genny?"

Eve's eyebrows winged up. "You're on a first-name basis with Yung?"

"We share an appreciation for the same types of music. This is her brother's wife? Denzel's wife. I met them once, when Genny had a musical evening at her home. I didn't recognize her, but Genny always spoke so warmly of her."

"The judge is clearing the road, seeing that we have full access and in a speedy fashion."

"You don't suspect the husband?"

"No, but you've got to look. COD's the broken neck?"

"Yes. Someone very strong and very skilled. It wasn't from a fall. The report said she was found at the bottom of a stairway."

"A short one, and no, not a fall. She didn't fall. They put her there when they were done, tried to make it look like a mugging. It wasn't."

"She has some minor injuries. Facial bruise, the injured lip, both from a blow — a hand, not a fist —

slight bruising around her mouth, bruising on her right wrist, slight bruising on both knees and her left elbow, the abrasion on the heel of her right hand."

"Knees and hand. Like she skidded on some kind of rug or carpet?" Eve held up her hand, shoved the heel of it forward.

"That would be my conclusion. I found fibers in the hand abrasion, and sent them to the lab."

"Blue fibers?"

"Yes, as your notes stated you found on her pants. You'd marked for Harpo, so I sent her the ones I removed."

"Good."

"I've barely started on her, and don't have much."

"Any stun marks? Any tox?"

"Very light marks from a stunner, just above her left shoulder blade."

"I'd figured no on that," Eve murmured, hooking her thumbs in her front pockets as she walked closer to the body. "If you want it to look like a mugging, leaving stun marks is seriously stupid. Your average mugger's not going to have access to a stunner. They use stickers. Shoulder blade," she continued. "He took her down from behind."

"Yes, and I'd say a very low stun, just enough to incapacitate her, daze her for a moment or two. I'll go over her very carefully. I've sent off a blood sample for tox screening. I can flag it."

"Wouldn't hurt." Eve walked around the body, taking her own study. "Grab her when she comes out of the office building — not inside unless they could shut down security, and why do that, why leave bread crumbs? Slap a hand over her mouth, shove or toss her in a van, that's quick. Stunning her — maybe the killer's another woman, or small, worried she'd fight back, get away."

"The slight lacerations on her knees and hand read like a fall on a carpet. In the apartment?"

"No rugs or carpeting there. Tarps — beige. No blue. But tossing her into a vehicle with carpeting on the interior floor, yeah. And she's dazed from the stun and doesn't catch herself, skids over it. She could've gotten the bruises on her knees, the fibers on her pants from the transpo. They didn't walk her eight blocks to the murder scene, so he or they had transportation."

"Harpo should be able to identify the carpet type, the manufacturer, the dye lot."

"Or lose her crown, yeah. One person could do it," Eve mused as she walked around the slab. "Stun her, push her in the back of a van or a car, but she'd come out of a light stun pretty quick. You have to keep her quiet and contained, drive, get her out, over, unlock the door. It's likelier two people, one to drive, one to deal with her."

"Big hands," Morris said. "I don't think whoever manhandled her was small. The pattern of the bruising indicates large hands."

"Okay. Okay." The need to stun Dickenson made less sense now, but facts were facts. "So, just taking no chances. Maybe the mugging gambit was last-minute. Either way, they took her to an empty apartment, lower level, direct access, no sign of break-in. They want her scared, scared enough to be cooperative, to give them what they want, tell them everything she knows. Backhand." Eve swung her own through the air. "She goes down — face bruises, elbow knocks the floor. When they're done, and it doesn't take very long, one of them snaps her neck. Manually?"

"Yes, almost certainly, and left to right. From the angle, the bruising, the break, my conclusion is left to right, from behind."

"Behind again. He's right-handed. Strong, trained. It's not that easy to snap a neck. Prepared, controlled enough not to mess her up too much, but not especially professional. Military maybe or para, used to kills on the field where you don't have to clean things up before the cops get there. I found a little blood on a paint tarp bunched up on the floor. Apartment's being rehabbed. It's going to be her blood."

"I found no defensive wounds." Gently, Morris lifted the victim's hand. "Nothing under her nails, in her teeth. So yes, I'd say it will be her blood."

"It all went according to plan, except for the blood they missed, and the fact the owner hoped for some nookie and brought his date over so we found her quicker. But I wonder if they got what they were after. Did she have it? Did she know it?"

"I can't tell you that, but the lack of any sign she fought back? No indication she was bound? No signs of torture, only relatively minor injuries . . . It reads as if she'd have given them what they wanted if she'd had it."

Eve thought of the condo again, family-friendly. Photos of happy kids, the big dog.

Yes, she'd have given them what they wanted. If she'd had it.

"Rough her up first, scare her, hurt her just enough, then tell her if she tells them or gives them what they want, they won't hurt her again. They killed her from behind. He didn't need the rush of face-to-face. A job, a duty, a task. And he probably didn't see the need to draw it out, give her more pain or fear.

"It wasn't personal."

Though Morris nodded, he touched a hand to Marta's shoulder. "I imagine she feels differently about that."

CHAPTER
THREE

Eve pushed and dodged her way through Central at change of shift. Cops going off tour, coming on, or those like her who'd caught something and were trying to get in or out to follow up.

She stopped by Vending to study her choices, decided they all sucked, and settled for something laughingly billed as a blueberry Danish.

She plugged in her code, her selection. And got nothing but a grinding hum and blinking lights.

"Come on, bitch." She repeated the process, and this time received a few weak beeps. "Damn it, I knew it wouldn't last."

Her poor history with machines haunted her, and now she wanted that damn anemic-looking excuse for a breakfast pastry on a matter of principle.

She gave the machine a solid kick.

Vandalism or physical force on this machine or any others on the premises can result in termination of Vending privileges for a period of thirty to ninety days. Please insert coin, credit or authorized code, and your selection.

"That's what I did you useless piece of junk." She reared back to kick it again.

"Hey, Dallas." Baxter, the slickest dresser of her detectives strolled up. "Problem?"

"This miserable pile of junk won't give up that blob of crap disguised as a Danish."

"Allow me." Whistling between his teeth, Baxter keyed in his own code, selected the Danish.

It slid smoothly into the slot. Eve eyed it while the machine cheerfully listed its mega-syllabic ingredients and dubious nutritional value.

"There you go, LT." Baxter pulled it out, offered it. "My treat."

"How do they know it's me? Why do they care?"

"Maybe it's body chemistry, something to do with energy."

"That sounds like bullshit."

"Well, you got the Danish."

"Yeah. Thanks for that."

"So, Trueheart and I closed the double murder. Ex-girlfriend who didn't want to be the ex."

She toggled back into her mental files. "The bludgeoning in Chelsea."

"Yeah," he continued as they walked. "Beat them both to shit and back again with a tire iron. I figured the didn't-want-to-be-ex hired somebody or sexed somebody into doing it. That kind of damage? You don't expect a woman."

"Why?"

"Well, you know, LT. Women typically go for poison, or something less gruesome. Especially seeing as this one's barely five feet tall and a hundred soaking wet.

Just didn't figure she had the chops or the muscle. Trueheart broke her down."

"Trueheart." Eve thought of the clean-cut, kindhearted uniform she'd given to Baxter to train.

"He stuck with the 'hell hath no fury' bit from the jump. Wouldn't let go of it. And he played her, Dallas, played her in Interview like a shortstop plays an infield grounder."

She heard the pride in his voice, still some big brother in it, but that's what worked.

"It was beautiful, I gotta say. He's all sympathy and understanding, talking about having his heart broken." With a grin, Baxter thumped a hand on his heart. "Getting the whole simpatico deal going, getting her worked up about how he done her wrong and all that shit."

"Good angle," Eve praised.

"Oh yeah, and he got better. He pulls out how he bet it hurt her, deeply, to see her ex's new lady wearing that sexy leopard print nightie — he even said nightie. And the stupid bitch can't resist saying how it was a tiger print, and that flat-chested slut didn't have the tits to fill it out.

"The dead woman just bought the thing — tiger print, which my boy knew — that afternoon, so the ex couldn't have seen her in it, unless she was in that bedroom. The boy took her apart from there. Got a full confession. How she'd climbed up the fire escape — the dead ex always left the bedroom window open a little, fresh air fiend. Bashed him first, then went to town on the new skirt, went back whaled some more on the ex. Then went down to the basement laundry room, he hadn't changed his codes on that. Washed her damn clothes, cleaned up, walked out. Tossed the tire iron in the river."

"That's good work. Does the lab have the clothes?"

"Yeah. I'm leaving it to the boy to follow up there. We both figured her for involvement, but he's the one who saw her with the tire iron, swinging for the fences."

He paused a moment, and knowing there was more, Eve waited.

"He's lost his green, Dallas. Well, he's one of those who'll probably always be fresh, but you know what I mean. He's earned a shot at detective."

She'd promised to consider it, and though Baxter's second pass was a little ahead of schedule, she couldn't fault his logic. "The first of the year. If he wants it, he can take the exam then. That'll give him time to get a little more experience under his belt and study up. Let him know. You've done good with him, Baxter."

"He's gold, boss. I figured him mostly for ballast when you tossed him my way, but he's gold. Appreciate it."

"Prime him," she warned. "The exam's not for pussies."

"He's a sweetheart, but he ain't no pussy."

When they walked into the bullpen, things were already hopping. She gave Peabody the come-ahead and kept moving into her office where Eve headed straight for the AutoChef and coffee.

"Morris confirms COD is the broken neck. No apparent defensive wounds. The bruises she has could be — most likely are — the result of the snatch, the backhand. Manual neck snap."

"Big ouch."

"I don't think she felt much. He stunned her first — extra careful maybe — light stun, on the shoulder blade."

"Like an ambush, from behind."

"Yeah, and I'm betting the fibers on her pants, and the ones Morris took out of the heel of her right hand are from the interior of the vehicle used to transport her. I'm going to set up the board and book. What have you got?"

"McNab's already in and started on the 'link. EDD's waiting for the go-ahead for the rest of the electronics. Carmichael and Santiago are on tap for the search, and Uniform Carmichael's on the canvass. I put an alert out for the wedding ring and the wrist unit, and went ahead and contacted the husband about the earrings so we could alert all of it. She had on these gold heart-shaped studs the kids gave her last Mother's Day. I really hope we get them back. Something like that . . . Anyway, we could get lucky there if the killer decides to pawn or sell."

"They're not pros, so we could get lucky."

"I started a run on the financials — vic and spouse. They both have life insurance — and plenty — but they're solid money-wise. He makes considerably more than she did, but she didn't do half bad. They've got investments, the low-risk, long-term growth type, and already have college funds started for the kids."

She took out her notebook, swiped through just to refresh. "They own the condo, and have a mortgage going on a house on Long Island, in Oyster Bay. One vehicle — family-style cargo deal, late model, but not flashy. Some art and jewelry. Dickenson and Grimes started their firm eleven years ago, took on the other partners along the way. They have a good rep. The vic worked for Brewer and company for about the same amount of time, moving up, time off for each of the kids with standard maternity leave. The nanny's been with them since the first kid came along. I have her data."

"Okay, we'll talk to her, to the vic's work people, to the law partners."

"Crossing, there are some clients popping on each, and I've got a couple so far who've used or are using the wit's firm."

"Run it through, then we'll work the matches." She glanced down when her unit signaled an incoming. "There's the warrant." She ordered it to print, read the attachment. "Yung says the family's heading over to her place. Give Carmichael the warrant, and get them going. Give EDD the nod on the electronics. Be ready to — Sir."

She straightened her shoulders when Commander Whitney filled her doorway. She'd expected contact, and quickly, but wished he'd called her up to his office, given her time to prepare.

"I've been informed Judge Yung's sister-in-law has been murdered."

"Yes, sir. I've just come in from the field. I haven't written up my initial report, and am waiting for some lab results."

"Run it through for me."

"Peabody, get things started. Commander," she began, then gave him an oral report.

He was a big man in her small office, his dark face grim as he listened, as he walked over to stare out of her skinny window at the gloomy morning.

"You're not leaning toward the husband?"

"I'm leaning away from the husband," Eve told him. "But we'll take him through the process. Both he and the judge have been cooperative. I've got Carmichael and Santiago heading over to the vic's residence to do a search, and EDD's picking up the electronics. McNab's already processing the husband's 'link. The upshot is she was snatched by person or persons unknown for reasons as yet undetermined. But it wasn't random, it wasn't a mugging, and there's no evidence at this early stage to indicate Judge Yung is connected to that reason. I'm going to take a harder look at the wit, and his partners, and find out what the vic was working on, or has worked on, her current clients."

He nodded, turned back to her. "The wife of a prominent judge's brother, the media will stir that. We'll have the liaison issue a statement, save you time."

Sing "Hallelujah." "Thank you, sir."

"I'm acquainted with Yung, as most of us are. You should know she and her husband and Chief Tibble and his wife are friendly."

"Understood."

"Keep me informed."

"Yes, sir." The minute he left, she opened the murder book, then set up her board, centering Marta Dickenson's photo. She ran through the time line again, scanned the interview with the wits, then the spouse. For a moment, she studied the printouts she made from her crime scene record.

Blood drops on the tarp, she mused. Sloppy cleanup. Quick grab — timed well. Killing method, quick and brutal. Trained, she thought again, but not professional.

So who'd hired, or had on their payroll, a couple of thugs with training — spine-crackers, security, bouncers — who weren't above breaking the neck of a defenseless woman?

Start with why, she mused, and gathered her things.

Her 'link signaled again. "Dallas?"

"Lieutenant." Harpo with her spiky red hair popped on screen. "Figured to give you a quick heads-up on those fibers."

"You ID'd them."

"Give me a challenge next time. Interior carpet on the Maxima Cargo, Mini Zip, and 4X Land Cruiser. Color's Blue Steel, and comes standard with Indigo exterior, but you can order it custom. GM intro'd the color last year, so the model is either a '59 or '60. But the fibers were coated with the factory sealant so it hasn't seen much wear or use."

"That's good, quick work, Harpo."

"Like I said, no challenge. The ones from the morgue match, blood trace on them. I checked with the blood

48

boys, so I can tell you the blood on the tarp and the blood on the fiber both came from your vic."

"Really good, quick work."

"A lot of us have testified before Judge Yung. So . . . I'll send along the reports."

"Yeah. Thanks, Harpo."

"We do what we do," she said. "I do it best."

At the moment, Eve couldn't argue.

"Peabody," she said as she swung through the bullpen.

Peabody snagged her coat and jogged to catch up. "McNab's finished with the 'link. Everything corroborates Dickenson's statement. Vic called, said she'd be working late — chatting about food, kids, domestic stuff. She contacted him again at just after ten to tell him she was heading home. He pushed her to call their car service, but she brushed that off, just as he said. She also said she was bringing some work home, but she was going to deal with it in the morning — that she'd arranged to work at home until noon."

"He forgot to tell us that."

"McNab's sending up a copy of all transmissions. He says you can clearly see the vic pulling on her coat, a scarf, even a hat and gloves while she talked with the husband. She had him on her desk 'link. McNab says she had the briefcase Yung described, and a red handbag also with shoulder strap. Wedding ring, wrist unit, and the heart stud earrings."

"Good." McNab might have been Peabody's main man, but that didn't affect his work.

"They talked for just over three minutes, and she told him to pour her a big glass of wine, how maybe he'd get lucky. He joked back, no, maybe *she'd* get lucky. It makes it sadder. It just does."

"Sad isn't part of the equation right now," Eve said as they walked out of the elevator and into the garage. "The transmission backs up the husband's story, and also gives a picture of their relationship. Add that, the initial interview, his demeanor, their financials, and he's looking clear. Unless we find he had a sidepiece, he's got no clear motive for having her done."

She got behind the wheel. "Harpo came through. We're going to need to run Maxima Cargos, Mini Zips and 4X Land Cruisers, with Blue Steel interior carpet. Either '59 or '60."

"That's a good break."

"It's a break anyway. The blood on the tarp and some trace on the fibers are the vic's. So we've confirmed she was grabbed, tossed in a vehicle, transported, taken inside, killed. Coat, hat, gloves, scarf, jewelry taken, dumped outside."

"I'll start a run, see if any of the names we've got has a vehicle that matches."

"Let's find out what work she was bringing home, and see if we can figure out why."

Knowing her job, Peabody pulled out her PPC as Eve zipped out of the garage. First things, first.

"I've got Sylvester Gibbons as her immediate supervisor. If I'm figuring this right, she works in a division that does independent audits. Businesses, corporations, trust funds."

"Audits. That's when they're looking for something hinky."

"I guess. Or just making sure everything's right."

"Something hinky," Eve repeated. "One way to screw up an audit or at least delay it — kill the auditor."

"That's pretty harsh and extreme. And if numbers are hinky, it's going to come out anyway, right?"

"Maybe they need time to fix it. You snatch the auditor, find out what she knows, what she's put on record, who she's talked to. Get the information, kill her, set it up as a mugging. Now you've got some time to fix the numbers, or if you've been dipping into the till, put the money back. If it'd gone smooth, everybody thinks Marta had some really bad luck. They don't start poking around in her work straight off. We could be ahead of them. Contact Judge Yung."

"Now?"

"Preemptive strike. No money guy's going to want to hand over a client's documents to the cops. We need a warrant, one that covers everything the vic's worked on in the past month. Yung will clear the way for that, save us time."

"It's like having a judge on tap. I didn't mean that in the bribery, judge-in-the-pocket kind of way."

"Uh-huh. Don't give her any more information than necessary. We want to be thorough, cover all bases. You know the drill."

"I've never drilled a judge before. And that still comes off shady. Or uncomfortably sexual."

"Just get the warrant, Peabody."

Eve thought about something else she had on tap. She happened to be married to a numbers geek. Money was his language, and he was seriously fluent.

She hunted for parking, and considered it her lucky day when she found a spot curbside only a block and a half from the victim's office building.

"The judge says she'll make the warrant happen," Peabody reported, "but it may take a little time. Sensitive material, privacy issues. If we can show reasonable evidence the vic was killed due to her work, it'll slide right through."

"We might show evidence if we looked at the work." But she'd figured as much. At least the wheels were already grinding.

The sky began to spit an ugly, icy sleet, causing other pedestrians to quicken their pace. In seconds, an enterprising street vendor hauled out a cart, popped it open to reveal a supply of umbrellas for about triple their usual rate.

In seconds more, he was mobbed.

"I wouldn't mind one of those," Peabody murmured.

"Toughen up."

"Why doesn't it just snow? At least snow's pretty."

"Until it's in grimy black mounds against the curb." Shoving her hands in her pockets for warmth, Eve quick-stepped the last half block. She shoved through the lobby doors, shook her head like a dog, and shot out little drops of cold.

She badged the man at the security podium. "Brewer, Kyle, and Martini."

"Fifth floor. Is this about Ms. Dickenson? I heard the media report before I came on."

"Yeah, it's about Ms. Dickenson."

"It's true then." His lips tightened as he shook his head. "You gotta hope it's a mistake, you know? She's a nice woman, always says hi when she comes in."

"You weren't on last night?"

"Off at four-thirty. She logged out at ten-oh-eight. I checked the log when I came in, because of the report."

"Did she work late routinely?"

"I wouldn't say routinely, but sure, sometimes. All of them do. Tax season?" He waved a hand in a *forget about it* gesture. "They might as well live here."

"Has anybody come in, asking about her?"

"Not to me. I mean she gets people, clients, and whatever who come in asking for her and the firm. They have to sign in."

"Any problem showing us the log for the last week or so?"

"I don't see why it'd be a problem."

"How about making a copy for our files."

Now he shifted, foot-to-foot. "I'd like to clear that one with my boss. If you're going up, you could stop back on the way out. I think he'll be okay with it, considering."

"Good enough. Thanks."

"She was a nice lady," he said again. "Met her husband and kids, too. They came in to pick her up now and then. Nice family. It's a damn shame, is what. A damn shame. First bank of elevators on the right. I'll talk to my boss."

"Thanks again. Check in with Uniform Carmichael," she told Peabody. "See if he's got anything."

"If the security guy knows, the office knows," Peabody pointed out.

"Yeah, kills the element of surprise."

"And makes it just a little less awful."

Not so much, Eve thought when the elevator doors opened. She heard someone weeping, the sound muffled behind a closed door. The two people — one man, one woman — behind the reception desk stood, holding each other.

No one sat in the dignified — and boring — cream and brown waiting area.

The woman eased away, made an obvious effort to compose herself. "I'm very sorry, all appointments are canceled for today. We've had a death in the family."

"I'm aware." Eve took out her badge.

"You're here about Marta."

"Lieutenant Dallas and Detective Peabody. We're investigating her death. We need to speak with Sylvester Gibbons."

"Of course. Yes." She pulled some tissues out of a holder. "Marcus?"

"I'll get him, right away." The man dashed off.

"Would you like to sit down? Or coffee? I mean would you like some coffee?"

"We're good. How well did you know Ms. Dickenson?"

"Very well. I think very well." She dabbed at her eyes. "We — we took an exercise class together, twice a week. And we talked every day, I mean every workday. I can't believe this happened! She's careful, and it's a good area. She wouldn't have fought or argued with a mugger." Tears welled and overflowed again. "They didn't have to hurt her."

"Has anyone been in asking about her?"

"No."

"Have there been any problems between her and someone in the office, someone in the firm?"

"No. I'd know, you hear everything on the desk. This is a good company. We get along."

Nobody got along all the time, but Eve let it slide. "How about a client, any trouble, complaints?"

"I don't know. Maybe. I don't know."

"People don't like being audited. Has anyone caused any trouble about that, about the work she did?"

"Legal handles that sort of thing. I don't understand. She was mugged, so —"

"It's routine," Eve said. "We need to be thorough."

"Of course. Of course. I'm sorry. I'm so upset." She choked on the words as she dug out fresh tissues. "We got to be pretty good friends with the class we took."

"Did she talk about her work with you, about the audits?"

"Marta wouldn't gossip about an audit. It's unprofessional. And if she'd gossiped, it probably would've been with me. You get, well, loose, when you're sweating together. And sometimes we'd go have a drink after — a reward. We talked about our kids, and clothes, and that sort of thing. Men — husbands." She smiled weakly. "Neither of us wanted to talk about work when we were out of the office."

"Okay."

"I — oh, Sly!" She said the syllable on a smothered wail, then dropped down in her chair, covered her face with her hands.

"Nat." A stringy man with flyway blond hair and watery blue eyes stepped around the reception desk, patted the woman on the shoulder. "Why don't you go home?"

"I want to stay, to help. We couldn't reach everyone who has an appointment. I just need — a few minutes." She rose, dashed off.

"It's going to take longer than minutes." He passed a weary hand over his face, turned to Eve and Peabody. "Lieutenant Dallas?"

"Mr. Gibbons?"

"Yes. Ah, we're not ourselves this morning. Marta —" He shook his head. "We should go back to my office." His movements ungainly, as if he couldn't quite deal with the length of his limbs, he led the way through a cubical area — more tears, more watery eyes — and down a short hall where office doors stayed closed.

"Marta's office . . ." He stopped, stared at the closed door. "Do you need to see?"

"We will, yes. I'd like to talk to you first. Is the door secured?"

"She would have locked it when she left, that's policy. I unlocked it when I came in, after I heard . . . Just to see if there was anything . . . Honestly, I don't know why. I locked it again."

They passed a break area where a few people sat speaking in muted voices, and to the end of the corridor.

56

Gibbons's office took a corner, as supervisors' often did. It struck Eve as minimalist, efficient, and scarily organized. His desk held two comps, two touch screens, several folders neatly stacked, a forest of lethally sharpened pencils in several hard colors, and a triple picture frame holding snapshots of a plump, smiling woman, a grinning young boy, and a very ugly dog.

"Please sit down. I — coffee. I'll get you coffee."

"It's all right. We're fine."

"It's no trouble. I was getting coffee," he said vaguely. "I was in the break room, trying to . . . comfort, I guess. We're not a large department, and we're part of a, well, tightly knit firm. Everyone here knows each other, has interacted, you could say. We — we — we have a company softball team, and we celebrate birthdays in the break room. Marta had a birthday last month. We had cake. Oh my God. It's my fault. This is all my fault."

"How is that?"

"I asked her to put in some overtime. I asked her to work late. We've been shorthanded this week, with two of our auditors at a convention. They were due back, but there was an accident — a car accident. One has a broken leg, and the other's in a coma. Was, I mean. I just got word he came out of it, but they've put him under again for some reason. There's no brain damage, but he has broken ribs and needs more tests and . . . I'm sorry. I'm sorry. That's not why you're here."

"When did you ask Marta to work late?"

"Just yesterday. Yesterday morning when I talked to Jim, the one with the broken leg. They won't be able to travel back. They're in Vegas, at a convention. I told you that. Sorry. They won't be able to come back to work for several days, at least, and we had audits pending. I asked Marta to pick up the slack. I worked until eight myself, but then I took the rest home. Marta was still here. She said thanks for dinner, Sly. I ordered us some food about six. For myself, Marta, and Lorraine."

"Lorraine?"

"Lorraine Wilkie. She and Marta both worked late. Lorraine and I left at the same time, but I'd given Marta the bulk of the work. She's the best we have. She's the best. I didn't know she'd stay so late. I should've told her to leave when I did. I should've gotten her into a cab. If I had, she'd be all right."

"What was she working on?"

"Several things."

He took out his pocket 'link when it signaled, glanced at the readout, hit ignore.

"I'm sorry, that can wait. Marta was finishing up an audit of her own, had just begun another. And I gave her three more — one assigned to Jim, and the others to Chaz. And I asked her to look over some work done by a trainee."

"Would Marta have told anyone about these assignments — details, I mean — names?"

"No. That information would be very confidential."

"We're going to need to see her work. I'll need you to give me access to her files."

"I . . . I don't understand." He lifted his hands, palms up, like a man offering a plea. "I'd do anything to help. But I can't give you confidential material. I don't understand."

"Mr. Gibbons, we have reason to believe Marta wasn't the victim of a random mugging, but was abducted when she left the office, taken to another location where she was killed. Her briefcase was taken. That would have contained at least some of her work, some of her files."

As his hands lowered, he simply stared. "I don't understand what you're saying. I don't understand you."

"We have reason to believe Marta Dickenson was a specific target, and that she may have been killed due to her work."

He sat down heavily. "They said — on the report — it was a mugging."

"And I hope they'll keep saying that for the time being. I'm telling you it wasn't, and I'm telling you to keep that confidential. Who knew she was working late last night?"

"I . . . I did; Lorraine; Josie, Marta's assistant; Lorraine's assistant. My admin . . ." Head slightly bowed, he pushed his hands repeatedly through his thin hair. "God. My God. Anyone might've known. It wasn't a secret."

"Cleaning crew, maintenance, security?"

"Yes, well, the crew came in to clean while we were working. And security requires logging in and out. I don't understand," he repeated.

"Just understand we need to see what she was working on."

"I — I — I need to talk to Legal. If I could, I swear to you, I'd give you everything, anything. She was my friend. You think someone killed her because of an audit?"

"It's a theory."

"I don't see how this can be." He began to rub his fingers across his brow, back and forth, back and forth.

"Talk to your lawyer. Tell him a warrant's in the works. We'll get it. Judge Yung will see to it."

"I hope she will, and quickly." He pushed to his feet. "I think you must be wrong, but if there's any chance — any — I want you to have what you need. She was my friend," he repeated. "And I was responsible for her here, in this workplace. I don't know how I can ever tell Denzel . . . It's my fault, any way it happened. It's my fault."

"It's not," Eve said flatly, because she thought he needed it. "It's the fault of the person who killed her."

CHAPTER
FOUR

Gibbons gave Eve access to Marta's office, then, as requested, went to find the assistant.

Though smaller than her supervisor's, Marta's office held the same level of organization, efficiency. She'd brought her own touches, Eve mused — the family photos, a lopsided pen/pencil holder that had to be the work of a child, or a very untalented adult. Some sort of leafy green plant stood lushly in the window.

Eve noticed the sticky note stuck to the front of a mini-AutoChef.

"Five pounds."

"To remind herself she wants to lose it before she programs something fattening. You've never had to worry about your weight," Peabody added. "When you do, you use all kinds of tricks and incentives."

"She liked her work, according to every statement. But this wasn't a second home, the way some offices are. She made it comfortable, but she doesn't have a lot of personal stuff. The photos, the pencil holder, not much else."

She had more in her own, smaller space at Central, Eve realized. Little things — the paperweight mostly to give her something to pick up, fiddle with; the sun catcher in her tiny window, just because she liked it there; the silly talking gun Peabody had given her, because it made her laugh.

She'd had a plant once, but since she'd nearly killed it with neglect, she'd passed that off.

Eve turned to the desk 'link, ordered a replay of the day before.

Inter-office stuff, nothing that popped. A couple communications with clients, which she noted down, another with Legal on a thorny question Eve didn't even understand, one to the nanny to tell her she'd be late, and could she stay and help Denzel with dinner for the kids, then the final two with her husband.

As she shut it off, she glanced up, saw the pale, tear-ravaged face of the woman in the doorway.

"I heard her voice. I thought . . . When I heard her voice."

"Josie Oslo?"

"Yes. Yes, I'm Josie. I'm Marta's assistant."

"Lieutenant Dallas, Detective Peabody. You should sit down. We need to ask you a few questions."

"I didn't hear before I came in. I never turn on the screen in the morning. I never have time. When I got here Lorraine — Ms. Wilkie — she was crying. Then everybody was crying. Nobody knew what to do."

She looked around the room in a helpless search that had her pressing her knuckles to her mouth. "Sly — Mr. Gibbons was a little late. He tried to contact Marta's husband, but nobody answered, and he tried to talk to someone at the police, but they didn't tell him anything, not really. And he said we should cancel any appointments for today and tomorrow. We could go home. Nobody really went home, not yet."

"It helps to be around other people who knew her," Peabody said, and gently led Josie to a chair.

"I guess. When I heard her voice, I thought, *See it's a mistake*. I've been trying to tell everybody it has to be a mistake. But it isn't."

"No, I'm sorry, it isn't a mistake." Eve leaned back against the desk. "How long have you been Marta's assistant?"

"About two years. I came on right out of college. I'm going to grad school part-time."

"Have there been any problems lately?"

"Marta's printer broke. But I fixed it."

"Anything out of the ordinary," Eve qualified.

"No, I don't think so. That's not true! I forgot. Jim and Chaz were in an accident, a car accident in Las Vegas. They went to a convention out there and were supposed to be back yesterday, but they were in a cab that got hit, and Chaz — that's Mr. Parzarri — and Mr. Arnold were hurt. That's why Sly had to give Marta and Lorraine the extra work. That's why Marta was working late. That's why."

"As her assistant you know what she's working on. You keep a log of incoming contacts, appointments."

"Yeah, sure. Yes."

"Have there been any contacts recently that caused concern, that were upsetting or unusual?"

Josie's eyes cut away. "No."

"Josie." Eve spoke just sharply enough to have the woman's gaze zipping back to hers. "You need to tell us."

"Marta said I wasn't supposed to say anything."

"That was before." Peabody sat down beside her. "You want to help Marta, to do what's right for her and her family."

"I do. I really do. She didn't want Sly upset, and she said she'd take care of it."

"Take care of what?" Eve demanded.

"It was just . . . Ms. Mobsley. Um, Marta was doing the audit on her trust fund because the trustees ordered it. Marta was just doing her job, but Ms. Mobsley was really upset, really mad about it. How it's her money, and she wasn't having any dried-up numbers cruncher giving the assholes — that's her word, okay — any lever to cut her off. She said Marta was going to be sorry if she didn't do what she wanted."

"What did she want?"

"I think, I guess, she wanted Marta to, you know, tweak some numbers so everything looked fine. But the thing is, I'm not supposed to talk about accounts and people."

"You're relaying information to the police about a possible threat," Eve reminded her.

"It's just I helped run some of the numbers, research some of the data, and well, Ms. Mobsley was sort of cheating. She was taking funds she wasn't supposed to, and covering it, sort of, so it looked like approved expenses. And the trustees are the client, so Marta had to give them a clean report. Marta told her if she kept harassing her she'd have to report the communications to the trustees, and the court. And Ms. Mobsley got mega-steamed. Marta had me come in and close the door, and she told me — I heard some of it anyway — but she said since I was assisting on the audit, I needed to know. And I needed to tell her asap if Ms. Mobsley or anyone else contacted me about the audit, or tried to pressure me about it."

"Has anyone?"

"No. People like Ms. Mobsley don't notice assistants, I don't think. I was supposed to tell her — Ms. Mobsley — if she contacted the office again that Marta was unavailable. But to log the call and everything she said. If it didn't stop, she was going to tell Sly, and they were going to inform the trustees."

"Do you have Mobsley's full name and contact information?"

"Yes, sure. Candida Mobsley. I can get you her address — addresses," Josie corrected. "And the trustees. Should I tell Sly? Do you think I should tell him?"

"I do, but for now, tell me about yesterday. Did Mobsley try to contact Marta?"

"Not yesterday. We were so busy, and upset, too, because of the accident. Marta took on three audits, and two of them were barely started. I stayed late to help, but she told me to go home about eight, I think. I went home. I was really tired. My roommate just broke up with this guy, so we just hung for a couple hours."

"Okay. Get Detective Peabody that information, and why don't you ask Lorraine Wilkie to come in."

"All right." Josie rose. "She was a great boss, I just want to say. She was mag to work for, and taught me a lot."

Peabody waited until Josie went out. "Candida Mobsley's all over the media. She's been in and out of rehab for illegals and/or alcohol abuse, which is the excuse used when she wrecks another car, smacks another rival, tears up another hotel suite or whatever. Travels a lot. Third- or fourth-generation money that she's apparently pissing through as fast as she can."

"And you know this because?"

"McNab and I like to watch the gossip and celeb channels sometimes. It's fun. She's been engaged I don't know how many times, and was married for about five minutes after a mega-multi-million-dollar wedding on this private South Sea Island estate. They said her dress alone cost —"

"I don't care."

"Sorry, got caught up. What I'm saying is, she's really rich, really spoiled, and has a history of violent behavior."

"Someone who could afford to hire a somewhat sloppy hit on an accountant she was pissed at."

"Yeah, she could. Plus she ran with some rough types a couple years ago. The type who'd know how to hire a somewhat sloppy hit."

"Okay, get her info, and we'll have a talk with her. And why don't you go on down, see if the security guy's got the copy of the logs for us. If not you could try a little pressure there."

"I love this job." Bouncing a little at the prospect of interviewing the rich and infamous, Peabody walked out just as another woman came to the door.

Where Josie had been soft-featured, young, dewy, and clad in cutting-edge fashion, Lorraine was whittled down like a finely sharpened pencil. Thin and angular, with no-nonsense steel gray hair hacked short, she wore a mannish pants suit in banker navy with a crisp white shirt.

Her eyes might have been puffy, but they remained dry and steady as they sized Eve up.

"You're in charge of finding out who did this to Marta."

"I'm the primary investigator."

Lorraine nodded briskly as she entered. "You look capable." She sat, crossed her legs, folded her hands in her lap. "What do you need from me?"

Eve ran her through the basics. It seemed clear Marta's coworker knew nothing about trouble from Mobsley. Added to it, she wasn't as easy to manipulate into divulging information about the work as the soft-featured assistant.

"What we do here is very sensitive. We have an obligation to confidentiality. And the fact is, Marta and I worked on different accounts. We don't overlap as a rule. In case of illness or termination —" She broke off, pressed her thin lips together briefly. "I'm speaking of employment termination — Sylvester will assign one of us to an audit or client."

"Such as the accident requiring you and Marta to take on other work."

"Exactly. This firm has a reputation, earned and deserved, for accuracy, discretion, and efficiency, and our department's part of the reason for that reputation.

Clearly Chaz and Jim will be unable to work for several days, if not weeks. The work can't wait."

"Due to the sensitive nature of the work, have you ever been threatened or harassed?"

"For the most part we're dealing with corporations and large businesses. Their lawyers may jostle with ours, but most usually they're too busy jostling with the courts who approved or ordered the audit. There have been times, over the years, when an individual learns who is doing the actual figures, and there are — on rare occasions — angry calls, rarer still a personal confrontation here at the office. In those cases, one has to assume there's a reason for the anger and fear." She lifted bony shoulders. "For the most part we work in peace and quiet, and in a very pleasant atmosphere."

"How about bribes?"

Now Lorraine smiled. "Oh, it's not unheard of for someone mired in an audit to offer the auditor or one of the other staff a bribe to cover up what the audit would expose. Taking one means the risk of prison or a very stiff fine, the loss of a hard-earned license, termination from the firm."

"Bribe's sweet enough, it could be worth it to some."

"Maybe so, but it's foolish and shortsighted. Numbers don't lie, Lieutenant. Sooner or later, they'll add up correctly, and that quick, easy money will have proven a very poor choice. Marta would never make that choice."

"There's no question in your mind on that?"

"None whatsoever. She enjoyed her work, and was well compensated for it. Her husband enjoys his, and is well compensated. They have children, and she would never, never risk embarrassing her family, exposing her children to scandal. And at the core of it, of her? Integrity."

For the first time Lorraine's voice wavered, and those dry, steady eyes went damp. "I'm sorry. I'm trying not to be emotional, but it's very, very difficult."

"I understand. You've been very helpful. If you think of anything, please contact me. Any detail at all."

"I will." Lorraine rose. "I walk that way in good weather. In fact, Marta and I often walked together. I live only two blocks from where they said she was found. I like to walk in the city. I've never worried about walking in that neighborhood. My own neighborhood. Now I . . . It will be some time before I walk easily there again."

"One more thing," Eve said as Lorraine started out. "Do you have any business with or knowledge of the WIN Group?"

"Win? As in win or lose?" She pursed her lips at Eve's nod. "It sounds vaguely familiar, but I can't place it. I don't recall ever doing any work for or on them."

"Okay. Thank you."

She made the rounds with the rest of the staff, with Peabody when her partner returned with the log copy. While the statements filled in the picture of a woman well-liked by her coworkers, there were no real revelations. She couldn't claim surprise when the warrant bogged in legal mires, but she left the offices with every confidence Yung would find a way.

And she had one lead out of it.

"We'll track down this Candida Mobsley, but I want to go by the crime scene first, and I want to follow up with the two wits and a talk with Whitestone's partners. Start that search for the snatch vehicle."

She pulled away from the curb. By the time she'd maneuvered the handful of blocks, Peabody was asleep with her PPC in her hand.

Eve jabbed her with an elbow.

"Yes, sir! What?"

"There's a deli up the block there. Go, fuel up. Get me whatever."

"Yeah, okay. Sorry. We hung with Mavis and her gang until about midnight. It's catching up with me."

"Take a booster if you need it."

Peabody scrubbed her hands over her face, and yawning, crawled out of the car. Eve skirted around the hood, walked in the opposite direction through the insistent sleet to stand in front of the building where Marta Dickenson died.

It looked good, she decided, even in the crappy weather. Dignified, old-school, and very, very fresh. She imagined the owners would have little problem filling those spaces.

If they ignored the small detail of murder.

Standing in the sleet, she closed her eyes.

Park the van or the four-wheel, because a mini struck her as absurd for abduction, near the front of the office building. She has to come out sooner or later. Waiting's just part of the job. Security cams don't scope all the way to the sidewalk. Let her come out.

Get out of the vehicle, she imagined. Let her walk by, step in behind her, stun her, muffle her, muscle her in the back in seconds. One in the driver's seat, one in the back with her. Hold a hand over her mouth, hold her down when she struggles or makes noise. Short drive. One gets out, unlocks the door — one way or the other — comes back.

Muscle her inside. It wouldn't take more than seconds.

How wasn't hard, Eve decided. How seemed pretty straightforward. The why was trickier.

"Lieutenant."

She turned, watched Officer Carmichael approach, his heavy uniform coat wet, his face pink from the cold.

"I saw Detective Peabody in the deli. We were about to go in for a meal break."

"Whatcha got?"

"Not a lot. Nobody we've talked to heard anything. We dug up one possible wit, other side of the street, fourth-floor apartment, facing this way. She thinks, maybe, she saw a van parked over here last night."

"What kind of van?"

"Dark," he said with a wry twist of his lips. "Maybe black, maybe dark blue, maybe dark gray. No idea of make, model, plates. Her privacy screen hung up, and she was trying to fix it, thinks she saw a van over here. And she says she's sure the lights were on in the lower apartment. She noticed that especially as she's been watching the rehab progress. She figured the van was one of the crew, working late."

"What time?"

"About ten-thirty, she says, give or take a few minutes. She messed with the screen awhile, then went for her cohab. He was sleeping in his chair, kicked off watching the screen. I talked to him via 'link. He doesn't remember one way or the other. We knocked on a lot of doors. In a neighborhood like this, people mostly open up for the cops. But a lot of people were out during this canvass. We'll follow up in a few hours."

"Good enough. How did Turney do?"

Carmichael smiled a little. "She don't give up."

"Take her on the second pass if she wants it." Let her see, Eve thought. Homicide, like most cop work, was walking, waiting, asking questions, and paperwork.

She walked down the stairs, broke the seal, entered the apartment.

Nothing to see, really. Same as it had been, but for the fine layer of dust left by the sweepers, and that on-the-edge-of-nasty chemical smell that clung to the air.

They didn't take her farther than the front living space. No need to drag it out. Privacy-screened windows — lights showed through, but not movement, not activity. Good soundproofing. A dozen people might have walked by on the sidewalk, they'd never have heard her scream.

They took her briefcase, that was more than show, more than cover. That was part of the job. Take her work, her files, her memo book, her tablet, whatever she'd carried.

The woman had two kids at home. She wouldn't have played the hero. And for what? Numbers, someone else's money? She'd have told them whatever they wanted to know, if she knew it.

She didn't fight back. Did she believe they'd let her go if she told them, gave them, cooperated.

"Makes the most sense," Eve murmured as she circled the room. "Tell us, give us, what we want, and it doesn't have to get ugly."

She'd believe them because the alternative was too terrifying.

Peabody came in and brought the scent of something wonderful with her.

"Chicken noodle soup and twisty herb bread. They make it on site, right there. I got us both a large go-cup. Did Carmichael find you?"

"Yeah. Possible wit on a van parked out front, but no description of said van other than dark. Push the search on that, on the Cargo." Eve took the go-cup Peabody offered, sniffed, sampled. "Jesus. That's freaking good."

"It's freaking uptown squared. I started mine on the way back. The smell nearly killed me. It tastes a lot like my granny's."

"There's probably something illegal in here. I don't care." She hadn't realized how far she'd been flagging herself until she felt her energy rise up again.

"They got what they wanted from her," Eve stated. "If she'd said she didn't know, didn't have, whatever, they'd have messed her up more, broken some fingers, blackened her eye, hurt her until she gave it up, or they were sure she didn't have it. They got what they wanted, pretty quick, pretty easy."

"And they killed her anyway."

"They were always going to kill her. Whatever she knew, had, did — they couldn't have her pass it to anyone else, talk about it. Her work, and this place, either the owners or somebody on the construction crew. My money's on the owners, but we'll see about the construction people. A job like this, they went high-end. High-end construction firms make plenty. And I bet audits aren't out of the ordinary."

Eve bit off a hunk of bread. "Got to be illegal. Let's go talk to the wit and his partners."

"You still want to talk to Candida, right?"

"After, if you can stay awake long enough to track her down."

"I'm totally charged up again. Maybe I should go buy a gallon of that soup. No! I'll e-mail my granny, and I'll sweet-talk her into sending me some."

"You have no shame, or guile." Eve led the way out, still sipping soup. "You e-mail her and tell her you just had some soup that's as good as hers — subtext, maybe better — and it made you think about her, blah blah. How good it was, on a cold, crappy day in New York, yadda, yadda. She'll cook up a batch and ship it out to prove hers is better."

Peabody slid into the car, stared at Eve. "Have you met my granny, because that's exactly what she'd do. That's brilliant."

"That's why I'm the LT, and you're not."

"Too true. Are you going to eat all your bread?"

"Yes."

"I was afraid of that." Peabody pulled out her PPC again, and went to work trying to locate Candida Mobsley.

"She's in town," Peabody reported, "according to her personal assistant. Her appointment calendar is full, I didn't say cop. I didn't say I wasn't a cop, but saying cop would've maybe had her blowing before we get to her."

"At last, some guile."

"It must've been the soup."

Eve parked in Midtown. The sleet had eased off, but the cold held tight. She blessed the soup for keeping her bones warm as they moved into a towering office building.

She badged security, gave her destination, and squeezed her way onto an elevator.

"Dallas, there are over two thousand Maxima Cargos — '59 and '60 with New York registrations. More than double that if we include New Jersey."

"Dark color. Black, dark blue, dark gray."

"That *is* just dark colors."

"Try using the Blue Steel interior to eliminate." She considered Harpo's report on the factory sealant. "And stick with 2060 models for now."

Eighteen crowded floors later, she pushed off, strode to the menu of choices. "WIN Group." She pointed, took a left jog, found the nameplate on a set of double doors.

"Over eight hundred registered," Peabody reported. "New York alone."

"We'll do a standard search and match with the names we have. If nothing pops, we widen it out."

She pushed through the doors. Inside the small reception area they'd gone for energy — lots of reds, bright whites, chrome. The smoldering brunette behind the counter offered a slow, liquid smile.

"May I help you?"

"Lieutenant Dallas, Detective Peabody." She set her badge on the counter.

"Oh, this is about that poor woman Brad found last night. Did you find out who mugged her?"

"We need to see Mr. Whitestone," Eve said.

"Of course. Sorry. He's really shaken up about it." She tapped her earpiece. "Brad? The police are here. Yes, Lieutenant Dallas. I will." She tapped again. "I'll take you back to his office. Would you like anything?"

She might never want anything again after the soup. "We're fine. Are Mr. Whitestone's partners available?"

"Jake's at a business lunch and should be back by two. He has a two-thirty. Rob's in with a client. I can let his assistant know you're here if you need to speak with him."

"Do that."

Before she could open the door, Whitestone stepped out. Like Lorraine's his shirt was crisp and white. His suit perfectly tailored. But shadows dogged his eyes.

"Thanks, Marie. Lieutenant, Detective, I hope you're here to tell me you found the mugger." He stepped back to let them into a small, slick office. A good window, she noted, a counter for an AC and a minifriggie. Contemporary art, a glossy black workstation, and a couple of visitors' chairs in that energetic red.

"We've confirmed that Marta Dickenson was killed inside your apartment —"

"What? *Inside?*"

"It wasn't a mugging. When's the last time you were in the apartment?"

"I —" He sat down. "Day before yesterday. I went by to talk to the crew supervisor about a couple of details."

"Name."

"Jasper Milk. Milk and Sons Contractors. They're third generation. They're artists. And they're reputable. They *always* secure the building. We have an alarm system."

"Yes. I saw it. Who has the codes?"

"I do, Jasper. My partners. And, ah, the designer. Sasha Kirby. City Style. If this person broke in —"

"There's no sign of a break-in."

Eve watched his expression change, shift from puzzlement to understanding, then to stubborn denial.

"Listen, I trust, absolutely, everyone who has the code, who has access. I don't see how anyone could have gotten inside my apartment."

"Evidence doesn't lie, Mr. Whitestone."

"Maybe not, but it sure as hell doesn't make any sense. That's a brand-new system."

"Brewer, Kyle, and Martini. Accounting firm, auditors. The victim worked for them, and there's some cross between the clients of your firm and theirs."

He no longer looked puzzled or stubborn, but slightly ill. "I don't know that name offhand. I can have my admin check, but — if you tell me the clients we have in common —"

"Peabody."

At the ready, Peabody reeled off the short list of cross-matches she'd already found.

"Those aren't mine. I recognize Abner Wheeler. He's one of Jake's. And Blacksford Corporation, that's one of Rob's. Those I'm sure of, but to confirm any others, I'd need to check files, or talk to Rob and Jake."

"We're going to need to speak with your partners."

"Absolutely. I don't understand. Why would anyone use our new place to kill that woman?"

"Good question," Eve responded.

CHAPTER
FIVE

Whitestone took them into a small conference room, apologizing for its size and sparseness.

"It's one of the reasons we invested in the new building. We need the space. We've been moving some things over here and there, so we're in flux right now."

"It's no problem. Business must be good."

"It is." His face lit up. "We've been growing steadily, building a solid client base, a good reputation. And the building uptown has character, looks important. Perception's reality in finance."

"In a lot of things."

"Let me hunt up Jake and Rob."

"Before you do, why don't you give me a little backstory. How long have you been partners?"

"Officially? We're finishing our fifth year. Rob and I went to college together. We invested in our first property our first year of grad school, this dumpy little retail space on the Lower West Side."

He relaxed as he spoke, and nostalgia clung to the edges of his tone. "His idea, and he had to talk me into it. I like money," he said with a grin, "I like the deal, calculating risk and reward, and I was cautious about investing in a little commercial space. Rob wouldn't give up until I threw in with him. Best decision I ever made, because it jump-started us as a team. We worked like dogs on that place, did most of the work ourselves, and I learned a lot about sweat equity. When we flipped it, made a nice profit, we dumped most of that profit in the market, as partners, played the market together, made some more."

"It sounds like you worked well together."

"We did, and do. After college I went to work for Prime Financial, and he worked for Allied, but we'd get together and talk about forming our own company. Rob met Jake at Allied, and the three of us just clicked. The three of us bought another place together. Once we turned it, we had what we called the WIN investment fund. We started this place with it. Jake's uncle — he's the Ingersol in Ingersol-Williams Corp — gave us one of his subsidiaries to manage, and my father let us take over the management of a small lead trust and we were off and running."

"It's good to work with friends," Eve said simply. "If you can find yours, we'll get this done and out of your way."

"Give me a minute. Oh, help yourself to coffee or whatever. The coffee's good here."

Maybe, Eve thought, and decided to check it out by programming a cup for herself and one for Peabody. "He's enthusiastic," Eve commented.

"Yeah, but if you're not excited about your work, life's crap."

"He also doesn't strike me as a moron, which he'd have to be if he arranged or took part in the killing, set it up in what will be his apartment, then, oops, discovers the body."

"If he wanted the attention, wanted to put himself inside the investigation."

Eve shook her head. "Not him, and not this murder. This was a hit, not a mission." She narrowed her eyes as she tried the coffee. "This is Roarke's blend."

"Oh God. Our own small miracle."

"Business is good," Eve said again.

Whitestone came back in. "Rob's just finishing up with a client, and he'll be right in. Jake's heading back from a lunch meeting. It shouldn't be long. Do you need me to stay? I've got a client coming in, but I can reschedule."

"I think we have what we need from you for now."

"All right. Listen, I know it sounds crass, but can you give me an idea when the crew can get back into the apartment? I'm just trying to work out a time line."

"We should be able to clear it by the end of the day, tomorrow latest."

"Okay."

"I'd advise you to change the codes, and to be very careful who you give them to in the future."

"You can count on it. And here's Rob. Lieutenant Dallas, Detective Peabody, Robinson Newton."

"A pleasure to meet you, despite the circumstances."

He strode into the room covered in an aura of absolute confidence with hints of power. She recognized the combination. Roarke had it — in spades. Robinson Newton cultivated the aura with a meticulously tailored suit in slate gray pinstripes mated with a shirt in a subtly deeper hue, and a bold red tie.

Under the suit he was built like a quarterback, muscled and tough and honed.

He wore his hair in a dark skull cap that brought out the ice-pick cheekbones in a face the color of Peabody's coffee regular. His eyes, a direct and bold green met Eve's, then Peabody's. He offered a hand to each — smooth, firm, dry — then gestured to the conference table.

"We're a little Spartan at the moment, but please have a seat. I'm sorry I kept you waiting."

"No problem."

"I heard about the mugging early this morning. It's terrible, but when Brad told me you were in charge, I felt better about it. I've followed some of your cases, particularly since I read the Icove book. In fact, I just scored tickets to the premiere." He gave his partner a thumbs-up. "Six, so round up a date. And I apologize," he said quickly. "You're not here to talk about Hollywood and red carpets. What can we do to help?"

"You had access to the apartment."

"Yes. We all have access to every area in the building."

"Can you tell me where you were last night between nine P.M. and midnight?"

"I can." He reached in his pocket, took out a date book, keyed into it, then set it on the table in front of Eve. "Dinner with my fiancée and her parents at Tavern on the Green, they like their traditions. Eight o'clock reservations, and we left a little after ten. Lissa and I caught a cab, then met up with some friends at Reno's Bar, that's downtown. We didn't stay all that long. Maybe an hour. Then we cabbed back to our place. We got home about midnight. Are we suspects?"

"It's routine," Eve said automatically. "The victim was taken inside the apartment, you have access. It's helpful to know where you were. I'll need the names of the people you were with, just for the files."

"I'll have my assistant get you a list of names and contacts. But we didn't even know the victim. Did we?" he asked Whitestone.

"I didn't. But she worked for one of your clients' accounting firm. Blacksford."

"She was with Brewer, Kyle, and Martini? I have three — I think three — clients with them." He took his book back, slid it into his pocket. "But I don't remember having any contact with her. I work with Jim Arnold."

Eve took out Marta's ID photo. "Do you recall having seen her, having met her?"

"I don't. I'm sorry. I've had lunch with Jim several times, and with Sly — Sylvestor Gibbons, but I never did business with this woman."

"It would help if you got me the names of any clients you have who cross with the victim's firm."

"That's simple enough. You don't think this was a random mugging? A random opportunity? I'm sure anyone in that neighborhood knows the building's being worked on, isn't tenanted yet."

"It wasn't a break-in," Eve said.

"Maybe the crew left the apartment unsecured."

"They never do," Whitestone reminded him.

"Mistakes happen, Brad."

"We're investigating all possibilities," Eve began, then stopped when she heard voices.

"That's Jake." Whitestone slipped out, and stepped in again a moment later with his other partner. "My appointment's on the way up. If you don't need me —"

"We'll be in touch," Eve told him.

"Jake Ingersol, Lieutenant Dallas and Detective Peabody. I'm in my office."

"What a mess, huh?" Ingersol offered his hand, quick, hearty shakes, then dropped down at the table. "Hell of a thing to happen. Brad's been sick about it."

Where Whitestone projected cheerful competence and Newton smooth confidence, Ingersol was like an energetic puppy, all movement and avid eyes.

Like his partners, he wore a good suit, a perfectly knotted and coordinated tie, and shoes with a mirror gleam. Sun-streaked brown hair curled around his face, made him seem very youthful, somewhat innocent. But his eyes, though warm brown, were sharp, savvy.

"Café Diablo," Newton said mildly.

"What can I say, it's what the client wants. I start out hyped," he told Eve, "add a couple of double Diablo Locas and I'm overwired. I'm getting bits and pieces of what's going on. Brad said they were inside the apartment? *Inside?*"

"That's correct."

"We put in damn good security. I don't get it."

"We believe they had the codes."

He opened his mouth, shut it again, and sat back. "Jesus, Rob. One of Jasper's crew?"

"We don't know that," Newton said quickly.

"Do you have any reason to suspect someone on the construction crew?" Eve asked him.

"Just doing the math." He rose, grabbed a bottle of water out of the friggie. "Not that many people have the codes. We sure as hell didn't kill anybody."

"Jasper and his people worked on my place for six months before they started on the building," Newton pointed out. "There was never so much as a coffee mug missing."

"I know, hey, I know, and I like him, too. A lot. I guess somebody didn't lock up, that's all, and whoever killed that woman got lucky."

Eve nudged Marta's photo toward Ingersol. "Do you know her?"

"No, I don't . . . wait a minute." He shifted a little closer, studied the photo. "Maybe, but I can't pin it down."

"She worked for Brewer, Kyle, and Martini," Newton said before Eve could speak.

"That's it!" Ingersol snapped his fingers, right hand, left hand — pop, pop. "That's where I've seen her. We coordinate with our clients' accountants, on taxes, investments, portfolio strategy. I've got some clients who use that firm. I work with Chaz Parzarri and Jim Arnold, but I met her awhile back. Just in passing. Wow. I met her."

"Can you tell me where you were last night, between nine P.M. and midnight?"

His mouth dropped open, briefly. He lifted the water bottle, swallowed. "And another wow. Are we suspects?"

"It's routine," Eve said again.

"Well, sure, I was . . . let me think." He pulled out a date book. "I had drinks with Sterling Alexander, Alexander and Pope Properties, and that's one of the clients I share with Chaz. We, ah, met at about six-thirty at the Blue Dog Room. I think he left about seven-fifteen, close to that. He was going out to dinner, I think. I finished my drink, then I hooked up with some friends — a woman I'm seeing and another couple — for dinner. Chez Louis. I guess we left about ten-thirty. Alys and I went back to my place. We stayed in."

"I'd like a list of names and contact information, for the files."

"Sure." He looked at Newton again. "This is really weird."

"I'll also need a list of any other clients you have who cross with the victim's firm." Done, Eve got to her feet. "We appreciate your cooperation."

It took some time to get all the names and contacts she needed and the receptionist was chatty.

She learned she'd only copped the job a year before, when the expanding client list had warranted a separate receptionist rather than the assistants riding herd. The partners planned to connect with a small law firm, establishing them in the new building. They hoped, within the year, to take on an associate.

"An interesting mix," Eve commented when they walked out of the offices.

"I think it works for them. Smooth operator — and slap my ass, is that guy built!"

"I noticed."

"I love McNab's skinny ass and bony shoulders, but *mama*! Anyway, Newton's the smooth one, Whitestone's the charisma, and Ingersol's the hamster."

"Hamster?"

"On the wheel. Go, go, get it done."

"Something like that."

"They're all alibied up."

"We'll run the alibis through, but I expect they'll hold. Mr. Body probably has the muscle to snap a neck, but he'd be too smart to use his own place for it. Maybe he, or Ingersol, wanted to flick a little dirt on Whitestone — a twofer — but they wouldn't get their hands dirty. They're serious suits."

"But run them anyway," Peabody said.

"You bet."

"None of the three of them have a Cargo registered. Not in their names or the company name."

"Check Newton's finances, and their families, their family businesses."

Once more she got behind the wheel. The boost of magic chicken soup wouldn't last much longer, but she wanted to cover more ground.

"Let's see if we can have a conversation with Mobsley."

"Hot damn."

"And try not to be a dick."

"I know how to behave," Peabody huffed. "I'm in a vid, you know. I've had a scene with vid stars. I'm going to a major premiere, and *I* didn't have to score tickets. They were given to me."

"Yeah, yeah."

"Come on, you have to be a little juiced. Mavis said the dress Leonardo designed for you is mag to the extreme."

She remembered, vaguely, it was magenta — according to Leonardo who'd sided with Roarke when she'd said she already had fancy dresses, and why couldn't she just wear black anyway.

"I don't know why they have to make so much fuss over a vid. You go to it, you watch it, and eat popcorn."

"It's about *us*. Plus," Peabody added slyly, knowing her target, "it's really important to Nadine."

Nadine Furst, ace reporter, screen personality, best-selling author — and, damn it, friend. No getting around it. "I'm going, aren't I?"

"We're going to look fantabulous, mix with celebrities — and we actually know them — and walk the red carpet. Like stars. I think I'm going to be sick."

"Not in my vehicle. And right now, I'm just a little more concerned with who the hell killed Marta Dickenson than standing around on some stupid red carpet while people gape at me."

Peabody wisely neglected to mention the pre-premiere prep she and Mavis had already worked out, which included hair and makeup by Trina.

Eve had Trina fear.

"What's that look for?" Eve demanded.

"It's my 'serious about murder' face."

"Bullshit."

"I am serious about murder," Peabody insisted. And nearly sighed with relief when the in-dash 'link signaled.

"LT." Detective Carmichael came on screen. "We finished the search at the vic's residence. Nothing out of line. We went through the vehicle. Same deal. McNab went through their electronics, fine-toothed them. Nada."

"Figured it. We're working on a warrant for her office data, client list."

"McNab said there was some work stuff on her home unit."

"Is that so?" Eve smiled. "Take it. The warrant covers it. Have him make copies of everything. I want you and Santiago to go have a chat with a Sasha Kirby, designer with City Style. She designed the crime scene, so to speak, and had access." She checked the time, calculated. "After, I've got some alibis for you to run down."

"You got it."

Eve clicked off. "Peabody, contact Yung and tell her the residence is clear. See if you can get any kind of ETA on the warrant. We got a little break here," she murmured. "Could be something relevant on her home unit. Could be."

It was the day for penthouses and the Upper East Side, Eve decided. This time she had no choice but to wade through security, cool heels in the gold and white lobby jammed with flowering plants. As she'd figured on a hassle, she only lifted her eyebrows when security politely cleared her.

"I figured Mobsley would tell us to stick it," Eve said as they rode up.

"Maybe she's curious. Or guilty. According to the gossip channel she's always doing something."

"Which is why the expected stick it."

With a shrug, Eve stepped off into a foyer done in sapphire blue and emerald green. More flowers, this time in tall white vases, flanked by candles as tall as she was.

A man in unrelieved black with white-blond hair and nearly as many earrings as McNab stepped out of wide blue doors.

"Please come in. Candida will be with you shortly. We're serving catnip tea today."

"We'll pass on that."

"I'd be happy to prepare another choice." He gestured them into a huge space that looked like a small palace under a snowstorm. Every inch was white — sofas, tables, rugs, lamps, pillows. The only spot of color came from the white-framed portrait — their hostess reclining naked on a white bed. Her endless tumble of blonde hair and deeply red lips jumped out of the canvas.

Even the curtains on the wall of windows were filmy white so the city beyond seemed to float on clouds.

But not, in Eve's mind, in a good way.

Something moved in the snowbank. She realized a huge white cat, its eyes blinking vivid green, stretched on some sort of divan. It watched them while its tail flicked lazily.

She liked cats. She had her own. But this one, like the room, like the filmed windows, gave her the creeps.

"We're fasting today, so I can't offer you food. Or caffeine, but we have some lovely water, harvested from snowmelt in the Andes."

"That'd be great," Peabody said before Eve could decline for both of them.

"Please be at home."

"I'd like to see what water from snowmelt in the Andes tastes like," Peabody said when he left them.

"I bet it tastes like water. Who could live in this place?"

"It's sort of giving me a headache. It hurts my eyes, and I have to keep blinking to see where things actually are. Oh Jesus, that's not a pussycat."

"Huh?" Eve glanced back. No, not just a cat. A *cat*. Maybe a lion — small scale, but . . . Or a tiger, or —

"A white panther cub."

Candida, draped in a white sweater, snug white pants, white diamonds in a hard sparkle, glided in on bare feet. Her hair tumbled around a face as beautiful and as hard as her diamonds.

"Delilah." She stroked a hand over the cub as she passed by. "Is Aston getting your tea?"

"Water," Eve corrected. "We appreciate you taking the time to speak with us."

"Oh well." She laughed, waved a hand, then curled up on a curvy white sofa, all but disappeared into it. "I spend a lot of time talking to the police, or my lawyers do. I know who you are, and I'm interested. I thought you'd be older."

"Than what?"

She laughed again. "I'm going to the premiere of your vid."

"It's not my vid."

"I love premieres. You never know who you'll see, or be seen by. Never know what might happen, and there's nothing like seeing what nightmare dresses some women wear. Leonardo's doing yours."

"I'm not here to talk about my wardrobe."

"Too bad. I could talk about clothes for hours. There you are, Aston. Will you make sure Delilah has her snack?"

"Of course." He set her tea on the table beside her, walked over to offer the two glasses on the tray to Eve and Peabody.

"So, why are you here? I don't have much time. I have appointments."

"Marta Dickenson was murdered last night."

Candida stretched her arms, shifted into recline pose. "Who's Marta Dickenson, and why should I care?"

"She's the accountant doing your trust fund audit. The one you've threatened."

"Oh her."

"Yeah, her."

"If somebody killed her, it doesn't make any difference to me."

"Doesn't it?"

"No, I asked Tony, and he said they'd just have somebody else fuck with the audit. But maybe they won't be such a bitch about it."

"Who's Tony?"

"Tony Greenblat. He's my money guy."

"One of the trustees?"

She made an ugly, dismissive sound. "He's not one of those tight-assed old farts. He's my personal finance manager, and he's my lawyer, too. One of them. He's working to get *my* money from *my* trust."

"So Tony advised you it wouldn't do you much good to kill Marta Dickenson."

"Yeah. No!" Face sulky now, she angled herself up again. "You're trying to trick me. I'm not stupid, you know."

No, Eve thought, you go beyond stupid. "Why did you ask him about her?"

"Well, she's dead, right? I thought maybe that would work for me. But Tony said it wouldn't, so . . ." She shrugged it off, sipped her tea.

"If you didn't know her, as you stated when I asked, why did you ask Tony?"

Candida's eyebrows drew together in what Eve assumed was deep thought. "So what? So I knew who she was."

"*So what* is you lied to a police officer during a murder investigation. If you'd lie about something as simple as that, I have to believe you'd lie about more important things. Like whether or not you arranged Marta Dickenson's murder."

In a bad-tempered move, Candida slapped her white cup down on the white table. "I did not either."

"You threatened her. You harassed her. You made angry, threatening calls to her, and she responded by

93

informing you to cease and desist or she would inform the trustees and the court. Now she's dead."

"So what?" Candida demanded again. "I can say what I want, there's no law against it."

"You'd be wrong about that."

"It's, like, freedom of speech. It's, like, the Fifth Amendment or whatever. Look it up!"

"I'll be sure to do that," Eve murmured. "Since we're talking about rights, let me read you yours, just so everybody understands."

Candida went back into sulk mode as Eve recited the Revised Miranda. "Like I haven't heard all that before."

"Well, it bears repeating. So you understand your rights and obligations."

"Yeah, BFD."

"Why don't you tell us what you said to Ms. Dickenson when you were exercising your interpretation of your constitutional rights?"

"What?"

"What's your version of your conversation with Marta Dickenson."

"Jesus, why didn't you just *say* that? All I did was ask her to ease off — it's *my* money, and it's just stupid I have to go begging to those tight asses every time I want more. And I was *nice* to her. I sent her flowers, didn't I? I said how I'd give her ten thousand under the table if she'd just clear it. Ten thousand's a nice chunk for some bookkeeper bitch."

"You suggested Ms. Dickenson doctor the audit in your favor, and in return you'd give her ten thousand dollars?"

94

"Yeah. I was *nice*. And she got pissy about it. So I said fine, fine. Make it twenty, and she's all 'I'll have to report you if you keep this shit up,' like that."

"Peabody, your cuffs or mine?"

"Can we use mine?"

"What're you talking about? You stay away from me." Candida cringed back on the sofa. "Aston!"

"Ms. Mobsley, you've just confessed to offering a bribe to Marta Dickenson in the amount of twenty thousand dollars in exchange for her altering a court-appointed audit. That's a felony."

"It is not!"

"Look it up," Eve suggested as Aston rushed in. "Step back, pal, unless you want to be restrained and charged."

"What's the matter? What's happening?"

"They're trying to say they can arrest me for being nice to that stupid dead accountant. I just said I'd give her money."

Obviously, a bit more evolved than his employer, Aston shut his eyes. "Oh, Candida."

"What's the matter? What's the problem? It's *my* money. I was going to give her some."

"Lieutenant, please, Candida didn't understand the implications. Can we just take a moment, just take a moment? I'll contact her lawyer. He'll come immediately."

"Let's try this first. Come clean, absolutely clean. Answer questions without the bullshit, and we'll see."

"Absolutely. Absolutely. Now, Candida, you need to answer the lieutenant's questions. You need to tell her the truth."

"I did!"

"You lied with your first answer. Try again."

"I didn't recognize her name at first, that's all."

"Peabody. Your cuffs."

"Okay, okay. Jesus! I was just playing it a little frosty. No big. I admitted I knew who she was, didn't I?"

"You threatened her."

"Maybe I said some things. I was upset. It's the trustees that're the real dicks. And my grandfather for being such a tight ass. And my parents, for God's sake, because —"

"I don't care about the trustees, your grandfather or your parents, though I pity them all. I care about Marta Dickenson."

"I didn't *do* anything. I just said how I'd give her money, like a favor. You do this, I pay you. I pay lots of people to do stuff."

"Lieutenant," Aston began.

"Quiet." She glanced down at a familiar sensation to see the white panther cub rubbing and winding itself between her shins. Weird.

"You contacted her numerous times, threatened her if she didn't cooperate."

"I was upset! I was nice to her at first, and she was pissy to me. So I got pissy."

"You were going to make her sorry."

"Damn right. I know people who'd make sure she was sorry."

"Is that so?" Eve questioned when Aston moaned quietly.

"I was working on it, too. The tight asses always want me to make wise investments, right? So I've been working on buying that stupid place where she works. Then I could fire her ass."

"Your plan was to buy the firm and fire her?"

"Damn right! Tony said how they weren't interested in selling, but people always fall in when you hand them enough money. And he said — Tony — that even if they did, the stupid courts would just get another firm for the stupid audit, but it was the *principle*. I've got principles just like anybody."

"And knowing people like you do, maybe you know people who'd know how to scare her. Rough her up a little."

"Huh? Like —" Candida mimed punching. "Come on!" Now she laughed. "If I wanted to smack her, I'd smack her myself. But if I smack anybody for another like eighty-one days, I have to take more anger management, and that's so frigging boring I can't stand it. Probably she pissed somebody else off. I figured that out when I heard somebody killed her. People who mess with other people's money piss people off."

When the cub tried to climb up Eve's leg, she gave it an absent scratch between the ears, then nudged it away. When it moved away, stretching then curling up in a ball, she concluded it had more brains than its owner.

"All right."

"All right what?"

"That's what we need for now. We'll be in touch if we need more."

Aston gripped his hands together. "Should I call the lawyer?"

"Not at this time. Sending flowers is nice; bribery's not nice," she told Candida. "It's illegal. Try to remember that. Peabody."

When they stepped back into the elevator, Eve sighed hugely. "Conclusion?"

"I thought she'd be cagey and canny. I mean all that money, you'd think she'd be smart. But she's dumb as a brick. Dumber. Too stupid to have arranged murder — or if not, too stupid not to admit it — like she was just paying somebody to do her a favor."

"Agreed. Buy the firm so she could fire the auditor." Eve shook her head. "Because she's got principles."

"And her Fifth Amendment rights — or whatever."

"Yeah. She should've invoked it instead of incriminating herself on the bribe."

"But she was just being nice."

Eve shook her head on a laugh. "So, how was the Andes snowmelt water?"

"Wet."

CHAPTER
SIX

Considering the time, Eve opted to send Peabody to interview Jasper Milk. She wanted a follow-up with Alva Moonie. Bradley Whitestone's date and co-witness might add more insight into the three partners.

She found Alva at home, not a penthouse this time, but a pretty brownstone on the Upper West.

Eve approved the security, especially when it didn't dick around with her. Within moments, Alva opened the door wearing a slim, short purple dress and bare feet.

"Lieutenant Dallas, what timing. I just got in from work."

"Work?"

"I put time in with a nonprofit group. A family foundation thing. Come in."

The foyer boasted walls nearly the same color as Alva's dress and a tile rug in geometric prints. Alva moved through, to the left and into a wide, high-ceilinged living area that hit somewhere between the Dickensons' and Candida's in style. Rich — Eve recognized it in the art, in the fabrics, the scatter of antiques. And comfort in deep cushions, more color, a softly simmering fire in the hearth.

"I was about to have a glass of wine — long day. Can I offer you one?"

"Thanks anyway, but go ahead."

"Sissy's getting it. My housekeeper," she explained. "She was my nanny once upon a time, and she's still looking out for me. Please, sit down. I expected I'd hear from you again. Have you found out what happened to that poor woman?"

"The investigation's ongoing."

"Brad got in touch about an hour ago." Alva sat, curled up her legs. "He said you'd come to talk to him and the others. And that you think she was killed inside the apartment. That she was a specific target."

"He saved me time explaining."

"Shouldn't he have told me?"

"It's fine." She glanced over when a tall, attractive brunette came in with a tray holding a bottle of red wine, two glasses, and a little plate of cheese and fruit.

"Thanks, Sissy. This is Lieutenant Dallas. Cicily Morgan, my rock."

"It's good to meet you." She spoke in an accent Eve thought of as classy Brit. "Can I pour you a glass of wine?"

"On duty, but thanks."

"Coffee? Tea?"

"I'm good."

"I'll leave you to talk."

"Sissy, sit down and have a glass of wine with me since Lieutenant Dallas can't. Is it all right?" Alva asked Eve. "I've already told Sissy the whole story."

"It's fine," Eve said. "I'm just here to follow up. Maybe you can tell me a little more about your relationship with Bradley Whitestone."

"We met at a fund-raiser a few weeks ago. He's courting me." She smiled as she poured wine in two glasses. "My portfolio anyway. I don't mind. He has good, fresh ideas, an appealing approach."

"So it's not a personal relationship."

"Not yet determined. I like him, but I'm careful. I wasn't always, was I?" She patted Sissy's hand, got a quiet smile.

"You were young, perhaps a bit headstrong."

"A bit?" Alva tossed back her head on a laugh. "Sissy's discreet. I went through a wild stage, not that long ago in the scheme of things. Clubs, clubs, more clubs, parties, men. Even a couple of women just to say I had. Throwing money away because it was there. Then I was wild with the wrong man. He hurt me."

"I'm sorry."

"To keep the story short, he beat me unconscious, raped me, then beat me again. He stole from me, tossed me out of my own apartment — naked. If one of the neighbors hadn't heard me, gotten me inside, called the police, I don't know what might have happened."

"Did they get him?"

"They did. It was an ugly trial. I was on trial as much as he was. My family, which includes Sissy, stood by me. Even after everything I'd said and done."

"I don't remember hearing about this."

"It was in London. I'd moved there, more or less. It was about four years ago. Sissy moved in with me, took

101

care of me. I went to counseling, and I came home. I came home a different person, and a better one than when I left."

"You came home the person you always were," Sissy corrected. "It just took you some time to find her."

"I didn't want to lose that person again, so I asked Sissy to come back with me, stay with me. She's my compass. I bought this place, and I'm trying to deserve the second chance. Which concludes the condensed version of my life story."

"It's a nice place. It feels . . . content."

"Thanks, that's exactly what we want."

"I just came from one that didn't feel so content. Do you know Candida Mobsley?"

"Yes, I do." With another quick look at Sissy who only sighed, Alva sipped more wine. "She was one of the so I could say I did. We cut quite a foolish swath for a few months back in the bad old days. We don't, let's say, have the same lifestyle anymore, but I see her now and again at an event or a party. She hasn't changed much. Is she . . ." As surprise flickered across her face, Alva lowered her glass. "Candida's not involved in this?"

"I don't think so, no."

"She's wild, and a little crazy, and frankly not very bright."

"Yeah, I got all that."

"She's the person she wants to be," Sissy added, then immediately straightened. "I'm sorry. That was harsh and unnecessary."

102

"And true," Alva added. "If she's using, which is a lot, she might pick a fight. Slap someone, throw things — actually more a tantrum than a fight. But I can't see her doing anything like this, not what was done to that woman."

"She has enough money, and connections, to hire someone to do it for her," Eve pointed out.

"No, not even that. If she had a problem with someone, she'd have her tantrum, throw money around, threaten, throw more money. But murder?"

Alva picked up her wine again, settled back. "Honestly, I don't think it would occur to her, or that she has it in her. If for some reason she did, she — not being very bright — would brag about it."

"Interesting," Eve commented. "That was exactly my take."

"Maybe I should try law enforcement." Alva laughed again. "And not in a million years. So . . . You haven't asked, but I'll answer. I can't see Brad doing anything like this either. It's true I've only known him a few weeks, but I'm a much better judge of character than I used to be. And Sissy?"

"Yes. I like him. He has manners, humor, and enthusiasm."

"My compass," Alva repeated. "Last night, we had a really good time, relaxing, fun, easy. Dinner, then drinks. I said something about how interesting it must be to refurbish an entire building. I liked that he'd built his company with his friends, that they were revitalizing this building. We talked about it a little, and he said since the building was just a couple blocks away, maybe I'd like to see it."

"So the idea evolved," Eve prompted.

"Yes, exactly. And I did want to see it, to see what he and his partners had done. He was excited to show me, pleased I wanted to see it. And I think, possibly, we might have shifted that relationship into the personal. But after . . . We were both so shocked. He took me home, came in awhile. Neither of us wanted to be alone. He caught a couple hours' sleep in the guest room."

"What about his partners? What do you know about them?"

"I've met them. The Bod —" Laughing, Alva fanned her hand in front of her face. "We had dinner with him — Rob and his fiancée, and Jake and a date. No business. Part of the courtship, I'd say, but very pleasant. I've also had my father do some research on them, professionally, and personally. I don't take chances anymore. He likes what he sees. It's unlikely he'd shift his allegiances, but he's fine with them if I decide to."

"All right. That should do it."

"Have you been working since I saw you this morning?"

"That's the job."

"I can't imagine it. Sissy and I read the Icove book. We're going to the premiere."

"Alva, you take a date."

"I am." Alva slid her arm through Sissy's. "My choice. We really enjoyed the book."

"It was fascinating," Sissy said. "I feel sorry for those women, the young girls, the children."

"So do I." Eve got to her feet. "I appreciate the time, and the candor. From where I'm standing, you're doing a good job with that second chance."

She put her vehicle on auto, partly because she was bone-ass tired and because she wanted to do a few more runs on the way home. She started standards on every member of the victim's firm, every member of Whitestone's firm.

What she needed, Eve decided, was to dig into the files McNab had copied from the victim's home office unit. That gave them a leg up until Yung finessed a warrant.

And, she admitted, there was no way she could comprehensively analyze financials, numbers, audits, whatever the hell it was unless she cleared her head, recharged.

As she drove through the gates, she rubbed her gritty eyes and thought home had never looked so good.

November's cold and blowing winds stripped the last of the leaves from the trees rising over the wide green lawn. But that just left the view of the house, its towers and turrets, the castlelike gray stone, open. She could already imagine herself inside — in the warmth, the color, the quiet.

She'd grab a shower first, hot, hot, hot, with all those jets pounding the endless day from her body. Maybe twenty minutes down for a quick power nap. Then some food at her desk while she trudged her way through a bunch of numbers she hoped she'd understand.

She pulled up to the grand front entrance, left her car and, so relieved to just be there, all but sleepwalked into the house.

Summerset stood in the foyer, the nightmare in her dreamscape. His bony body clad in his habitual black suit, he eyed her critically while the fat cat Galahad sat at his heel.

"If the cat had dragged anything in, it would be you."

Deliberately, she stripped off her coat, tossed it over the newel post. "Only because he'd have figured you weren't worth the effort." A little lame, she thought, but coherent.

The cat in question trotted over, started to rub against her leg. He froze, arched, sniffing at her with a wild gleam in his bicolored eyes.

Then he backed up, stared up at her. And hissed.

"Hey!"

"Apparently it's you he doesn't appear to think worth the effort."

For a moment she was both puzzled and mortified. This was *her* cat — and he had very genuinely saved her life. Twice.

Now he stood like a bloated version of a Halloween cat, back arched, hair on end, snarling.

And she remembered the panther cub.

"It's not my fault. I was conducting an interview. She had a freaking baby panther. I didn't invite it over for milk and kibble."

Galahad, obviously finding her excuses as lame as her daily insult, turned away, stuck up his tail in a nonverbal *fuck you*, and padded back to Summerset.

"Fine. Be that way."

Grumbling to herself she stalked upstairs. "Who brought you into this cat palace anyway?"

She sulked her way to the bedroom. Stopped long enough to turn to the house comp.

"Where's Roarke?"

Good evening, darling Eve. Roarke is not in residence at this time.

"Fine." So she couldn't even bitch about the cat to her husband.

Fine.

She stepped onto the platform, sat on the edge of the huge bed to take off her boots. She kicked them aside.

"Hell with it," she managed before she crawled on, lay facedown across the bed, and tuned out.

An hour later, Roarke walked in. He'd had a long, rough day of his own, wanted his wife and a large glass of wine, more or less in that order.

The same tableau greeted him.

"The lieutenant's upstairs," Summerset began as Galahad — semi-arched now — crept over to sniff at Roarke's trousers.

"Good."

"She looked exhausted."

"Small wonder. What's this?" He bent to scratch at the cat who continued to sniff.

"Apparently he's mistrustful you've been loyal, as he smelled another cat on the lieutenant."

"Ah. Well, I haven't had time for cats today." As Roarke stripped off his topcoat, Summerset held out a hand for it. "Thanks. Let's go up then," he said to the cat. "I'm sure she'll make it up to you."

He started up, the cat strolling behind him.

If she'd gone to her office, he'd pour some wine into both of them, Roarke determined. And talk her into a short lie-down. He could use one himself. But he wanted out of the bloody suit first.

And he found her, still facedown across the bed.

"That works."

He took off the suit, changed into loose pants and a long-sleeved T-shirt. Wine could wait, he decided, and slid onto the bed beside Eve. She stirred a little when he wrapped an arm around her, muttered something that sounded like *numbers*, then settled again.

The cat took a running leap, bounced on the bed beside Roarke's hip. With his wife curled to his front, the cat to his back, Roarke, in turn, tuned out.

Dreams took her through the day, in their own strange way, into white landscapes, onto frigid sidewalks, through empty offices where weeping echoed and echoed.

She stood in the Dickenson penthouse, hands on hips.

"It's not here," she said to Galahad, who ignored her. "Nobody asked you to come, but I'm telling you it's not here. Nothing's here but grief. Here's clear."

She stepped out of the door and into the apartment still under construction. "Just a little blood, but they shouldn't have missed it. Sloppy, sloppy. Leave her on the doorstep? Was that a statement, and if so, for who?"

For Whitestone? But he shouldn't have found the body. An early morning passerby, maybe, more likely one of the construction crew.

And she couldn't see a link between her vic and anyone on that crew.

She turned a circle, saw the framed photographs of the victim's kids, the husband. Happier days.

"Family meant everything." Daniel Yung sat on the comfortable sofa, his hands neatly folded in his lap. "She'd have done, given, said anything to protect them."

"Yeah, she'd have thought of them after the snatch, of getting home to them. Of the kids, especially. That's what mothers do, right?"

She smelled her own, saw Stella sneering from the doorway. "She'd have thought about herself, like everybody. She hated being stuck in this place with a sniveling kid. Just like me. She's no better than me."

Eve studied her a moment, the bitter eyes, the sneering mouth, the bloody throat slit by McQueen's blade. And felt little but mild annoyance.

"Fuck off. I don't have time for you. Everything's not about you."

"You think she thought of a couple brats, or the asshole who stuck them in her?"

"Yeah, I do. She thought of her kids, her life, and she gave the bastards who killed her whatever they wanted.

109

But she still *knew* whatever it was, or enough of whatever it was. Money, audits, portfolios, investments. It's numbers. Somewhere they won't add up. How the hell do I find the right ones, the wrong ones?"

Roarke stepped beside her, stroked a hand down her hair. "Do you really have to ask?"

"Oh yeah. I've got you."

She opened her eyes, looked directly into the wild, wild blue of his.

"You're muttering in your sleep."

"I am? Was?"

"'I've got you,' you said, and so you do. I have your back."

Still groggy she stroked his hair as he had hers in the dream. "I was sort of running the case in my sleep. It's about money, big money, I think. The kind that gets invested and audited and tucked around in special accounts. So you were there, in the dream. At the crime scene."

"And what did I have to say?"

"Just reminded me that I have an expert on big money in my pocket. I'm pretty sure I'm going to need one."

"Always happy to serve."

"McNab found a file I need to look at, or have you look at."

She started to push up. He simply rolled on top of her.

"I want my fee in advance."

"I warned somebody about bribery just today."

"You can arrest me after." He hit the release on the weapon harness she hadn't taken off. "I'd prefer you unarmed at the moment. And undressed."

"You always prefer me undressed."

"Guilty as charged." He laid his lips on hers. "There you are."

It felt like days since she'd been home, in bed, with him. It felt like a gift to be back, to have her body respond, to allow her mind to turn away from the work, from blood and death and grief, and toward pleasure.

"For once you're not wearing too many clothes." She tugged the shirt up and off, then slid her hands down his back.

"I thought ahead." He pulled her up to slip off the harness, peel off her jacket. "You didn't."

"I was just going to recharge." She grinned as he dragged off her sweater. "Still am." She wrapped around him, still wearing her tank, trousers, and the baby-fist diamond on a chain he'd given her.

Hooking her legs around his waist, she over-balanced him, reversed positions until she straddled him. "I think the power nap set me up." She pulled off the tank, tossed it aside. "But I could use a hand."

"I have two." He closed them over her breasts.

"Yeah, you do." She closed her eyes, let the sensations soak in.

She leaned down to him, sank into a kiss that was welcome and lust wrapped in promise.

Slim and strong, he thought. Shadows of fatigue dogging her eyes, but energy revving in her body. His Eve, his gift at the end of a long, hard day.

When he flipped her he heard the laugh in her throat, heard it go to a purr as he replaced his hands with his mouth. Her heart beat under his lips, its pace kicking up as his hands roamed over her. She boosted up her hips when he tugged at the trousers, and his lips trailed down — torso, belly. As he teased, glided, possessed, her breath caught and the fingers stroking his back dug in.

She coiled, released. Moaned soft as silk with pleasure.

He knew what to give, what to take. He always knew. With him, she could love, without fear, without doubts and know she was loved the same way. She reached for him, reached for that love, for the welcome, and once more looked into the wild, wild blue of his eyes.

When he filled her, joy married pleasure. Movement echoed need. Slow, slow, then building into a rise and fall that shut out everything but that mating, that merging. She took his face in her hands as each thrust took her higher.

In his eyes she saw herself fly. And saw him fly after her.

Since her body clock was already inside out and backwards, she didn't see any reason not to just lie there a few more minutes. Maybe the mind-clearing/recharging agenda hadn't gone exactly as she planned.

But this was better.

"I've talked to too many people today," she commented.

"Tell me about it."

She stared up at the sky window above the bed, wondered when it had gone full dark. "You never get tired of talking to people."

"You'd be wrong about that."

"You can pay people to talk to the people. Even pay people to talk to the people talking to the people you don't want to talk to."

Amused, he linked his fingers with hers. "And who would talk to them?"

"You could do it all by text or e-mail and never have to speak to a living soul. I can only dream of days like that."

"Ah, but if I paid people to talk to the people — which I actually do when necessary, and then paid more people to talk to the people I paid, there's no doubt some things would be lost in translation, and I'd end up having to talk to even more people after it all got bollocksed up."

"Maybe. But you like people more than I do."

"That's probably true, until you factor in you risk your life for people every day."

"Not today, especially."

"Then we should celebrate. God, I want a bloody glass of wine."

She lifted his head with her hands, took a long look. "You had a bad day."

"No, a bumpy one, a long one, but in the end not bad at all. Especially the homecoming portion."

"Well that part goes without saying."

"It should always be said." He nudged up to kiss her.

"Then I'll say it, too. And I want a shower, maybe some wine, and since I paid you in advance I want you to look at the vic's file."

"A deal's a deal. Shower, wine, food — and my end of the bargain."

"I had food before."

"Before what?"

She laughed, rolled out of bed with him. "I had a fake Danish this morning, and magic chicken soup this afternoon."

"More cause to celebrate."

They walked into the shower, with Roarke already resigned to having his skin boiled off.

"It was really good soup from a deli near the crime scene." She ordered jets on full, one-hundred-two degrees.

He winced and bore it.

"How about you?"

"Food?" He couldn't recall she'd ever asked that question of him. "I had an actual breakfast, then lunch in the exec dining room where I talked to entirely too many people for entirely too long. It quite spoiled my appetite."

"Is there a problem? Should I hock some of the zillion pieces of jewelry you've given me?"

"I think we can muddle through. No problem." But he circled his neck under the spray. "Just a few people who needed to be reminded of their priorities, and who pays them."

"Were you Scary Roarke?"

114

He smiled, flipped a finger down the dent in her chin. "I may have been. In any case, it's done, and shouldn't have to be repeated anytime soon."

"You got to kick ass today. I didn't. That would've been good. But I did intimidate a really rich idiot, so that's something."

"Anyone I know?"

"Probably. Candida Mobsley."

"Ah yes. She is an idiot. Is she involved?"

"I don't think so. She's too much of a moron to have planned any of this, and if she'd paid to have it done, she'd have bollocksed it up when I was grilling her."

He smiled at her use of his slang. "I suspect you're right about that."

"Anyway, I've got a whole list of firms — why do they mostly always have three names — I want to run by you. Just for an opinion if you know them."

She stepped out, into the drying tube while he cut the water temperature by ten degrees and sighed at the reprieve.

Back in the bedroom, she put on comfortable clothes and frowned at the cat.

"He fucking curled his lip at me." Thoroughly insulted, she turned to Roarke. "How does a cat curl his lip? Get over it, fatso," she ordered. "I ditched the pants. I showered. It's over."

"He's annoyed, Summerset tells me, as you were around another cat."

"It wasn't a cat. It was a goddamn panther."

"You were at the zoo?"

"The rich idiot has a white panther cub to go with her white penthouse, which made me snow-blind. Everything's white, except her assistant wore black. I figure so she can find him in that snowstorm she lives in. And I need to check and make sure she's got the proper license for that panther. What kind of idiot keeps a jungle cat as a pet?"

"She would, if someone told her it was fashionable or rebellious."

Eve narrowed her eyes. "Did you do that moron?"

Roarke shook his head. "That's a very crass term considering our personal welcome home. No, I didn't do, bang, nail, or bounce on that particular moron."

"Because?"

"*Moron* would or certainly should be self-explanatory. Add she's not, in any way, my type. Booze, illegals, stupidity, reckless behavior, and spoiled right down to the marrow."

"Good to know. How about Alva Moonie?"

"While not a moron, no, I've not done, banged, etc., Alva Moonie. Is she involved as more than a witness?"

"No. No, not that I can see, or feel. I liked her. She said I met her before."

"It's likely we exchanged greetings at some fund-raiser or event. Any other women on the list I may have potentially banged?"

She grinned at him. "Not really. I wondered about those two since you're all filthy rich."

"You've some grime on you, Lieutenant."

"That's just transferred grime." She held out a hand. "You're going to come in handy on this one because you're filthy rich and you're not a moron, *and* you actually understand portfolios and all that crap."

"All that crap is what's paid for the wine we're both going to have — and the food."

"I get a paycheck," she reminded him. "I say I paid for the food tonight."

"As you like." He gave her hand a tug, brought her close, kissed her again. "But I'm by God not having pizza after this endless day."

"Good. I want a steak. A really, big, fat steak."

"There we are in perfect accord. Let's eat, drink, and talk murder and money."

She let out a satisfied breath. "I love you."

CHAPTER
SEVEN

In years past, the closest Eve came to real cow-meat steak on a cop's salary was an anemic soy burger. She'd have matched that with fake fries, burying them in salt and been fine with it. Now a perfectly grilled New York strip sat on her plate, beside actual fried potatoes piled like golden shoestrings, and crispy green beans mixed with slivers of almonds.

Not a bad deal.

But the better one, better than real meat and potatoes, was having someone sitting across from her she could run through the case with. In those years past most of her meals, such as they were, had been eaten alone or on the fly. Maybe she'd catch something with Mavis, and there'd been plenty of crappy food chowed down with another cop.

But sitting in her own home, with a real meal, and a man who not only listened but got it? She'd won life's trifecta.

"You've eliminated a personal motive," Roarke commented after she'd laid out the basics.

"It was business. I can't find one whiff of personal for motive or in execution. I'm going to ask Mira for a profile," she added, referring to the department's top shrink and profiler. "But this was what I think of as a semi-professional hit."

"Semi-pro? Not quite good enough for the majors?"

"I'm thinking no, not quite good enough. There was a . . . bullishness about it. Charging in. She didn't know she was working late until that afternoon, so not much planning ahead. Still, a decent plan. Stun — though the stun feels unnecessary — snatch, grab, transport, and get her inside for privacy. The killing method, that takes training, and again, it's impersonal."

"I doubt the victim thought so."

"She thought they'd let her go, or she sure as hell hoped they'd let her go, right down to the instant. And he took her from behind, again, impersonal. He — they — got whatever information they asked for, plus whatever she had in her briefcase. Then they used the standard cover of a botched mugging."

"A homicidal classic."

"It might've worked. But what kind of mugger stuns a mark, smacks her around, then snaps her neck from behind?"

"A particularly vicious one, but no," he continued before Eve could speak. "If you're a mugger lucky enough to have a stunner, you stun, take the valuables, and run off to stun another day."

"Agreed."

"If you're particularly vicious, you don't bother to stun. You'd want to do some damage and you'd inflict it."

"Also agreed. Plus why? She was a mugger's dream. A woman walking alone who doesn't fight back. No defensive wounds. If she'd screamed or shouted for help say, and spooked him, someone would've heard it. And in that neighborhood, would likely report it, or at least tell the cops on canvass. And *if* he was spooked —"

"And had a stunner." Roarke picked up her train of thought. "Quicker, easier to jam it against her throat and kill her that way."

"That's why the stunner doesn't make a lot of sense, but the marks are on her. And one more plus. She had no business being that far from the office, that far from home. It was too cold and too late for her to walk it, and she'd told her husband she was just walking to the subway — a block and a half from the office."

"All that, yes. And the blood on the tarp."

"That's the big one as it proves she was inside the apartment. To get her inside, they needed the code."

"Ah, well . . ." He only smiled, wiggled his fingers.

"If they could afford or had a B&E man good enough to get through that security without a trace, they could afford a pro hit."

"There wasn't much time to recruit."

She pointed a finger at him. "Exactly." Pleased he followed the same line, she lifted her wine to drink. "She gets passed the accounts, the audits, just that afternoon. That's the most likely motive. Maybe, maybe, it was one of the other, older deals, and she'd just reached some stage on it that sent up the red flag, but the probability's higher if it was new because it reads like a rush job."

"New to her."

This time she toasted him. "Exactly. Word gets back to the client, or the auditee — is that a word? — or the person involved with the business who doesn't want somebody fresh coming in, can't afford it. She's only had a few hours, hell, maybe she didn't even scratch the surface. But you can't take the chance. Things are a little confused, a little bogged down at Brewer and company, with the two accountants in a Vegas hospital. It's a smallish department. Everybody knows everybody. You can bet anybody who needed to know could find out who's working on what. Nobody's going to think a thing about a question like, say, who got slammed with Jim's or Chaz's work? Or the supervisor told the interested party who'd be handling the audit when they contacted him to express concern."

"Not to worry, Mr. Very Bad Man," Roarke began, "Marta's one of the best. She does excellent work, and in fact, will be burning the midnight oil right here tonight to catch up."

"As simple as that," Eve agreed. "Then Mr. Very Bad Man calls in a couple of goons, tells them to find out what Marta knows, get the files, and get rid of her."

"Which they do, but Lieutenant Very Smart Woman detects the subtle mistakes in their work."

"They shouldn't have taken the coat." She cut a bite of steak before gesturing with her knife. "It's a little thing, but it was overkill. Or if they took the coat, they should've taken the boots. They were good boots, pretty new. Probably worth more than the coat. And if they wanted it to look like a mugging, they should've used a sticker. Messy, sure, but putting a couple of holes in her would read more like a mugging. Using that apartment was convenient, but not smart. It gave us the connection."

"WIN to Brewer to the vic's new audits."

"I know at least eight clients at this point who cross, and three who had audits assigned to Marta on the day of her murder. We may find more yet." She plucked up a fry, frowned at it. "Too fucking convenient."

"Why not one of the construction crew? One of them could have finessed the codes."

"Not impossible, and I need to dig into Peabody's report more thoroughly. So far, nobody's popping. And it seems to me one of the crew would be more likely to spread that tarp back out. They'd know how the place looks every morning. Leaving it bunched up just brings more attention to it. And when you straighten it out, you're more likely to spot the blood."

"As you did."

"Yeah. Still, panic equals mistakes."

"He could've assumed you wouldn't go inside."

"That's what's bone-ass stupid. For Christ's sake, we find a woman outside an empty apartment, it just follows we'll go in and look around."

"Then take a closer look at — who's the W in WIN again?"

"Whitestone, Bradley."

"Right. Who also happens to be right on the spot to report the crime."

"Makes him look suspicious, yeah. And it's obvious, not so subtle here. Moonie gave me the rundown of her evening with him, and she's the one who brought up the new building. He didn't push it. We'll keep looking at him, but I like the other partners more."

"Why?"

"If you're arranging for somebody to be murdered, and you've arranged for them to use your place, and you're an ambitious money guy, do you take someone you're hoping will be an important client — and one you'd like to bang — to the scene so she discovers the DB with you?"

"Well now, that's a bit of a circular route, and a foolish one. Still, you could call it an alibi."

"You could call it an alibi," she agreed, "but a smarter one, and he comes off smart, is to stick with the potential client, stay away from the area, and find out when the cops come to call."

"Some like to insert themselves."

She liked him playing devil's advocate, making her think through the steps and details.

"Some do, not him. Just not." She shook her head when Roarke lifted the bottle to pour her more wine. "Added, there's that ambition. He's proud of the company, and that building. It can't be good for business when clients find out some woman got killed — even if we bought mugging — right there, dumped right on his doorstep. It puts people off, and especially people with lots and lots of money."

"There's a point." Roarke leaned back, enjoying her, enjoying the moment despite death. "Aren't the other partners proud and ambitious?"

"I'd say yes. I also say this was spur of the moment, driven by the moment, and a little panic. We've got a place, we'll use it — the cops will never figure it's us. It's just random, just her bad luck. Whoever ordered the hit tells the muscle to make it quick and clean, and make it look like a mugging. Take her valuables. And I'll bet your fine ass a week's pay whoever killed her has never been mugged and has never mugged anyone. Or he'd know better how to make it look."

"Whose week's pay? Mine or yours?"

"Since you make more in a week than most people make in a bunch of decades, we'll stick with mine. Which circles back to why you're so useful. If there's something hinky with the books, the files, you'll spot it."

"Fortunately I like being useful," and added, "I'm looking forward to the opportunity to poke about in someone else's financials." He smiled when she frowned at him. "Using the power for good, of course. Why don't I get started on that? I'll work in here. Easier, I think, if I have a question for you, or you for me."

"Okay. I can use the auxiliary. I need to set up my board, but I'll get you started first."

"Are the files on your unit here, or at Central?"

"I told McNab to copy and send, yeah."

"Then I can be a self-starter."

Just as well, she thought. As he'd put the meal together, she was stuck with the clearing up. But fair was fair, and like the magic soup, the meal and the reprise had her energy back in tune.

A nap, sex, and a hot shower may have played into that. Either way, she calculated she had a few good hours in her.

She noted that Roarke dived right in, and that the cat watched her suspiciously when she came out of the kitchen to set up her board.

She decided her best tactic there was ignoring Galahad until he pretended nothing was wrong and never had been.

She studied the board as she worked, and went to her auxiliary unit to print out more ID photos. She pinned Candida and Aston to her board, and Alva Moonie's housekeeper.

Connections, she thought, and began to make them. Candida to Alva — former friends, lovers. Both rolling it in. Candida to the vic through the audit. She added Candida's money man, and a note to do a run on him.

She aligned the vic's family on one side, her coworkers on the other. And took a good look at James Arnold and Chaz Parzarri, making another note to contact the hospital and get the rundown on injuries and prognoses.

Roarke, she saw, was in work mode. With his hair tied back, sleeves pushed up, he looked relaxed about it. Who knew why some people found numbers so damn fascinating.

She sat at her auxiliary unit, and dived into what she considered the much more interesting prospect of digging into people's lives.

Arnold, James, age forty-six. On his second marriage, nine years in. The first gave him two children, one of each variety, and hefty child-support payments. He'd added another kid — female — with the second marriage.

He *looked* like an accountant, she decided. At least the clichéd image of one. Pale, a slightly worried expression on his thin face, faded blue eyes, thin sandy hair.

The sort who looked both harmless and boring. And, she knew, appearances were often deceiving.

He had an advanced degree, and had been a teacher's assistant and a dorm monitor in college.

Nerd.

He'd worked for the IRS for six years, then had gone into the private sector with a brief and unsuccessful two years between trying to run his own business out of his home.

He'd been with Brewer for thirteen years.

Decent salary. She figured anyone who crunched numbers all damn day probably deserved one. Good thing, as his oldest kid's college tuition took a greedy bite.

No criminal, but a shitload of traffic violations, she noted. And, hmmm, the second kid had some juvie knocks. Shoplifting, illegal possession, underage drinking, vandalism. A long stint in rehab. Private rehab. Pricy.

His wife had recently given up her professional parent stipend to go back to work as a paralegal.

While finances balanced, as far as she could tell, money had to be tight. How did it feel, poring over all those accounts loaded with cash, stocks, trusts, whatever, while you had to work and calculate just to make the mortgage?

Interesting.

Chaz Parzarri, age thirty-nine, single, no offspring. He had the kind of dark, sulky looks some women went for. Chiseled bone structure, a lot of wild curls. He didn't, to her mind, look like an accountant. But he, too, had the advanced degree and the government experience — was all that required?

She glanced up, over to Roarke, wondered if he knew, but didn't think it was important enough for the interruption.

His education advanced largely on scholarships — Chaz was a bright boy, she mused. Born in New Jersey to a waitress and a cab driver, with three siblings. Tight money again, at least in his background.

He'd turned that around, steady work, smart investments — she assumed — and had himself a condo on the Upper East Side only blocks from work.

No criminal. Traffic knocks, too, but not in Jim Arnold's league. Mostly speeding.

Some people were always in a hurry. Maybe Chaz was in a hurry to get rich.

She put them aside to let them stew and read Peabody's report on her interview with Jasper Milk, then Carmichael's on her and Santiago's interview with the interior designer.

Still letting it stew, she got up, programmed coffee, and came out to set a mug on the desk for Roarke.

"Thanks." He leaned back to look up at her. "What's the cost?"

"A couple of answers and/or opinions."

"I can afford that."

"Are you getting anywhere?"

"Of course." He smiled, picked up the coffee. "Let me tell you up front, this is unlikely to be a snap. Two of these are big companies with subsidiaries, charitable foundations, payrolls, expenses, depreciations, and so on. I'll need a basic overview on all of them. Don't expect I'll find a handy column marked Monies I've Embezzled or Misappropriated or That Were Never There in the First Place."

"What does that last one mean?"

"That sometimes companies or people within them fudge in the opposite direction to mollify stockholders, potential clients, or investors and their BODs — and hope to make up those numbers. It's . . . optimistic cheating," he decided. "And usually flawed."

"Okay."

"I've one audit here due to a potential merger, another due to by laws, another by court order. It appears your victim had done the same as I'm doing here. She got a feel for them first. She has some questions noted, on all three of these. Nothing major, but she hadn't worked on them very long."

"Is your opinion she didn't — at least at the time of her death — know anything particularly damaging?"

"I can't say absolutely, but I think that's probably accurate."

"Okay. I've got a handful of suspects. Let me run one by you. This guy owns his own company, a generational deal. About a dozen years ago, things got very, very thin. He held out, but barely. Had to take out loans, sell off some assets. He took a lot of smaller jobs, and sometimes lost money on them."

128

"Keeping his hand in. Employees?"

"Yeah. They'd built up to about fifty, and in the thin went down to about twenty. I'm no business expert, but it looks like he'd have been smarter cutting that by half. He wouldn't have had payroll eating up the profit so he lost money on some of those jobs."

"He kept as many of his people as he could working. It may not be sound business in the short-term, but it is in the long. You know who's working for you, they know they can count on you."

"All right, I can get that. He's got thirty-two employees now, and some of them are from before the thin, ones he had to let go."

"Loyalty? He'd done well for them while he could, brought them back in when work picked up."

"Maybe."

"Is the company private or public? Are there stockholders?" he asked.

"No, it's his deal. His family's deal. The construction guy."

"Ah. About a dozen years ago things were thin in that area. In real estate, in housing. The bubble burst."

"What bubble?"

"The housing bubble. And not the first time. People lost their homes, and when that happens people who service homes and buildings, who rehab them, repair them, build them don't have the work. It's a hard time for many, and for those willing to take the risk, an opportunity."

"For what?"

"For taking some risks and reaping rewards — long-term. I acquired a lot of real estate during the thin. You don't think this man killed your victim."

"No, at least I'm not sold on the idea. But like you said he or one of the crew could've been paid to pass on the code."

"You don't like that one either, less now that you've looked into this man more thoroughly."

"No, I don't like it. Not enough time, as far as I can see, to find the right person, offer the right incentive. Unless they were already involved, and I can't see that connection."

She edged her hip on the corner of the desk as she sampled her own coffee. "I get the same, basically, from the interior designer. Good rep, up front with the cops I set on her, what appears to be a good relationship with the construction guy, and with the clients — the partners."

"Then even if you don't — or can't — absolutely eliminate them, they're well down the list."

"Yeah, unless inadvertently they passed the codes." She shifted around to look at her board. "That leaves me, so far, with the three partners and the accountants whose work the vic took over. Or one of the others in the accounting firm, but from what you just told me, that doesn't hit the mark."

"They'd have known she had nothing to speak of, and there was no reason to kill her. Arrange to mug her and take the briefcase, the handbag in case she took files home. Then, if they had access to the offices as employees, it's not that difficult to access a locked office after hours, corrupt files on her comp. Easier, cleaner than murder."

"That's my take. That leaves me with the partners, clients who cross, and the two accountants in Vegas. One couldn't talk to her as he was in a coma, and the other could only speak to her in a limited way. Too much curiosity, and it looks off. Plus he's pretty banged up."

"Hard for either of them to order the hit."

"Yeah. I can't quite see some accountant calling in a hit from his hospital room in Vegas. The hit came from somewhere else, but if it came due to the files, one or both are in this. They're too good at what they do not to have seen something off."

"Have you looked at their financials?"

"Yeah, and one of them lives close financially. Two marriages, three kids, one with a hefty college tuition, another who's been in some trouble and did a stint in expensive private rehab."

She pointed to her board and Arnold's photo.

"He's got a house in Queens and three vehicles he's paying for. To want something you have to know about it, see it, imagine it — and if you see it a lot, deal with it a lot, and it's always someone else's?"

"You want it more, or some do. I did."

"Yeah. On the surface, he looks like an average guy, but that's surface. The other's single, came from blue-collar, hard-scrabble, studied. Got a good ride on scholarships."

Again she gestured, zeroing in on Parzarri.

"He's made money with his money, which you ought to be able to do when you know money, I guess. He's not swimming in it like a money pond, but he's solid. Scholarship kid, going to good schools, really good schools and coming home to a tough neighborhood in Jersey. You see how the other half lives, and that can be rough. You're the one who's there because you're smart, not because you've got money. You don't have the nice clothes, you take the bus instead of driving the car Daddy bought you. It can piss you off."

"So you'll make sure you'll eventually be the one with money, with the nice clothes and the fancy car?"

"Maybe. They look clean, but . . ." She tapped her computer. "There's something there."

"But no pressure."

She laughed, shook her head. "You'll find it. But meanwhile, I need some input. You're the expert."

"On greed and avarice?"

"On how the greedy and avaricious work. If there's something in there, and there damn well has to be, would the accountant in charge of the account know, or am I just assuming and suspicious?"

"You're suspicious, but yes, almost certainly the accountant in charge would know. There's some wiggle room there if the person — if it isn't indeed the accountant skimming, cooking or finagling on his own — who's finessed the numbers managed to do so without having it show. A thorough audit's bound to turn over some of those rocks."

"So the person doing the audit would know, or find what's under them."

"In a firm like Brewer? You could count on it."

"Would the financial guy — the money managers, brokers, whatever term you use for WIN — would he know?"

"Again, there's that wiggle room, particularly if the client and the accountant worked it together. But to make more? To keep it smooth, and actually simpler? You'd want the money manager in the pocket as well."

"At least three people," she considered. "Simpler maybe, but it gets sticky. The more people who know, the easier for something to slip."

"Didn't it?" he returned. "Someone's dead."

"Yeah." She looked back toward the board. "Someone is."

"It's business," he continued. "As you said about the murder itself. Not personal, just business. Cheating, stealing, shifting funds, kickbacks, payoffs, burying profits — whatever it might be — it's business. To do business, and do it well, to do it profitably, you need advisers, managers, workers. And, to keep it smooth, again simple, you'd want those people to have a foot in each door — the legal business, and the criminal."

"Yeah, okay, that's how I was leaning. I thought about Oberon, how she ran her department, all those cops — and used her hand-picked to run her dirty cop sideline. You need some in each camp, to keep the legit business going, and to use that legit business for the dirty one."

She considered it as she finished her coffee. "And if it runs like that, if that's a good comparison, the money guy, the accountant, they're not in charge — they're

133

tools. The one in charge," she tapped her computer again, "is in there."

"But no pressure," Roarke repeated.

"You eat pressure for breakfast, ace."

"Some days a man just wants a full Irish."

"Me? I get that every day." She rose, walked back to the board. "He — or she — or them. Not up here yet. Not yet. But the tools are. I just need to figure out which ones up here do the cooking."

She went back to her auxiliary, and back to work.

He saw the moment she started to flag, how she rubbed at her eyes, scrubbed at her hair, as if it would keep her awake and alert.

He thought he could manage another hour or so. It was all so bloody interesting, how others set up their businesses, their books, their investments. He'd find what she needed, nothing else would do the way she'd put her faith in him. Challenged him, of course, very purposefully, he knew. Put his ego and his competitive spirit on the line.

He wouldn't have it, or her, otherwise.

But he wouldn't find it tonight. He'd found some potential questions, but as he wasn't a shagging accountant, he'd have to check some tax codes.

Tomorrow.

For now, he rose, walked over, pulled her to her feet. "I'm just —"

"Going to bed. With the exception of your short nap, you've been up and doing nearly twenty-four hours. And so have I. We both need some sleep."

"Did you get anywhere?"

"I need to check some codes tomorrow, and I want to start a separate search for secondary, unreported accounts. That would be fun."

"Anybody stand out?"

"Not as yet. And for you?"

She shook her head as she fought to stay upright on the way to the bedroom. "The accountants haven't been cleared, medically, for travel. Parzarri's had some BP spikes, and some other medical crap I don't quite get. But they're both stable, just not cleared for travel for another couple days. I want face-to-face."

"We can go to Vegas. Sweat accountants and gamble."

"I don't have enough to sweat them. Yet." But boy, she'd enjoy making them sweat. "If I made the trip, whoever's in charge would know or suspect I know, and I want him thinking he's clear."

In the bedroom she undressed, dragged herself to the bed. And realized as soon as she hit the sheets, he was right. She needed some sleep.

Dreamless, she hoped, though the last hadn't been bad, hadn't been a nightmare. Those were fading again. But it was still death and dying and murder. And mothers, she mused, trying to turn it off as Roarke slid in beside her, drew her in.

But it nagged.

Who was right? Was she right claiming Marta had thought of her kids, of her family, when terrified, when hurt? Or was Stella right, and she'd only been able to think of herself and survival?

It didn't matter, and the answer couldn't be known.

Put it away, she ordered herself.

Then it came so clear. She'd missed it, too wrapped up in the rest of the investigation.

"She thought of them."

"Hmm?"

"Marta — the vic. She thought of her kids, her husband, when they had her. She thought of them because she didn't tell them everything. I figured she'd told them everything, but she didn't. She didn't tell them she'd copied the files to her home unit. They hurt her, they scared her, they threatened her and in the end they killed her. But she protected her family."

"What she loved most," he said and brushed his lips over her hair. "Sleep now. Rest that brain."

For reasons she couldn't understand, knowing she'd been right, the mother had protected the children, she closed her eyes and slipped into a deep, dreamless sleep.

CHAPTER
EIGHT

She woke to the scent of coffee and a quietly simmering fire — and to Roarke in one of his slick dark suits monitoring the stock reports from the sofa of the sitting area.

She considered it an excellent way to start the day. Or it would be as soon as she had that coffee and cleared the fog from her brain.

She rolled out, shuffled over, and poured a large mug from the pot Roarke had on the table.

"You look rested, Lieutenant."

"Feel that way. Mostly." She gulped coffee on her way to the bathroom.

When she came out, wrapped in a robe she suspected was cashmere, bowls of berries, rashers of bacon, and plates of French toast sat on the coffee table. Grateful he hadn't decided, as he often did, she needed oatmeal, she dropped down beside him.

"Nice."

"I thought we both deserved a bit of a treat." Roarke lifted his eyebrows when she broke off a piece of bacon and offered it to the cat who sat staring holes through her.

"For him, this is makeup sex. That's all you get," she said when Galahad inhaled the bacon then affectionately butted his head against her calf.

"Just FYI, if you let another man rub up against you, and I sniff it out, you won't be able to buy me off with bacon." He handed her the syrup pitcher so she could drown her French toast.

"So noted. What's on your slate today?"

Once again, Roarke lifted his eyebrows.

"What? I can't have an interest in how you bring home the bacon?" She bit into a piece, smiled. "And okay, I'm trying to get a feel for what these guys do on any given day. The money guys, the guys with the money. I'm going to have to look at the big shots in the companies the vic was auditing. You're the biggest shot around, so . . ."

Saying nothing, Roarke took out his appointment book, keyed in the day, handed it to her.

"Seriously?" She shook her head as she ran through his day. "You've already had a holo-conference with these dudes in Hong Kong, and talked to this other guy in Sydney?"

"And fed the cat, that's not in there."

"Ha. Later this morning two more 'link conferences and an R&D meeting on something called Sentech."

"Would you like me to explain Sentech?"

"No. I really don't. Later, another holo about the Olympus Resort. How's Darcia doing?" referring to Roarke's police and security head on Olympus.

"Very well."

"You know I hear Webster's gone up there twice since she was here, and they . . ."

"Developed a relationship?" Roarke suggested.

"Yeah. Weird. Anyway, then you've got this lunch deal with these other dudes, a note to 'link up for this auction thing. What are you buying?"

"You'll find out, won't you, once I do."

"Hmm. More meetings, more conferences, more 'link shit. I'm getting a headache just looking at this."

She forked up some French toast, cleared her head. "You could assign people to do half this stuff. Probably more than half."

"And often do."

"So you're up before dawn doing business, and you come in here and check this out." She gestured toward the reports scrolling on the screen. "You're looking at what your stocks are doing — your companies, your investments, and your competitors."

"You'll do smarter business if you know the field, which is always in flux."

"Okay, I sort of get that. Then you spend the rest of the day moving and shaking, wheeling and dealing, checking up on stuff in the works, putting more stuff into the works, and buying stuff."

"In a nutshell." He took the appointment book back, put it away.

"You do it to make money, and make stuff, but you also do it because you get off on it."

"In a manner of speaking."

She was a boss; she knew how it worked. Her department was small scale compared to the Universe of Roarke, but a lot of the same rules applied.

"And if I asked you about any given employee, especially one who'd have the security level to access or gather information about funds or properties or investments — whatever — if you didn't have the information on that employee in your head, you'd be able to have it in about ten seconds."

"Anyone in particular?"

"No. See, you've had a couple people who work for you screw around, but when you consider the kazillion people who work for you in one way or another, but especially on the higher rungs, your system's gold. And part of that gold is your immersion in it, because it's your money, your people, your companies, your rep."

"All right."

"You've been audited, right?"

"Internally and externally."

"And if there was anything hinky, you'd know it before the auditors. You'd fix it."

One way or another, but there was no point thinking about that.

"That makes me wonder if the brass of the companies the vic was auditing know what's what, and if they don't, why? More, one of those companies — at least one — has something going on they'd kill for. How high does that go?"

"It's usually best to start at the top and work down."

"I'm thinking the same. Another round with the partners," she continued as she ate. "Another with the vic's firm. Tightening the circle if I can until you dig out whatever needs to be dug out. I'm going to give a copy to one of the department's forensic accountants, too."

"Are you telling me that to stir my competitive juices?"

"No, I need to do it. And okay, that's a factor, but I need to do it. And run some of this by Mira, once I talk to a few more people."

"Your day's starting to look like mine."

"Don't say that, I'll be forced to hide under the bed until tomorrow."

"Darling Eve, the motives and the methods may vary, but our days aren't so very different. Now, since you're going to interview some of the top businessmen in the city, what are you wearing?"

"Some sort of clothing."

"That's a start."

He rose, walked into her closet. "Subtle power, I think. Authority, but not threatening."

"I like being threatening."

"As well I know, but you'll want to draw out rather than beat out information. And what you wear will send a message — I can swim in the same pool as you, and mine's even bigger."

She scowled over a last slice of bacon. "It's your damn pool."

"Shut up before you annoy me and I pick out something that makes you look weak and foolish."

Amused, as he'd intended, she polished off her breakfast. "Do I have something like that?"

"It's all in the combination, the presentation, the geography, and the time of day."

"All that," she muttered, and figured this time he was being absolutely serious.

"By the way, your dress for the premiere's here. Have you bothered to look at it?"

"I saw it." And automatically rolled her shoulders when they tensed. "You know something might come up."

"Stop." He came out with a pair of dark gray trousers with silver rivets, a simple mock turtleneck in pale apricot, and a jacket caught somewhere between red and orange.

"The color makes a statement. You're not afraid to be noticed, and the cut says profession. Combined it's 'Don't fuck with me, as I'm in charge.' It's rich fabric, but doesn't flaunt it."

"Why don't clothes ever talk to me?"

"They do. You don't always listen. And, to circle back, you'll enjoy the premiere. I'm arranging for Peabody and McNab and Mavis and Leonardo to go with us in the limo. That makes a statement, too. You're partners. You're friends."

"They'll be all over that. I hate the gawking. Half the damn people I interviewed yesterday are going to the thing, and . . ." She paused, considered. "Hmmm."

"And there you are. Now you can consider it part of the job."

"I might be able to make it work for me. Something to think about."

He tapped a finger to her head. "Always busy. Black belt and boots."

"Even I could figure that out."

Now he brushed his lips over her head, then walked to her jewelry case, scanned, selected. "Studs, subtle again, and classic, with the pop of the carnelian that picks up the color of the jacket."

"I thought carnelian changed colors."

"Very funny." He handed them to her. "Wearing this, you'll be like a chameleon in the ivory towers of business."

Once she'd dressed, he angled his head. "Very nice. You know, a scarf would polish it up."

"Oh sure, I'll hang something around my neck some bad guy can grab onto and strangle me with."

"Forget I mentioned it. I'll give some time to your business today. If I find anything, I'll let you know."

"With that schedule I don't see how you have time to take a leak much less do side work."

"Yet somehow I manage." He slipped his arms around her, laid his lips on hers. "You look out for my cop now."

"I'm so well-dressed nobody'll make me for a cop."

"Care to wager on it?"

She shook her head and laughed. "You can look out for my gazillionaire."

"I'll be sure to do that."

Even as she turned to leave, her pocket 'link signaled. She frowned at the readout. "It's the supervisor at Brewer. Dallas," she said.

"Lieutenant, it's Sly Gibbons at Brewer, Kyle, and Martini. There's been a break-in."

"What sort of break-in?"

"I — I came in early. I wanted to have some time . . . Someone's been in Marta's office. On her computer. Files are missing from her computer, and, and the backups, they're gone, too. I —"

"Have you alerted building security?"

"Yes, first thing, but when they checked the discs they said there was some sort of glitch. I don't understand it. I was the last one out of the office yesterday. I secured it myself. I don't —"

"I'm on my way. Stay where you are, tell security I'm coming in, and I want to see all security discs."

"Yes. Yes. I'll be right here."

"Tidying up," Roarke said when she clicked off.

"Yeah. They had her keys, her codes, whatever she had in her handbag, her briefcase. Screwed with the security cams. Had to get rid of the files, probably several that don't apply just to cover. Maybe make it look like a malfunction."

"Not difficult, unless you look carefully."

"Which we will. They don't know about the copies she sent to her home unit. Unless they looked carefully. I've gotta go." She contacted Denzel Dickenson first.

He looked, to her, unbearably weary.

"This is Dallas. Have you had anyone contact you or attempt to get into your apartment?"

"I don't know what you mean."

"I'm sending a couple of cops over, just to take a look. I don't want you to answer the door to anyone else. Understood?"

"Yes, but —"

"Just a precaution. Are your children with you?"

"Yes. My sister's coming over later this morning. We have to . . . start making arrangements."

"Just sit tight."

She grabbed her coat from the newel post, dragging it on as she rushed out the door.

Her car sat out front. She had to give Summerset points for putting it back, since she knew he always garaged it in the evening. Jumping in, she contacted Dispatch, arranged for the detail, then tagged Peabody.

"I need you and McNab at the vic's office. They had a break-in. I want a geek going over her office unit. We don't need the warrant for that now. Have him contact Feeney so he knows I've grabbed one of his e-men."

"You got it. We're on our way."

She zipped through the gates and punched it.

Somebody'd been doing some calmer thinking, she decided, and had concluded sooner or later — most likely sooner — another accountant would be assigned to the audit. It didn't pay to keep killing accountants. Better to get rid of the files. Then generate new ones at some point. Doctored ones, maybe. Or you'd insist the audit be conducted when the accountant in your pocket was back in business.

Or . . . Outrage. You're taking your business elsewhere, or you're going to court to demand another firm handle your audit.

The key word? *Stall*.

Pushing through traffic, she contacted Mira's office, wheedled a short meeting out of Mira's ferocious admin. Wheedling wasn't easy, but she'd finished the job as she pulled up to Gibbons's office building. She double-parked — screw it — and flipped on her On Duty light.

She badged her way through the door and dealt with the same security man she'd met the day before.

"I know Mr. Gibbons thinks he's had some trouble up there. But I've got no record of anybody coming in or out of the building after hours."

"Cleaning crew?"

"Yeah, sure, but they logged in."

"I'm going to need copies of the discs."

"I'll have them for you."

"I've got an e-man on the way. Show him your security."

"No problem."

With a nod, she stepped onto an elevator. And stepped off to a hand-wringing Sylvestor Gibbons.

"This is terrible. Someone stole those files, Lieutenant. They were on Marta's computer. She worked on them on the day — on that day. Her unit's secured, passcoded. That data is highly sensitive and confidential. We're responsible."

"I get it." She moved into the office with him. "Why were you on her unit?"

"I wanted to copy her work. It has to be reassigned. There are deadlines. We'll get extensions, obviously. But the work needs to be done. And if you get the warrant and confiscate her files, I wanted another set of copies."

"You said it was passcoded."

"Yes, but I have a master code. As supervisor I have to be able to access any data necessary. I contacted Mr.

146

Brewer personally, discussed it with him, and he agreed."

"When did you contact him?"

"This morning. Early. I didn't sleep well, and I was up. I thought about this, and knew I had to discuss it with Mr. Brewer."

"Okay." Which probably put Brewer in the clear. The timing didn't work. "Let's have a look at her office."

"It was secured," he told her as he unlocked the door. "There was nothing out of place, nothing I can see. I bypassed her passcode, began the copies, and I saw files missing."

"How many accounts or clients?"

"I counted eight before I contacted security, then you. I was afraid to do anymore. That I'd compromise the evidence? The scene? I'm very upset."

"But you checked for the backups?"

"Right away."

"Where do you keep them?"

"Oh, sorry. I'll show you. I have a safe in my office. All copies of sensitive material stay secured."

"Who has the combination?"

"Besides me? The bosses and the head of security would have it on file."

"No one else in the office?"

"No. No one."

"How often do you change it?" she asked as she studied the compact safe inside a small closet.

"I . . . I've never actually changed it. It's the factory default, and we've never had any trouble. There never seemed to be any reason to reprogram."

"I bet sometimes when you're securing sensitive material in this safe, someone might be in here. Your assistant, one of your accountants, one of their assistants."

"I . . . Yes." He dropped down in a chair, dropped his head into his hands. "This is a nightmare. The parties involved will have to be notified their data may be compromised. The work done, if not complete and already copied to clients or courts will have to be regenerated. And our reputation . . . I'm responsible."

"The person who killed Marta Dickenson and compromised her data is responsible."

"You think it's the same person."

Eve just looked at him. "What do you think?"

"I don't know what to think."

"Was anything else taken? Anything that wasn't Marta's work?"

"I don't think so. I didn't look thoroughly."

"Look thoroughly now. I'm going to have a crime scene team process the offices, and my e-man will analyze the security discs, and the system. What time did you leave the office yesterday?"

"About four. We closed early. The partners came in, spoke to everyone, and told us to go home. We're closed today as well. I stayed a little longer, then I locked up. I went to Mr. Brewer's office. I just needed to talk to someone. Mr. Kyle and Mr. Martini were still with him. We talked about having a small memorial here, in the offices. I went to Marta's apartment, to offer Denzel my condolences. I know it's for family

148

right now, but we were. Are. And when I got home, I had several drinks. My wife was very understanding."

He paused, shook his head. "There was some petty cash, three hundred dollars. It's gone. Otherwise, it's just copies of Marta's files. I count ten now. There must be two more missing from her computer."

He stared down at his hands. "It can't be one of us. It can't. We're family."

Eve didn't bother to tell him families often stole from each other, and weren't above familial murder.

When Peabody arrived, Eve gestured her into Marta's office. "Ten missing files, so they're trying to work another cover. Still not real smart about it. It may look like system error when McNab gets to it, so he'll need to dig past that."

"He will. He's going over security with the guy downstairs."

"They got into Gibbons's office safe, took the copies, which kind of negates a system glitch. Helped themselves to the three hundred in cash in there."

"Waste not, want not."

"Sounds true. Gibbons never reprograms the combination, and he admits he's not always alone in there when he opens it to put something in."

"So anybody who works here could, potentially, have the combination. Plus they had Marta's security data most likely if she kept it in her bag or briefcase. Even if not, whoever they're working with inside, if so, could have given them a way in."

"It's a clean job. No ransacking, no mess, no violence. That semi-pro feel again. Professional enough to cover your tracks, stupid enough to leave a trail taking the cash and the files. Leave the fucking three hundred, just corrupt the files."

"Rushed again, like the murder," Peabody commented. "A good plan, but not thorough."

"Still got the job done. Nothing for us to do here," Eve concluded. "I've got CI coming in to process, not that they'll find anything. The rest is for McNab. I think we should go talk to some hot-shot business guys."

"You got that hot-shot outfit."

"Don't start on my clothes."

"I can't compliment your outfit? Strict."

"You're wearing pink cowboy boots. What do you know about fashion?"

"You gave me the boots," Peabody reminded her, "and I get compliments on them all the time. So there."

They went downstairs, and Eve hunted up McNab.

As fashion statements went, Ian McNab occupied a world of his own. Eve imagined the many pockets of his bright purple baggies came in handy, but for the life of her couldn't figure out why he'd matched it with a pullover made up of eye-aching, multicolored swirls. Over it he'd tossed a long, sleeveless purple vest, presumably to discreetly cover his weapon. But the neon hearts dancing over the back of the vest over-balanced discretion.

And Roarke said she didn't pay attention to clothes.

He lifted his head from his work, the silver rings in his ear jiggling. Like Roarke he wore his hair — straight and blond — pulled back in work mode. But McNab's trailed halfway down his back of pulsing hearts.

"Somebody knew what they were doing," he told Eve, and pushed back a bit from the main comp. "Jigged it up to look like a hiccup, and that can happen on these older systems."

"But it didn't."

"Nope. He left fingerprints."

She all but leaped at the word. "You ran prints?"

"Not that kind of print. E-prints. If you'd just done a standard check run of the system, you'd go, yeah, damn hiccup. You push through a couple levels, and you find a shutdown code blended in with the rest. It's a little hide-and-seek, and pretty damn good. I need to run a few more checks, but I think they did it by remote, and that's excellent equipment and a mega excel tech."

"Okay. When you're done here, see what you can tell me about the vic's office unit."

"Gotcha." His deep green eyes narrowed in his thin, pretty face. "Mega excel tech," he repeated. "Shut down the cams, the locks, the alarms, one, two, three. It's an older system, but it's not crap."

"It didn't do its job." The man who walked in looked like someone's kindly grandfather in a three-piece suit. "It's crap. What system would you recommend?"

"Well, ah . . ." McNab looked at Eve.

"I'm sorry. I'm Stuart Brewer, senior partner of Brewer, Kyle, and Martini. You're Lieutenant Dallas."

"Mr. Brewer." He'd saved her time tracking him down, she thought. "I understand Mr. Gibbons contacted you early this morning."

"Yes. Twice. First about the files, Marta's files. Neither of us, neither of my partners thought of it yesterday. We were all reeling, and we let that slip between the cracks. It's unconscionable, and we're paying for that now. When Sly called back to tell me of the break-in, I realized we'd opened ourselves for it. And this system, as the young man said, is old. I'm also a member of the conglomeration that owns this building. We've updated the system regularly, attached the patches — that's the correct term?"

"Yes, sir," McNab told him.

"We did that to save money rather than invest in a new, more efficient system. And now . . . do you know if any other offices were compromised?"

"I have a forensic unit on the way, and we'll have uniforms canvass the building. But I think it's clear your audit offices were the targets, and Mrs. Dickenson's files the primary goal."

"Marta was killed for them, this is what you think. She was young, her life and her children's lives all ahead of her. And she was killed for information? Information is power and money, a weapon, a defense. I understand that. But I don't understand murder. You do."

"The new files she was given the day of her death. Are you personally acquainted with the individuals in those files?"

"No, but I intend to be by the end of today. I started this business sixty years ago with Jacob. Jacob Kyle. Twenty-eight years ago, we brought Sonny on as a full partner. I intended to retire in about six months. I think now I'll need to put that off. I started this firm, and I won't leave it until I know I leave it clean."

★ ★ ★

"I feel sorry for him," Peabody said when they walked outside. "For Brewer. I know he's a suspect, technically, but he looked so tired."

"Here's why he's not a suspect, at this point. He has access to the information that was taken. He's top dog, and if he wanted the files, he could just take the files. If there was something hinky and he was involved, rather than assign an auditor, he could just say, Hey, I need to get my hand in. I'll take that/those accounts. The same for the other two — Kyle and Martini. If you're smart enough to keep a business like this going for half a century or more, you're smart enough to cover your tracks without killing off an employee."

Eve's hands slid into her pockets. Not as cold today, she thought, because the wind was down. But damn cold enough.

"And if you're not," she continued, "or if killing the employee seemed more efficient, you sure as hell wouldn't break into your own offices and take files after the fact."

"Makes sense. I'm glad because I did feel sorry for him."

"Right now, we'll focus on the businesses in the files the vic sent to her home unit. She didn't give that away, even when they hurt her. She had a reason to send those files home, a reason she wanted to work on them there, and a reason she didn't tell anyone."

"She found something," Peabody ventured as they got into the car.

"Maybe. Or felt something. She had questions, made notations. So, it follows she wanted to dig out the answers. We'll make the circuit. The closest offices are Young-Biden. Health company — health centers, hospitals, clinics, meds, supplies, and all the junk that goes with it."

Young-Biden comprised five floors, with the busy hub covered with marble, glass, and bright, hard colors. Five people manned a curved central counter, all of them looking fit, healthy, and youthful.

Wall screens showcased various health centers, labs, rehab centers, and clinics worldwide.

Eve approached the counter, waited until one of the five behind it made actual eye contact.

"Yes, may I help you?"

"I need to speak with Young or Biden."

The woman arched her eyebrows so dramatically they all but merged with her hairline. Eve heard the distinctive sniff. "Do you have an appointment?"

"I have this." Eve laid her badge on the counter.

"I see." She stared at the badge as if Eve had laid a fat, hairy spider on the counter. "Ms. Young is out of the country. Mr. Young-Sachs is in house, but in meetings, as is Mr. Biden. If you'd care to make an appointment . . ."

"Sure, I can do that. I can make an appointment to have Mr. Young-Sachs and Mr. Biden brought down to Cop Central for questioning. When would that be convenient?"

Now the eyebrows lowered to beetle over very annoyed eyes. "I'm sure that won't be necessary. Excuse me a moment."

She swiveled in her chair, presenting her back to Eve, and murmured rapidly on her headset.

154

When she swiveled back she kept her eyebrows level, her face impassive. "Mr. Young-Sachs will see you shortly. If you'll go up to the forty-fifth floor, someone will meet you."

"I'll do that." Eve walked over to the elevators, rolled her shoulders. "That felt good."

"Why do people like that get so pissed off about having the boss talk to a cop?" Peabody wondered. "I mean, really, it's not their ass in the sling."

"I don't know, but I'm glad they do." Eve stepped into the elevator, ordered forty-five. "It gives me a lift."

CHAPTER
NINE

Floor forty-five shifted the mood to calm and plush with warm colors, thick rugs, leafy plants, and stylish waiting areas.

A six-foot blonde in towering heels and a short black suit greeted Eve with a pleasant, professional smile.

"Officer?"

"Lieutenant Dallas, Detective Peabody."

"Lieutenant. I'm Tuva Gunnarsson, Mr. Young-Sachs's admin. May I ask what this is in reference to?"

"Police business."

"Yes, of course." The smooth voice and manner didn't ripple. "If you'll come with me."

How the blonde managed to glide on the stilts seemed like magic, but glide she did, through the waiting area, through glass doors into a window-walled corridor, all the way to the wide double doors. She opened them both with a kind of flourish into her boss's big, swanky office.

More glass, more plush in two conversation areas, a slick silver wet bar, three wall screens, and a command console in that same slick silver backed by a high-backed leather chair in fresh-blood red.

"Mr. Young-Sachs will be with you in a moment. Can I get you anything?" She opened a wall panel to reveal a kitchen area, complete with full bar and a gleam of ruby-colored glassware.

"No, thanks. How long have you worked here?"

"Six years, four as Mr. Young-Sachs's admin."

"What's his title?"

"He serves as CFO. Ms. Young remains CEO. She's currently out of the country."

"So I heard. And Biden?"

"Mr. Biden is COO. Mr. Biden Senior is retired." Her face changed subtly as she glanced toward the door. Eve detected a bump of heat as the boss walked in.

She could all but smell the cool admin's pheromones pump out.

Late thirties, Eve concluded. Poster boy handsome in the requisite excellent suit. He had a rich man's tan, a gym-fit body, and a quick, crooked smile women probably found charming.

He also had the pinprick pupils of the high if not the mighty.

"Sorry for the wait. Carter Young-Sachs." He took Eve's hand, squeezed it rather than shook, did the same with Peabody. "Let's have a seat. Tuva, how about some of your amazing coffee. She does something special."

He winked.

"I'm sorry, they didn't give me your names."

"Lieutenant Dallas, Detective Peabody."

"I thought I recognized you." He wagged a finger, and the carved band on his middle finger glinted.

"Roarke's wife and the center of some Hollywood in New York excitement. Ty and I are going to the premiere. Tuva, we're entertaining celebrities here."

"Police," Eve corrected. "We're not here to be entertained or for the amazing coffee."

"Might as well have some. I'm looking forward to the premiere, especially now that I've had this chance to meet both of you." He settled back, spread his hands, every movement just slightly exaggerated with that chemically induced energy. "And what can I do for you?"

"Are you acquainted with Marta Dickenson?"

"Doesn't strike a bell. Tuva?"

"She was the auditor from Brewer, Kyle, and Martini. She was killed."

"Oh. Right." He maneuvered his face into serious lines for a moment. "Old Man Brewer called me personally about that. Slipped my mind. She wasn't the original auditor. That was . . ."

"Chaz Parzarri," Tuva supplied as she brought out a tray of coffee.

"Right. Nice guy. He had some kind of accident. Bad luck for Brewer and the rest."

"Can you tell me where you were night before last from nine to midnight?"

"Night before last?" He looked as if she'd asked where he'd been five years before, on a Tuesday, at two-fifteen sharp.

"You attended Poker Night at your club. Your driver picked you up at seven," Tuva told him.

"Right, right. I couldn't win a damn thing. Just tanked, but what the hell, all for a good cause."

"What time did you leave the club?" Eve asked.

"I'm not sure. Since I got my butt kicked, I left early. Maybe nine-thirty or ten."

"And you went home."

"Well, no." He glanced at Tuva, shrugged. "I went by Tuva's place. I could tell you we worked late, but, hell, we're all adults here. I'm not sure when I left."

Color high, Tuva stood very straight. "At just before one in the morning."

"She'd know." He offered that quick, crooked grin, another wink. "No big deal. We're both single. Hey, Ty, come meet the city's own Lieutenant Dallas and Peabody."

Another poster boy, dark to Young-Sachs's light with the broody, sulky looks some women found as appealing as the crooked grin. He dropped down in a chair as if exhausted.

"Tuva, how about another cup here? I could use some coffee." He gave Eve a subtle smirk. "So, hunting for clones?"

"For killers," she countered. "Marta Dickenson's killers."

"Who?"

Once again, Tuva gave the information, and brought the fresh cup.

"I don't see what that has to do with me — us. Sorry about the woman, but they'll just put another number-cruncher on it."

"I'd like your whereabouts from nine to midnight, night before last."

He rolled his eyes, but pulled out his date book. "I took the corporate shuttle down to South Beach, to a party. You wanted to do that poker thing," he said to Young-Sachs. "Said you were feeling lucky. He lost." Biden jerked a thumb at his associate. "I got lucky. Came back about ten yesterday morning."

"We'll need to verify both of your alibies."

"Over some accountant?" For the first time, Biden showed some interest and annoyance.

"Yes, over some accountant who was, at the time of her murder, conducting an audit on your company, and whose office was broken into last night. Her copies of your files were taken."

"For crap's sake. That can't be good." As if unsure, Young-Sachs looked at Tuva.

"You would be wise to immediately inform your financial advisers and your lawyers," Tuva began. "To change all passcodes, to —"

"What the hell kind of dick-all security do they have over at . . . Where the hell is it?"

"Brewer, Kyle, and Martini," Tuva supplied.

"We're firing their asses, you can bank on it."

"We aren't clients," Tuva told him. "They were assigned by the courts."

"Then get the damn lawyers, and get somebody who's not a fucking idiot assigned."

"Are you aware," Eve put in, "that Marta Dickenson's body was found by Bradley Whitestone, outside of the building under remodeling for the WIN Group?"

160

"Goddamn it, get Rob on the 'link," Biden ordered. "And give Roarke's get-out-of-jail-free card here the names of our lawyers. We're done."

Eve rose slowly, and whatever he saw in her face had Biden shifting. "No offense."

"Considerable taken. You want to be careful about offending cops, Mr. Biden, especially when you're mired in a murder investigation."

"Talk to the lawyers. I'm done." He shot to his feet. "And get Rob *now*, send it to my office." He stormed out.

"I apologize," Young-Sachs began. "Ty tends to lash out when he's upset."

"Interesting. Someone certainly lashed out at Marta Dickenson. Thanks for the coffee. We'll be in touch."

"It was really good coffee," Peabody murmured as they walked back to the elevator.

"Chocolate. Just a little chocolate in the coffee."

"Are you sure?"

"I know chocolate."

"Well, *damn*. I'm off sweets until after the premiere. It doesn't count, right, because I didn't know it was there."

"Right." Eve stepped on the elevator, muttered, "Asshole."

"I know. Both of them, really, but Young-Sachs was kind of a benign asshole. Maybe due to being a little high."

"Which makes him stupid as well as an asshole. The admin knows more than both of them put together. She's hot for the boss. She'd lie for him, no question.

161

But he hasn't got the belly for murder. Not in person anyway. The other? He could order it up like lunch."

"I'll start runs on them."

"You do that. Next up. Alexander and Pope."

The offices of Alexander and Pope opted for fussy dignity. Heavy furniture, art in thick gold frames — lots of paintings of people riding horses with dogs running alongside.

Everybody spoke in hushed tones in reception, as they might in a surgical waiting room.

But as Eve and Peabody were escorted back, she heard the busy sound of 'links beeping, voices dealing, feet scurrying.

Sterling Alexander's office reflected his reception area with its deep tones, deep cushions, gracefully faded carpets, ornately framed art.

He sat at his desk, a prosperous-looking man with dark hair. The perfect touches of elegant white at the temples added distinguished to his sharply chiseled features.

He gestured Eve and Peabody to chairs with a flick of his hand, and dismissed his silent assistant the same way.

"Pope will be here momentarily. I've already spoken to Stuart Brewer, and to Jake Ingersol — you know who they are. I've also spoken with our legal counsel. I understand you have a job to do, procedure to follow, but my partner and I must act quickly to protect our company, our investors."

"Understood. Were you acquainted with Marta Dickenson?"

162

"No. We worked with Chaz Parzarri. His supervisor informed us he'd been seriously injured while out of town, and our audit — which is required by our bylaws — would be taken over by this Dickenson woman. Then we're told she's been killed. And now the office is compromised and our confidential financial data stolen. It's obvious what's happened."

"Is it?"

"Parzarri's accident must have been engineered so this woman could get her hands on our data. Whoever did that, dealt with her. One of our competitors, I suspect."

"Do you have competitors that aggressive?"

"It's an aggressive market, as you should know as your husband is certainly fully involved in real estate."

"It seems unnaturally aggressive to put one auditor in the hospital and murder another just to access financial data. But," she said before he blustered in, "we're investigating all avenues. As we are, I need to ask where you were on the night of the murder."

A red flush bloomed across his cheekbones. "You would dare?"

"Oh, I would. If you refuse to answer, which is your right, I'll take that in a way you wouldn't care for."

"I don't like your attitude."

"I get that a lot, don't I, Peabody?"

"Yes, sir, you do."

"Young woman —"

"Lieutenant," Eve slapped back.

Alexander's chest heaved twice. "My father founded this firm before you were born. And I've run it for the last seven years. We brokered the governor's country home."

"That's nice. I still need to know your whereabouts. It's routine, Mr. Alexander. It's not personal."

"It's personal to me. I took my wife and a few friends to dinner at Top of the Apple."

"That would be after you met Jake Ingersol of the WIN Group for drinks."

Like Galahad before breakfast, Alexander stared holes in her.

She wasn't tempted to offer him bacon.

"Yes. We discussed business that I have no intention nor obligation to disclose to you. I returned home to meet my wife, and the car took us to the restaurant for our eight o'clock reservations. We didn't leave until nearly midnight."

"Okay."

There was a soft tap, something like a mouse scratch at the door.

"Come!" Alexander boomed out, and the mouse scuttled in.

"I'm sorry I was held up."

The painfully thin man with a long face flanked by enormous ears offered Eve a soft-palmed hand. "Lieutenant Dallas, I recognize you. And Detective Peabody. It's very nice to meet you, and before the premiere. My wife and I are looking forward to it. And you and Zelda, too, Sterling."

"We don't have time for small talk," Alexander snapped.

"Of course. I'm sorry. I'm Thomas Pope."

164

"We need to get this mess sorted out, Tom."

"I know." Pope held up his hands. "I know. I've contacted everyone we discussed. It'll be all right, Sterling."

"Someone's trying to sabotage us."

"We don't know that. Don't upset yourself. We weren't the only account taken. And a woman's dead. She's dead." He glanced at Eve. "She had two children. I heard that on the media report."

"Yes. I need to ask you your whereabouts on the night she was killed."

"Oh. My. Of course, of course. I was home. We spent the evening at home, my wife and I. Our daughter was out with friends. We worry. She's sixteen. It's very worrying. We stayed in all evening, and our daughter came home at ten — on time." He smiled when he said it.

"Did you see or speak with anyone that evening, other than your wife and daughter?"

"Ah . . . Actually, I spoke to my mother. Our mother," he corrected, glancing at Alexander. "We're half-brothers."

"Is that so?"

"Yes, I meant to tell you, Sterling, but everything's been so upside down, I forgot. I spoke with my mother, and, oh yes, my on-the-right neighbor. When I walked the dog." Every sentence contained a hint of apology. "I forgot to say I went out and walked the dog. We have a dog. And my neighbor and I usually walk our dogs together when we can. We did. About nine o'clock."

"All right. Thank you. This audit, it's required by your bylaws?"

"It is," Alexander confirmed. "My father wrote it in when he formed the company. He believes in full accounting."

"It's a way to keep your house clean." Pope cleared his throat. "My mother always says that. She initially joined the firm as an associate, then became full partner. Though she and Mr. Alexander Senior parted ways on a personal level, they remained business partners until their mutual retirement."

"There's no need to wave around family business," Alexander snapped out.

"It's interesting," Eve countered. "Has there ever been any problems with previous audits?"

"Absolutely not." Pope spoke first, then winced as he glanced at his half brother. "I don't mean to speak out of turn, but while there have been a few minor issues, immediately resolved, we're very proud to run that clean house."

"Any chance I could get copies of those previous audits?"

"Absolutely not." This time Alexander spoke first, and with an entirely different tone. "Now that's all the time we can spend on this. Look to competitors. It's obvious this woman got caught up in something that cost her her life. We're the victims here."

"Yeah. You're the victims. Thanks for your time."

Eve bared her teeth when she and Peabody rode down to the lobby. "Another asshole."

"The world's full of them. You'd never know by looking or listening to the two of them that they're related."

"Alexander doesn't consider them related. He considers Pope a pain in the ass when he's not considering him a go-fer. And Pope knows it. Alexander's playing the victim card, and hard — and that buzzes for me. And Pope's just a little too self-effacing."

She replayed the interview in her head as they crossed the lobby. "Alexander plays the big deal, but his 'link didn't ring while we were in there, and you can bet your ass he didn't order a hold on communications for us. Pope's pocket 'link hummed two different times."

"I didn't notice. I did notice how clear Alexander's desk was. No work on it."

"I bet Pope does most of the down-and-dirty work, the inside work, while the other plays big-shot. Doing the down-and-dirty gives you a lot of access."

"He doesn't seem the type to steal, cheat, and kill."

"A lot of people who steal, cheat, and kill don't, Peabody. That's why they steal, cheat, and kill until we catch them. Let's hit the next."

The offices of Your Space spread over a two-level downtown lot. Eve figured a family of four could live there comfortably, particularly as the design reflected a home rather than a work space.

Seating ranged around a sparkling fireplace topped with a mantel holding candlesticks and flowers. A second seating area aimed toward the wide window. In this second space a woman demonstrated something on a tablet to a young couple who appeared to be engrossed.

Rather than security, assistants, or hard-eyed admins, one of the four founders of the firm greeted Eve and Peabody personally.

"Latisha Vance." The tall, ebony-skinned knockout offered a brisk handshake. "Angie's with some new clients, but I have some time. We can talk upstairs if you like. Can I get you anything? We have some fresh cookies. They're deadly."

"No, thanks," Eve said over Peabody's quiet moan. "Are your other partners available?"

"Both Holly and Clare are out on jobs. I expect both of them back before long." She led them up floating stairs painted candy pink. "You're here about the woman who was killed, Marta Dickenson."

"That's right."

"I talked to Mr. Gibbons that day, and he explained about the accident, and assured me it wouldn't cause any delays."

"Had you ever met or spoken to Mrs. Dickenson?"

"Yes." Latisha walked them past a bedroom and into a spiffy, organized office where a woman worked at a computer station topped with shelves. "I'm sorry, Kassy, I need the room."

"No problem. I'll pick it up in the sitting room."

Latisha sat on a curvy gray chair as the woman slipped out. "Kassy's our office manager. Yes, I met Marta. The four of us went into the Brewer offices before we hired them. We like to get a feel for things. We liked the feel there, quite a bit. We liked Marta, and hoped she'd be able to take on our account, but at that time she didn't have room for us. Jim's great though, and we're hoping he makes a full recovery, and quickly. But Mart . . . I just talked to her a week ago."

"About?"

"Her hiring us."

"For?"

"We organize. When Angie and I started, just the two of us, we focused on private homes — rooms, really. Going in, designing a system, helping the client purge, and that can be a challenge, redesigning the space if necessary, and so on. It was the Angie and Tisha show for about six months, then Holly and I started talking at the gym."

Latisha shifted, crossed well-toned legs. "She worked for an interior designer, and was considering going out on her own. Instead, she came in with us. Angie brought in Clare who was, in fact, an office manager. She opened us up to helping organize, reorganize, redesign office spaces. This space was Clare's idea."

She gestured to indicate the loft. "Offices don't have to look like offices to be productive and efficient, and we'd also be able to show clients what can be done, how much productivity and comfort they can pack into their space without clutter.

"Sorry, that was off topic."

"No, it's good to know."

"Marta contacted me. She wanted to surprise her husband, redo his home office space and their bedroom. We'd set up an appointment to go look at the site. Angie and I were to meet her there next Monday."

"Did you speak with her after she took over your audit?"

"No. I intended to e-mail her the next day, just to touch base. We were all concerned for Jim, and I wanted to give her a little time to acquaint herself with our file. And then . . ."

"You've been in business about five years?"

"As we are now, yes."

"Business is good."

"It is." She brightened up again. "Most people don't know how to get started, how to let go, repurpose, reimagine. That's what we do."

"And this audit is due to a potential merger."

"That's right. We were approached by a company that designs and makes organizing equipment and tools. They do a nice online business, but haven't been able to keep up more than a small storefront otherwise. What they need is an influx of cash, and a connection. We're in talks about merging them into Your Space. Before we move to the next step, we wanted solid figures, ours and theirs, so we insisted on full audits. If we do this, it's a big step. It would mean expanding, finding a retail and office space for that new end of the business, staffing it. We need to be sure we're ready, financially, and both parties have to be sure the foundation's there."

"Your financial adviser is on board with this?"

"Fully aware, yes, and was working with Jim. I know, too, from the media reports that Marta's body was found right there, at the new WIN building. It's . . . disturbing to have so many connections to murder."

"You work with Jake Ingersol at WIN."

"Yeah. A lot of energy," she said with a smile. "Enthusiasm. We always say we feel like we could organize the world after a session with Jake. Angie talked to him just . . . Here she is."

The compact brunette moved quickly, striding in, sticking out a hand to Eve, then Peabody. "Angie Carabelli. I have to say it's great to meet you even though it's terrible. Our goal around here is to organize Roarke World."

"Angie." Latisha winced.

"Oh, come on, it's a fact. We're all so sorry about Marta. We liked her, and we were looking forward to working with her. What do you need to know?"

"We can get this out of the way if both of you can tell me where you were on the night of the murder, from nine to midnight."

Angie looked at Latisha. "Don't you get tired of always being right?"

"No."

"Tisha said the cops would come, and they'd ask that exact question. I said, They will not. Why? And she said —"

"Connections," Latisha finished.

"So we talked about it, all of us."

"To get your stories straight," Eve said mildly.

"God, that's just what that sounded like." Angie let out a choked laugh. "No, just to prepare, especially since the reports said you were in charge, though we still figured you'd just send some other detectives. But I was hoping you'd come because I have this Roarke goal. Professionally," she added with a smile.

"If it's in Angie's head," Latisha put in, "it generally comes out of her mouth."

"That's true. Why hedge? It's not efficient. And here you are, asking the question. I prepared but it still made my stomach jump."

"Why don't I take this?" Latisha suggested. "We were all here — all five of us — until about nine-thirty. We had an after-hours staff meeting, and Clare made Irish stew."

"She likes to cook," Angie put in. "Kassy left first. She got married last September and wanted to get home to her honey. Then Holly left to meet this guy she's been seeing. He was taking her dancing. Nobody takes me dancing. She looked completely iced, didn't she, Tisha?"

"She did. Angie and Clare left together."

"We shared a cab. We live in the same building. One of our neighbors was having a party, so we hit that."

"And I locked up, went home because I currently have no life," Latisha finished. "I walked. It's only five blocks."

"I wish you wouldn't walk alone at night," Angie admonished.

"I have a black belt in karate, and I carry Back-Off. I was in bed by eleven. Alone."

"Your own fault. If you gave Craig another chance, I think —"

"Angie, I don't think Lieutenant Dallas or Detective Peabody are interested in my lack of sex life at the moment."

172

"Everybody's interested in sex, right?" She grinned at Peabody.

"It's hard to argue that."

"Can I ask you a question?"

Peabody blinked. "All right."

"Was it totally surreal investigating the murder of the woman who plays you in the vid? She sort of looked like you, especially in the publicity shots. It had to be really weird."

In her curvy chair, Latisha just sighed.

"It was strange, yes."

"And a total scandal, which just adds delicious juice — don't roll your eyes, Tisha, it *does*. I'd kill to go to the New York premiere. I don't mean literally," she said quickly. "I'm sorry. I'm actually nervous, and I don't get nervous. I have no nerves, except now I do. I've never been interviewed by the police. And then it's you, the Icove police. And Roarke's cop. And God, I'm sorry, but I seriously love your boots," she said to Peabody.

"Thanks. I do, too."

Latisha rose, got a bottle of water from a cabinet, handed it to her friend. "Sip, breathe. Breathe, sip."

"Thanks." She breathed, she sipped. "We're some smart, ambitious women who put their heads and talents together and made something. And we're working on taking that up a level. We do good work, we make a good living, and we have a lot of fun doing it. And we're really sorry about what happened to Marta."

Latisha reached over, gave Angie's hand a squeeze. "That's about it."

"Just a couple more things," Eve put in. "You're aware of the break-in at Brewer's company?"

"Yes. Mr. Brewer called us personally, about an hour before you came," Latisha told Eve. "It feels as if they're getting slammed over and over."

"Will the theft of your financial files cause you any problems?"

"I don't know. I don't think so. We're a relatively small outfit, and what's in the files would've been shared with the reps of the company we're considering merging with. It's a problem because it may hold up the merger, but we're not in a hurry."

"We want to take our time with that," Angie added. "It feels like a good fit, but so did those fabulous shoes I bought last week, and ended up giving to Clare after they put blisters on my blisters. You know what I'm saying?"

Peabody had to grin. "Oh boy, do I."

"In any case," Latisha continued, "Kassy talked to Jake about it. The upshot is, we've been smart and clean, so if the data gets out, it's all good. And we've already changed all our passcodes, alerted our credit companies, and so on. It sounds like someone's screwing with Brewer more than with us."

"Not assholes," Peabody concluded as she climbed back into the car.

"No, but not assholes also cheat, steal, and kill."

"I don't see any motive."

"Maybe there's something off with this merger. Maybe one of them's skimming and the others don't know about it." Eve shrugged. "I don't get a buzz either, but the connections are there."

"I liked them. I wonder how much they charge. McNab and I could use some organizing at our place."

At the moment, Eve was more interested in organizing her notes and her brain. "I've got a consult with Mira coming up, and I want to put some of this together before we hit the WIN partners again. You start checking alibis, top to bottom. I'm going to reach out to Vegas PD, see what there is to see on this accident that started this ball rolling."

CHAPTER
TEN

She had considerable to deal with back on her own turf. Detectives needed to run investigations by her, or update her on the status. She had to read and decipher McNab's report on the Brewer building security and on his progress on the vic's desk unit.

Her own board and book required updating. Then she needed coffee and a few quiet minutes to process.

As she added the last photos to her board, Trueheart tapped on her doorjamb.

"Sorry to bother you, Lieutenant. Have you got a minute . . . Hey, I know her."

"Who?"

He stepped in, tapped Holly Novak's picture.

Intrigued, Eve gave the photo of the Your Space partner another study. Attractive, mixed race, leaning Asian. A dark wedge of hair around a lively face with light green eyes.

"How and where?"

"I'm looking for it," he said. "Oh yeah, they hired her — her company — to organize and streamline my mother's office. I mean, the office where my mother works. I was over there one day, and met her. Is she a suspect?"

"I don't think so, but give me a take."

"Friendly, energetic. Ruthless my mom said, but in a good way. Mom liked her, I know that. She said how she wished my aunt would hire her. She's kind of a pack rat, my aunt. And when she found out I was a cop, out of Central, she said how she bet we could use a good organizer, made kind of a joke about fighting crime through spacial efficiency. I thought it was pretty funny."

He scanned the board as he spoke. "She and her company are connected to the Dickenson murder."

"There are a lot of connections to the Dickenson murder."

"Big business, big money." At Eve's questioning look, he flushed just a little. "That's Young-Sachs and Biden. They get a lot of media, business, and gossip. The new breed of movers and shakers, and that kind of thing."

"Take?"

"Well, for me spoiled, entitled, and showy. That's probably not fair since it's media stuff, and that gets overblown."

"No, I'd say it's fair and accurate in this case. And add assholes."

"I guess that one was my take, too."

"I'd say that sums it up. What do you need, Trueheart?"

"Oh, sorry, Lieutenant. Nothing really. I . . . just wanted to thank you for giving me a chance at the detective's exam."

"You earned the chance, and Baxter made a solid case for you. The rest is up to you."

"Yes, sir. I won't let you down. You took me off sidewalk sleeper detail," he continued quickly. "You brought me into Central and assigned me to Baxter so he could train me. He's taught me a lot, Lieutenant. A lot about a lot. I'm not going to let either of you down."

"You do good work, Trueheart. As long as you do, you can't let anybody down."

"Yes, sir. All I want is to do good work. And a detective's shield," he added with a quick and easy grin.

"Don't screw up the work, study, you'll have the shield. Now beat it."

Alone, she closed her office door, got her coffee. She sat at her desk, propped her feet up. Drinking, she studied the board.

Spoiled, entitled, and showy for one group. She'd define another as pompous, angry, and envious — with a side of timid thrown in.

And the third? Ambitious, tightly woven, and efficient.

But did any of those attributes equal murder?

Your Space. It just didn't click. Maybe there was something she wasn't seeing — yet — but she'd set them aside for now.

Young-Biden. They had more than the previous generation, and did less to earn it. Young-Sachs, not only sleeping with his admin, but depending on her for everything. From what Eve could see, he knew dick-all about his own company's workings, and cared less if he got high during working hours. Maybe Biden knew more, she'd have a look-see on that, but from what she'd taken away from the brief meeting, he enjoyed his expensive suits, expensive lifestyle, and had no problem flinging insults around.

Alexander and Pope. Big-shot reveling in his big-shotiness. Treated his half brother like an underling, which Pope appeared to accept. Eve suspected Alexander treated everyone like an underling. Some Mommy resentment there, too, she thought, as the mommy had had the bad taste to give birth to Pope.

Was it funny or telling that Roarke's name had come up in each interview?

She'd have to think about that, too.

She rose, rearranged her board. She had fifteen before her Mira consult. Enough time for another hit of coffee and a little more processing.

She didn't manage to get her ass in the chair before somebody knocked on her door.

"Damn it."

Peabody poked her head in. "Sorry, Lieutenant, but —"

"I need a moment." Gennifer Yung pushed in. "I've been told all morning you were unavailable."

Eve signaled Peabody to go out, shut the door. "I've been in the field." She stepped over, started to turn her board around.

"There's no need for that. I've seen a murder board before."

"Have you seen one centered on a family member?"

"I'm not a novice at this, Lieutenant. Leave it. Please."

Yung stood, shoulders rigid, back stiff, and stared at the board. "You've been busy."

"Yes, I have. Your sister-in-law's murder is my top priority."

With a nod, Yung rubbed at the back of her neck. "I apologize for pushing my way in here. Waiting is misery, Lieutenant, and can be destructive. I made myself be patient regarding the warrant for the files in her office. I know these matters can be delicate, can take time. I'd already pushed, so I told myself to wait it out, to give the process time. And now someone took advantage of that time to steal valuable evidence. Evidence that might have led you to Marta's killer."

"Your Honor, you know I can't discuss the particulars of the case with you, but I will tell you we're analyzing and processing considerable data, following all possible leads, interviewing those we feel may connect to her death in some way."

"You sent a unit to my brother's home."

"As a precaution after the break-in at your sister-in-law's office."

"Yes. All right. It's easy to become accustomed to being in charge, to having the authority. It's difficult to find yourself in a situation where you're not in charge, you don't have the authority. You have to leave that in the hands of someone else. It doesn't matter if you know those hands are capable. They're not your hands."

She held hers out, looked at them, closed them.

"I went with my brother to see his wife this morning. To see Marta. Of all the things I've seen, of all the things that have come through my courtroom, nothing has been as horrible." She cleared her throat.

"My brother and his family will stay with me and mine for the time being. He thought it would be easier for the children to be at home, with their own things around them. But it's too painful for them, for all of us. He'll be with me if you need to reach him."

"Again, I'm sorry, sincerely sorry, Your Honor, for your loss. When I have something I can share, I'll let you all know at the first possible opportunity."

She nodded, then looked back at the board. "Do you think her killer is up there?"

"I don't know. But I think the reason for her murder is up there. The reason leads to the person or persons."

"I'll take that away with me, and let you get back to work."

As the door shut behind Yung, Eve dragged a hand through her hair. Grief, she thought, always left a weight on the air.

She grabbed the jacket she'd tossed off when she'd come in, and left that weight behind to keep her appointment with Mira.

She put some speed on, unwilling to face a spanking by Mira's admin if she was so much as a minute late. She zipped up to the dragon's desk with — according to her calculations — thirty-three seconds to spare.

And still earned a scolding scowl.

"The doctor has a very busy schedule today."

"That's going around."

The admin folded her lips, tapped inter-office comm. "Lieutenant Dallas is here to see you."

She sniffed. "Go right in."

Mira stood, drawing pretty teacups from her office AutoChef. She wore a suit in a smoky sort of lavender with plum-colored heels and a trio of silver chains. Her soft brown hair swept back from her face, and her soft blue eyes warmed when they met Eve's.

"Yes, I've made you tea, which you're not very fond of, but can use. You've had a long, difficult couple of days."

"That's the job."

"It is. And still, it's good to see you look reasonably rested, and very smart today."

"Roarke put the outfit together. I had to face off with a lot of business moguls."

"An excellent choice. Powerful but not hard, fashionable but not flashy, authoritative but not threatening."

"Clothes talk to you, too."

"They do, and too often say: Buy me. Have a seat." She chose one of her cozy scoop chairs, passed one of the pretty cups to Eve. "How is Judge Yung?"

"Hanging tough."

"I like her very much, personally and professionally. I actually met Marta a few times. She struck me as a lovely and loving woman."

"She's coming off that way. She's dead because she drew the short straw."

"I'm sorry?"

"Everything points to it. Two auditors get banged up, put out of commission. She inherits some of their files. Hours later, she's dead in what the killers hope we'll see as a violent mugging. Hours after that, the offices where she works are compromised, her computer messed with, and the files — and the master copies — go missing.

"Short straw."

"Yes, I see. I agree, insofar as her murder was impersonal and poorly masked. You call it semi-pro in your report. I think that's very accurate."

"I've got these honchos, okay? Companies I'm taking a hard look at. I've got Roarke doing his thing — who knows business and numbers and money better — so he may give me more to take a hard look at, or eliminate some I'm looking at now. But the honchos all have, let's say, attributes that could have them order the murder of an accountant. She's just a tool, and the wrong tool at that, which makes her a potential liability."

"It was rushed. Both the time frame and the profile of the killing were rushed. Still honchos as you say can afford full professionals."

"Can afford," Eve agreed, "but maybe don't see the need to pay. You've got security of some kind on the payroll already. Put them on it, give them a little bonus on the side. She's just a droid, basically, no big deal."

"Their needs outweigh hers." Mira nodded as she sipped tea. "They can't concern themselves with the lives of those who work for them, work under them." Mira sipped again and considered. "I'd like to read your interview reports from this morning."

"I'll get them to you."

"I would say you're dealing with brutish, cold-blooded, and physically trained individuals for the actual killing. Those who do what they're told, but don't think for themselves. Taking the victim away from her workplace, leaving her body blocks from where she would have been shows a lack of logic."

"She was supposed to walk to the subway, but they didn't know that. They, or the one who hired them, may have assumed she'd walk home. Added to it, the location was convenient."

"An empty building, and one it appears they could easily access."

"Not worried about the connection, maybe because it's rushed, it's convenient. It's just a mugging, it's just an accountant."

"Whoever hired them, if they were indeed hired, also doesn't consider the long view. It's immediate, quick gratification rather than careful planning and finesse. The concern is the files, the data, which may be incriminating in some way, not the victim. She is disposable. It's not cruelty. It's callousness."

"It's business."

"Yes. It's business. And how do you run and maintain a successful business when you aren't inclined to look at the long view, at the details, when you brute your way through a problem?"

Eve sat back. "You inherit it."

Mira smiled. "Cynical, and in this case high probability. The killers themselves, as I said, brutes. No sexual aspect, no rage, no personal agenda. Though the actual killing is a kind of showing off."

"Showing off?"

"*I'm strong. See how strong — I can snap a neck with my bare hands*. Quickly and cleanly according to Morris's report. They have a stunner, which is lethal used on full with contact, but go with brute force. Yes, showing off, and completing the kill with his own hands rather than a weapon or tool. He's the weapon."

"Okay." Eve tried it out in her head. "Yeah. Okay. And maybe he needed to show off since he stunned an unarmed woman in the back, and that's cowardly. He . . . had to offset that maybe."

"I believe so. And the source? Impatient, impulsive, accustomed to having what he wants and quickly, with a distinct lack of compassion or attention to those who do the work so that he can live as he lives."

"That pretty much eliminates four of my suspects."

Mira smiled. "Which four?"

"Four women, five counting their office manager. Your Space. They didn't inherit anything, they came from the middle-class pool, and they pay attention to details. It's part of what they do. They're organized and they're efficient. If they'd targeted the vic, I think it would've been done right. It would've been very tidy, very clean."

"Is that a compliment?"

"It is, actually. And they understand time-budgeting. The vic didn't have time to get that far in the files. Killing her was inefficient. Okay, I can't take them off the list, but I can keep my focus elsewhere. It saves me time. Thanks."

"I'll let you know what I think after I look at your interview reports."

185

"Good enough." Eve rose, surprised to find her cup nearly empty. She didn't remember drinking the damn stuff. "So . . . I thought I should tell you I had this dream last night."

Concern clouded Mira's eyes. "Dream?"

"Yeah. Not a nightmare. You could call it a kind of review of the day, sort of going over the murder, at the scene. Sometimes I get a different aspect of the vic that way, or the killer, or some line, some angle. Anyway, she was there. Stella."

"I see."

"It didn't bother me, in the dream. It didn't upset me or twist me up. I just told her to fuck off."

Mira beamed at her as if she'd won a gold medal. "Perfect. Progress."

"I guess. The thing is, her being there, it gave me that angle. I don't know why exactly, except for the fact she never thought of me, never put me first — or anywhere. She not only didn't protect me, she was one of the monsters under the bed. Mothers are supposed to think of their kids. You don't have to say she wasn't my mother in any sense but the DNA," Eve said before Mira could. "I get that. I'm dealing with that. But it turned it on Marta. And I realized she thought of her kids, of her family. She'd copied the files to her home unit, but she didn't tell her killers. They'd have gone after the husband, at least they'd have gone after the files. She knew that. I don't know if she believed they'd kill her anyway or not. But I believe she'd have died before she put her family in the crosshairs.

"Anyway, it made a difference to me, when I woke up, when I came out of it. Thinking how Stella would have killed me herself if she risked so much as a paper cut. And how this woman would've died to protect her family. I slept easier, I think, knowing that."

"You're a resilient woman, Eve. Nothing Stella did will ever break you."

"Dented me some. But I'm doing okay. I wanted you to know I'm doing okay."

"I'm here when you are, and I'm here when you're not."

"I know. That helps me do okay. I've got to get back. Thanks for the time."

Mira rose to walk her to the door. "I'm looking forward to the premiere."

"Oh, man."

With a laugh, Mira patted Eve's shoulder. "I'm prepared to be absolutely dazzled by the celebrities, the fashion, the glamour. I made Dennis buy a new tux. He's going to look so handsome."

"He always looks good." Eve's soft spot for Dennis Mira smoothed out some of the anxiety over the event. "If I don't close this before, you can get an up-front look at my suspects. Plenty of them are going to be there."

"More excitement."

"I guess." A little surprised at Mira's attitude, Eve headed out.

She decided to swing into EDD, check on McNab's progress, and spitball it with Feeney if he had the time. She braced herself for the noise, the constant movement, the saturation of colors that looked as though they'd soaked in neon then baked on the rings of Saturn.

She found McNab chair-dancing in his cube, his bony butt bouncing, narrow shoulders jiggling as he talked to the vic's office comp in the incomprehensible language of geek.

She tapped those rocking shoulders, half expecting him to jump as he was so obviously in his own world. But he only swiveled around.

"Hey, Dallas."

"How's it going here?"

"It's up. I'm getting the same buried code as I did on the building security. Same guy hacked it, the same method. It's like a fingerprint."

"So you said. How can I use the fingerprint?"

"When I get done here, I figured I'd do some research, see if I can find out who wrote the code. It's a style, you know. Like shoes."

Shoes and fingerprints, she thought. E-style.

"Okay."

"Here's the thing. I'm not seeing any access of her outgoings. Me, if I'm hacking in, I'm hacking all, and looking through. But it's like the job was get the files, compromise the unit, move on. I don't think whoever did this bothered to find out she'd copied them. She did it from a disc, see?"

He gestured to the screen where she understood nothing at all.

"If you say so."

188

"I totally do. It's right there. I figure accountant types are anal types, right? Back up your backups, then make a spare copy in case the world blows up. So she backed up the files on the discs, then went ahead and copied to her home unit from the discs, one disc for each file. Me, I'd've put it all on one, just separate docs, but the one for each is careful to analyze."

"Okay."

"She probably had the backup with her in the briefcase. In fact, she pretty much had to have them with her with the analysis factor. So when they got them, they figured they were covered. You have to be anal to deal with analysis."

That she got. "So, it's reading to you like someone got an assignment, did exactly what that entailed. Nothing more. No 'let's just be thorough.'"

"That's the zip. Most hackers are going to play around some, scoot around. Hey, you're in there anyway. This one didn't. Straight through, no detours." McNab zoomed his arm through the air. "At least nothing I've found yet."

"Good, it fits."

She left him to his bouncing and rocking, wove her way through the prancing and dancing traffic of other e-geeks to poke her head in the door of Feeney's mercifully calm, dull-colored, and motionless office.

He sat at his desk in a beige shirt. As he still wore a shit-brown jacket over it she assumed he'd come in from the field. He'd loosened his shit-brown tie but hadn't pulled it off, so he might have planned to go back out again. His hair, a combination of ginger and salt sprang untidily around his sleepy basset hound face.

He worked a touch screen and keyboard simultaneously.

He might've dressed like a cop, thought like a cop, walked like a cop, but he could outgeek McNab and the rest of his department combined.

She gave the doorjamb a quick rap. "Got five?"

Feeney held up a finger, continued to do whatever the hell he was doing, then gave a satisfied grunt.

"Now I got five. Son of a bitching cyberstalker. Thinks he can terrorize women, slide in through their security, rape and rob them, then stroll away whistling a tune? He's going to be whistling in a cage before much longer."

"You got him?"

"Got his signature, got his location, and now the primary has them. If he can't bust the asshole now, *he* should be whistling in a cage."

"Who's on it?"

"Schumer."

"He's good. He'll close it."

"Yeah." Feeney scrubbed his hands over his face. "Long couple days. You, too."

"Yeah. Looks like yours is wrapping up. I can't say the same."

"The boy's working on it."

"Yeah, he's pushing through. I appreciate you letting me have him on this, especially when you've been in a stranglehold."

"No problem." He reached into his bowl of candied nuts when Eve eased a hip on his desk.

190

"I got bad guys who get the job done, but don't go an inch further to do it right. They kill a woman because that's the job, but the woman doesn't have to be killed to reach the objective. They come in after the fact to clean up, and don't check all the corners. They use a location for the kill that rings bells. Vic's an auditor — big money. Crime scene's the property of financial advisers — big money. And the two firms have some overlaps."

"Sloppy."

"Yeah, but like half sloppy. Like if I were doing an eval report, I'd put down 'Does the job, but doesn't think outside the box, isn't able to access the situation as it evolves and adjust accordingly.' Trueheart's going for the detective's exam after the first of the year."

Feeney swiveled back and smiled. "He's come along."

"He has. See, he's not green anymore, but he's still fresh. He's always going to be fresh because that's who he is. But I know if I sent him out on assignment, he wouldn't just get the job done. He'd tie up the details, he'd adjust as the situation called for it. He might make a mistake, he doesn't have much time on him, but he wouldn't make the same mistake twice."

"No argument."

"Trueheart gets credit for that, because, yeah, it's who he is. Baxter gets credit for that because he's trained him and trained him well. I get credit because I saw there was something to be trained and brought him over. And I get credit because I'm the boss of both of them."

"And you get the blame when they fuck up or do something half-assed."

"Exactly. So you've got a couple goons, that's how I see it. The killing wasn't slick, it wasn't messy. It was down, dirty, done — with little screwups."

"Broke her neck, right?"

"Yeah, which Mira says was showing off, and that rings true. You've got the brute for that. Then you've got a hacker who knows his business and gets through decent but not stellar security, through more security into the vic's comp, into her supervisor's safe. He got the job done, but he doesn't run it through and see that the vic made copies of the goddamn files he's gone to all that trouble to steal. He did his job. The goon or goons did theirs. But —"

"Bad management."

"Yes!" She lifted her arms to punch her fists lightly in the air. "Bad fucking management. Now you're all pissed off because the cops are coming in the door when you practically put out the welcome mat for them. And still I can't be sure who it is."

"Do you have any who it isn't?"

"Yeah, I got some of those."

"It's a start."

"They're all various kinds of assholes, and looking at them, I can see any one of them doing this, ordering this. Even if I figure out who, it's likely to be circumstantial right now. And I haven't figured out the why, not altogether. It's money. It's got to be money. It's greed, or Roarke used avarice. That's classier greed, right?"

Feeney poked out his bottom lip with a nod. "Sounds classier."

"Avarice. You've got it so you're wading through it, but you want more. You'll cheat, steal, and kill for more, and to protect yourself."

"Have you got your rich guy looking at the financials?"

"Yeah."

"If anybody can find the why. Look at the spouses."

"They don't all have one."

"I bet they all get sex somewhere. The spouse either knows or just spends the money without giving a rat's ass. If they're not banging anyone specific regularly, then you find out who they pick up, hook up with, or pay. Greedy people like to talk about money, how much they have."

"He doesn't see the people who work for him," she continued. "I don't know if that includes a spouse, but it would be a licensed companion, a hookup, a sidepiece. Sex and money, always a winning combo."

She took a handful of his almonds, popped one as she rose. "Thanks. Something to poke around in."

"Greedy bastards who kill women deserve a cage just like sons of bitches who cyberstalk and rape them."

"Fucking A."

"Hey," he called as she started out. "The wife says I have to rent a monkey suit for the premiere thing."

"I don't know, Feeney. Mira just told me she made her husband buy a new one."

"What kind of crazy shit is this? Who needs to wear a monkey suit to watch a damn vid?"

"I've got to wear a dress, and stilts, *and* put crap all over my face. Don't cry to me because you have to wear a tux."

"Crazy shit," he complained.

"Fucking A," she agreed and went on her way.

CHAPTER
ELEVEN

Back in her office, Eve ran a search through gossip and society sites, hoping to mine a couple of gems. While it worked she contacted Vegas PD, and did the dance necessary to score a copy of the police report on the accident that had injured Arnold and Parzarri. Another contact garnered the information that both men would be cleared to travel the following day.

She intended to hit both of them for interviews as soon as possible.

While she waded through gossip — clothes, hair, hookups, breakups, tune-ups — she ran yet another search on Alexander's wife, Pope's wife, Tuva Gunnarsson, and Newton's fiancée.

Enough, she decided, enough to start. Gathering her things, she walked out to the bullpen.

"Peabody, with me."

"I can't find anyone on the list who owns the Cargo van." Peabody said, stuffing her arms into her coat as she caught up with Eve.

"Relatives, friends, rentals."

"Nothing that's hit, yet, but I'm still digging. Did you know, for instance, Chaz Parzarri has fourteen first cousins, and eleven of them live in New York or New Jersey?"

"I did not have that information." Eve squeezed onto the elevator wondering why the hell it was always so crowded when she needed to use it. "Unless one of them owns a Maxima Cargo I don't need that information."

"Well, just saying that's a lot of first cousins and none of them owns a Maxima Cargo. But I'm digging on the people as well as their potential vehicles. Just looking for any red flags. Gambling, whoring, unusual travel."

Good management, Eve thought and gave herself a mental pat on the back. Good management contributed to good work.

"And?"

"So far your sort of expected gambling, whoring, and travel. Except for the married guys and the engaged guy on the whoring thing. If they're tapping LCs, they're doing it with cash, and with care."

The woman wedged in the front corner wearing a skirt the size of a dinner napkin, high-laced boots, pink foaming hair Eve hoped was a wig, and a whopper of a black eye snapped an impressive wad of gum.

"You gotta report the cash," she said conversationally. "You can give a credit discount if you want 'cause you don't have to pay the credit fee, but you gotta report it."

"Is that so? Note that down, Peabody. How'd you get the mouse?" Eve asked her.

"An associate and me had a difference of opinion about a client. Bitch popped me. I just filed a complaint 'cause you gotta have it on record, right? Officer Mills was real nice about it. He didn't even want a free BJ."

"That's . . . nice."

"I'm all about giving freebies to cops, and firefighters, when I can. To show my support."

"And the city of New York thanks you."

The woman beamed, snapped her gum, then sailed off the elevator when the doors opened on the main floor. Grateful nearly everyone else in the car exited along with the LC, Eve shifted for some breathing room.

"Okay, Peabody, pick it up."

"I guess she hasn't figured out offering a free blow job to a cop's considered a bribe."

"Just trying to do her civic duty."

"Right. Where was I? Oh yeah. The Young-Biden team likes gambling. Win some, lose some — and I say that as if winning and or losing more than I make in a year at the tables or on a horse is no big deal. They, Alexander, and Ingersol, travel a lot. Bunches, to really frosty places, including some I've never heard of. Newton does some traveling, and likes sports betting — minor league stuff on the betting. Just friendly amounts. Whitestone travels mostly for business, but does it up right. He also likes to scuba, and he's taking some trips with that at the center."

"They all live within their considerable means, or so it appears," Eve said as they got off on her level of the garage. "And live according to what we'd call their privileged or semi-privileged lifestyle. And that lifestyle includes spouses, fiancées, lovers, exes, LCs — and, you bet your ass, sidepieces."

"You don't really think that mouse bait Pope has a sidepiece."

"That type can surprise you and bang like a drum."

"Have you ever been banged by mouse bait?"

"No." Their footsteps echoed. Somewhere on a higher level, someone gunned an engine. "But Mavis dated this guy for a while back in the day who looked like one of those garden gnomes. She said he went at it like a rabid mink. Don't trust appearances."

"That's true." Peabody jumped in the car. "Take McNab. He's adorable, but he's got that skinny frame. But he can go like a turbo thruster."

"Jesus, Peabody, I don't want to hear about McNab's thrusting abilities."

"They're exceptional. Just the other night, he —"

"Don't, don't, don't." Eve slapped a hand at the corner of her eye when it twitched, then bared her teeth at Peabody's muffled chuckle.

"You did that on purpose."

"I just wanted to see if it still worked."

"It'll always work. Just like my boot will always fit up your ass."

"They're nice boots," Peabody said cheerfully. "But Angie at Your Space liked mine."

"You must be proud. We're going to start with exes," Eve continued before Peabody could brag on her boots — again. "Young-Sachs has one who runs a fancy boutique in the Meat Packing District."

198

"How do you know?"

"You're not the only one who can troll for gossip."

The fancy boutique offered screens scrolling a constant shift of outfits highlighting one feature. The leopard knee boots with the short black dress, the short black dress with silver heels and a complicated silver scarf, the silver scarf with jeans, a red top, and a vest.

Little beams of light spotlighted each piece at its place on rack or shelf as they appeared on screen.

It made Eve mildly dizzy.

Compact and curvy, Brandy Dyson stood on heeled boots and moved like a lightning bolt until Eve managed to corner her.

"Sorry." With a bright smile and lashes so thick and heavy Eve wondered how she managed to keep her eyes open, Brandy pulled a small blue bottle from the jeweled holster on her belt, took a gulp. "Energy drink — legal. You wanted to ask me something about Carter. Is he in trouble?"

"Should he be?"

Brandy laughed. "That's a loaded question to ask an ex. Being a dick isn't illegal, right? If it were, half the guys I've dated would be doing time."

"What kind of a dick is Carter Young-Sachs?"

"And that's a strange question for a cop to ask, but the selfish, self-absorbed, lying, cheating kind."

Understanding where Eve was heading, Peabody put on her just-us-girls tone. "Maybe you could give us an anecdote or example."

"Standing me up on my damn birthday, without so much as a text, and claiming later he'd been called into an emergency meeting — when what he did was zip off to Capri with another woman. That was the last time he lied and cheated on me. Not the first, but sometimes it takes a while to cut through the sparkle and see the dark."

"That's harsh," Peabody said. "Your birthday."

"Yeah, it was. He started out so attentive, really went after me, you know? The whole pursuit thing, and it just swept me up. I'd just started dating this other guy, a really nice guy, and I broke it off for Carter."

Her shoulders lifted with her sigh before she turned to make a minute adjustment of the position of a mammoth handbag in zebra stripes.

"I was stupid, and I walked away from a sweetheart. And once Carter had me wrapped up, the dick came out — metaphorically as his anatomic dick had already made a few appearances."

Enjoying the woman's style, Eve had to grin. "How did the metaphorical dick rear its head?"

Brandy shook back her own head and laughed. "Good one. Well, to start, I was supposed to drop whatever I had going for what he had going. He made fun of my shop, subtly at first, just kidding, you know? But it got old, and it got clear he didn't respect what I'm doing. You know, just because my family's got money doesn't mean I should sit on my butt and not try to make something."

She let out a breath. "Whew. I'm still pissed. What did he do?"

"I don't know if he did anything, other than being a dick," Eve told her.

Under her impossible lashes, Brandy's eyes hardened. "Well, if he did, you can bet his conjoined twin's in on it."

"Tyler Biden?"

"That one doesn't even pretend not to be a dick. He *likes* being one. His dickhood's like his mission in life, and he's really good at it. Smirking, sneering, superior-assed fuck. Sorry," she added. "I really am still pissed."

"No need to apologize," Eve told her. "My impression of him runs parallel."

"Good, because I'll tell you something else, they don't know half as much about business as I do. They wouldn't be in charge of cleaning the floors at Young-Biden if they hadn't been born into it. Carter especially. Just try to have a conversation with him about supply and demand, or marketing, or net returns, customer base and growing same, and it's clear he's clueless. He's kind of an idiot really. An idiot dick, which makes me an idiot for giving him eight and a half months of my life."

"So he didn't like to talk about business, his work, his company?"

"More like he couldn't. He liked to talk about the company, but only to brag. About his money, and how he liked to spend it, or the trips. He'd bitch about his mother now and then when he'd had a couple drinks or . . ."

"I've already figured out he uses," Eve told her.

"Well . . . He'd complain that his mother pushed him too hard, or expected too much, how she wanted him to live and breathe the company. I don't know, she didn't strike me as bitchy the few times I met her. But in my family we're expected to make something, to be involved. Maybe we don't have the Young kind of money, but if we did, I can tell you it'd be the same. You want something, work for it. I've got three years in this place, and I've worked my ass off. I figured out before long that Carter mostly sits on his."

She sighed again, adjusted the bag again. "But there was that sparkle. He's great-looking, he's charming when he wants to be, and he can make you feel really special. For a little while."

"Did you ever meet his financial adviser?"

"No. But now that you mention it, early on, when he was really going after me, he'd talk about how I should hook up with his guy if I really wanted to see my portfolio zoom. How his guy knew all the ins, all the outs, all the little corners. My family has a firm they've worked with for years. I stuck with them. I trust them. I didn't know anything about his guy, and maybe I was dazzled by the sparkle, but when it comes to my bottom line, I'm careful."

"And what did we learn, Peabody?"

Peabody pulled her gloves on as they walked to the car. "Other than I really want that snakeskin belt with the sapphire blue buckle I can't afford? That Carter Young-Sachs is a dick who, if she's any judge — and I think she is — doesn't know squat about his own company. And could care less. He'd cheat on his girlfriend on her own birthday, then lie about it. A stupid lie because she's going to find out. He resents his mother expecting him to actually work, and Biden's smarter and meaner."

"All that. And."

She sidestepped a couple of women loaded down with shopping bags, bubbling over with excitement over some sale, and not watching where the hell they were going.

"He likes going after what's not his, then doesn't appreciate it once he's got it," Eve added. "He's tight enough with his financial guy to push him on someone else, and does it in such a way that indicates said money guy isn't above skirting around the edges."

"That, too."

"Which doesn't mean he'd kill or arrange for a killing. But it does confirm he's stupid enough to do it, and do it half-assed. I want you to go talk to a few more exes, feel them out."

"Good times."

"Yeah, I figured you'd see it that way."

People hustled or breezed or wandered by. Some talked on 'links like the guy pleading into his for Michelle to give him five minutes, just five minutes, baby. Some took vids, like the group of Asian tourists in I Heart New York ski caps posing in front of a storefront. Others ate on the run, like the man chomping down on a loaded soy dog.

The buzz of voices and varied languages, the movement and pace typified New York to Eve.

But right now she wished they'd all just get the hell out of the way so she didn't have to weave through them.

"I'm going to do another run at the WIN Group. Then I'm going to my home office, see what I can put together," she told Peabody. "We're going to push at Arnold and Parzarri tomorrow, as soon as they're back. It's one of them, one of the WIN Group, and one of the four dicks we talked to today. Or two of the four. We'll whittle it down. If we can pin any one of them, we've got all of them."

She heard the faint whine, felt the pressure thump into her back, just between her shoulder blades. Instinct kicked in, had her driving at Peabody and knocking her partner to the ground.

"What the —"

"Stunner!" Eve rolled, coming up with her weapon as she surged to her feet. Through the crowds — New Yorkers who barely flicked a lash, tourists who stopped to gape, she spotted the big man — six four, two-fifty, Caucasian, ski cap, sunshades, black scarf and coat — execute a quick pivot and run.

"Move!" she shouted to Peabody and sprinted off in pursuit. Forced to dodge and weave — and leap over the pedestrians the man mowed down like bowling pins — she lost some ground. She saw him charge up the stair access of the High Line. For a big man he moved fast and well — athletically, she thought as she bore down and bolted up after him.

People strolled, sat on benches, took personal vids — while others stumbled back off the pebbled trail as her quarry cut through them. She ignored the shouts, the curses, long jumped over a planting to cut his lead. Her lungs burned, but she told herself she was gaining ground.

With barely a hitch in his stride, he snatched a toddler off the ground, coldcocked its father with an elbow to the jaw, and threw the shrieking kid through the air like an arena ball with limbs.

With no choice, Eve cut left, trampling native grasses, and set to receive.

The force of the kid's body knocked her up, back. Knocked her flat and knocked her hard. The kid's skull rammed like a hurled rock into her chest. She felt her bones sing, and her burning lungs expelled what air she had left. Desperately she tried to suck in oxygen, and her throat wheezed and burned from the effort.

The toddler's galloping heart thwacked against her — even that hurt, but it assured her he'd lived through the flight and landing. She had a moment to think at least the impact had knocked the air out of the kid, too, as the shrieking stopped. But with a mighty gasp, the child let out a scream so sharp she wondered the air around them didn't split in two.

Her ears rang in a chorus of crazed church bells.

"It's okay, you're okay." Panting, Peabody lifted the kid — its sex undetermined in its bright red hat and coat. "You're just fine now, little man. Just fine."

With the pressure somewhat relieved with the lack of the kid's weight, Eve wheezed in air. "How do you know it's a male?"

Peabody patted the kid as she crouched down to Eve. "Are you okay? How bad are you hurt?"

"I don't know. Not bad." Unless she counted the throbbing in her chest where the kid hit, in her ass where *she'd* hit, in her head where it had slammed, and some singing in her just healed shoulder. "Fucker."

Peabody winced, straightened to turn toward the hysterical woman running toward her.

"My baby! My baby! Chuckie!"

The father, eyes glazed, face white but for dribbles of blood, staggered after her as the crowd moved in.

"He's fine. Just fine. Hey, Chuckie, here's your mama. Everybody move back!" Peabody ordered.

Mother and son clung to each other, sobbing while Eve pushed herself up. The world did a little shimmer and dance, then righted.

"Move back, please!" Peabody repeated, and took the father's arm. "Sir, you need to sit down a minute."

"What happened? What happened?"

"I'm going to call the medicals. Please, just sit down here. Ma'am, I want you and Chuckie to sit right there. I'll call it in," she told Eve. "You oughta sit down, too."

"I'm okay. Just knocked the wind out of me."

"You caught him." The mother turned her tear-streaked face to Eve. "You caught him. You saved my baby."

"Okay, let's —"

And she had the wind knocked out of her again as the woman grabbed her, digging the kid's feet into her groin in the desperately grateful embrace.

The singing in her shoulder became an anthem.

"Peabody."

"Ma'am." Peabody shifted her tone to croon as she peeled the woman off Eve. "I want you to sit right here. You and your family. I'm going to need to get some information, okay?"

Eve stepped out of the trampled grass, gritted her teeth against the twinges in her ass, her shoulder.

Fucker, she thought again, scanning the High Line.

He was long gone.

"What the hell," Peabody managed when they'd finally turned the family and the situation over to uniforms and MTs.

"Son of a bitch. Son of a bitch stunned me in the back. Fucking coward asshole bastard."

"He *stunned* you? How did — your magic coat!"

"Yeah." Eve rubbed a hand over the leather. "It definitely works. I felt the impact, like a thump on the back, a slight burn. Milder and slighter, let me tell you, than you get with standard vests. I caught the whine of it. He had you zeroed in next."

"So you tackled me. Thanks for that. My coat's not magic."

"Bastard could move. Really move. He went up those stairs like they were a glide. I couldn't fire, not with all those damn people swarming everywhere, but I was gaining on him. A little."

"I couldn't keep up with either of you, but I was trying to get some backup while I trailed you. Then, Jesus, all I saw was that kid flying through the air."

"He didn't even hesitate. Barely changed his stride. Hit the father — elbow to jaw, grabbed up the kid and hurled him."

"You made a hell of a catch."

"Yeah." She rubbed her chest where the kid had slammed into her. "Fucker," she repeated.

"Chuckie's going to grow up on the story of the cop who caught him on the High Line, for a game-winning TD."

"He also has to live with the name Chuckie for — that's it! That's how he moved. Football or Arena Ball. Like a freaking running back. Fast, nimble, hard. I bet he's put some time in on the field. Goddamn semi-pro."

"I didn't get a good look at him."

"Hat, sunshades, scarf — I didn't get a good look at his face. But his build, his shape. It's something." And now she'd run with it. "Go on and get to those interviews. I want to hit the WIN Group again, then try to find this asshole."

"You took a hard hit, Dallas."

"And I won't forget it."

She didn't limp into the WIN offices, but that was pride. She wanted to go home, soak her aching body in a hot tub of swirling jets, but had to push on this angle.

That was the job.

Even as she stepped — gingerly — off the elevator, Robinson Newton turned from the reception desk. His eyes widened when he saw her, but before she could judge if the look of stunned surprise equaled guilt, he rushed forward.

"Lieutenant Dallas! I need to shake your hand."

"Okay."

"It was amazing! Amazing what you did," he said as he pumped her hand and made her abused body weep.

"What?"

"Chuckie. You caught him right out of the air, like a high fly. I just —"

"How do you know?" She shifted her feet to a plant, laid a hand on the butt of her weapon.

"It's all over the screen, the Internet. I've already watched it a half a dozen times. Are you all right? It looked like you went down pretty hard."

"I'm fine."

"Amazing. Just amazing. That little boy . . . Who would do something like that? He's not even two."

"Did they get a shot of the guy who threw him?"

"Not that I've seen. There are a couple of different angles where people caught the catch, and one that's from some security angle I think. I've never seen anything like it. You should come sit down, let me get you something. Coffee, some water. Some champagne."

"Thanks all the same. I just want a quick word. Are your partners here?"

"Yeah, we're about to head over to the new building. It's cleared, and we're meeting the designer about a couple details. Come on back, and I'll get them. The reports weren't clear, just that you were chasing this man, and he injured some pedestrians, then tossed that little boy. What did he do, I mean before that?"

"Killed Marta Dickenson."

Newton stopped, eyes wide again. "Oh my God. Who is he? Why did he kill her? Did you catch him?"

"If I could speak with all three of you?"

"Yes, of course. I'm sorry. It's so . . . so everything." He led her into the little conference room. "Have a seat. Give me just a minute."

She stood as she'd already discovered during the drive over that sitting wasn't her friend.

Jake came in first, moving fast, face wreathed in smiles. "Super-woman! Sign her up! Mega-maniac catch. We were all, 'Man! We know her.' You caught the kid when you were chasing a murderer. It was like third and goal."

"They said the little boy's just fine," Whitestone put in. "Just some bumps and bruises. Were you really chasing the person who killed that woman?"

"I believe so. He's white, about six four and two-fifty. Broad shoulders, big hands. Square jaw." Or so she believed with the very brief glance she'd managed. "Sound familiar?"

"That's pretty big." Whitestone lifted his shoulders as he glanced at his partners. "I don't know anybody, personally, who sounds like that."

"Do you remember seeing anyone who fits that description around your new building. Or this one?"

"I don't." Whitestone eased a hip onto the table. "Rob said you were chasing him. Do you have a name, a photo?"

"Not yet, but I will. I imagine you often go to the client rather than the client coming to you."

"Sure."

"Then I'll ask all of you." She nodded toward Newton and Ingersol. "Do you remember anyone who fits that description at or around either Alexander and Pope or Young-Biden?"

"I —" Newton hesitated, scrubbed a hand over his hair. "I don't honestly know. I don't know if I've paid any attention. I don't understand. Young-Biden's a solid company, one of our biggest accounts. You don't really believe they're involved in a murder?"

"I keep an open mind. How about you? You're in charge of those accounts," she asked Ingersol.

"They've got some big guys, I guess. Security, maintenance. And Mr. Pope's admin's a tall one. Yeah, easy six four, but I don't think he's that big. Leaner than two-fifty. If this is about the murder, their audit's really just a formality. An internal check, really. From my end, their finances are in very good order."

"From your end," Eve repeated. "What if an audit turns up a problem, a discrepancy?"

"I can't imagine it will." He sort of bounced to the friggie, took out a power drink. "If it did, it would depend on what kind of problem or discrepancy. Rob and Brad will tell you, audits sometimes, a lot of times, turn up a couple little things, a different interpretation of some tax code, or a payment or withdrawal coming out or going into the wrong pocket. That kind of thing's easily resolved."

"What about something not so easily resolved?"

He shook his head. "I can't see it in these accounts. If something big was off, I'd have found it, or the accountant would, or the tax lawyers. Somebody."

"It's why we coordinate," Whitestone told her. "Why we work with their accountants, their legal department, and why they work with us. Checks and balances, and minimizing time, maximizing profit."

"All right."

"We think it might be corporate espionage." Whitestone spread his hands as Newton sighed at him. "That's what we've been talking about since we heard about the break-in at Brewer's," he insisted. "It sounds like somebody hired somebody to access all those files, and maybe the Dickenson woman was part of it. I know she's dead, and that's terrible. But we've been told several files were taken. It sounds like a big operation looking to access and analyze data, trying to undermine competitors."

"That's a theory."

"But not yours," Whitestone said.

"No, not mine. Just taking the two companies I asked you about, they're not in the same businesses or areas. They're not competitors. They don't have anything in common, except you and Brewer. So . . . Thanks for your time."

She'd done what she needed to do, Eve thought — and did limp a little once she got down to the lobby. She'd planted seeds of doubt and unease, at least in the mind of the guilty.

And now she was going home, soaking her aching ass.

She bore down again as she maneuvered her body out of the car at the base of the steps of home. Just had to get by Dr. Doom, up the stairs, into the tub. A solid soak would do the trick.

Breathing carefully, she stepped inside.

Summerset scanned her, top to toe. "I suppose it couldn't last forever."

"What?" Just had to get up the stairs that, right that minute, looked like the towering side of an alp.

"Getting through the day without injury."

"Who says I'm injured?"

"Slamming into the ground as you did would jar the body, bruise the points of impact."

She imagined that was his delicate way of referring to her ass, but she still didn't like it. When the cat wound his pudgy way through her legs, she realized she'd probably whimper out loud if she tried bending to pet him.

"There was a lot of grass."

"Regardless. Oh, don't be an idiot," he snapped at her. "Take the elevator."

"I'm fine. Just a little stiff." She started for the steps, gave up. Crawling up them lost more pride points than just walking past him to the damn elevator.

"I assume you refused any medical attention. You want ice and heat, on and off. And a blocker."

He was probably right, but she wanted that damn tub like she wanted to breathe. "I'm fine," she repeated.

"You're young, fit, quick, and have excellent reflexes," he said as she walked to the elevator. "Because of that a child is being pampered and spoiled by his parents right now instead of lying in a hospital.

Or worse. Take a blocker. He'll only make you when he gets home, and he's on his way."

Summerset held out a little blue pill. "Take it now, and I can tell him you did."

Simpler to just take it, she decided, because he was right again. Roarke would shove one down her throat if she didn't. And that was stupid all around.

"Fine." She took it, swallowed it.

"Ice," he repeated.

"I don't want ice unless it's in a really big drink." She stepped into the elevator.

"Master bedroom," Summerset ordered before she could do so herself.

So she just closed her eyes, leaned against the wall, and let it take her where she wanted to go.

She'd been hurt worse, she reminded herself. A hell of a lot worse. Despite that dubious qualifier, she felt as if every muscle, bone, and tendon in her body had been pulled, knocked, and strained. The blocker would help, for now, but it wouldn't help the aches and stiffness tomorrow, and they'd be a distraction, an annoyance. They'd just be in her way.

So she'd deal with them.

When she stepped out into the bedroom, heard the elevator door whisk closed behind her, she allowed herself a long, heartfelt, moaning sigh.

And that was enough self-indulgence.

She eased out of her coat, blessing it for its stun-proof lining. But at the moment it felt impossibly heavy. She started to pull off her jacket, realized when her shoulder pinged that sometime during the dash, leap, twist, catch, and fall, she'd wrenched it good and proper, and it had barely healed from a much nastier injury during a life-and-death struggle with Isaac McQueen a few weeks before.

She fumbled with her weapon harness, carefully slipped it off.

And Roarke walked into the room.

He studied her carefully, nodded. "Nice catch," he said.

CHAPTER
TWELVE

She'd expected worry, concern, stroking and soothing, so his matter-of-fact comment threw her off balance.

Probably his devious plan, she decided, to trick her into going to a health center.

"Thanks. It was an unexpected play."

"At the least. How bad is it?"

"Not very. I took a blocker."

"So I heard. Well, let's have a look."

Now she smiled. "You just want to get me naked."

"My life's work," he said as he walked to her. He could see in her eyes it was more than "not very." "As it is, I'll tend to that myself." He started to draw her sweater up and off, heard her hiss of pain.

"Okay, ouch. Just a second." She pressed her hand on her shoulder, trying to re-angle, decrease the twinge.

She saw the change in his eyes, that flash of ice blue heat, and knew he thought — as she did — of McQueen.

"The same shoulder?" he said gently.

"It figures, doesn't it? It's — okay, it's ouch, but mostly just sore."

"I'll cut the sweater off."

"The hell you will. This is that cashmere stuff. And I like this sweater."

"Is that so?"

"Yeah, that's so. I can like a sweater. It's soft, and it's warm, and we're not hacking it up. We'll just go easy, okay?"

"All right then." Keeping his eyes trained on her face, he brushed the back of his hand over her cheek. "Relax now, loosen up and relax, and let me do it."

She breathed, shut her eyes, let him carefully lift the wool. Not bad, not bad — shit, shit — okay, better.

"See? No hacking, and —" She followed the direction of his gaze, looked down at herself and found herself mildly stunned by the bruising blooming across her chest above her tank.

"Wow, colorful. I think the kid's head plowed into me. He came at me like a mortar. Pow! Skull meets tits. Tits lose."

"Have a seat, let me get your boots off."

She did, watched him. His cool tone told her he was very, very angry, and much too worried. She could pin his response on her previous injuries. Not enough time between bouts, she decided. The only way she knew to offset his reaction was playing it light, playing it easy.

"I like sexy undressing better than you thinking about tranq'ing me unconscious and hauling me to the health center undressing."

"I considered just that."

"Come on. What kind of reward is that for making a really excellent catch?"

He met her eyes, and she saw him relax, just a little. "You've been hurt worse."

"That's what I said — thought."

"Pants next."

She smiled again. She still hurt, but some of the aches and twinges were buried under a layer of cotton from the blocker. "I will if you will."

"It pains me to refuse such a generous offer." He just unhooked her trousers, drew them off. "You've more bruises here and there." He stroked his hands over the back of her head, carefully. Then relaxed a bit more when he found no knots or lumps. "But from watching the mini-vid all over the media, I'd say you've worse on your ass."

"It's kind of numb right now, but yeah. Tits and ass took the brunt."

"Two of my favorite parts. Up you come." He held her upright, and gently for a moment, brushing his lips over her temple.

Just banged up, he told himself. It wouldn't be the first time, or the last.

"Have you seen the vid?"

"No. Kind of unnecessary as I was there."

"I think you need to see it." Gently, he drew her support tank up, bit back a curse at the trail of bruises over her ribs. "Two seconds later, or if you'd misjudged the — I suppose I'll say arc and velocity — that little boy would have more than some bruises."

"It was so damn fast. That fucker? The way he moved — speed, agility. He scooped the kid up with one hand, elbow-jabbed the father with the other arm, did a smooth half pivot, hurled. He's played ball, Roarke. Serious ball at some point. And he's strong. I figure the kid for a solid twenty-five pounds."

"Twenty-seven, according to the parents in an interview."

"Twenty-seven, and he hurled it like the kid weighed two. Some of that's adrenaline, but it's serious, solidly strong."

He'd slipped off her underwear and stood studying her ass.

"What? How bad?" She craned her neck, tried to see for herself.

"There's one here that looks a bit like Africa, another that resembles Australia. Then there's a small chain of islands."

"Great, I've got a world map on my ass." She managed to turn, get a reasonable look in the mirror. "Jesus. It is a world map."

"You've not much meat back there."

"Are you complaining?"

He traced his fingers over her, featherlight. "Only about its current state."

"It'll be better when I soak it, and the rest of me in a hot jet tub."

"It's ice you need."

"I don't want ice. Ice is cold."

"Is it? I need to write that down. On the bed with you."

"The tub'll be soothing."

"So will this. Ass up to start," he ordered as he moved into the next room.

She really wanted the tub, and figured the sooner she got the ice portion over and done, the sooner she'd get what she wanted. Plus it felt good to stretch out on the bed, at least once she'd adjusted for throbs and twinges.

Roarke came back, knelt on the bed beside her. "Why were you in that area?"

"Something Feeney said, so I wanted to get the feel from some of the suspects' exes. Exes may say it all ended friendly, no problem, but they're usually ready to serve the guy up to whoever asks for a slice."

She started to protest when cold met her aching butt, then the relief eked through. Maybe ice wasn't so bad.

"And you got the slice?"

"Yeah, on Carter Young-Sachs. He fits Mira's profile, and my sense of the type who'd arrange a killing on impulse. Then again, he's not the only one. I was telling Peabody to hit up a couple more of the exes, and I'd go by and take another pass at the WIN Group, and the asshole tries to stun me. In the back. Cowardly fuckhead."

Roarke's hands paused. "He fired at you, on the High Line?"

"No, he fired at me below the High Line." And she realized, belatedly, she'd just told her husband she'd been fired on, without any kind of preparation. "I heard the whine of the stream — not sure why — and felt this thudding between my shoulder blades. So your most excellent still-in-development anti-stun material has now been field tested."

She held up a thumb, gave it a jerk up.

"That's desperation," she continued. "And more impulse and stupidity. Firing a stream at a couple of cops in the middle of the Meat Packing District, with people swarming everywhere. It was a damn good shot, which tells me it's not the first time he's fired a stunner, which tells me — since there's no way he's a pro and has weapons illegal to civilians at his disposal, he's been on the job, in the military, or part of a paramilitary deal. Possibly he's got a collector's license, but I'm leaning toward military. Former, and currently in the employ of one of my bigwigs as security or personal bodyguard. Something along those lines."

She heard the hum of a healing wand, felt the mild pressure.

"Stunning you wouldn't have accomplished anything. He'd need to finish it."

"Yeah. I caught the movement, mostly just the movement. He'd have hit Peabody next, and she doesn't have the magic lining. I tackled her. We both probably have some bruises from that now that I think of it. When I rolled over and up, I didn't get a solid look again. All those people. But again, my sense is he was moving in, figuring I took her down when I fell from the stun. He'd just need to get to us, take us both out at point-blank, and get gone. Sloppy, brash and sloppy. But he thought fast, moved fast. I'm not sure I'd have caught him even without the flying toddler."

"Security cameras must have captured him. You must have his face."

"Not so much. Ski cap, sunshades, scarf. And he kept his head down. He's not a complete idiot. We sent what we've got in, and they'll run facial recognition. If he was in the military or on the job, we could get lucky with that. I've got some basics — he's a big guy, about six four, two bucks-fifty. Strong build. Strong. I really think he played some ball. Arena Ball or football. So it's another angle to poke at. He could've snapped the vic's neck. He's got the muscle for it."

"And as he'd attempt to kill two cops in broad daylight, in a crowded area, the nerve and the lack of, let's say, moral center. Turn over now, let's see what I can do about those pretty breasts."

"They've been prettier."

"Still mine," he murmured, gently kissing both when she turned.

"Attached to me."

"I take a dim view of someone who'd bruise my wife's pretty breasts."

"You're saying it like that to get a rise out of me."

"You do happen to be my wife," he reminded her, and used a gentle hand with the cold pack. "And they are very pretty breasts."

"Chuckie had a head like a brick." But she smiled. "It feels better. Why don't you lose all those clothes so I'm not naked all by myself?"

He gave her bad shoulder a little poke, made her hiss.

"That was mean."

"And why I'm not naked."

He put another cold pack on the shoulder. It hurt, she realized, but she supposed in a good way. Who knew?

"It's Alexander/Pope/Parzarri/Ingersol or Young/Biden/Arnold/Ingersol. Or any of those with Newton. I don't think Whitestone because he's just too smart to — oops — discover a body on his own doorsteps with the client of his wet dreams. But any three of the WINS could access each other's accounts. They're just that intertwined."

"Which one are you leaning toward?"

"That's the thing. Alexander, Young-Sachs, and Biden are all such assholes. And Pope's such a measly little no-balls, he's annoying. That colors it. They all fit neatly enough. Ingersol? He says too much, talks too fast, pushes too hard. A lot of impulse there, I think. On the other hand, Newton's contained, genial, smooth — and that equals clever and smart to me. Somebody in this mess has to be smart. I need to push on the auditors, and that's tomorrow. If one of them rings for me, that'll fit the lock. But it's just gut and circumstances without solid evidence. So I need to break one of them down, once I figure out which one."

"Sterling Alexander's considered a bit of a tool in some circles," Roarke began as he ran the wand over her shoulder. "Those who respect him do so — according to those I spoke with — primarily for what he's inherited, not what he's done with it. The sense is he spends far too much on personal travel, income, perks while holding the line at a contrasting low end for employees."

"None of that surprises me, but it's good information."

"Pope's hardly considered at all," Roarke continued, "but those who bother see him as the one dealing with the internal glitches, problems, numbers. Both Alexander Senior — Sterling's father — and Pope Senior — the mother they share — hold controlling interests, though both have essentially retired. I'm told if it was discovered anything underhanded was going on inside the company, the mother would come down like the wrath of God."

"What about Alexander Senior?"

"Apparently he's enjoying his golf —" Roarke rose, moved into the bathroom. She heard the water spewing into the tub. "And his current wife. That would be wife four who's a full half century younger."

"Gee, could it be love?"

"Cynics say no, and I can guess which camp you'd fall in." He went to a panel in the wall, tapped it, and took out a bottle of red wine. "He made his fortune, and to his and Mum Pope's credit, built good facilities, donated generously, funded a number of excellent causes. Now he's firmly entrenched in enjoying his later years with his five iron and his — some say — dim-witted young wife.

"Into the tub now."

"It's a big tub. Why are you still wearing clothes?"

Roarke shook his head as he poured wine. "Does getting bruised from head to foot make you think about sex?"

"I think it's more having you tend to the wounded. You're a pretty sexy nurse."

He laughed. "Into the tub, Lieutenant. We'll see how you do with a soak and some wine."

"You said I should relax and loosen up." She held out a hand for him to help her up, then slid her body against his.

"So I did." He answered her kiss, but gently. And when she started to lift her arms, wrap around him, she gasped.

"Okay, the shoulder's still a problem," she admitted. "That just means you have to do all the work."

After setting the wine down, he took off his tie, his jacket, his shirt — watching her smile spread, and the gleam light in her eyes.

He picked her up, taking care, gave her a soft, warm kiss as he carried her into the bath. And slowly, gently, lowered her into the warm, frothing water.

"Oh God, yes." She moaned in glorious relief. "That's what I mean."

"Relax," he said again.

"Hey!" She scowled after him when he walked out.

She wanted some sex, so what? Some nice, loosen-up-the-aches-in-the-bubbling-tub sex. Bubbling tub he'd put something in she realized with a sniff. Something that smelled good and probably had some medicinal purpose.

She gave him a steady stare when he came back with her wine, with a second glass, and with some sort of cream in a bottle.

"What's that?"

"Something that will help ease up that shoulder. Have some wine." He passed hers off, set down the rest as he finished undressing.

"That's more like it."

"I haven't finished giving you my report, have I?"

On a sudden, uncomfortable thought, she studied her glass with suspicion. "You didn't tranq the wine, did you?"

"You took a blocker like a good girl. You've tolerated the ice packs with minimal complaint, and had a session with the wand. You're stiff and sore, and will be tomorrow, but you don't need a tranq. Still, the shoulder troubles me."

"I bet it troubles me more."

"You don't take stupefying love into account."

"Stupefying," she said as he eased in behind her. "Not even love could make you stupid."

"I'm in this boiling pot, aren't I? Here now." He rubbed the cream between his palms, then began to spread it over her shoulder.

"If I'm going to have a sore shoulder, I wish I'd gotten it kicking his ass."

"You saved a baby."

"Save the kid, lose the killer. But not for long. I'm going to get that fucker."

"I have every faith. To continue," he said as he increased the pressure slightly, working steadily into the muscle and joint. "Carter Young-Sachs is considered a bit of a git. His mother in particular indulged him, and he hasn't seemed to have outgrown his youthful dependence on that indulgence, or his affection for doing whatever he pleases whenever he pleases. He enjoys women, and doesn't mind paying for them. He also enjoys a wide and colorful variety of illegal substances."

226

"He was high when I talked to him."

"Which, again, shows his assumption he can do as he pleases with impunity — as he always has. He puts in time at the business — he's required to be in the offices or on company business for twenty-five hours a week in order to receive his generous salary and benefits."

"Twenty-five hours a week? It's a wonder he's not suffering from exhaustion."

"Time, according to those in the know, is about all he puts in. He's charming and personable when he chooses to be, attractive, enjoys sports, and does well when he's doing no more than entertaining clients."

"He knows less than jack about company business," Eve put in. "Every question I asked, he had to refer to his Nordic goddess admin who he's banging."

"It's difficult to resist a goddess."

"She's banging for love. He's in it for the bang. His ex — and she's a looker, with money and family connections — gave me the picture of a man who wants what he doesn't have, or someone else does. He goes after it, gets it. Forgets it. Mira would probably say something about his inner child. I just figure his inner child needs a good spanking."

Whatever was in the cream, she thought, definitely did the job.

"I don't know if he's smart enough to screw around with the books, to skim or twist around some deal, plus he'd just figure he was entitled to it anyway. But I could see him ordering up a murder to get his hands on something that wasn't his. Somebody else's data, but only if he knew what the hell to do with it. That's a puzzler."

"The younger Biden in Young-Biden would know. He's smarter, cagier, more ambitious, and I'm told fairly ruthless."

"Yeah, that jibes with my information."

"He also has a quick trigger on his temper. He enjoys the life he's been born into, and why shouldn't he, but at the same time, he comes across as someone never really satisfied. There's a cold, cruel streak from my research there. Both in business and in his personal life."

"You spent some time on this."

"It's not difficult to get people talking. Gossip is one of the fuels of business. I have some nibbles on some of the others in the files you gave me."

"I'll want those, but it's going to come down to one of these four, or a combination of them."

Cautiously, she rolled her shoulder, barely felt a twinge. "It's better. A lot. Maybe you won't have to do all the work after all."

"I disagree. No point in overtaxing an injury. Relax."

"I am relaxed."

"Not enough." Gently, he stroked his cream-slicked hands over her breasts. "Chuckie wasn't the only one who flew."

"What?"

"Watch the vid. You didn't just go down, you flew back a few feet first. It must've been like catching a cannonball. Then after you hit, you lay there, obviously dazed — and sheet white — for a few seconds." He pressed his lips to her shoulder as he stroked. "Then, my darling Eve, when the child started screaming in obvious shock and terror, you just looked annoyed, maybe a little puzzled. I could all but hear you think: *Well now, what the hell do I do with this now that I've got it?*"

"Did I think it with an Irish accent?"

"It was that expression on your face that let me breathe easier again. Even though I knew you'd come through it all right before I watched, I breathed easier when I saw that annoyed bafflement on your face. And then the faithful Peabody was there."

"You changed around your schedule, probably canceled some multi-zillion deal to be here."

"Stupefied in love."

She closed her eyes while his hands glided over her. "None of the people I'm looking at understand that. Maybe that's why it's so easy for them to kill — more pay for it. It's colder, I think, when you can't even do the killing yourself. Like hiring people to fumigate your house or office. You're not going to actually deal with the bugs. That's too nasty. You'll just pay to have it done. Money for money. Not for love or passion, not for need. Even then you don't think it through, don't bother yourself with the details. Just get it done, you think — order — and don't clog up my day with the details."

"Why come after you?" He knew, but wanted to let her talk it through.

"I bothered him. I got in his face, into his business. That's insulting, and a little frightening. Get rid of me, and Peabody, and brush your hands off. Which is stupid again, for the same reason killing Dickenson was stupid. Somebody else just picks up the ball and runs with it."

"It buys time."

"That's true, but kill a cop? Two cops? Wrath of God hits about even with the wrath of the entire NYPSD. And neither of those hits the level of the Wrath of Roarke."

"It's already been stirred," he stated.

"I know it, but I'm good. I'm here. I'm good." She hooked her good arm up and around his neck. "They're jealous of you, all of them. That's another kind of greed. Of avarice. They want what you have."

"They can't have it."

"And they know it. More of a pisser. You're not second- and third-generation money and business. You upstart."

He laughed at that. "Now I'm insulted."

"Irish street rat upstart with your shadowy past and your cop wife. Yeah, it adds a layer of pissiness having Roarke's cop in their face. We'll just teach them both a lesson."

"They don't know my cop." Carefully, he turned her so they faced. "But I do."

He kissed her, sweetly, then just took her hands in his when she started to reach for him. "No. You started this, and now you'll just have to lie back and take it."

"Oh, I can take it."

"Let's see."

Just his mouth on hers, just that kindest of contacts. He'd wanted only to tend to her, to soothe her aches,

230

ease her hurts. Only that, but he understood she needed more. Needed him, and needed to show them both she wouldn't be beaten, or even slowed down.

Part of it might have been those memories of being hurt, of being so close to death by McQueen's hands, of coming so close to taking his life while the pain and shock ruled her.

It didn't matter why, he thought. She needed, and he'd give.

But gently, slowly, and with that fine sugary layer of sweetness.

He felt her body go pliant, go soft against him, as he knew it would only for him. She, who never surrendered, would surrender to him, for him. Would give him that most intimate treasure.

He murmured to her as he used his hands, his lips to comfort and arouse. *A ghra*. My love.

He took her down, away from hurts, from worries, from all but silky, shimmering pleasure. Weighted her body with it, clouded her mind. And his words, so lovely, stirred in her heart.

My love.

The water foamed and frothed around them, scented, pulsing. She thought she could float away on it, on him, on what they brought to each other that no one else ever had, ever could.

He gave her comfort before she knew she needed it, and he gave her love when her life had been so empty of it for so long.

He'd come home to her, to bring her both before she'd thought to ask.

"I love you." She turned her cheek to his. "For everything."

For everything, he thought as he slipped slowly inside her. For all. Forever.

Because he filled her, lifted her, loved her, she floated away. And linking her hand with his, floated away with him.

CHAPTER
THIRTEEN

Better, Eve thought, when she switched to work mode. She wouldn't want to go hand-to-hand with a Zeused-up chemi-head, but she could if she had to.

And she was pretty sure, considering the circumstances, she could talk Roarke into pizza and brainstorming at her desk.

In her office she went for caffeine — cold-style in a tube of Pepsi — while he had another glass of wine. And for comfort in one of her oldest T-shirts, a pair of navy flannel pants, and thick socks.

If work didn't beckon, it was just the sort of thing she'd put on to curl up with Roarke and watch one of his old vids.

But work beckoned.

"So I thought I could bounce some things off you while —"

"Didn't we just do that in the tub?"

"Perv." She gestured with her icy tube toward her board. "I'm getting a more rounded picture of some of the players, from your POV. A business guy's POV. Maybe, using that same POV I can get some more hypotheticals, run more probabilities."

"We can do that."

"Great. We can bounce and eat. Let's keep it simple, just grab some pizza."

"We can't do that. I'd say the evening calls for something a bit more nutritious after the day you had."

"I'm not that hungry." She felt her cheesy pie slipping out of reach. "I feel okay. Plus, pizza gets a bad nutrition rap."

"Mmm-hmmm." With that, he left her for the kitchen.

Probably in there programming gruel or broth, she thought, with a little bitterness. And she felt stuck as he'd taken care of her, and was — as usual — willing to devote a large portion of his evening to her work.

So she'd choke down the stupid gruel.

She went to her board, did some additions, some rearranging.

She couldn't see, not really, the difference between her top suspects. On the surface, sure, plenty of differences, but she didn't *get* them.

She pulled out her pocket 'link when it signaled, noted Peabody on the display. "Yeah?"

"Hey, I'm sending you my notes from the interviews with the exes. I don't know how much light they shed, but I can tell you I got an earful from Biden's last ex. Can you spell *bitter?*"

She glanced over as Roarke brought something out from the kitchen — thought of pizza vs. gruel. "Yeah, I can."

"Whitestone's last serious relationship's mostly sad, a little resentful. It's the 'Spent more time at work and with his friends than with me' routine. Ingersol doesn't really have a genuine ex. More like several women he sees or stops seeing off and on. The upshot there is fun guy, but commitment phobic."

"I'll look at it," she said as Roarke went out, came in again.

"I didn't hit up Newton's fiancée, figuring she's only going to tell me the good, but I thought it wouldn't hurt to try for some juice on him. I tried a couple of her friends."

"That's a good angle."

"I thought it would be — and if happy, in love, suited, perfect for each other, adorable, and so on are what we're after, it was a great angle. Just no dish in that area."

"No dish is still information."

"Okay, I really tagged you to see how you were. Are you okay?"

"I'm good."

"There's a vid of the catch — well, a couple of them all over the Internet, all over the screen."

"So I hear."

"It was a really sweet catch, and too damn bad none of the people doing the vid got a decent capture of the suspect we were chasing."

"We'll have EDD see if they can finesse anything there. Meanwhile the two auditors in Vegas are being transported back, and straight to Stuben Health and Wellness. Meet me at the ambulance bay, eight hundred."

"I'll be there. Maybe you can get checked out while we're there."

"I'm fine, Peabody." And to dispense with any more fussing, she cut her partner off.

She wandered over to see what Roarke had set on the table.

Some sort of stir-fry, she noted. Some sort of healthy deal, his dinner version of oatmeal.

It wasn't gruel, but . . .

"That's a lot of vegetables."

"It is, yes, and if you eat them like a good girl . . ." He lifted the silver lid on another plate, revealed a small pizza, with pepperoni arranged into a smiley face.

She tried to give him a stony stare, but the laugh won out. "You think you're cute, don't you, pal?"

"Adorable."

"In this case, you can have adorable. Ow!" She managed the stony stare when he slapped her hand away from the pizza.

"Vegetables first."

Now the stony stare came naturally. "I've pummeled men for less."

"Want to give it a go?" he offered, and forked up a bite of his stir-fry.

"I might, except the smiley pizza earns points." She tried the stir-fry, discovered it wasn't half bad. In fact, not bad at all with whatever sauce he'd programmed. It actually had a nice little bite to it. "So greed," she began, "and envy, and in a sense gluttony. Maybe lust, too, and for some of them, definitely sloth. What's left?"

"Of the seven deadly sins? I believe wrath and pride."

"Okay, they can squeeze in there, too. The biggest that show in this group are the greed and envy. They're deadly sins because they lead to others, right? They're roots."

"That would be one way of looking at it."

"You've got some of them — well, everybody does — but they work for you. Not sloth. You're not lazy, and to acquire, because acquisitions feels like another root here, you work. Physically, mentally. You think, plan, put time in. More than a lot of people who could easily coast put in. That's the lust part."

"I thought we had the lust part in the tub."

"Lust for business." She pointed her fork at him. "I get that lust from Whitestone, too. A lust for what he does, a desire to get up in the morning and do it again. It's what builds success."

"Well, that and a talent for doing what you do. You can want it, be driven to do it, but if you're not skilled, all the lust in the world won't bring you success."

"Good point. In the case of my four top suspects, the lust doesn't seem to me to root from what they do, but from the results and benefits of what others have done before, or are doing."

"Lust for gain, which toggles back to greed."

"Yeah. What is this, exactly?"

Roarke glanced at the bok choy on her fork. "Tasty."

Because it wasn't *not* tasty, she couldn't formulate a reasonable argument. "Anyway, if you're doing what you're doing for the result, for the benefits, with no real lust or skill or basic appreciation for what generates the benefits, you're going to look for ways to do less of what generates while pumping up the benefits."

"Passing the work off to others, and/or cheating."

"Others built something, figured it out, had to be good at it, and you're plopped into the big leather chair and expected to keep it all going, and add to it. Maybe that's privilege, sure, but that's also pressure."

"Remind me of that when we have children. It's important to give them enough for a foundation, and not enough they can do nothing."

She sure as hell wasn't going to think about that now.

"On the other end of that, Alva Moonie's family appears to have instilled work ethic and responsibility. So after her wild phase, she likes what she does and wants to do it well. It's not money that corrupts, necessarily. It's —"

"Greed. Once again."

"I figure." She ate in silence a moment, considering. "That covers them all, except — possibly — Pope. He's either the mouse he appears or he's really good at pretending to be one. We need to look for private accounts, hidden accounts and property. These types are bound to have some."

"I've already started a search on that, but now that you've narrowed in, I'll do the same and focus more keenly on the top of your list."

She nodded, pleased she'd finished the stir-fry and could now reach for a slice. "You know how to think like a cop." At his silent rebuke, she smiled. "To avoid and outwit cops, if we're sticking with roots. And you've served as expert consultant, civilian, plenty. You're also the biggest of the business big shots. You know how to think in business, in big-shot style. I can get a feel for it, apply it to the case, but my POV on

238

running a company is largely colored by what I see you do, and that's not what I'm seeing here. At least in my limited view."

"You've investigated and closed countless cases that fall into areas you're not familiar with."

"Absolutely. But I don't always have the most expert of expert consultants eating a slice of my pizza."

"Who said it was all yours?" He toasted her with it, took a bite. "That would fall into the category of greed, and gluttony."

"Smart-ass. Anyway, I keep going over the board, my notes, the tones, the shades, and I feel like I'm missing something. Some, I don't know, nuance that would narrow it down. You'll find the motive in the files, in the numbers and the books and the tax codes and all that bullshit. But you're going to find, I'm betting, plenty of little slick deals and shoving through loopholes that aren't quite big enough and require greased palms. Like that."

"I have already, a bit here and there. Not enough, to my way of thinking, to justify murder or panic. Some adjustments, some penalties and interest, a fine or two — and some of those would be forgiven with a smart tax or corporate attorney making a case for misinterpretation or clerical error."

"Harder for me to judge that part. Even if I could find it. You asked me before who was I leaning toward. I'm going to ask you the same thing."

He shook his head, sat back with his wine. "I'm not a cop, not a trained investigator. Moreover, I haven't spoken with any of your suspects, and am far from finished analyzing the financial data."

She peeled off a piece of pepperoni, popped it in her mouth. "You've got a gut, same as me. You know business, business leaders the way I never will. You understand that world because you live in it. I'm just asking if you were me, which one would you give the hardest look?"

It surprised him how much he wanted to backpedal. He was used to watching her pick her way through the people, the evidence, the timing, the reasons, used to enjoying the way her mind and instincts played together on her hunt.

"And if I'm wrong? If I lead you in the wrong direction?"

"Direction's what I want, right or wrong. It's up to me to figure out what to do, how to do it. And up to me to take the direction or not. You're the expert here. I'm consulting you. I want your opinion."

"All right then. Sterling Alexander."

"Why?"

"Start with elimination." He rose, and as she so often did, circled her board. "Young-Sachs. Use your deadly sins here as a springboard. He's got more sloth than greed or lust. He'd prefer to do nothing at all, and has an admin who knows more than he does about his company. That's laziness and carelessness. No one should know more than you do about your own. And if he wanted more, he'd just ask his mother. He's got no reason to cheat or steal, and hasn't enough ambition to do either. And he's just not smart enough."

240

"I liked him."

"Did you?"

"I mean I liked him for it because I didn't like him otherwise. And that's been part of the problem. They all gave me a buzz, one way or the other."

"Very possibly you get a buzz because your instincts tell you none of them are thoroughly clean. They've all got pockets where they tuck some dirty little secrets."

"Maybe. Young-Sachs flaunting his illegals use and his complete lack of competence as CFO. He's using the company to get access to illegals. I know it. Then there's Biden going out of his way to insult and offend, and I'm betting finding ways, maybe just little ones now, to dip into the till. And Pope so damn accommodating, so willing to take his half brother's disdain. But what you're saying makes sense."

"So your instincts tell you all of them are wrong in some way."

"Yeah, that's been a problem."

She rose now as well, joined him at the board. "So, elimination. Keep going."

"All right. How do you massage your books — and it has to be in the books — if you don't understand how they work in the first place? Young-Sachs is dim and incompetent. Greedy, sure, but more lazy."

"Okay, let's bump him down for now. Take another."

"All right then, staying with the same company we'll take Tyler Biden. He's a loose cannon. Quick temper, and has difficulty instilling loyalty in his employees. He's got an idiot as the CFO."

"Yeah, which made me think it would make it easier for him to screw around the numbers."

"Agreed, but his CFO has, by all appearances, a very bright admin, who's also sleeping with the CFO. And if you're any judge, she's in love with him, or at least emotionally attached. More difficult to persuade said admin into covering something up that would, should it come out, blowback on her lover. And on her as it would be well known through the company that she's doing her boss's job."

"That's a good point, but —"

"Not finished," Roarke said, getting into the spirit of it now. "He's an ambitious, angry man, who'd know that many believe, perhaps rightfully, he only has his position with the company due to nepotism. He has a lot to prove. He enjoys the money, the status, yes, but he wants respect. Whoever's doing this, or involved, would have to align several others, as you said, in order to pull it off. And they'd know he couldn't make it on level ground. That would be important to him."

She followed the line of thinking, but wasn't quite convinced. Still, she nodded. "Okay, we'll bump him down for now, too."

"As for Pope," Roarke continued. "Sometimes things are exactly what they seem. The man does his job reasonably well according to my information. He lives comfortably, but not ostentatiously. He yields power and authority to his half brother. His older and more domineering half brother. He's well liked by those who work with and under him, though he's certainly considered a lightweight. If he wanted more, he could have more simply by asserting himself, but that falls outside his comfort zone. It's difficult for me to see him orchestrating something illegal through his mother's company — his devotion to her is well known — and ordering or condoning the murder of the auditor. A mother herself."

"Okay, I couldn't really see him either. We could both be wrong and he'll turn out to be some criminal mastermind, but it doesn't play for me. Pretending to be a schlub all the time would be too damn much work, and for what?"

"Schlub?"

"Yeah, he comes off as one. Alexander despises him."

"Yes, and that's an open secret on the business world's grapevine."

"If something's open," she pointed out, "it's not a secret."

"True enough. It's a poorly kept secret."

"Okay, so we've got the why nots. Let's hear your why."

"I want coffee."

"Me, too," she realized, then huffed out a breath when he cocked an eyebrow.

"I'm the expert on this one," he reminded her.

"Yeah, yeah." She grabbed up the dishes on her way to the kitchen to deal with the coffee.

"You know," he said from behind her, "we could have a droid take care of that — clearing the dishes, serving the coffee."

"I see enough of Summerset."

"Amusing."

"I thought so." She shoved the dishes in the washer. "Why would we need a droid looming around up here?" Especially since they almost always gave her the mild creeps. "It only takes a minute to deal with."

"Agreed. A lot of people at a certain level of privilege wouldn't think of doing something so simple for themselves as clearing a table or making their own coffee. Maybe taking care of a few small, basic tasks helps keep a person from sliding too deep into any of those seven deadly."

She handed Roarke his coffee, picked up her own, leaned back on the short counter. "You're betting Alexander doesn't load his own dishwasher."

"I'm betting he's rarely, if ever, spent any appreciable time in his own kitchen. Pride's as hungry as greed in some, and he's proud of his status, his wealth, his position. He employs five full-time domestic staff, three part-time, and subsidizes them with three domestic droids."

"How did you find that out?"

"Ask the right question of the right person," Roarke said simply. "In contrast, Pope has two part-time domestics, no droids. Alexander also keeps two shuttle pilots on twenty-four-hour call, which is showy and wasteful. He insists on certain perks any time he meets with a hospital board — petty things. A certain type of bottled water, for instance, and a seat at table's head. His wife often flies her favorite designer into New York from Milan. And he keeps a mistress."

"Mistress?" Eve shoved off the counter. "I didn't find a mistress. Where did you get a mistress?"

"I don't currently have one as my wife is so often armed. Alexander is rumored to have one, long term, very discreet."

"I need to find her, talk to her."

"Rumor has it, again, she's someone he's known for years, and his father deemed inappropriate. My best guess would be a woman named Larrina Chambers, a widow, billed as a close family friend. I haven't had time to confirm or eliminate," he warned, "so rumor is all it is. The point is, as mistresses go, Alexander is a staunch Conservative, one who often bangs the political drum, and likes to trot out his family as examples of those values, those idealogies."

"The wife has to know. You said long term. So the wife knows. Exposure there wouldn't do more than embarrass him. It wouldn't hurt his bottom line, would it?"

"Business-wise? I can't see how. He'd been seen as something of a hypocrite, but that's personal. Still, pride again."

Pride, she thought. One of those seven deadly again. "So maybe part of it is payments to or gifts to the mistress, or housing, travel, what have you. And how he's pulling that money from the business. An audit would show that."

"It would."

"Murder over that?" She shook her head. "People kill for less than nothing, but Jesus, it doesn't feel like enough for this. Not enough for other people to be involved and invested."

"I agree. There must be enough money at stake to spread around, and I'm wondering if that, too, may be long term. Or planned to be. Even before murder, it's a lot to risk unless the rewards are fat enough."

"So, it goes back to the books, the audit. Okay. You should focus on Alexander and Pope, see what you can dig up. And you were going to do that anyway."

"I was, yes." He smiled at her. "I'll leave the rest to you."

"You talked a good case."

"I'm flattered, Lieutenant. If I'm right, will I get a promotion?"

"If you're right I'll fix dinner *and* clear the dishes. Not pizza," she added at his long look.

"Acceptable. How's the shoulder?"

"It's fine. A little sore," she admitted.

He moved to her, brushed his lips over her shoulder, then drew her in. And just held her.

"I've done my share of cheating, of stealing. For survival, and for the fun."

She knew it. She knew him. "How many innocent mothers of two have you killed?"

"None so far." He drew her back. "I won't apologize for cheating and stealing or regret those days are done. Because here I am with you, and there's nowhere else in the world I'd rather be."

"Naked on a tropical beach?"

"Well, now that you mention it." When she laughed, he touched her lips with his. "But no, not even there. Just right here, right now."

"It's a good place."

"And we can see about that tropical beach after the holidays, which are coming right along."

"I can't think about the holidays." The idea had panic rising up in her belly. "I don't even want to think about this premiere deal everybody's all jazzy about."

"We'll have some fun with it. Try not to get any more bruises between now and then. Your dress shows a lot of skin."

"See? One more thing to worry about? I'm going to look for a mistress."

"I'll look for corporate misdeeds. And we're already having fun."

She poured more coffee, and since Roarke settled at her desk, once again took the auxiliary station. She noted Galahad had come in at some point and now stretched out like overfed roadkill on her sleep chair. And all around the office Roarke had designed for her to resemble her old apartment, her old comfort zone, the big, beautiful house stood quiet.

No, she thought, there wasn't anywhere else she'd rather be, right here and now.

She wrote up her notes first, reviewed, fiddled, then shot them off to Peabody. After reading her partner's notes, she took a few minutes, feet up, eyes on the board to consider everything Roarke had said.

Young-Sachs too lazy, Biden too proud, Pope too self-effacing (and potentially just too honest).

Highlight on Sterling Alexander.

Maybe, she thought. Just maybe. And if so, the probability ran high that folded in Jake Ingersol and Chaz Parzarri. Smaller possibility, but still possibly,

Robinson Newton, playing fast and loose with one of his partner's clients.

She looked forward to her first face-to-face with Parzarri. That could turn the tide here. Kick him when he's down, she decided. Hurting, weakened after a serious accident.

Maybe try to convince him it wasn't an accident, though she'd vetted the report. A trio of just-out-of-college guys, drunk, celebrating a minor win at the casino, plowed straight into the cab transporting Parzarri and Arnold from their own casino trip back to their convention hotel.

Everybody involved did some hospital time, and she'd found nothing on the three drunk idiots to lead her to conclude they'd been hired to bash up a couple of auditors and themselves.

Just an accident, the luck of the draw, and an innocent woman was dead.

Yeah, she thought, yeah, she could use that, all that to try to crack Parzarri.

Meanwhile, she'd take a look at Alexander's mistress.

The first thing she noted regarding Larrina Chambers was her age. At fifty-seven the woman didn't qualify as a young, gold-digger bimbo. Next, she noted Chambers and her dead husband had opened an eatery in New Jersey twenty-two years before that had blossomed into a national chain over the following decade, and took the woman out of gold-digger status. As she'd copped a scholarship to MIT at the age of eighteen, and had earned her master's in business at twenty-five, bimbo didn't likely apply.

Eve's suspicious mind nudged her to research how the husband met his demise, then had to set the idea of foul play aside. Neal Chambers died during a sudden squall off the coast of Australia when his sailboat was swamped. At the time, the widow was in New York, helping her mother recover from minor surgery. The investigation into the drowning — Chambers and four others, crew and passengers — had been thorough. She couldn't find any holes, or indeed any motive.

As she poked, prodded, dug, she found no evidence Larrina Chambers was, as the term went, being kept. She had very deep pockets of her own. But she found considerable that indicated Larrina and Alexander were connected, and over the just shy of nine years since the husband's death, had very likely rekindled the spark that had flickered during their early twenties.

Might be worth a conversation, Eve mused, and wrote up some notes.

Alexander, Ingersol, and Parzarri, she thought again, and began to slowly, methodically dig deeper into each man's life.

CHAPTER
FOURTEEN

He was onto something. Roarke felt it shift and slide, very much like a lock under the pick.

He'd already found three off-shore or off-planet accounts for Alexander — two of them absolutely legal if not wholly, technically, ethical.

He wouldn't quibble with wholly, technically ethical as Eve might. They had a different threshold there. Even the one — technically again — illegal wouldn't equal serious damage or problems. Fines, a naughty-boy finger wag and a bit of hot water for his money manager.

And the manager could, very likely, lure more clients with the incident.

But those accounts had been playfully easy to find, especially for someone who knew where and how to look for such things.

Which caused him to believe there would be more, not so playfully easy to find, and not at all legal.

He'd find them, Roarke thought. People had patterns and tells, habits and rhythms. It was simply a matter of finding them, using them.

But there was more, he felt that, too.

He remembered the sensation, from ago as he thought of it, of popping a lock and finding more than expected. That frisson of heat and energy in the fingertips.

Exciting, he recalled, in an almost mystical way no one but another thief would recognize or truly understand.

But ago was then, and this was now. He found nearly the same heat and excitement from tapping into the vault of secrets and misdeeds, to work with his cop.

Thinking of her, he glanced over. Ah well, he thought, she was done. She didn't know it yet, but he knew the signs. Her body had begun its droop, her eyes were going a little glassy. Left to her own devices she'd have worked until her head just dropped down on her desk.

When he checked the time, he noted it was nearly half-one. No wonder.

Even as he watched her sliding, the cat butted its head against his shin.

"All right, I see, don't I? It's off to bed for all of us."

Considering her injuries, she needed that bed, a reasonable night's sleep in it. So he programmed what he could of his work in progress to auto, copied and saved the rest before he rose to go to her.

"I'm calling time."

"Huh? I'm . . . just taking a harder look at Ingersol." She scratched her fingers in her hair as if to wake up her brain. "Nothing works with Newton in this, with him crossing into Ingersol's client base. I mean, it would be pretty clever, but that's predisposing you'd get caught and have the patsy waiting."

"And people like these rarely if ever believe they'll be caught."

"They just don't. So, anyway. You said once to look at insurance. Ingersol's got heavy coverage, mostly on art. Way over the listed value."

"Which could mean he fudged the value initially so as not to raise flags on where he got the money to buy it. Or he'll make a claim and skin the insurance company."

"I didn't see any claims here, but —"

"You can look more tomorrow. We need some sleep."

"It's not that late," she began, then looked at the time. "Oh. I guess it is."

"Tomorrow." He drew her to her feet, felt her body tense. "You're feeling that fall you took."

"A little stiff, that's all." But she didn't argue when he leaned down, manually saved her work.

"I've a couple of lines to tug," he told her as he led her out of the room. "And I'll have a better grip on them tomorrow."

"What lines?"

"Some tucked-away accounts — two legal, one questionable. Some transactions that bear a closer look. I expect the auditor in his pocket, if indeed he's in the pocket, would have tidied it all up. And so I expect I'll find more that hasn't yet been cleaned. He's listed travel expenses, business expenses, and the locations weigh heavily toward places that have large gambling draws and generous tax codes."

"It's a way to launder money."

252

"A time-honored method for a reason," Roarke said as they entered the bedroom.

While she readied for bed, he brought out a med-pad. "You'll sleep better for it," he said before she could object. "And for the blocker you'll take. A good night's sleep will put you back in tune to catch the bad guys. Let's see the back door."

She rolled her eyes, but she turned so he could study her ass.

"You're still carrying Africa, but it's eroding at the edges."

"Great. We're destroying the Dark Continent."

He laughed, gently applied the pack to her shoulder, then gave Africa a soft pat. "Hopefully its land mass will have further eroded by morning."

"With or without Africa, I'm going to push Parzarri in the morning." She slid into bed. "Those accounts you found, that's something to push on. Oh, Larrina Chambers isn't what you'd call a mistress," she added, relaxing as Roarke lay beside her. "She's got plenty of her own. They're connected, I'm damn sure, but it's not a being kept kind of deal. I don't know if I'll be able to work her. I have to think about it."

As her voice had already thickened, he began to rub her back, lightly, lightly, to lull her under. "The wife's gotta know. You can't hook up like that for what looks like about six or seven years without the wife figuring it out. Unless she's another idiot.

"I'm not an idiot."

Smiling, Roarke continued to stroke. "I'll keep that in mind when I decide to have a long-term affair."

"Yeah, you do that. They'll never find your body," she murmured, then dropped into sleep.

His smiled warmed, and feeling well loved, he dropped off with her.

She woke to see Roarke in his usual spot, already dressed and with the numbers and codes scrolling on screen as he worked on a tablet.

She sat up carefully. Stiff, a little sore as predicted, but no twinges or grinding. Good sign.

"How is it?" he asked her.

"Pretty okay." Her shoulder didn't grind, but it did groan a little when she rolled it. A hot shower, she decided, would take care of it.

He circled his finger as he had the night before, and as she had the night before, she rolled her eyes and turned. "More like South America now," he decided. "An improvement."

But he didn't like the sickly yellow bruising across her chest.

"When I find that fucker, he's going to have a continent on his ass."

"Go for Asia," Roarke suggested. "It's bigger."

"An Asian ass-kicking. I can do that."

He thought she'd have to beat him to it, but didn't mention it.

She angled around to take a look at her butt in the mirror. Better. A lot better. "I dreamed about flying babies. You can't catch them all."

"That's . . . unfortunate."

"I'll say. They'd hit the ground and *pow*." She threw her hands up in the air. "All this stuff came gushing out."

"Really, Eve, you'll put me off breakfast."

"Not guts and stuff. It was like little weird toys and shiny candy. Like they were those piñata things people bust up for what's inside."

He lowered the tablet to study her. "You have such a busy, fascinating brain."

"And the vic's there, too, sitting on one of those benches on the High Line. She keeps saying two and two makes four. Over and over. I mean I get it, numbers don't lie, numbers add up, but she's sitting there, chanting that and working on one of those ancient adding things."

"An abacus?"

"What's an abacus? Oh, right, one of those —" Standing naked but for the pack on her shoulder, her hair in tufts, she slid her fingers through the air. "No, it was one of those —" Now she tapped her two index fingers in the air, then swiped her hand.

"An adding machine."

"Yeah. I'm trying to catch all those flying babies and she's tapping away, muttering basic math. It was distracting. I probably missed a few because she wouldn't give it a rest. Anyway, weird."

Weird indeed, he thought as she went into the bathroom, but not a nightmare.

He rose, got a fresh med pack, the wand, programmed coffee. After a brief consideration, he opted for cheese and spinach omelets. Enough cheese and she wouldn't

255

bitch about the spinach. He thought she could use the protein and the iron.

When she came out, wrapped in a robe, he had the food and the first-aid tools set out. She eyed them both suspiciously.

"What's in those eggs?"

"Eat them and find out. I've been playing with some of the data my auto-search spit out. It's interesting."

"What have you got?"

"Eat and find out."

She sat, but went for the coffee first. "Does two and two make four?"

"I think not in this case. There's a payment here of just over two hundred thousand to IOC. A search for IOC turns up several companies and organizations including a porn site billed as the Intense Orgasm Companion, which deals in vids, toys, enhancements, real-time vid or VR sex with a licensed companion, contacts to LCs who are affiliated with the site and will make house calls. And so on."

Sex, she thought, never failed to sell.

"I don't think Alexander funneled two hundred K out of his company for porn."

"I tend to agree. I lean toward Investment Opportunity Corporation, a smallish outfit based in Miami, but claiming national coverage. They buy and sell properties — primarily commercial, but also residential. Developed or zoned for development."

"Isn't that basically what Alexander and Pope already does?"

"It is, so it's odd — not illegal — but odd they'd pay out six figures, under the label of operating expenses, to another company. IOC is also connected, if you follow the dots carefully, to yet another company. Real and Exclusive Properties. This one's based in the Caymans, claims global coverage. It caters to, according to its site, investors looking for exclusive properties, as individuals or groups. One of their services is analyzing clients and properties and matching them up."

"What, like a dating site?"

He grinned at her. "I suppose so. They have a few properties on their site, and some testimonials from satisfied clients. They suggest direct contact for further information, and of course, exclusive property investments."

"And you smell fraud?"

"Well, it fairly stinks of it, darling. This sort of thing is ripe for fraud."

She thought she could see it, more or less, but wanted clarity. "How?"

"The basic con here would be to lure the client, and the money, in. Then make some reasonable payoffs as you would in any hustle to prime that pump for more. I suspect some of the land doesn't exist, or is well overestimated in value thanks to payoffs or grifters on the payroll who can spin the con."

"How do they get away with it? If they skin clients, there'd be noise."

"You'd keep it fairly small, the dollar amounts. Keep it under the radar of the Security and Exchange Commission or its global alternative. Deposit in several accounts, again, keeping those deposits under the radar. Run the con, shut down, take the money, launder if necessary, then set up elsewhere. Different name, different look, different place. Same basic con. That's the simplest."

"Okay." Yeah, she could follow it. "Alexander gets his share — the elephant's share —"

"Lion's share, as you perfectly well know."

"Elephants are the biggest, and he takes the biggest."

"Your logic is . . . unarguable."

"See? So, he's the elephant, then he has to wash the money, then bury it, or just bury it."

"He has another easy system for laundry with the real estate. Arrange to purchase a property below market value, giving the difference in cash to the seller. He saves on taxes. Then you resell at market a few months later and make a legitimate profit. The money's now clean."

"He's in the perfect position for that."

"He is. Now, there are plenty of other ways, more complex, and more profitable to pump up the profits. Set up a loan company, for instance, which I expect to find. The client takes out the loan to purchase the property. Then you diddle with the loan, make some on that, the property turns out, when legitimately assessed, to be worth a fraction of that loan. If you keep it small, a few thousand here and there so the IRS doesn't take note, you can draw cash out of those loan accounts — wash it, and it appears clean. If and when the client defaults on the loan as he's in deeper than the value, you also have the land."

258

She listened as she ate. "It seems like a hell of a lot of work. And it seems like you could make the money just doing it legitimately."

"That doesn't factor in the thrill, the greed — there'd be skimming and circling around the tax codes — and the enjoyment some have from screwing over others."

"Get rich quick is usually a scam and always for suckers."

"And there's never a shortage of suckers," Roarke pointed out. "I expect the bulk of the clientele falls into two categories. The naive, novice investor, and the overconfident who believes he can con the cons."

"Did you ever run this sort of thing?"

"I've enjoyed the feel and scent of freshly laundered money." He smiled as he topped off their coffee. "Lieutenant. But not the real estate scams. I could have," he considered. "But I liked the game on its level playing field. And I'm good at it. I liked to steal. It's hard to apologize, even to a cop, for having an aptitude and affection for the illegal. I stole to survive at first, but there's no question I developed a taste for it. But the con? Not as much. And now."

He leaned over and kissed her cheek. "I enjoy putting my talents to your use. Which I'll do today. I have some of my own to see to, but I believe I can do that from home. Then I'll see what I see with all this two and two makes four."

"I may break Parzarri down. He's hurt, and I could use some of this if I have to for pressure."

"You've got enough to bring Alexander in on the fraud. What I have already paints a picture."

"Maybe, but I don't want him on fraud. It's a good lever, but I want him on murder. I want them all. Conspiracy to murder, murder for hire. If I push on the fraud straight off, he could cover and the feds are going to come swooping down on me. They won't care about Dickenson as much as busting up a big-ass land fraud operation with a hefty side of money laundering and tax evasion. I'd rather he thinks he's getting away with that end, keep him worried about me on murder."

"He could try for you again."

"He could. He's probably stupid enough. I have my magic coat. Don't worry," she said because she knew he did. "He couldn't take me before, and I have to admit I wasn't expecting it. Now I am. His trigger has to be on his payroll somewhere. I don't think he's quite stupid enough to have tagged Thugs 'R' Us."

"They do sell an inferior product."

"I couldn't find the fucker on a search through employees, but he's there. I'm going to pass it to Feeney for a matchup. I'm still betting former cop or military. He'll pop sooner or later. But the auditor's priority."

She rose to dress.

"If I manage to get my own done, and solidify any of yours, I'll come in to Central to fill you in."

"Okay with me, but you might want to tag me first. I may be out in the field."

"I'll find you."

When she strapped on her weapon harness, pulled a jacket over it, he stretched out on the sofa with his tablet, and the pudgy cat sprawled over his feet.

If you didn't know better, she thought, you'd see a man completely at his leisure.

Then again, the way he approached the work, that wasn't far off.

"Is that how you work?"

"For the next twenty minutes." He looked up at her, smiled, crooked his finger.

She leaned down, easing in for a kiss.

"I meant to tell you, I've arranged an after-premiere party at Around the Park."

Her eyes went to slits. "You waited to tell me until I'm damn near out the door so I couldn't complain."

"Isn't it a testament to our relationship, how well we know and understand each other?"

"I'll give you a testament," she muttered, and started out.

"Mind the exploding babies," he called after her, and heard her laugh.

Chaz Parzarri felt fine and good. But then he'd flown on the private shuttle, compliments of the insurance company of the shitheads who'd busted him up, and the cab company for their substandard safety features. And he'd flown on the really good drugs the in-flight nurse kept pumping.

They said he'd be laid up a couple more weeks, and he'd need a couple weeks of PT after that — but he was fine and good with that, too. As long as the drugs kept coming.

He had work to do. He could do that from the hospital in the private suite, also courtesy of the insurance companies. The audit wouldn't take long, and being willing to do it earned him points with his supervisor and with Alexander.

The accident, now that he didn't hurt like fuck every time he blinked an eyeball, had actually worked out for him. He'd get a big-ass settlement, paid time off, piles of sympathy and attention. In fact, he planned to run some numbers for himself. A big enough settlement, and he might just retire, go live the good life in Hawaii the way he'd intended to do in another six-point-four years.

When he'd first come out of it, he'd been scared. Really piss-pants scared. That maybe he'd die, or maybe they'd find irreversible brain damage with all the tests they'd run. When he stopped being scared of that — or mostly — he'd been scared about the audit. He'd barely started on it before the convention.

Okay, maybe he'd procrastinated some, but there'd been plenty of time. Should have been plenty. And he had the framework for the adjustments, the doctored figures, the clean monthly files he'd kept carefully buried on his home unit.

A couple of days to implement, run an analysis, do a recheck, and boom! Done, clear, and a fat fee wired to his holding account, then wired — by himself — to his numbered, anonymous, and tax-free account in Switzerland.

Still all good, he told himself. Just a few days later to finish it all, and still comfortably ahead of the deadline.

He hadn't been able to contact Alexander. They hadn't allowed him a 'link in his room, but then again, he'd been barely able to talk until yesterday. He'd take care of that as soon as he was tucked into his medical suite.

Jim Arnold hobbled over on his skin cast. "How ya doing, partner?"

"Cruising, partner."

As Jim sat, stuck out his casted leg, he winced a bit. "I can't wait to get back, get home. The Vegas doc said they'll probably let me go home after they check me over. Maybe keep me one night, but then spring me. I'm sorry you weren't as lucky."

"Yeah." Parzarri put on a grim face, though he liked the idea of a few days in the hospital, people fussing over him, bringing him food. "I guess I used up my luck at the blackjack table."

"You were rolling. I wanted to tell you Sly just texted. He'll meet us at the hospital. I told him he didn't have to do that, but he texted back he wanted to see us for himself. You know Sly. We're going to land in a minute. Look, my wife's meeting me at transpo, but I can ride in with you if you want."

"Forget it. Go ahead with the wife. Hell, you already stayed on an extra day until they let me travel."

"Can't leave a buddy behind. We've been through the war together now, partner."

"You bet." Parzarri lifted his hand for a high five.

He drifted in and out, comfortable and secure on his gurney as the shuttle made its landing.

Good old New York, he thought. Would he miss it when he settled down with palm trees and ocean views?

He didn't think so.

Maybe he'd buy a little tiki bar, get somebody else to run it. It would be fun to own a bar, hang out, watch all the half-naked women sipping mai tais or whatever.

Maybe he'd learn how to surf.

Smiling to himself, he kept cruising as they rolled him out of the shuttle, fixed the gate to slide him out. He felt the sudden, wicked cold — closed his eyes and envisioned balmy breezes, sun-washed sand and surf.

"I'll be right behind you, Chaz." He opened his eyes briefly, gave Jim a thumbs-up, then saw his associate's pale face light up. "Hi, honey!" And his Vegas compatriot hobbled away and into the arms of his wife.

"Happy reunion," Parzarri mumbled as they lifted him into the back of an ambulance. Warm again, he let out a sigh. He heard voices — the in-flight nurse giving a report to the MTs, Jim's wife babbling, Jim's happy-I'm-home laugh.

Then the ambulance shifted a little with the weight as the MT levered himself inside, slammed the double doors. With a rumble, they began to move.

"Don't forget the good drugs." Parzarri smiled, looked up at the ceiling and thought of women in tiny, tiny bikinis with skin gold from the sun, wet from the sea. "Aloha."

He felt so warm, his body so heavy. He turned his head, with effort when he felt the straps clamp around his wrists. "What's that for?"

"Keeps you where you are."

Puzzled, Parzarri turned his head again, stared into a familiar face. "Hey. What're you doing? Your boss order security for me?"

"That's right."

" 'Preciate it."

"He wants to know if you talked to anybody."

"Huh?"

The man reached up, turned the clamp on the IV. "Mr. Alexander wants to know if you talked to anybody about the audit, about anything."

"Jesus, I was in a coma half the time, getting poked and prodded and imaged the rest. Who'm I gonna talk to? I need those drugs, man. It's starting to hurt."

"Mr. Alexander wants to know if you have any documents or files."

" 'Course I do. I'm the accountant. I've got everything I need to finish the audit. I can do it from the hospital once I get the files and my notebook. He can send Jake for them. He'd know what I need."

"Mr. Alexander wants to know if you have any documents or files, or any information on his business in any other location?"

"What the fuck? Turn the drip back on, will you? Come on, man." The pain shot through him like lava when the fist rammed into his healing ribs. As he drew in his breath to scream, the driver hit the sirens, drowned him out.

"Answer the question. Do you have any documents or files or any information on Mr. Alexander's business in any other location?"

"No! God! Why would I? I'll take care of it, like always. I'll do my job."

"Mr. Alexander says you're terminated."

With that he clamped his big hand over Parzarri's mouth, pinched his nose closed. While the sirens screamed, the lights flashed, Parzarri's body bucked from the lack of air, from the pain. His eyes wheeled like a terrified horse's.

Blood vessels burst in the whites of his eyes, so it seemed he shed bloody tears. His fingers clawed at the gurney, at the air as his hands strained against the straps.

His bladder voided, and those reddened eyes rolled back, and fixed.

Removing his hand, the big man pounded a fist on the ceiling. The driver cut the sirens, the lights, and drove onto the broken ground of an underpass. Both men got out, the big one hefting the Pullman Parzarri had taken to Vegas and back. He tossed it in the trunk of the waiting car before getting into the passenger seat.

He liked sitting in the big, roomy car, he thought, being driven around like he was *somebody*. And now that he'd done it — twice — he liked to kill even better.

Eve stood inside the ambulance bay where she'd been directed. According to the log, Parzarri was being transported via ambulance while Arnold, ambulatory, was on his way in, driven by his wife.

"How do you want to play it?" Peabody asked her.

"I want a look at him for myself, see what kind of shape he's in. We'll let him get to his room, interview him there. I want to read him his rights straight off, not only to cover it all, but to scare him a little. You should look grim."

"No good cop?"

"I don't think we need good cop."

In her pink boots, Peabody did a little heel-toe dance. "Yay!"

"We need to talk to Arnold, too. We can get him out of the way while they're fooling around with Parzarri." She stopped when she spotted Sylvester Gibbons.

"Lieutenant Dallas. Detective. I didn't expect to see you here so quickly."

"We need to speak with your last two employees."

"Of course. Sure. Ah . . ." He let out a breath, rubbed his face with one hand. "Can you give me a few minutes with Chaz? Jim knows about Marta. But I asked him not to say anything to Chaz. The poor guy was in such bad shape, and they didn't want him overly excited or upset. They even banned 'links and screens. I want to tell him myself, what happened. I don't want him to hear it from cops, no offense. I think it'll be easier to hear it from a friend."

"We'll talk to Mr. Arnold first."

"I really appreciate it. That's Jim's car. There he is. That's Jim. God, he looks like he's been through the wringer."

Eve watched an attendant roll up a wheelchair, and the man — walking cast, pale, drawn face — maneuver from the passenger seat into the chair.

"Jim!" Gibbons pushed forward. "How ya doing? How do you feel?"

"Been better." Jim took the hand Gibbons offered. "And believe me, a coupla days ago I was worse. I'm so damn glad to be back."

"It's good to have you back. They're going to take good care of you and Chaz. I don't want you to worry about anything. Anything you need, you just let me know."

"I just want to get checked out and go home." His gaze shifted to Eve, crossed over Peabody, and back again. "Police?"

"Lieutenant Dallas," Eve said, "Detective Peabody."

"Marta." His eyes watered up. "I can't believe it. I don't know what to think or do. I didn't tell Chaz," he said to Gibbons. "I don't know if I would've known how even if you hadn't told me not to — and the doctors said that was best, too. I don't know how he's going to take it, Sly. He's a hell of a lot more hurt than me. He really took the brunt of it. Where is he?"

"He's not here yet."

"They left before we did." With obvious concern he tried to swivel in the chair, look around. "My wife and I just sat in the car for a few minutes, but they took him off in the ambulance right away. I guess they hit some traffic. Came a different way?"

Uneasy, Eve signaled Peabody. "We have a few questions," she began as Peabody hurried off.

"We really need to get the patient into exam," the attendant said.

"I want to wait for Chaz. Honey." He reached out to a woman, eyes pink from weeping, when she came in. "The ambulance with Chaz isn't here yet."

"They must've gone another way." She crouched down beside him. "Don't worry now. Don't. He's fine. Everything's going to be fine."

"Lieutenant."

268

Peabody's tone, her face, told Eve the news wouldn't be good. She stepped over. "What have we got?"

"They can't reach the ambulance. They don't answer the dash 'link or the emergency call."

"I want the names of the medicals sent to pick him up."

"Got them. Communication's trying their personal 'links. They have LoJacks on all emergency vehicles. They're tracking it."

"Keep an eye on these people," she ordered, and strode off to Communications. She heard the angry voices before she reached the station.

"And I'm telling you, I got shifted to nine. So did Mormon. Ask him!"

"You're on log, right here, for the transpo station pickup."

"I *was* on the pickup, until I got the schedule change."

"When did you get the schedule change?" Eve demanded.

"Who the hell are you?"

In answer she pulled out her badge.

"Jesus, now a schedule screwup's illegal? I got the tag about six this morning. Instead of seven on, and the pickup, I'm nine on and standard rounds. Look." He yanked out his 'link, pushed incoming, shoved it at Eve.

She read the message. "Where's this Mormon?"

"We were in the eatery, catching some breakfast. He ran out to get some of that fancy coffee from the van when it showed up. He'll be back in a minute."

"Have you located the bus?" Eve asked.

"I've just got it. It's way off route," the woman said with a frown. "And I don't know who the hell's driving

269

it because we've clearly got Mormon and Drumbowski on that run, and Drumbowski's standing right here."

"It's not my screwup," Drumbowski insisted.

"No," Eve said, "it's not. Give me the location. Now!"

"What the hell's going on?" Drumbowski threw his hands in the air.

But Eve just took the location, sprinted away. She already knew Chaz Parzarri wouldn't be transported to the hospital. But she was damn sure he'd be transported to the morgue.

CHAPTER
FIFTEEN

Eve expected to find Chaz Parzarri dead. A dirty accountant, she concluded, could be replaced. Still, she had Peabody call in for uniform response to the GPS location as she ran hot across town.

"Two units responding," Peabody told her, squeezing the chicken stick in a death grip while she prayed the safety and maneuvering features in her partner's DLE were all they were touted to be.

Her heart did a flip into her throat when they shot vertical, skimmed over the bright yellow snake of Rapid Cabs with a couple of layers of paint to spare. She decided her heart might as well stay where it landed as the car tipped to her side like a banking plane before they boomeranged around a corner.

"It's *stupid* to kill him." Eve slammed back to the street, punched through a hole in traffic. "But they're stupid. I should've factored that in. The goddamn stupidity."

"He knows a lot," Peabody began.

"Because he's dirty. Throw money at him to stonewall me. They don't know Dickenson made those copies. Stonewall me, doctor the books, *then* kill him. Or just ship him off. He's got no real ties here. Ship him off to someplace we can't extradite him, give him a new identity, and keep him on the payroll. Why bring yet another goddamn number cruncher in? It's inefficient to kill him. It's wasteful."

"Maybe that's what they're doing. Trying to get him gone, hide him."

Eve only shook her head. "They'd have plucked him out in Vegas. No point bringing him here to send him somewhere. And no goddamn point to bring him here to kill him. Why not do it out there where there's distance between you? Stupid. They're stupid."

Murderously stupid.

She fishtailed, righted, then swung beside a black-and-white.

The thunder of traffic roared overhead when she got out of her vehicle. A uniform stood beside the open rear doors of the ambulance, another at the driver's side. She noted two more talking, or trying to talk to a jittery funky-junkie.

"DB in the back, Lieutenant. He's still warm."

She peered in, visually identified Chaz Parzarri. "Peabody, they had to have another vehicle here. See what you can find on any traffic cams in this area. They can't have more than a fifteen-minute window, probably less. What have we got over there?" she asked the uniform, jerking a head toward the junkie.

"We found him trying to get into the bus. Nothing locked on it, but he's so strung out he couldn't work the handle." The uniform set a hand on his hip under his Sam Browne belt. "Says he was just checking to see if anybody was inside. Just being a good citizen."

"Right."

"Yeah, we figure he's messed up, but a junkie like him can smell drugs a mile off. The guys are working him some, but he claims he didn't see anything."

The timing said otherwise, Eve thought as she did a quick scan. She spotted the pile of rubble and trash behind one of the pillars. "Is that his hive over there?"

"That's what we figure."

"I'm going to talk to him. Stand by here."

"Good luck."

The man wore a filthy army-green coat and torn orange sweatpants over the gaunt frame with the distended belly typical of severe malnutrition. His red-rimmed, watery eyes — sunlight wasn't the funky-junkie's friend — skittered over at Eve as she approached, then squinted out of a grimy pair of sunshades with a crack in the left lens.

His hands moved, picking at the ragged fringe of the black scarf wrapped around his neck. His feet moved, shuffling inside scarred army boots with no laces and silver tape holding the soles together.

He could have been anywhere from thirty to eighty with that pale, ravaged, soot-streaked face.

He'd been someone's son, might have been someone's lover once, or father. He'd had a life at some point before he'd offered it up on the altar of funk.

"Just walking by," he chanted — moving, moving, moving. "Yep, yep, just walking by. Hey, lady, got anything to spare? Don't need much."

She tapped her badge. "See this?"

"Yep, yep." But those ruined eyes watered and blinked.

273

"It's a badge. A lieutenant's badge. It means I'm not a lady. Give me a name."

"Whose name you want?"

"Yours."

"Doc. Tic-tock doc, the mouse and the clock."

"Doc. Do you live over there?"

"Not hurting anybody. Keep myself to myself, right? Check? Double check."

"Check. Were you at home when the ambulance got here?"

"Just walking by." Those ruined eyes did their skittering dance again. "Just walking."

"Where to, where from?"

"Nothing, nowhere. Nohow."

"You were just walking from nothing to nowhere, and happened to see the ambulance parked there, maybe twenty feet from where you live?"

When he smiled, he offered Eve a full view of the unfortunate results of really bad dental hygiene. "Yep. Yep. Check."

"I don't think so, Doc. I think, you were tucked up at home. Wrapped up warm on a cold day like this, not walking around without more gear. I bet you've got more layers over there you put on when you head out to look for spare change, when you go out to find some funk."

"Just walking," he insisted with his voice creeping toward a whine. "Didn't see nothing, nowhere, nohow. I don't see good. I got a condition."

Yeah, she thought, called chronic addiction. "Wait here."

274

She went to her car, checked the glove box. As expected she found a couple pair of sunshades either Roarke or Summerset had stocked as she constantly lost them.

She imagined either pair cost more than Doc saw in ten years of panhandling on the street, but grabbed one. She walked back, waved them at Doc.

"Want these?"

"Sure! Sure!" Something desperate came into his abused eyes. "Wanna trade?"

"Yeah, but not for your sunshades. You can have these if you tell me what you saw. No bullshit. Tell me the truth, and they're yours."

"I know a true! Stop clock, tic-tock — true two times every day."

"How about that? No." She pulled the shades out of his reach. "I want the true about what you saw here. About that ambulance."

"I didn't go in. Just looking. Just walking."

"Who got out?"

He stared at her, bumped his shoulders up and down.

"Okay." She started to turn away.

"Make the trade!"

"There's no trade until you tell me. You tell me the truth, I give you the shades. That's the deal."

"White coats get out. What you think? White coats in the am'lance. Not gonna take me, no way no how. I set down."

He skimmed his palms on the air in a downward motion. "Don't need no white coat, no am'lance."

"How many white coats got out?"

"Two. Prolly two. I don't see good. Two. Then no white coats. In the trunk."

"What's in the trunk?"

"The white coats' coats, what you think? In the trunk of the big car that's here when I wake up. Big car. Shiny. Smooth. Can't get in, all locked tight. Just to look," he said quickly. "Just wanna look, but locked up tight. White coats with no white coats in the big shiny car, and drive away!"

"What did they look like?" A long-shot question, considering, but she had to ask. "The white coats without white coats who got in the big shiny car?"

"One's big, one's small. Don't see good, but one's big." Doc spread his arms wide as he lifted them into the air and gave Eve an unfortunate whiff of amazing body odor.

"Okay, how about the car? Was it like white or like black?"

"Dark, dark. Maybe black. Dunno. Shiny. All true. Trade."

"Okay." Calculating she'd mined all she could expect, she passed him the glasses. "No, you keep those, too," she said when he offered his broken ones. "We're trading truth for shades. We're done."

When she stepped away one of the uniforms fell into step beside her. "Do you want us to take him in, Lieutenant? To a rehab shelter?"

It's what — technically — should be done, and maybe, she thought, morally. But realistically? He'd be out within a week, have lost his turf, and very likely be worse off than now.

He sure as hell wouldn't be better off.

"No, let him go. Maybe cruise down here once in a while, take a look at him."

The uniform nodded. "He's got a halfway decent spot here, mostly out of the weather and it looks like the hyenas leave him alone. It's about the best he's going to get."

Sometimes, Eve thought, you had to settle for that.

Peabody jogged over as Eve started back to the ambulance.

"I had EDD patch with traffic. We've got a vehicle coming out eastbound at eight-twenty-three. They thought about the traffic cams, Dallas, smeared up the license plates, front and rear. But we've got the make and model. Black Executive Lux 5000, current year. The windows, including windshield, were privacy screened — and that's illegal — but it also means we've got nothing on the occupants."

"See if McNab has time to run it, against Alexander personally and the company for a match. And I need another run from traffic. They had to get it here, and I'm guessing very early this morning. So another vehicle followed it in."

"Three vehicles for one accountant? That's a stupid way to do this."

"Yeah, it is, but they are."

"They're lucky the one they drove out wasn't busted to shit and stripped."

"If Doc, that's the funky-junkie currently wearing my sunshades, had stirred up his brain cells, he'd have busted the window to scavenge. Smarter to have a third party meet them or just walk the hell out and hail a damn cab. It tells me the one giving the orders doesn't have a freaking clue how things work on the street — or under them. It's all about privilege."

She sealed up as she spoke, then boosted herself into the back of the ambulance. "Let's get the sweepers on their way, and have EDD go over to the hospital, see what we can get from security on when and how that ambulance was taken."

Though she knew his identity, certainly knew the approximate time of death, Eve used her tools and gauges to confirm. With her recorder on she studied the lockdown straps, wrists and ankles, the broken blood vessels in the eyes, the bruising around the nose and mouth.

Like his live associate, he'd been pale and banged up. From the older bruising, the signs of medical treatment, the portable IV, she'd say considerably more banged up than Arnold.

Lifting the top lip, she studied where the teeth had ground into the soft flesh, the smears of blood.

She'd miscalculated, she thought. She'd planted seeds, wanting to tangle the money manager in some vines. Give him something to sweat.

But she hadn't considered anyone would be stupid enough to hand her yet another link in the chain, would order murder rather than bribery or a bonus. Would so quickly discard a well-honed tool.

"Bruising and lacerations on the wrists and ankles," she stated. "Looks like he twisted, strained, twisted."

Rising, she bypassed a secured locker with her master. The drugs inside would have been worth a nice chunk on the street, as would the medical equipment, some of it very portable.

No time, or no inclination to make some extra, to take a nice little bonus. Do the job, move on.

She moved into the cab of the vehicle, using a penlight to search under the seats, under the dash, hoping for some little mistake. A candy wrapper, a go-cup, a scrap of anything.

Finding nothing, she sat back on her heels, studied the dash. She checked the log, ran the last outgoings.

Base, this is Mormon with Drumbowski, Unit Seven, confirming pickup at East Side Metro Transportation Center of Parzarri, Chaz. Sheet shows private shuttle from LVI, tail number Bravo-Echo-Niner-Six-Three-Niner.

This is base, confirming. Advise when you're loaded and en route for return.

Roger that Unit Seven out.

As she listened, Eve tapped her fingers on her knee.

Base, Unit Seven, loaded and running.

Copy that. Condition of patient?

Stable. He ran through what Eve assumed was an acceptable range of blood pressure, pulse, other vital signs, then signed off.

Peabody opened the side door. "McNab's looking now. Sweepers and the meat wagon on the way."

"Has to be the hacker," Eve said, as much to herself as Peabody. "The driver. He'd have to know who was on, the unit number assigned to the pickup, the basic give and flow of how they communicate. Hack into the hospital system, get the log, listen to a few runs. Hospital dispatch isn't expecting a hijacking. They've got no reason to push the communication. It's all A-fucking-OK."

She marked the communication center for EDD. "And now we have his voice print. Stupid asshole. I want to see if EDD can enhance as well as print. See if they pick up any chatter from the back."

Peabody nodded as she texted the instructions. "Do you have a line on COD?"

"Smothered him. Strapped him down, covered his mouth, pinched his nose. The bruising's like a signpost for it. Face-to-face this time," she considered. "They knew each other. It's more personal. Still business, just doing the job, but it's like firing a coworker. It's got that personal element. I want this area secured. We need to find Jake Ingersol."

"You don't think —"

"I didn't think they'd kill the accountant." She shoved at her hair. "Listen, I'll find out where Ingersol is. You contact Gibbons. He should know Parzarri's dead. And we're going to have the media hum this time, as soon as they put together that two accountants from the same firm were murdered within days of each other."

"Not much we can do about that."

Maybe a preemptive strike, she thought. And wondered if she could squeeze in enough time into coaxing, maneuvering, or bribing Nadine into spinning the story as she needed it spun.

She contacted the WIN offices as she drove. "This is Lieutenant Dallas. Is Jake Ingersol in?"

"All three partners are meeting at the new offices this morning, Lieutenant. Do you need the address?"

"I've got it."

"Would you like me to contact Mr. Ingersol and tell him you're hoping to speak to him?"

"No, don't bother."

As she drove back across town yet again, she heard Peabody murmuring condolences to Gibbons, and skillfully, she'd give Peabody the chops there, evading direct answers on the murder.

"Set me up another consult with Mira, will you?" she asked Peabody when her partner ended the conversation. "Her admin's less likely to try to fry out your eyeballs over the 'link. I need some direction on these assholes."

She rubbed at the back of her neck, thinking of Parzarri, strapped down on the gurney, watching his killer's face as he smothered. Twisting, struggling, helpless.

He'd been dirty, that was clear to her. But not a killer. Or he hadn't had the opportunity to decide if he could or would take part in the murder of his coworker. He'd never known.

Now, he was dead because she hadn't anticipated, she hadn't seen the logic in killing him, in eliminating what must have been a valuable cog in the wheel.

Maybe she should've taken Roarke up on that trip to Vegas, confronted him then and there. Or met the damn shuttle instead of going to the hospital.

Hindsight, she thought, was a cold, hard bitch.

"You've got a meet with Mira when you can work it in," Peabody told her.

"That's it? Just like that?"

"I played nice."

"Okay, that does it. You're making all my session appointments with Mira. I freaking surrender to her admin, just like I'm going to freaking surrender — again — to vending machines. It's not worth the aggravation."

"It's not our fault." Peabody let out a sigh, leaned back. "I'm pretty good at the self-blame game. I can usually win. It's hard to lose anyway when I'm playing myself. But Parzarri isn't on us."

"I miscalculated. He's dead."

"Maybe you miscalculated, but how do you calculate this? You were right before when you said killing him was stupid and wasteful. How do you run a mega-million-dollar company when you make stupid, wasteful decisions? He was incommunicado, they knew that. He didn't know about Dickenson, so he had no reason to betray them even if he'd wanted to. He's been raking in the dough, and finding ways so they rake it in. As far as they know the files on them are all in their possession, so those numbers can be manipulated before they're reaudited. Why wouldn't they keep their same guy on that?"

"I figured they would. I was wrong."

"No — I mean yes — but they *shouldn't* have killed him, not with the scenario that's in place. If they worried about letting it ride, that you'd keep building a case, keep digging, okay, move him out. He's in the wind — and in the wind, hell, Dallas, they could've laid it all on him somehow. They could've planted bogus evidence that made it look like *he* ordered the hit, or that he'd been working with somebody who ordered it. He's off doing the mambo in Argentina or wherever, still keeping the books — new name, new face. It's a good investment. And they pin it on him, maybe even have him fiddle around so it looks like he skimmed from them. Now they're a victim, too."

Eve ran it over in her head. "That would've been smart. Keep the accountant, aim the light on him, but keep him fat and happy somewhere else. They should've thought of that, should have tried it."

"They've got somebody who's running their numbers, cooking their books, helping them run scams, but they kill him during an audit they need fixed up? It's dumbass."

"Impulse again, instant gratification. They could always get rid of Parzarri if he didn't go along, if he made any of the wrong noises. They didn't give him a chance, either way. They had an accountant, a money guy, a hacker, and the muscle."

"Now they're down an accountant."

"Yeah." Impulse, instant gratification, Eve thought. "They may compound the stupid by going after the money guy. But more — think about this — by killing the accountant, it gives us something they didn't know

283

we had — that connection. Now we know Parzarri was involved. So maybe they hope to shine that line on his corpse, with less time to plan it through, less time to implement. But that's the impulse, the quick trigger again. And back to greed. Fucking greedy bastard. Why invest in the accountant? You figure you'll just bribe another, start him out on what's it — entry level. I bet Alexander thinks that's smart business. The ultimate layoff."

"No severance package."

"If he's going to try to hang it on the dead guy, he needs the money guy's cooperation. Or he needs him dead, too." Considering the pattern, Eve hit the sirens and floored it.

"Here we go again," Peabody sighed, and grabbed the chicken stick.

Eve swung to the curb in front of the building, slapped On Duty as she double-parked, and ignored the bitter fury of other drivers. She scanned quickly for a dark Exec Lux 5000, saw none as she jogged up the steps to the main entrance.

She jabbed the buzzer.

In under ten seconds, Whitestone opened the door with a welcoming smile. "Lieutenant Dallas, we were just —"

"Ingersol."

"Jake?" Whitestone stepped back as she strode straight into the spacious lobby that smelled of fresh paint and gleamed with smooth surfaces. The unmanned reception counter formed a central, wide U backed by a shimmering silver wall with THE WIN GROUP in large, fancy script.

"We need to talk to him."

"He just stepped out. He should be back in a few minutes. Why don't I give you the tour while —"

"Where?" Eve demanded. "Where did he go?"

Puzzlement edged toward worry. "I don't know, exactly. We're getting furniture delivered this morning, some other things. Rob and Jake and I wanted to make sure it all went smooth. Rob's back in his office, trying to coordinate deliveries. Jake got a call on his 'link and said he had to go take care of something and wouldn't be more than an hour. He's only been gone about twenty minutes, maybe a half hour. I didn't pay attention."

"Peabody."

"I'm on it," she said, and walked away to follow the unspoken order for a BOLO on Jake Ingersol.

"On what?" Whitestone demanded, more agitated. "Is there something wrong? Something to do with Jake?"

"Chaz Parzarri was murdered this morning."

"What? How? Jesus Christ. Rob!" He turned, moved right, shouting. "Rob, get out here. He was in the hospital, right? Are you sure it was murder? Maybe he was hurt worse than we thought. I just can't —"

"What the hell, Brad, I'm in the middle of — Oh, sorry, Lieutenant. I didn't know you were here."

"She says Chaz Parzarri from Brewer — she says he's been murdered."

"When? Where? He's in Las Vegas, or no. God, he was coming back this morning. I talked to Jim Arnold last night. They were coming back this morning. Jim? Is Jim all right?"

"He's fine. Do you know where your other partner went when he left here?"

"Jake? He had a client with some crisis or problem. He just said he was meeting the client for a quick coffee and reassurance. He'd be back. Why?"

"I need to speak with him. Urgently."

"Let me just tag him. He's going to be upset about Chaz. They worked together on several accounts." Newton pulled out his pocket 'link.

"I'd appreciate it if you didn't mention the murder. Just find out his location. I'll take it from there."

"It went to v-mail. Let me text him. We have a code when it's urgent."

"How did he behave when he was contacted by this client?" she asked Whitestone.

"Ah, I don't know exactly what you mean. Maybe a little annoyed. We're really trying to get this place up and running within the next two weeks. The crew finished here, and in my apartment. They've just got a few things to do, what they call punch out, in a couple of the rental units. We're ready to move in."

"If he was meeting a client for coffee in this area, where would it be?"

"We usually use Express. It's just a block south."

"He's not answering," Newton reported.

"Stay here," Eve ordered. "If he contacts you, tell him to stay where he is, and let me know. Peabody."

"Why won't you tell us what's going on?" Newton complained. "If there's something up with Jake, if something's wrong, we need to know."

"I'll let you know when I know," she said and strode out.

Halfway to the car she stopped, turned, and stared at the door of what would be Whitestone's apartment.

"Jesus, could they be that arrogant? That goddamn bold?"

Changing direction, she walked down the stairs, glanced back at Peabody, drew her weapon.

"You really think?"

"It's right here. Pretty damn convenient. He's sure as hell not meeting a client for coffee."

With her left hand, she took out her master, slid it slowly, quietly through the slot. She held up three fingers, two, one.

They went through the door together, fast and smooth.

She saw they could be that arrogant. They could be that bold.

Jake Ingersol lay on the newly finished floor, eyes staring up at the freshly painted ceiling, and his brutalized head swimming in a pool of his own blood.

Eve held up a hand. "We clear it first."

She didn't believe they'd find the killer hiding in one of the closets or curled into a kitchen cabinet, but they worked through, room by room before she holstered her weapon.

"Get the field kits, Peabody. I'll call it in."

"He beat him with a hammer." The weapon lay beside the body, covered in blood and gore. "Beat his head to pulp with it. Spatter's everywhere. Jesus. And look at the blood on the pants. He must've kneecapped him with it."

"Yeah. He put some effort into this one. I'd say he's starting to enjoy his work."

CHAPTER
SIXTEEN

While Peabody went out for field kits, Eve stood studying the scene, the body, the spatter patterns on the freshly painted walls, the gleaming floor.

She calculated they'd missed the killer by minutes, missed preventing murder by perhaps thirty.

She could see how it happened, the movements, the horror, the brutality — see it before the field kit and the tools and instruments.

The contact via 'link, text only, or with video blocked? She'd have lured her target that way. A simple statement, a flat demand. Mr. Alexander needs to speak with you, right away. He'll meet you in the apartment of the new building.

If the vic questioned, some cryptic or impatient answer could be given. Alexander said now, that means now.

Odds were the killer made the 'link tag from inside the apartment, gaining access through the hacker's skills, or because Ingersol had already passed on the new codes.

"Vic comes down after the 'link tag," Eve said out loud as Peabody walked back in with the kits. "The killer's already here. That's how he'd work it. He's a coward at the core. He'd take him from behind, an ambush. We know he's got a stunner, so he'd use it. He stuns Ingersol, takes him down, then beats him to death when he's helpless. That's his way."

"Why not quick and easy, snap his neck like he did with Dickenson? Or smother him, like Parzarri? Why this kind of ugly, personal mess?"

"Personal, exactly. And because he's experimenting now. He's into it now. He's not killing a stranger now." She took the kit from Peabody, began to seal up.

"So he not only knew Ingersol, but . . ." Like Eve, Peabody studied the body, the spatter. "Really didn't like him."

"Possible. Very possible. Ingersol pissed him off, or insulted him at some point, or he just didn't like his face. That gives him a reason — maybe it gives him permission — to whale away. Dickenson? That was thoughtless, ruthless. Swat that fly and walk away. The attack on us? Following orders. But was there a little thrill in there at the prospect of taking out two cops, in a public place? Maybe."

"Major fail on that one."

"Yeah." Taking out her gauges, Eve performed the basics — confirming ID, determining TOD. "Alexander wouldn't have been very pleased. Maybe he took his muscle to the toolshed."

"The toolshed? For the hammer?"

"No, you know. You go to the toolshed to get your ass whipped."

"You do? Oh, oh, you mean *wood*shed."

"Why does wood need a shed?"

"I don't know . . . well, to keep it dry. You can't start a fire with wet wood."

"Eighteen minutes. He's been dead for eighteen goddamn minutes." Anger spurted inside her, needed to be tamped down. "They came directly here from the underpass and Parzarri. He's riding on the boost from doing the accountant. Does he already have the hammer? Was it here?"

She looked around again but saw no tools, no materials. They'd finished in here. "The crew had cleaned up, so why would there be a hammer? Did he bring it with him? Did he stop to buy it? We find out. Either way, one of them, killer or hacker, makes the call."

She looked at the door again, calculated, then carefully lifted the victim's bloody, ruined shirt. "Yeah, stun marks. ME to confirm, but I think . . ." She fixed on microgoggles, all but put her nose on the broken chest. "Looks like it to me. He doesn't stun Ingersol from behind. Maybe he couldn't get in position to, or he just wanted to see Ingersol's face when he went down. So. Vic walks in, all rush, all business, and the killer stuns him."

She closed her eyes a moment. "If the hammer was here, using it was impulse. I don't think so, not this time, and a stray hammer's just too damn convenient. He's pumped up, wants *more*. He's greedy, just like the rest of them. All of them just want more. He could've walked over, put the stunner to the carotid, ended it. But he beat him to pieces."

"He'd have gotten blood all over him."

"If the hammer was here and it's impulse, yeah. But if he bought it, he bought protective gear, or he brought both with him. We need to know which. It'll play into profile."

She sat back on her heels. "Let's have EDD check the locks, get uniforms for a canvass — big guy with another guy, the vehicle. Maybe this time we'll get lucky."

"There's nobody left to kill, is there? As far as we know this involved Alexander, Ingersol, and Parzarri. And the hacker."

"Maybe they take out the hacker. More stupid waste, but why stop now? Alexander has other employees running these projects and scams. And maybe Alexander's through ordering kills, for now. But you do this." She nodded down at the body. "You've found another, very satisfying line of work. He's not giving it up."

She left Peabody to wait for the uniforms and sweepers, and went back upstairs to inform the partners.

"He's still not answering," Newton told her. "I can only think his 'link got turned off somehow. Otherwise —"

"He's not going to answer. He's dead."

She spoke flatly, coldly, wanting to study reactions. She saw anger surge into Newton's face, shock freeze Whitestone's.

"What are you talking about?" Newton whipped out the words. "That's ridiculous. What the hell are you trying to do?"

"To inform you your partner, Jake Ingersol, has been murdered. I'm sorry for your loss. Now sit down."

292

"Why would anyone murder Jake?" Whitestone managed. "It doesn't make any sense. It's crazy. Is this about the accountants? Is this some lunatic targeting all of us? A client? I don't understand. I don't understand. He was just *here*. Not an hour ago."

"Sit down," she repeated, more gently now as she saw the mix of shock and anger on both, and the dawning of grief.

Newton lowered shakily into an old folding chair. Whitestone just sat on the floor. "How? How?" he asked her. "You have to tell us what happened. He wasn't just our partner. He's our friend. Rob. Jesus, Rob."

"He met his killer in the apartment downstairs. Your apartment, Mr. Whitestone."

Color drained from Whitestone's face, leaving it a sickly green. "No. No. He was going out for coffee, meeting a client."

"No, he wasn't. He believed he was meeting a client — and more than a client, a partner in a land and investment fraud operation. Chaz Parzarri served as their accountant."

Newton lurched up from the chair. "That's bullshit! Fraud? Jake's dead and now you're trying to make him a criminal?"

"He made himself. We have significant evidence linking Ingersol, Parzarri, and another individual to fraud in several land and property schemes. You don't look very surprised," she said to Whitestone.

"I thought he was kidding around. I thought . . . The wrist unit, Rob, he said he got at an estate sale for peanuts. The painting he bought a few months ago after he said he'd hit it big in Atlantic City. And . . . other things. Oh God." He lowered his head to his knees.

"You don't seriously believe Jake was involved in fraud?" Newton demanded. "For God's sake, Brad."

"I don't know . . ." He rubbed shaky hands over his face. "About a year ago Jake and I were out at a club, and we got pretty toasted. You were off with Lissa, so it was the two of us. It looked like I might lose the Breckinridge account, remember? I was feeling pretty low. He laid out this whole idea for making money off land deals. Setting up dummy companies, pulling in groups and selling off more shares than you had, then buying up the land yourself. Inflating or deflating the assessments. He drew up a chart on cocktail napkins."

With a pleading glance at Eve, he rubbed and rubbed his hands on his knees. "I thought he was joking around. I swear I thought he was just messing around to cheer me up. I said it sounded good if you didn't mind cheating people, or going to jail for a couple decades. I even added a couple of ideas to it, Jesus. Jesus, Rob, I refined a couple of angles. He wrote them down. I thought it was joking, but he wrote them down. And I said something about it being too bad we were honest, too bad we'd worked all those years to get our license, build our business and our rep, things we didn't want to lose. And he said . . ."

"What did he say?" Eve prompted.

"Big money buys big rep. I just laughed at him, and said something like big talk buys shit, and it was his turn to get the next round."

294

"It was just talk," Newton insisted. "He wouldn't commit fraud or cheat a client. We built this business together, Brad. The three of us. Look at this place. We've done this. We've done this together."

"It's more than fraud," Eve told him. "It's murder. We believe Marta Dickenson was killed out of fear she'd discovered the fraud when she audited the accounts she'd taken over after the accident that put Parzarri out of commission and out of contact for several days."

"You can't think Jake had *anything* to do with that woman's death," Newton interrupted.

"I know he did. No sign of break-in? Because he gave the killer the codes. Maybe he thought they'd just take her in, rough her up, scare her, take the files. We'll never know for certain. But *he* knew, after the fact. He knew who killed her, why, and that he was complicit."

"I'm not going to believe that." Newton turned away, but Eve saw doubt and horror blooming on his face.

"But it's our building," Whitestone objected. "Why would Jake let anybody use our place for this? Bring this down on us?"

"She was supposed to be found in the morning. He didn't know, none of them did, that you'd stop by, bring a potential client. They didn't count on the police investigation inside the apartment, or finding anything if we did. If it had worked out the way they thought, it's just an address, just the sad story of a woman, a bad mugging, and the city."

"I can't believe he could do this," Newton mumbled. "Any of it. To himself. To us."

"Both Parzarri and your partner are now dead, within an hour of each other. Do you really believe that's a coincidence? Can you give me one viable explanation why Ingersol is dead in the apartment downstairs?"

"We built this place together," Newton repeated. "If you can't believe in, can't trust your partner . . ."

"I understand, but at this time the evidence puts your partner right in the center. It could have put you there," she said to Whitestone. "It could have put you in the ground."

"What are you talking about?"

"If you'd brought Alva Moonie by earlier, say before you went to the bar? If you'd walked in on the killer and Dickenson. What do you think would have happened to you, to Alva?"

Color drained from his face again before he dropped his head in his hands.

"We'll be confiscating all his electronics," she told them both. "Whatever he has here, at your other offices, at his home. Believe me when I say if you know anything, absolutely anything, it's imperative you talk now. Their method of tying up loose ends is murder."

"You think they could try to kill us?" Whitestone shot a panicked look at his partner. "Why? We're not part of this, we're not involved in any fraud. We're sure as hell not involved in murder. You can look through every file I have."

"Brad, we can't just turn over confidential client information," Newton began.

"They'll get a warrant, and I'm not willing to risk my life over this, Rob. You can't be either."

"Nobody's got any reason to kill us."

"Rob." Eve used his first name, hoping to draw him into trust. "If I'm wondering what Jake might have told you, or let slip, I can promise the people responsible for his death will wonder. They killed Marta Dickenson hours after she came into possession of the files. You've been partners with Jake for years."

"Let me think. Please." Newton paced the lobby. "I can't get my head around any of this. This is my partner, my friend. God, Jake introduced me to Lissa. We've . . . Lissa." He stopped dead. "My fiancée. Is she in danger? Could they try to hurt her?"

"I can have her protected. I can and will have all of you protected. I need your cooperation. Who did Jake spend time with?"

"Us." Whitestone lifted his hands. "He's seeing someone now, but it's not serious, and it's not exclusive on either side. He likes the clubs, likes the nightlife. Rob's backed off all that since he and Lissa got together, and, well, the fact is, I just couldn't keep up with Jake. I guess I didn't really want to. I like the clubs, too. I like getting out there. But not every night. He'd go out alone, or he'd hook up with somebody for a while."

"I want to call Lissa," Newton insisted. "I need to know she's safe."

"Give me her location. I'll send a protection detail now."

"She's at work."

He gave Eve the information, visibly relaxed when she ordered two officers dispatched. "You can talk to her after we're done here," Eve told him. "Now, again, if you know anything."

"I don't," Newton insisted. "I . . . He's been traveling more than usual in the last few months. He's largely responsible for bringing in new, out-of-state clients. He's good at it."

"Any recent trips to Miami or the Caymans?"

"I'd have to check," Newton said, "but his last trip was to Miami, about two weeks ago." He dropped back in the chair. "I can't believe this is happening. Can we see him? We should . . . whatever he did, we were partners. We were friends."

"You don't want to see him now. I'll do what I can to arrange it later if it's what you want."

"He's not close to his family," Whitestone told her. "And they're — most of them — up in Michigan. I think Rob and I will want to make . . . the arrangements. I think we should see him when we can. How did he die?"

She could tell them now, or let them find out when the media blasted the details. "He was beaten to death." She continued when Newton simply covered his face with his hands. "I need the medical examiner to confirm, but I believe he was stunned first, and most likely unconscious. If that's the case, he didn't suffer. He didn't feel anything."

"If he did what you think . . ." Whitestone spoke carefully in a voice that wavered. ". . . if he did these things, it was a game to him. It was wrong, but a game.

298

He liked being a player, liked being important. He made mistakes, bad ones, but he didn't deserve to die for them."

When Eve went back outside, the business of murder progressed. She watched the morgue team roll the body bag into the wagon, saw the sweepers moving in and out, and the uniforms keep the scene secured from the curious.

"I arranged details to keep an eye on the other partners and Newton's fianceée."

"You think he'd go after them?"

"I think he's unpredictable, impulsive, and having a hell of a good time now. He may not wait for orders, and I'm not taking chances."

"The team you had sent to the vic's apartment's transporting his electronics to Central."

"Any sign we didn't get there first?"

"They're going to review the security discs, but there's no overt sign of a break-in."

"Here either," she said as McNab came up the stairs to the sidewalk.

"Same deal," he told Eve. "The owner changed the codes, but they breezed right in. Maybe the vic unlocked the door."

"I think the killer was waiting for him. Ambush is more his style. I need you on the vic's electronics. The partners are cooperating so you can take everything. There's a unit here, but they claim it hasn't been loaded as yet. There's two more at their other offices. And a team's bringing in what he had at his residence."

"We're on it," he assured her. "That was some serious overkill in there. Not like the first vic. It doesn't seem like it could be the same guy."

"If it's not, we've got a bigger problem. Run those electronics, McNab. Find me that damn fingerprint you told me about. I want the hacker, hopefully before he ends up in a body bag, too. Peabody, with me."

Eve ignored the fact that Peabody and McNab did a quick pucker-up behind her back. She didn't have time to dress them down.

"Get Mira the preliminary data, the crime scene record on this and on Parzarri. I want her familiar with the details before I meet with her. Let's find out where Ingersol stayed when he went to Miami. I want to dig into where he went, who he met with. I don't know if there's a reason Parzarri would've traveled, same time, same place, but we need to find out."

"Got it. I figured we were heading back to Central."

"We are. I want to backtrack to the underpass. Try to calculate our killer's route. Where'd he get the hammer? Was it impulse? Did he stop along the route, buy it? Does he have his own little woodshed/toolshed?"

"The sweeper who bagged it said it looked new. It has to be processed, but that's an on-site observation."

"I had the same one. I have to go with probabilities. They're going to deal with two people in one morning, then they'd take the most direct and quickest route from the first killing to the second."

"They sure didn't stop for coffee and donuts," Peabody put in.

"Maybe after the morning's work. So if the hammer was impulse and new, he got the idea en route, stopped, made the buy. He had to see somewhere that sells tools."

"Okay. One minute."

"What are you doing?" Eve asked as Peabody went to work on her PPC.

"I'm plotting out the route, then I'm going to do a search for anywhere I can buy myself a hammer."

"Good thinking." Meanwhile, Eve kept her eye out.

"I've got two places," Peabody announced. "One's —"

"Big Apple Hardware." Eve pulled over, once again double-parking and raising the ire of fellow drivers. As she flipped on the On Duty light, she wondered just how many "fuck offs" she'd amassed just that morning.

She might've been approaching a record.

She stepped into the tiny shop with its myriad shelves and Peg-Boards holding various tools, bins full of screws, nails, bolts, stacks of tarps, protective gear, goggles, earplugs. Cans of paint, brushes, rollers, sprayers, toothy blades all crowded into the space.

She wondered how anything got built if the process required so many implements and choices.

A husky guy sat on a stool behind a jumbled counter watching some kind of action vid on a portable screen.

"Help ya?"

"Maybe." She pulled out her badge.

"Can't do no cop discounts. Sorry."

"No problem. I'm looking for a man with a hammer. Big guy, easy six four, two-fifty. Did somebody like that come in and buy a hammer this morning?"

"What kinda hammer?"

"The kind that bangs."

"You got your claw hammer, your ball-peen hammer, your sledgehammer, your —"

"Claw," Peabody said before he continued his litany.

"Curved claw, ripped claw or framing?"

"Mister," Eve said, "did an individual matching that description come in this morning and buy any damn kind and size of hammer?"

"Yeah, okay, I'm just trying to get the details. Yeah, I sold a thirteen-inch, high-carbon steel, smooth face, curved claw to a guy like that a couple hours ago."

Bingo.

Peabody stepped over, lifted down a hammer from a congregation of others. "One of these?"

"Yeah, that one. You know your hammers, girlie."

"I've got a brother who's a carpenter, and my father does some."

"I can give discounts to people in the trade," he began.

"We don't want to buy anything, and we don't need a discount," Eve interrupted. "We need to see your security disc."

The man glanced up to the camera. "Ain't nothing to see. We can't afford a real camera. That's just what you call a deterrent. Not that anybody bothers us. They gonna rob somebody, there's the liquor store down the block. People buy more booze than screws."

"How'd he pay?"

"Cash."

"Did you get a good look at him?"

"Nothing wrong with my eyes. He was standing right there where you're standing."

"I need you to come down to Central, work with a sketch artist."

"I can't close this place down to go work with no artist. I gotta make a living here."

"I'll send someone to you, Mister . . ."

"Burnbaum. Ernie. What the guy do, hit somebody over the head with the hammer?"

"Something like that. Peabody, I want Yancy."

"I'll get him."

"Now, Ernie, why don't you describe the hammer guy for me, and tell me what the two of you talked about."

"Like you said, he's a big guy. Big white guy."

"Hair? Short, long, dark, light."

"Short, buzzed, kinda medium."

"Eyes? The color of his eyes?"

"Ah, brown. Maybe brown. I think brown."

"Any scars, tats, piercings, anything that stood out?"

"No, can't say there was. Had a kinda squared-off jaw, I guess. Hard-looking guy. Tough-looking."

Yancy would get more, she thought. "What did he say to you?"

"He comes in —"

"Alone?"

"Yeah, just him. And he says he wants to buy a hammer. So I say, what kind? He just walks over there, takes the curved claw off the wall. He said, 'This one.' Pretty sure about that, how he just walked over and picked the hammer. I asked if he needed anything else, and he said he wanted a coverall. I asked what kind. He got a little irritated, I guess you could say, but you gotta know what kind. I showed him the stock in XXL, being he was big. He took one of the clear, full-body styles. I said something about what kind of project he had going, and he just said, 'What's the price.' So I rang it up, he paid cash, and that's that."

"Do you have the money?"

"Course I got the money. You think I ate it?"

"I'm going to need it. You'll get a receipt, and it will be returned to you in full."

"Yancy's on his way," Peabody told her.

"Get some sweepers in here. Maybe we can get some prints. That wall, the counter. I need the money, Ernie."

"It's all together." He unlocked the under-counter safe, took out a red zipper pouch. "Most people use credit or debit, but we get cash sales. I put the money in with the cash from yesterday and the day before. I don't know which was his money."

"All right, count it up. I'll give you a receipt."

"It's over five hundred dollars!" He clutched the envelope to his breast like a beloved child she meant to kidnap.

"And you'll get every dollar of it back. The man who came in here, bought the hammer, is suspected of killing two people this morning."

Ernie's jaw dropped. "With my hammer?"

"One of them. Ernie, your money's going to be safe. I'm going to put in for you to get a ten percent use fee."

His grip loosened. "Ten percent?"

"Yeah, and if you work with the artist, and your description and cooperation aids in the arrest of this individual, I'll put in for another fifty."

"A hundred bucks?"

"That's right."

He held out the envelope. "I still want the receipt."

After he'd carefully counted the cash twice, Eve printed out a receipt, added her card.

"What do I do if he comes back? Maybe he wants a skill saw."

Jesus, Eve hoped not. "I don't think he'll be back, but if he comes in, sell him whatever he wants. Contact me when he leaves. Did you notice which way he went, if he got into a car?"

"He went out the door. That's all I know."

"Okay, thanks for your cooperation." Eve went out the door as well.

"I'm going to drop you off at the lab," Eve began as she got behind the wheel. "I want you to take the money straight to Dickhead. He needs to run any prints he finds against military databases, police, private security. Eliminate females, anyone out of the suspect's age range and race."

"You want me to tell Berenski to run five hundred dollars in small bills, which have surely been passed through many fingers, for a set of prints. A set belonging to we don't know who."

"That's right. If we get a decent likeness, we can run a secondary search. He's Alexander's, we *know* that, but he's not his head of security. The head of security doesn't match the description. I think this is personal security, and not necessarily on the company payroll. Not that it shows. He's Alexander's strong-arm, probably travels with him, or travels ahead to clear the road. We're not going to find him on the company directory. I already tried that. So we'll try this."

"He's going to want a bribe. Dickhead, I mean."

"Tell him to go . . ." Eve reconsidered. "No, tell him I'll clear him for two tickets to the premiere deal tomorrow. VIP section. I think I can do that."

"That's a good one."

"Don't toss it out until he wheedles, and make it like you're going to have to pry it out of me. He'll think it's a bigger deal. I'll check with Morris, then meet with Mira. If we're lucky either Yancy or Dickhead will hit, and we can go after this bastard before he buys a skill saw."

"Eeww."

Eve couldn't argue.

"Feeney and I caught a hacksaw job a few years back, before you. Before he took over EDD. This guy killed his wife — she threatened divorce, and she was the money train. So he bashed her with this brass statue of a mermaid, then oh shit, she's dead, what do I do? He sawed her up into small pieces with a hacksaw he had in his little workshop, put it all in big waste bags, then dumped her in the river."

"I repeat. Eeww."

"It wasn't pretty. He told everybody she'd gone to Europe. But, oops, one of the bags got caught in this other guy's boat hook thing. It took awhile to put her back together, and not long to hook the husband. He tried the temporary insanity, diminished capacity, fugue fucking state bull crap. But since we had the saw, and CI determined it would take about six sweaty hours to cut her into the more compact and portable pieces, that didn't fly."

Peabody said nothing for a moment. "Do we lead interesting lives or really disgusting ones?"

"Both, depending. Out," she said as she swung toward the curb near the lab. "Get me prints."

CHAPTER
SEVENTEEN

She found Morris, with some sort of bass-heavy rock bumping out of his speakers, working on the seriously bludgeoned Jake Ingersol. Parzarri, chest still wide open, lay on a second slab.

"Two slabs," Morris said as he poked around in Ingersol's chest. "No waiting."

"I bet they'd have been happy to."

"No doubt. Your accountant had a standard mix of painkillers and relaxants in his system. He would've been quite happy before having his air supply so rudely cut off. Manually, and with a large hand."

"Any chance of prints?"

"Sorry, no. We can give you a reasonable reproduction of the size and shape of his right thumb and forefinger from the bruising, and estimate the size of his hand. I believe you'll be able to say with confidence, it's the same hand that bruised the first victim's face."

"That couldn't hurt."

"This second vic's hands and feet were restrained during the attack, and despite the drugs, the victim had a strong survival instinct. He struggled hard as you can see from the bruising on his wrists and ankles. As for the third victim, he never had a chance to struggle at all."

Morris, his hair in a long, sleek tail today, offered Eve micro-goggles. "Your observation at the crime scene was correct. You can see the discoloration from a stun stream, mid-body. A full charge from the look of it. He never felt what came after."

"I want to hear Mira's take, but I don't think he stunned him unconscious to spare him pain. He was dealing with a man this time, and not one hurt, doped up, or restrained. So he put him out."

"Taking no chances? Careful then, and you could say cowardly."

"I do."

"A careful coward with this much rage? A dangerous combination."

"Maybe. Rage, sure, but fun, too. Knees, groin — that one's personal — chest, face, head, hands."

"My analysis is the hands were crushed rather than broken."

"Crushed. More stomped on than hammered?"

"I believe so."

"He really didn't like this guy. He took Parzarri's travel case and Ingersol's briefcase and 'link and appointment book. And he left four hundred in cash on Ingersol, and a fistful of credit cards, a six-figure wrist unit. He didn't care about making this one look like a robbery. What's the point? And still, leaving the cash, the wrist unit . . . it tells me the hacker was most likely the one to take the cash out of the safe at Brewer's, and he either wasn't inside when this happened, or he's a little too delicate to root around in the blood and gore for profit."

She tucked her thumbs in her front pockets. "This is about money, more of it, greed for more. These two died for it, but money's not the killer's god."

"These two will have some explaining to do if and when they meet theirs."

"Yeah. It's tough to buy your way past those gates. I wonder how they, it, he, she, whatever keeps track."

"The higher power? Of the dead?"

"Yeah. I mean, think of the number of dead just you and I deal with. And we're just two people and one city. Then expand that pretty much by infinity. It's a lot. It makes you wonder if there's a bunch of people up there with ledgers, checking people off. Okay, John Smith from Albuquerque, too bad about that shuttle crash. Follow the green line to Orientation. And what if two John Smiths from Albuquerque happened to be in the same crash? It could happen. Plenty of room for clerical error there."

And over death, Morris smiled at her. "Entirely too much room. Let's hope the system's a bit more sophisticated."

"Yeah, but it makes you wonder."

She put existential musing aside and headed into Central.

She heard rolls of laughter as she approached Homicide, noted a small clutch of uniforms — that weren't hers — crowding the doorway of the bullpen.

"Has crime taken the day off, Officers?"

They scattered quickly, making a hole for her to go in.

She saw the reason for the party atmosphere in the person of Marlo Durn — vid star, celebrity darling, and the actress playing Eve in *The Icove Agenda*.

She'd let her hair grow and had gone blonde again, a vague relief to Eve as they no longer resembled each other closely. She sat on the edge of Baxter's desk, obviously in full flirt mode as she entertained the detectives and uniforms currently *not* doing any work.

Baxter looked like he'd been hit with a heart-shaped stunner.

Peabody spotted her first, dropped the cowboy boots she'd propped on her desk to the ground. "Hey, Dallas. Ah, look who's here."

"Dallas!" Wreathed in smiles, Marlo jumped off the desk and rushed to catch Eve in a hard, bouncing hug. "It's so good to see you. Matthew and I got into New York late last night, and I took a chance I'd be able to see you. We're all so excited about the premiere tomorrow."

"Yeah. It should be something."

"You'd rather be out looking for a killer than walking the red carpet, but it *will* be fun. Peabody said you're in the middle of a multi-murder investigation now."

Peabody hunched her shoulders as Eve slid her a stony stare. "You'll have this in Homicide. In fact, I'd wager every cop in this room has a case that needs attending to on his or her desk. Right now."

Immediately cops shifted, shuffled, opened files, picked up 'links.

"And you're busy. You wouldn't have just a few minutes?"

"I've got a few. Peabody, Dickhead?"

"On it. Bitchily, but on it."

With a nod, Eve gestured Marlo toward her office.

"I've missed it," Marlo began. "All this. I know it was just a set, but I miss the feel of the place. And —" She paused as she saw the murder board. "You are in the middle. I think about K.T., and all that happened. Matthew and I don't talk about it much, but it's there. Hovering, I guess. I've talked with Julian a few times. He's in rehab, taking a couple of days out now for the premiere, but plans to go back, finish the full program."

She turned away from the board. "I know it seems we're in and out of rehab like a boutique in our world, but I really think he's better. What happened with K.T., nearly dying himself, it pushed him to evaluate. It's terrible to say, but all that horror was probably the best thing that could've happened to him. You'll see for yourself tomorrow."

"I'm glad to hear it. Do you want coffee?"

"No, but thanks. The trial, the scandal, Joel — a major producer, a Hollywood icon like Joel Steinburger a murderer? It's dominating the media back on the Coast, and of course, by association Marlo Durn, Matthew Zank, Mason, Connie, and the rest of us. It's a relief to be away, though I expect we'll deal with some of that here, too."

"It'll pass," Eve said as Marlo wandered her office.

"Yes, it will. It's actually, in a terrible way, bumping up promotion for the vid, even for the studio. It's depressing, and I refuse to be depressed because — I wanted to tell you — Matthew and I are going to get married."

"Congratulations." Eve thought of the charming actor who'd played geeky McNab.

"I know it's fast, and that's another perception. Actors, always falling in and out of love, especially with other actors. But I do love him, so much. We're only telling a few people. We don't want a splash or the media hype. We went away for a while after the vid wrapped, after everything. It was good for us, good to be away, be together, have time to talk it all through. We love what we do, and despite all the shine, we live and work in a hard, stressful world. You understand hard, stressful worlds, and making a life, a real life inside one."

"I guess I do. As well as anybody can."

"I wanted to tell you because *being* you, so to speak, helped me understand and evaluate and decide on priorities. On what's really important. Good work, yes, in whatever you do. But when you find someone, the one, it changes everything. It changes you, and you're better for it. I have friends I can say that to, and they'd understand, but not the way you can. Because of that, I wanted to ask you a favor."

"Okay."

"Matthew and I are going to have a small, private wedding at Mason's and Connie's here in New York, the day after tomorrow. Will you stand up for me?"

"What?"

"Will you come — you and Roarke — and will you stand up for me? If you can. If you're not working."

"Marlo, you have to have people, friends you're tight with, someone —"

"I do, and I thought about it." Reaching out a hand to take Eve's, Marlo flashed her megawatt smile. "I want you, if you will, if you can. When I make promises to Matthew, I want someone beside me who really understands how important those promises are. We want to keep it simple, private. Later we'll have some big, crazy party back home, but this part — the promises — we want to keep the rest out of it."

Eve remembered when she'd understood, really understood that's what marriage meant. Promises, making them and keeping them.

"All right. Sure, if —"

"I know the ifs." Marlo looked back at the board. "And if one comes up, that's okay. Thank you, so much." She gave Eve's hand a grateful squeeze. "I was nervous to ask you. I feel much better now. Any time you need a favor, just ask."

"I could use two VIP tickets for tomorrow. I had to bribe someone."

"I'll take care of it. Just let me — and hello." The flirt went back on as Roarke stepped into the doorway. Then Marlo laughed, moved to him for a friendly kiss. "I didn't expect to be able to see both of you when I came in. This is an extra treat."

"How are you, Marlo?"

"I'm just about perfect. Dallas will fill you in as I've interrupted her work long enough. We're all looking forward to the after-party tomorrow. Plenty of time to catch up there."

"I'm sorry to interrupt. Marlo! How nice to see you."

When Mira came in, Eve thought: *What next? A brass band?*

Now she had to wait for all the *how are yous, you look wonderfuls*, and blah, blah, blah with people crowded into her office sucking up her oxygen.

Roarke sent Eve an amused look over Mira's head. "Marlo," he began, "I was about to go up to EDD. Would you like to come along, have a little look around?"

"I'd love to, and then I can fill you in myself. I'll see both of you tomorrow. And thank you, Dallas. Again. I'll take care of those tickets."

"Thanks."

When Roarke led Marlo out, quietly closed the door, Eve let out a huge breath. "God! Why are there so many people?"

"She looks happy," Mira commented. "You look impatient."

"She is. I am. I was coming to you as soon as I updated my book and board."

"I read the reports, studied the recording Peabody sent me, and I wanted to speak with you right away. He's evolving, Eve."

"I got that much."

Mira shook her head. "Update your board. Put this morning's victims and crime scenes up."

"Okay." She went to her unit to load the recorder, make the prints.

"I'm programming coffee," Mira told her.

"I've got some of that tea stuff you like stocked in there."

"I want coffee." While Eve worked, Mira programmed two cups.

"You see the first victim," Mira began. "A clean, quick kill, and the attempt to disguise murder as mugging."

"It was a job. He didn't know her. Business."

"I agree, as we discussed before. The second murder is unnecessarily cruel, would have caused suffering, and was done face-to-face."

"More personal. I get it," Eve repeated. "He knew the guy, and he's got a little taste for it."

"Face-to-face," Mira said again, "but a victim in a drugged state, and the restraints. You believe the killer is a big man, a strong man, yet he restrained the smaller, weaker man."

"He's a coward at the bottom of it."

"Yes, he is. The third victim, all but on the heels of the second, fast work, and in the last case, extremely violent. You believe the victim was stunned prior to the bludgeoning."

"Confirmed by Morris, yes."

"And that he lay in wait, lured the victim in, incapacitated him, then beat him violently. It's a very quick escalation, an experimentation in methods, perhaps, but more it's an embrace of that violence, one that, to escalate so quickly, has always been there. A big, strong man, capable of snapping a woman's neck, both physically and mentally. And yet a coward, and the cowardice, even more than the strength and violence, makes him very dangerous."

316

"Because he'll ambush, come from behind."

"It's more than that. Despite the relative ease of the first killing, he failed. It wasn't judged a mugging, and it turned the spotlight on his employer. The reaction to that?"

"Try for me and Peabody."

"Yes. Impulsively, and without any consideration for people who might have been hurt. And his cowardice is clearly shown — and has been touted all over the media — by using a child as a shield and weapon. Again, he failed, and this time he's been called a coward, a monster, while you're cheered as a hero."

"I caught the kid," Eve began. "It wasn't heroic, it was a good catch."

"I disagree, and so does the very vocal public. But the point is, he's termed a coward. You're termed a hero."

"All right. That'd be a pisser for him."

"Do you believe his employer ordered, or expected him, to carry out these two killings today with increasing violence? With no attempt at all to mask them?"

Eve shook her head. "Probably not. I expect the order was just, *Take care of this*. I don't think Alexander thinks things through any more than his muscle."

"No. Impulse, carelessness, cowardice, violence unleashed. He may not, very well may not, wait to be ordered before killing again. He'll see his last two murders as successes. He committed them his way, released that violence. Enjoyed it. He'll want that feeling again, that accomplishment, that release. And his first kill was a failure due to you, and Peabody. His second attack, on you and Peabody a failure."

"So he'll want to correct that mistake." Considering, Eve sat on the corner of her desk. "Okay."

"*Need* to correct it. He lost considerable face, considerable pride when those vids of you snatching that baby out of the air hit the media, the Internet. He was able to offset that by these kills, rack up success, feel accomplished, and enjoy the act. Increasingly. Whether or not his employer directs him, circling back to you will be imperative.

"And now you're calculating how you can use that threat to your advantage."

She wasn't the department's top shrink for nothing, Eve mused.

"If I can't, if I can't figure out a way to outsmart and stop this moron, I should be in another line of work. I figured if he got ambitious, he'd kill the hacker next."

"And he may. But he's feeling good about himself at the moment. The only fly in that ointment is you. You exposed him as a coward. He has to end you to prove he's not."

"So I draw him out. He won't want to wait long. Alexander may figure, incorrectly, that he's covered now. No loose ends, which would mean no fresh kills for his boy. If he kills the hacker, he'd have to explain why. But if he can get me, it's just cleaning up old business. I can work with this."

"He won't be controlled. He won't be logical. He will be vicious and violent, and he won't care who else may be harmed in his attack on you."

318

"So, I pick the time and place and circumstances. I can't just walk around the city hoping he'll make a move. I have to draw him a map. I think I have one. If I need it. We may be able to ID him today, then this is moot."

"Don't underestimate him, Eve. His impulse and unpredictability could work in his favor."

Maybe, Eve thought when Mira left her. But she believed cunning, experience, and a little manipulation would work in hers.

She contacted Nadine Furst.

"Ready for tomorrow night?" Nadine asked her.

"That's why I tagged you."

Nadine's cat-green eyes narrowed. "Don't pull the 'I'm too busy working a murder' card."

"I am busy working a murder. Make that murders."

Nadine shifted to reporter mode without mussing a hair on her streaky blonde head. "They're connected. The two this morning? And to Judge Yung's sister-in-law."

"The dots line up. How come I haven't done an interview on my excitement and anticipation of tomorrow's premiere?"

"Is that a trick question?" Those eyes narrowed again. "What have you got in mind?"

"I'm thinking about inviting one more person to the premiere."

"And that would be?"

"The killer. Get over here with a camera, and we'll issue the invitation."

Eve clicked off, sat back. It could work. Risky, sure, but workable. She started to reach for the comm to call Peabody in, then Roarke stepped up to the now open door.

"Alone again."

"Not anymore. Thanks for taking Marlo out."

"Easy enough as I wanted to speak with Feeney and McNab in any case. She's blissfully happy, and very grateful you agreed to stand up for her at the wedding."

"I couldn't find the wiggle room out."

"Didn't have the heart to wiggle hard." He tapped her chin, then set a go-cup from Vending on her desk.

"What's that?"

"Soup, as I wager you've had nothing since breakfast."

"I've been a little busy."

"As I've heard." He stepped over to her board. "Not cold and controlled any longer, but mean and bloody. Is the dog off the leash?"

"Maybe. Mira thinks so, in a lot of ways. She thinks killing opened up his taste for violence, and for killing. I'm with her on that. She sees him as a coward. Right there with her. Escalating, enjoying his work. Yeah. She also thinks that combination makes him more dangerous. She could have a point."

"A frightened animal's bite is as deadly as an emboldened one, but less predictable."

"Okay, that's her summary, or close enough. She figures I'm the fly in his lotion."

"Ointment."

"Same thing. He screwed up with me, so he needs to fix that so he feels good about himself. Plus the endlessly rolling vid of the flying baby damaged his internal rep."

"He'd hope to lure you into a trap or ambush." Roarke wasn't the department's top shrink, but he knew his wife. "And now you're planning one for him with yourself as bait."

"I wouldn't call myself bait in this case. More . . . an incentive. If we ID him before, we'll go scoop him up. If not, I've got an idea, and following Mira's profile, I can't see him resisting it."

He took a disc from his pocket. "I think you'll find everything on here to arrest and charge Sterling Alexander with multiple cases of fraud, embezzlement, and misappropriation of funds, with a side of tax evasion."

"You nailed it down?"

"Easily enough, once the dominoes started to fall. It's also easy enough to connect him to several other companies, some merely shells, and to individuals in those companies who would also be guilty of fraud."

"Does anything in there tie him to three murders, and attempted murder of a police officer?"

"It's easy, again, to draw the lines from his company, the other companies, to the recently dead accountant and the equally if more messily dead money manager. Were they alive, they'd have a lot of questions to answer."

"So we could say Alexander had them killed so they couldn't answer any questions. But without the trigger, we can't prove it. We get him on fraud, and push him for conspiracy to murder, he can claim he didn't have anything to do with it, had no idea."

She held out her hand for the disc. "I'll take it to the commander, and the prosecutor. And ask them to give me a couple days to cage him in on the murders. It's good work, Roarke. Thanks."

"How do you know? You haven't looked at it."

"Because it's your work."

He flipped a finger down her hair. "You're trying to soften me up so I won't make an issue of your . . . incentive to a murderer."

"That doesn't make it less true."

He sat in her miserably uncomfortable visitor's chair. "I suppose you'd best eat your soup and tell me what you have in mind."

Eve took off the lid, sniffed. "What kind of soup is it?"

"It was billed as minestrone, but it's your Vending."

"It won't be magic." But she sampled it. "It's not horrible. So, Nadine should be here before too long to do a quick interview with me about — woo-hoo — fun and excitement, glamour and glitter at the premiere tomorrow night. A premiere of the vid that's based on the case I cracked like a rotten walnut. Though modesty will prevent me from playing my own fiddle —"

"Tooting your own horn."

"What's the difference? They both make noise."

"I stand, if not corrected, forced to agree." In a futile attempt to find comfort in the chair, Roarke stretched out his legs. "You want to manipulate a confrontation with a violent killer at a public event?"

"I'm going to manipulate a killer into the open at an event he won't be able to resist because not only am I attending, I'm getting media play from it. It's splashy, and it comes right on the heels of his own media humiliation in the form of flying baby."

"And you see no downside to rubbing his face in it."

"I see that as a side benefit. Listen," she continued, knowing his reservations, "how's he going to lure me into an ambush? Maybe he tries to hit me when I'm driving home, or into Central, or when Peabody and I are in the field. We can take precautions on all that, but for how long? Or he goes at Peabody first when she's walking to the subway, or in the market for a bag of chips."

"All right, it's too open, too unpredictable."

"Exactly, and this narrows it down to a point. Tomorrow night, when I'm raking in the attention, he shows me — shows everyone, and more himself if Mira's on it — he can do the job."

He couldn't argue with her logic, or her strategy to ambush the ambusher. "And there'll be cops at the event, covering the event."

"Lousy with cops," she assured him. "And we should have a better description of him by then. It may be we'll be able to get him prior, but if not, we'll throw the net over him tomorrow."

And he'd be beside her, start to finish, Roarke thought.

"And when you have him, you believe you'll get him to turn on Alexander?"

"I will turn him, and they both go away."

"Well then, it promises to be an interesting evening."

"I need to clear it with Whitney, brief the men."

"And you can put any fine points on it, adjust as need be, consider more angles while Trina's dealing with your hair and makeup tomorrow evening."

"What? What? Why?"

"Lieutenant, for someone so clever, you really should have known that was coming."

"I know how to put the face gunk on."

"You'll have Mavis and Peabody for moral support. Not my doing," he added, holding up his hands. "And really, darling, if you can so courageously face down a killer, you should be able to tough out an at-home salon treatment with friends."

"Just another ambush," she muttered. "What kind of friends ambush you?"

"Your kind. And think how much more irresistible you'll be to your quarry when you've been glamorized."

She opened her mouth, shut it. Hummed. "That doesn't make up for it, but it's a point."

She glanced toward the door when she heard the sound of footsteps. "Prancing. McNab," she said moments before he bounced to her doorway.

"Lieutenant. I think I've got your hacker."

She forgot the misery of hair and face by Trina. "Who is he? Where is he?"

"His name's Milo Easton aka Mole. Milo the Mole, he's pretty famous in hacking circles. Have you heard of him?" McNab asked Roarke.

"As a matter of fact, yes. Young, isn't he, not twenty-five, and responsible for hacking into the NSA mainframe — still a teenager then. Draining the bank account of an Internet magnate he considered a rival, manipulating the odds boards before the Kentucky Derby."

"That's Milo," McNab confirmed. "He's only been caught once, and that was early on. He was only about fourteen, so they went easy on him. Big mistake as he stopped doing it for fun, and started doing it for profit. He burrows," he told Eve. "Himself — which is why he's hard to pin — and his work. He lost a lot of his shine in the community when it got out he'd tapped into retirement accounts. Going after big money from big companies or people, that's one thing. Sucking from regular joes? No frost on that. It's his fingerprint on the first vic's unit, and on the safe at the accounting firm. I'm sure of it."

"Where do we find him?"

"He burrows," McNab repeated. "You pop an ID on the guy, and you get one stream of data. Pop it again, you get another. All of them bogus. I'll work on it, but I can't pin his location yet."

"I think I can help with that." Roarke smiled at Eve. "It's, again, knowing people who know people. Then there's the money stream." Roarke nodded toward the disc on Eve's desk. "He's been paid. However he might funnel the money, however he might route it, that route has a beginning and an end."

Now he smiled at McNab. "Won't it be fun to find it?"

"Find Milo the Mole?" Sheer delight blasted over McNab's pretty face. "Fun doesn't begin. If we do that I'm King of the Hackers. Emperor of EDD."

"Let's go and get you that crown." Roarke rose, stepped over to kiss Eve's head. "I'll be playing with my friends."

And she'd better play with hers, so to speak. She contacted Whitney's office to ask for a meeting.

By the time she arrived she had a basic outline of her operation. She'd refine it, she thought as she stepped inside the commander's office. Nail down any loose ends, refine the layout.

"Lieutenant."

"Sir. I wanted to update you. Detective Yancy is working with the witness who sold the UNSUB the hammer used to murder Jake Ingersol. EDD, with McNab heading, has identified the man we believe served as the hacker on Dickenson's office unit, building security, and the hospital communications."

"Who?"

"He goes by Milo the Mole. Apparently if you're a geek, that name means something. They're working now to find his hole. We'll run Yancy's sketch for face recognition. If we can locate and bring in either or both of these individuals, we'll push them to roll on Alexander."

"I'll be attending Marta Dickenson's memorial later today. Judge Yung will have questions."

Stickier, she thought, and fortunately not her call to make.

"I don't know how much you feel appropriate to tell her, sir, but Roarke's compiled enough evidence through the copies of Dickenson's files re Alexander and Pope to bring them in on multiple counts of fraud and misappropriation of funds, tax evasion. There's money laundering in there, too."

"You've got him?"

"I haven't yet personally reviewed the data, but —"

"If Roarke verifies, it's so," Whitney finished.

"I will submit copies to you and the forensic accountant, but yes, sir, Roarke was confident. With time we should be able to follow that data and if payments to the killer and the hacker were drawn from any of the accounts therein, expand the charges to conspiracy to commit murder, murder for hire. As there will be issues of tax fraud and tax evasion, I expect federal agencies will take a strong interest in the actions of Sterling Alexander and in his company."

Whitney leaned back. "And you'd like to delay informing those federal agencies in these matters."

"Three people are dead. In addition an attempt was made on the lives of two NYPSD officers. I'd prefer he answer for that before the money matters."

"How long?"

"Thirty-six hours, at the outside. If we can ID and locate, we can bring in the killer and the e-man. If, however, we're unable to ID or unable to locate expediently, I have a contingency plan."

Leaning back, Whitney linked his fingers. "Go ahead."

"The New York premiere of *The Icove Agenda* has generated a lot of media interest and attention. It's well reported that Peabody and I will be attending. I believe, Commander, following the pattern, Doctor Mira's updated profile, and a ninety-six-point-six probability ratio the UNSUB will also attend in some fashion in order to complete the objective he failed to complete yesterday."

"You believe he'll try to get to you and/or Peabody at the premiere? With the crowds attending or watching the attendees arrive, the cameras, the security?"

"I do, not despite that but because of it. He failed, and was humiliated, on screen, with the replay of the baby catch."

"That was impressive," he agreed.

"Thank you, sir. The increase in the violence of his kills today — in his more personal involvement in those kills — indicates a growing taste for murder, and a passion that lacked with Dickenson. He's a coward, Commander, who needs to prove his ability, his strength. Every kill has been an ambush. This time, we'll turn that around."

"And ambush him?"

"Sir. With an interview with Nadine Furst, I can sweeten the trap, play up my attending, and more, my excitement about it."

Something close to a smirk played around Whitney's mouth. "Are you that good an actress, Dallas?"

"I can pull it off. He'll see the shine, not the trap. Moreover, if we don't close this down prior, Alexander will also be in attendance. He'll finish this job, in public, and in front of his employer. Commander, I strongly believe if we don't wrap this up before, he will make that attempt. I want to be ready for him. He killed two people in under an hour today. He's pumped, and so far he's only missed once. He needs to rectify that."

"There are easier ways to kill a cop."

"But none as expedient, or that fits his pattern of impulse. None that brings those cops down at the moment it seems they're most vulnerable. All dressed up, peacocking around. And all those people who saw his cowardice and humiliation on screen now get to watch his triumph. If we don't have him in a cage, Commander, he'll make his move tomorrow night."

"I tend to agree. All right, Lieutenant, what's your plan?"

CHAPTER
EIGHTEEN

Still needed some work, Eve thought as she walked back down to Homicide. Even with the commander's input, the op needed a tighter rein.

Calculating weak spots, soft spots, and dead ends, she stepped into her bullpen.

"Nadine's in your office," Peabody called out. "She said you'd asked her to come in."

"Yeah." She scanned the room. "I want everyone not needed in the field in whatever conference room Peabody can get. One hour. Peabody, get me the layout of Five Star Theater."

She left the mutterings behind her, went into her office.

Nadine paced the small area in skinny heels the color of kiwis that matched the waist-whittling jacket snugged over a black leather dress. She peppered questions and answers through an earpiece. They seemed to deal with timing, editing, and eight o'clock reservations. Nadine's cameraman sat in Eve's visitor's chair, and from the beeps and cheers emitting from his PPC, passed the time with a game.

When Nadine gave Eve a just-a-minute gesture, Eve turned to the camera. "Give us a few minutes."

"Sure." He hauled himself, his camera, his bag up, and still playing the game, strolled out of the room.

"If he wants it down to two-forty-three, I want Derrick to make the cuts. No, it has to be Derrick. I'll let you know when I'm done here. If I knew that, I'd tell you now, wouldn't I? Push it to eight-thirty. Just do it, Maxie."

Obviously steamed, she yanked off the earpiece. "This better be good," she told Eve. "I've got a special in post-production hell, an assistant who can't seem to put two clear thoughts together this week, and a last-minute fitting on my dress for tomorrow night."

"I don't know if it comes up to the extreme priority of a dress fitting."

"Don't be so snotty. Tomorrow night's important, and I'm damn well going to look sensational." She stopped, gave Eve a cold, hard look. "You didn't drag me down here to tell me you're skipping the premiere?"

"Just the opposite. I want you to interview me about attending the premiere, and make sure it gets some splash."

"Did you recently suffer some head trauma? From what I saw on the Amazing Baby Catch, you hit your ass. Then again . . ."

"Keep it up. I can get another reporter over here in ten seconds flat."

"Another reporter wouldn't go along with whatever you want to stir up, and in fact give it just the right stir." Nadine sat, crossed her excellent legs. "What are you after?"

"Some media attention, on this specific event. You'll have your own cameras covering it, right?"

"You bet your probably very sore ass."

"If this plays out, you're going to get a hell of a story."

Nadine flicked a glance at the board, then shifted back to Eve. "What does tomorrow's premiere have to do with the three murders?"

"We've got some lines, and may very well have that nailed down before the premiere. If not, we could nail it down *at* the premiere."

Nadine pursed her lips and got that reporter's gleam in her eye. "How?"

"The how's up to me and the NYPSD. The lure's up to you. He tried to take me and Peabody out once. I'm saying he'll try again, and I'm going to set the time and place."

"Tomorrow night, at Five Star Theater."

"It's probable he knows I'll be there. I want to remind him, toss it in his face, and give it some gloss so the idea of taking me down there is irresistible."

"You talking about the gloss, the glitz, the glam?" Angling her head, Nadine gave Eve a dubious study. "It's going to come off out of character."

"You play up that end. I'm about looking forward to seeing the investigation I headed hit the screens. You could ask —"

"Uh-uh." Nadine held up a finger, wagged it back and forth. "If I'm going to run this, we play by the rules. I can't lay it all out for you, practice what I say, you say. It's an interview or it's not."

"Okay. That's fair."

"And if this interview helps you catch your killer, you come on *Now*, do a segment." Nadine ticked her finger again before Eve could object. "That's fair, too. I'm going to have to juggle to get this — what by all appearances is a fluff piece — on air tonight."

"Fine. Done. Deal."

It didn't take long. Nadine angled Eve at the office window in a way that would give the illusion, on screen, of a bigger space, and a wide view of the city.

"Lieutenant Dallas," Nadine began, "are you looking forward to the premiere of *The Icove Agenda* tomorrow evening?"

"I am. It was a difficult case, a far-reaching case. The kind that sticks with you as a police officer. I'm very curious to see how the vid interprets reality."

"You had very little involvement in the production, by your own choice."

"I figure people like Mason Roundtree don't tell me how to run a murder investigation, and I won't tell them how to create a vid. I want to see how it turned out, how it angles. Your book got it right. I'm pretty confident the vid based on it will, too."

"Thanks. While you've been known to attend glamorous events as Roarke's wife in the past, this event centers on you."

"On the case," Eve said, instantly and obviously uncomfortable.

"On which you were primary. How do you feel about that end of it? The red carpet, the fashion — and commentary — the celebrities?"

And it would be out of character, she realized, to pretend any excitement or interest in fashion and glitz.

So she'd play it straight.

"The actors are just people doing a job as far as I can see. From what I saw when I visited the set, they did a good job. Actually, I just spoke with Marlo Durn today, and look forward to seeing her and the rest of the cast and crew tomorrow night."

"Rumor has it you'll be wearing something designed especially for you and the event, by your favored designer, Leonardo. Any hints on the dress for our audience?"

Eve was reasonably sure Nadine could have held a stunner to her throat and she wouldn't be able to describe the dress. "I'll only say Leonardo's favored for a reason. He never misses, so all I have to do is put on what he makes. Tomorrow — well, it's sort of a fantasy, isn't it? Fancy clothes, fancy people, red carpets, theater, a major vid. It's a break from what I do every day, a chance to step into the fantasy for one night before going back to the reality of the next case."

Nadine pitched a couple more soft balls, changed the camera angle, then wrapped.

"That'll work. Not bad, Dallas."

"The more air it gets, the better."

"I'll do what I can do."

Satisfied with that, Eve gathered what she needed to set up a briefing, walked out to Peabody. "Anything from EDD or Yancy?"

"Not yet."

"Let's get set up."

"For what, exactly?"

"I'll tell you while we set up." As they went out, Eve dug for credits.

"Here, get me a tube of Pepsi, and get whatever you want."

"You're really back on a Vending boycott?"

"It's safer for everybody. If we get leads on the hacker and the muscle, solid ones that lead us to them, this briefing will just be an exercise." She took the tube Peabody handed her, cracked it as they walked to the conference room.

"Otherwise, Mira believes, and I agree, he's going to try to take us out again — you and me."

"Well, that's not happy news."

"It is because we can work that. Did you get me the theater layout?"

"Right here. I wasn't sure if you wanted it on your unit or a hard copy."

Eve took the disc. "This for now. Go ahead and set up a board, standard for the current investigation."

As Eve loaded the disc, brought the layout on screen, and Peabody set up the board, Eve filled her in on the basics of her proposed operation.

"At the premiere?" Peabody interrupted. "Really?"

"Don't whine about it."

"I got a new dress. And shoes. I spent more for the shoes than the dress. And Trina's got this idea for my hair, and this whole new eye pallet to . . ." Trailing off, Peabody cleared her throat and got very busy with the board.

"I know about Trina. You bitch."

Shoulders hunched, Peabody carefully pinned up murder. "It's a special night. You'll look really good, and you won't have to do it all yourself. We won't want the NYPSD to fall short of the Hollywood crowd, right? Team pride!"

"Rah fucking rah."

"Really, Dallas, it'll be good, it'll be chilly, and we'll look abso-mag by the time . . ." She trailed off again, face lighting up. "We *will* look mag. And if we take down this killer at the premiere, with cams everywhere, it'll be all over the screen like the flying baby. And we'll look completely frosted."

"It's so good you've got your priorities in place, Detective."

"Catching killers, that's what we do. But if we get to do it at a big celeb event, there's no downside to looking most totally excellent. That's why you wanted Nadine and a camera. You wanted to push on this."

"She'll get me on screen, talking about looking forward to the premiere. Odds are it'll give him a nudge to try for us there — which playing the odds he'd try to do anyway — if we haven't taken him before. I need to set it up," she continued as she studied the layout. "Who sets up the carpet crap, the route, that stuff?"

"They have their publicist work with the theater's publicist." Peabody left the board, picked up a laser pointer. "They'll block off the street to vehicular traffic here, and here. They'll have pedestrian barricades along here, and down through here. Those with media passes can —"

"How do you know this?" Eve interrupted.

"Oh, well, I asked if I could have a copy of the setup, the schedule, and so on. So I could sort of practice, sort of get the feel for it. It's my first time," she said defensively.

"If the information wasn't so useful, I'd pity you. Run me through it."

"Okay. They'll let our limo through this block for the drop-off at the main entrance. People who want to catch a glimpse, try for autographs, take their own vids, they'll be behind barricades in these areas. The publicist thinks high volume there because the lead actors are A-list, the story's New York, we're New York, and because K. T. Harris was murdered during the filming. The house will be filled — SRO — invite only, but they issued a lot of VIP tickets. There'll be security for the producers, personal security, theater security, and an NYPSD presence."

"More than they know," Eve murmured.

"So, we get dropped here, and the red carpet goes right from the curb, down this way. At this point the media — those who obtained passes — can line up to take vids, stills, ask questions, try for quick interviews. And that goes all the way into the theater lobby."

"It's a big one," Eve commented, studying the layout.

"Yeah. McNab and I went there a couple weeks ago to scope it out. It's not one of your standard vid houses. It's like a palace. It has two full bars, and a little café, and —"

"We'll get to all that."

"Well, there'll be more media in the lobby. It's like a pecking order. The schedule calls for us to be there by seven-fifteen so we can do the red carpet, talk to reporters, do this mix and mingle. Then we'll have escorts take us to our seats. We're down front because we're V-VIPs."

"Security at all exits? And in each section?"

"I didn't ask about that — not knowing at the time somebody might try to kill me — but you have to figure it. They don't want people trying to sneak in. And if you really have to pee, they'd want security nearby because the media's allowed to stay in this smaller viewing room for the vid. If you want a drink or snack, each seat has an order plate. You key in what you want, they deliver it to you. No charge for us because —"

"V-VIPs. What happens when the vid's finished?"

"We're escorted out. Back out the main if we want, or either of these back exits."

"Okay. Okay."

She played it through her head as she walked back and forth in front of the screen. "He can't wait until it's over because he won't be sure which way we'll go. And he won't want to wait. He could mix with the crowds behind the barricades, but unless he's got something more lethal at that distance than a stunner, that's not going to do the job. He'll need to get close this time. Security or media, so it's going to be security. Easier for him to blend there."

She studied the screen, changed angles, zoomed in, enhanced, zoomed out.

"Finish the board," she told Peabody. "I need to work this out."

"If he hits us outside, he gets to do it in front of more people," Peabody pointed out. "The public."

"Yeah, that's a factor. But inside gives him a better chance of coming in close, and from behind. Smaller space. All those celebrities and VIPs corralled in there, grabbing drinks, showing off for the cameras."

She ordered the computer to give her an overlay of that sector, studied that, calculating the most likely escape route. Out of the theater, out of the area.

She routed the quickest, then routed what she considered the best. She'd run probabilities, but her instinct told her he'd go quickest. She didn't think he was smart enough to see the advantage of the longer, less direct route.

As she began to see the structure of her operation in her head, she used one screen for exterior, one for interior of the theater.

She highlighted potential routes, added highlights to maintenance areas, security areas, offices, employees only. She studied the layout — rest rooms, viewing rooms, bars, café, vending area, food sale area, ticket sale area.

Mentally she placed cops on sectors, like chess pieces on a board.

She glanced over as the door opened, turned when Detective Yancy came in.

"Lieutenant. Baxter said you'd be in here. I've got your likeness. Sorry it took so long. Some wits need more time." He offered her a printout and a disc.

Eve studied the image — the wide face, squared at the jaw; short, medium brown hair, buzzed at the crown; brown eyes heavily lidded, the slightly hooked nose, the more prominent top lip.

"How confident are you?"

"I think we're close."

Yancy slipped his hands into the pockets of comfortably worn jeans. "His overall impression was big, kind of surly, but he started to remember the details as we went along. It's a strong face. It comes off surly," Yancy added, "because that's how the wit saw him. But the features, I think, are close."

"Then we'll go with it. Thanks."

"No problem." When he glanced at the board, his young, attractive face hardened as he scanned Jake Ingersol's crime scene shot. "You'd have to be pretty damn surly to do that."

"Yeah. I think he's got an anger management problem."

With a half laugh, Yancy shook his head. "I hear they have good programs for that on Omega."

"We'll do our best to get him in."

"Let me know if you need more. See you around, Peabody."

"I had a sex dream about him once," Peabody said after Yancy left.

"Oh my God."

"It was before McNab. Well, before McNab and I were together. He's so fatally cute — Yancy, I mean. McNab, too, but —"

"Shut up now."

"It was a really good sex dream," Peabody said under her breath. "Speaking of," she added as Roarke walked in the room.

"One more word, and I'll get that hammer out of evidence and beat your tongue flat with it. Did you get the hacker?" she asked Roarke.

"Ian's nearly there. He asked if you'd excuse him from the briefing until he's finished."

"Yeah. He should stay on it. Why aren't you?"

"Because he's nearly there," Roarke repeated. "And I want to know what you're planning as I have a vested interest." He smiled over at Peabody. "Or two," he said and made her flush with pleasure.

"Aw."

"Peabody."

"Aw's not a word. It's a sound."

"Stop making sounds. I've got his face. Yancy's confident on it. I'll be running facial recognition, and I'm going to key in military and sports. If I'm right on either, it may cut back on the time, may bring us a quicker hit."

Roarke took the sketch to study it. "You think if he does try to infiltrate, it'll be as security."

"Look at that face."

"Yes, security's the most logical." He turned to the screens, scanned both. "It's a large building, numerous points of entry and egress on both levels, and more in the basement maintenance and storage areas. The security system is good, but it's not excellent. There's relatively little to steal, and there are standard alarms on the doors set during vids to discourage any attempt to break in and watch for free."

"How do you know?"

"I did a bit of research on it after you told me your plan."

"I don't think he'll break in. He'll blend in. The hacker could create a pass for him, a badge, whatever he needs. Or he could target someone legitimately on security, take him out, replace him. The security is to keep the public from getting too familiar with the celebrities, to keep them out of the theater, to be present. It's soft duty. He could bribe somebody, but he'd probably just kill. He's got a taste for it."

"He'll need to get close to you."

"That's right. He'll need to get close to kill me, and he'll need to get close so I can stop him from killing me and catch him. Remember that."

Meeting her eyes, Roarke skimmed a hand over her hair. "It's not something I'd forget."

She stepped back as cops began to shuffle into the room.

Feeney headed to her. "The boy's nearly got the location. I pulled Callendar off another duty so she can give him a hand."

"If he hits, maybe I'll be wasting everybody's time for the next half hour."

Feeney noticed the screen, pulled at his bottom lip as he studied it, as he understood where it led. "Well, crap. The wife's really looking forward to this shindig."

"Maybe we'll give her a kind of double feature. Better, we can pull this off quick and quiet. Nobody notices a thing."

"Somebody always notices," Feeney said, but walked off to sit, and hear her out.

She started to input the sketch disc, but Roarke took it from her. "I'll take care of it."

She left him to it, began counting heads. She'd need more, but she knew these cops, knew they'd run the op as she needed it run.

"Let's settle down," she called out. "Dickenson, Marta; Parzarri, Chaz; Ingersol, Jake. We believe this man . . ." She paused until Roarke flashed the sketch on screen. ". . . killed all three, with rapidly escalating violence. Yesterday, he attempted to kill two police officers."

"Hell of a catch, LT," Jenkinson said, and earned her quick applause.

She held up her hands, wiggled her fingers. "I have many skills. We'll be running facial recognition, and we hope to ID this baby-tossing killer. Until then, here's what we know."

She ran it through, quick, thorough, wanting her men to understand, all jokes aside, the target was dangerous, and not to be underestimated.

"As we have yet to ID him, and factoring Mira's profile, the very clear evidence, we're going to expect him to repeat the attempt on two NYPSD officers, if he's not been detained, at his earliest opportunity. He's got one, on a platter, tomorrow night."

She turned to the screens. "The Five Star Theater." She outlined the schedule, briefed them on the layout, adding more highlights as she assigned specific officers to specific locations and duties.

"Each one of you will have a copy of the target's image. He will be armed. If and when he's spotted, we'll move to block off his route, to separate him from civilians. If and when he's spotted," she continued, "I'll move to the least congested area. Contingency one, he's spotted outside."

She outlined the scenario, moved to containing him inside the lobby, inside the theater proper.

When she decided she'd hit it from every angle, addressed every element she could foresee, she paused again.

"Questions?"

Baxter wagged a finger in the air. "I got one, boss. Can I bring a date?"

"Sure," Eve said over the expected snorts. "Bring Trueheart. You look really cute together. If the op's a go, we meet here eighteen hundred tomorrow. Attired as suits assignments. I want those assigned to security or staff detail fully prepped, outfitted, and on site by eighteen-thirty. No later."

She gestured toward the board. "Look at what this asshole's capable of. Don't get sloppy. Dismissed."

"One moment, Lieutenant, if you will." Roarke pushed off the side wall. "There's an after-party at Around the Park. Once said asshole is where he belongs, you're all very welcome to attend. Again, Lieutenant, if you will."

She could hardly *won't*, when he pinned her that way. "It's your party," she said, then muttered about spoiling cops under the hoots and applause.

"Settle down. Get back to work. You want a party? Don't screw this up."

As cops headed out, McNab bounced in.

"Got him!" He punched a fist, gave Roarke a huge fellow geek grin. "I had to route it the way we said," he began. "His ISP and the echo spiked, then did the flutter. But once we filtered out the —"

"McNab," Eve interrupted. "Bottom line it. Now."

"Sir. Tribeca. Damn juicy neighborhood, too. I did a sat-scan once I had the location, and got a bird-bead on it. It's a big-ass brown stone. It looks like he may have the whole deal. Top to bottom. I did a resident search, too, and only got one. He's using the name James T. Kirk."

At Roarke's quick laugh, McNab grinned again. "Yeah, I know, right? Kinda rocking."

"What?" Eve demanded. "What's kinda rocking?"

"It's the name of the captain on *Star Trek*." Roarke explained. "Classic old screen and vids. Classic science fiction. A hacker with humor, and some taste."

"Yeah, but I think he should've gone for Chekov. He was more of an e-guy as the nav. Or Sulu. He's the helmsman, but —"

"Geeks," Eve grumbled. "Peabody, I want an eight-man team including the geeks here. Give me the sat-scan, McNab, on screen."

"You got it. Holy shit!" he said to Roarke. "We're taking down *The Enterprise*."

CHAPTER
NINETEEN

Eve studied the satellite image.

"A lot of ways in and out. We'll need imaging sensors to determine if he's in there."

"He'd be set up for that," Roarke told her.

"Has to be." Beside Roarke, McNab nodded. "Any kind of a probe, scan, snoop's bound to set off an alert."

"And likely a jam, divert and evade. Hacking's his world," Roarke explained. "He'd have programmed a system to block and disable any attempt to do the same to him. He's good. He'll have spent considerable time and money to be certain all his doors are bolted, all his windows latched and screened."

"Is he better than you?"

Roarke shifted his gaze. "If you think using my ego will help you, you're mistaken. Facts are facts."

"True's true, Dallas." McNab's hands slid into one of his countless pockets, jingled something inside. "The best hackers are paranoid because, hey, they *know* nothing's beyond reach. If we try imagery or bypass, he'll know."

"And he very likely has a rat hole to bolt into," Roarke added. "If he's in there, you won't get to him by conventional means. Unless we have time. We'd find a way around his system eventually. Nothing's beyond reach," he repeated to McNab and made the e-man grin like a kid on Christmas morning.

"Oh man, would that rock it out? Hack the Mole. We could run a hypo-analysis of his system factoring known and spec data."

"Yes. Extrapolate from that, reform, test the layers — in and ex. Play a dual and diversion."

"Man, I *love* that shit." McNab danced his fingers in the air, boogied his hips.

Considering, enjoying, Roarke rocked back on his heels as he studied the image. "We have samplings, the fingerprint, and the exterior views here. It's certainly doable."

"How long?" Eve demanded.

"Oh, with some luck and another two skilled men, maybe a week. With more luck, three days."

"Crap. Does it look like I have a week?" She paced away, then back. "I've got the resources of the entire EDD, I've got the ridiculous resources of the biggest, slickest, most conniving e-geek on or off planet —"

"Thanks, darling."

"And you need a freaking week to *outgeek* some skinny hacker who likes to call himself the Mole?"

Roarke only smiled at her. "That's about right, yes."

"Dallas, the freaking *Enterprise*," McNab reminded her. "You have to understand the complexities, the filters, the —"

"No, I don't." She pointed at McNab. "You do." She pointed again, more vehemently when he started to speak again.

"I *got* it!"

Eve swung around toward Peabody. "What?"

Peabody waved her PPC triumphantly. "It's the Kirk thing, *The Enterprise* thing. It reminded me I'd hit this name that made me snicker when I was running the van — the Cargo. Here it is. Tony Stark."

"Oh, baby." McNab blew her a double-handed kiss. "Good call."

"It's gotta be, right?" Peabody said to McNab. "It's his style."

"Who the hell is Tony Stark?" Eve demanded.

"Iron Man," Roarke told her. "Superhero, genius, innovative engineer, and billionaire playboy."

"Iron Man? You're talking about a comic book guy?"

"Graphic novel," Roarke and McNab said together.

"What do you bet it's him, Dallas?" Peabody asked. "Heroes from classic novels and vids. It fits. They used his van. It's Milo's van."

"Possibly. Okay, from the looks of you three, probably. We'll push on it once we have him, but first we have to get him. Now let me think."

So she paced, and she plotted. There was no way in hell she'd get this close and surrender to some ferret-faced electronic asshole who used aliases based on fictional characters from science fiction and comic books.

A geek, she considered. And one who liked to see himself as the hero, the smart one. Billionaire playboy? The one who got the women.

"Your high-tech can't beat his high-tech? We go low. We go goddamn classic. Peabody, ditch the jacket."

"My jacket?"

"Ditch it."

"Okay."

When Peabody took it off, Eve fisted her hands on her hips, took a hard study. "Unbutton the shirt."

Peabody's eyes popped, shocked brown balloons. "What!"

"Two — no three buttons down. Jesus, Peabody." Eve strode over to do it herself. "We've all seen tits before." She arched her eyebrows at the fancy lace number Peabody wore under the shirt, which nearly matched the color that currently heated her cheeks. "We could get blown up or something, and this is what you want people to see an NYPSD detective wearing under her clothes?"

"I wasn't planning on getting blown up today. Or undressed by my partner." She lifted a hand to draw the shirt back together. Eve slapped it away.

"Shove them up," Eve ordered.

"What?"

"Shove them up there."

"I'll do it."

"Stand down, McNab," Eve said mildly. "You know what I mean. Pump them up some."

When Eve started to do it for her, Peabody jumped back. "I can do it myself, thanks." Muttering, she turned her back. Her shoulders wiggled. And flushing furiously, she turned around again.

"Mmm. She-Body."

Ignoring McNab's comment, Eve circled her partner. "It's going to work."

"Classic," Roarke said.

"What's going to work? What's classic? I want my jacket."

"Forget it. You're going to walk right up to Milo the Mole's front door, and he's going to answer."

"I am? He is?"

"Damsel in distress, right?" Eve said to Roarke.

"A very alluring damsel. Clever, Lieutenant."

"Oh, okay. I get it. I look like I'm in trouble — all alone, unarmed. Harmless. Girl. He opens up to find out what's what. You should do it," Peabody told Eve.

"You're the one with the tits. Men are stupid for tits."

"Harsh," Roarke observed. "But largely true."

"Plus, you're the type, obviously, who appeals to skinny geeks."

"Oh yeah," McNab confirmed. "Completely."

"Maybe a short skirt and ankle-breakers. Somebody around here has to have them. All he sees is the half-naked woman with big tits knocking on his door. Lucky day. And while he's focused on the tits, we take him.

"McNab, go find me the skirt and shoes. Peabody, go slut up your face and hair and don't try to tell me you don't know how. I'll get the warrant and put this together. Move it."

As they moved it, she pulled out her 'link to arrange for the warrant. "You know how these guys think," she said to Roarke. "Help me put this together."

"Delighted."

Within the hour, Eve sat in the back of an EDD van a full two blocks from the target's building.

"We can't know he's inside." And she hated the uncertainty. "If he doesn't fall for the She-Body gambit, we move in, take down the door, clear the building."

"We'll need that ninety seconds to two minutes," Roarke reminded her, "to scan for booby traps, explosives. He's very likely built in some traps and self-destructs in the event of a forced entry."

"You'll get the time, but we go through the door."

"My money's on Peabody." McNab adjusted his screen. "She looks *whoa*."

"For all we know, he may go for your type," she told McNab. "Or yours," she said to Roarke. "For now, we go with the classic. The second the door opens, we move in. Roarke and McNab complete the scan. Peabody, you copy?"

"Affirmative."

"Baxter?"

"Right here."

"Roll it."

"Whee!" Peabody called out, and Eve heard the car engine rev. "Baxter's got totally mag wheels."

"Stop looking happy."

"I'm working up some tears, because my boyfriend's so mean to me."

With a laugh in his voice, Baxter responded. "We're rounding onto the block. Target's in sight."

"Give her room, everybody," Eve ordered. "Give her time. McNab, let's ease closer."

When he signaled the driver, the van pulled out, joined the traffic flow.

Directly in front of Milo Easton's building, Baxter peeled over to the curb. He sat, snarling in case Milo monitored the street. "At a stop," he said while Peabody snarled and pouted back at him.

"Give him a show," Eve directed.

"Sorry, Peabody."

He grabbed her; she struggled. For a few minutes they wrestled in the front seat. She slapped him, pulling the contact at the last second.

"Sorry, Baxter."

Face furious, eyes sheened with tears, Peabody shoved out of the car. She wrapped her arms protectively around her torso, and stood shivering — no coat, no bag. "You're a big prick with a little dick," she shouted.

Baxter shot a hand out of the window, speared up his middle finger, and sped off.

As instructed, Peabody chased the car for a few feet, teetering on high heels. "Come back here, you fucker! You've got my bag. You've got my 'link!"

She feigned a turned ankle, then began to limp back the way she came.

"That's the way," Eve guided when they picked her up on screen. "Pissed, but a little desperate. What do I do? Poor me. That's good, spot the house, don't even think about it. You need somebody to help you."

Her heart hammered with excitement and a little panic. Don't blow it, Peabody ordered herself. Don't blow it.

She pressed a buzzer, pretended to search for the intercom. "Hello!" she shouted, trying for a raspy, sexy voice. "Is anybody home? Hello? I'm in trouble. Can you help me?" She angled herself toward the cam, leading with her chest and willed a couple of tears down her cheeks. "Hello? Can I use your 'link? *Please*."

She shivered again, no need to feign that. She felt her nipples standing at attention, but maybe he wasn't even in there. Maybe her girls were on display for nothing.

"It's so cold. I don't even have my coat. My boyfriend dumped me out without anything. Can't somebody help me?"

"No way he could resist that," McNab declared. "He must not be there."

"Give it another minute." One more minute, Eve thought, then she'd clear Roarke and McNab to do the probe and scan.

"There. Do you see that, Ian?"

"I see it." McNab nodded at Roarke. "He's in there."

"How do you know?" Eve demanded.

"He's doing a sweep." McNab tapped his monitor. "Checking."

"Can he make us?"

"No, we're on the down-low. We'll read as standard comm."

"She can't keep buzzing and calling. Peabody, you need to look like you're giving up. Start to turn away, then just sit down on the step and blubber some."

"What am I going to do?" Sniffling, Peabody knuckled a tear from under her eye. "I don't know what to do." She started to turn, then she heard it. The faintest hum from the intercom. Forcing herself not to react, she took another step away.

"What's going on?"

"Oh, thank God!" She spun back toward the door, remembered to limp just a little. "Hello! Hello! Please, can you help me? My boyfriend left me. He took my bag. It's got my 'link, my money. Everything. It's so cold out here. Can I come in for just a minute? Can I just use your 'link? I could call Shelly. Maybe she can come get me."

"Who are you?"

"Oh. I'm Dolly. I'm Dolly Darling. I dance at Kitty Kat, over on Harrison? You know it? It's a nice place. It's classy, you know? Shelly's working this shift, so she could get off and come get me if you just let me in. He took my coat with him. I'm so cold."

"Did you have a fight?"

"I found out he was cheating on me. With my ex-best friend. Why did he want to do that? Why did he want to be so mean to me?" She put on her best sultry (she hoped) pout, and took an enormous breath to bring her breasts up to full potential.

"I've been sweet to him. I did *anything* for him. Honey, please? I'm so awful cold. Maybe you could just lend me a coat or something. I could trade for it, just for a loan. Give you a freebie, maybe. I've got a license. Well, not with me, because Mickey took my purse."

She *was* freezing, Peabody thought, and worked up some fat tears.

Her head came up when she heard the electronic click of locks disengaging. "Are you opening the door?

Oh, thank you! Thank you. I owe you so big, really, really big."

The door opened a few inches giving Peabody — and the team — their first up-close look at Milo the Mole.

He'd had some work since his last ID shot. Chin implant, Eve deduced, which he'd opted to spotlight with a narrow, horizontal strip of sandy blond hair. His eyes, an eerie green, couldn't stop drifting down to the display of Peabody's generous breasts. He'd chosen a neon rainbow of long dreads for his current hair style and wore what Eve thought of as typical geek baggies in pumpkin orange with a sunburst T-shirt that sat just as baggy on his skinny frame.

"Hi." Peabody gave the syllable a breathless, baby-doll huff, smiling into those eerie eyes as she heard the orders to close in, move in, through her earbud. "I'm Dolly. I really like your hair. Abso-mag. Can I come in for, like, two minutes? I'm just frozen. See?"

She held out a hand, palm up so he'd see it was empty. Then expanded her lungs yet again when he set his own on it. "Oooh, you're so warm. And so cute. Please, can I come out of the cold, use your 'link? I promise I won't bite, unless you want me to."

"Sure. We'll work out that trade."

When he opened the door wider, Peabody stepped in, then stopped, blocking him from shutting it. "Oh, ow! I hurt my ankle chasing after that *prick*."

"Maybe you need to lie down."

She giggled, gave him a teasing poke. "Maybe you could . . . warm me up before I borrow your 'link."

"I'll start here." He reached out, closed his hand over her left breast. Peabody smiled at him, eased a little closer.

In one fast move she had him pressed face-first to the wall.

"Want to party rough?" he began.

"The party's over," Eve said as she stepped around Peabody and yanked Milo's hands behind his back. "Milo Easton, you're remanded into custody. We've got a lot of questions for you, Milo. Peabody, why don't you read him his rights while we let the e-boys loose in this place."

"You can't just come in here. You can't touch my stuff. You can't —"

"Can, will, am," Eve corrected. "You're screwed, Milo. Take it apart," she told McNab.

"Can't wait." But he took a moment to lay Peabody's coat over her shoulders.

"Have the uniforms take him in, set him up," she told Peabody. "We'll let him cook a little while before we talk to him."

Eve watched Peabody haul him out, then smiled at Roarke. "All for a pair of tits."

"They are lovely ones."

She only shook her head. "Men. I'm betting you want to stay here, get in on the geek extravaganza."

"You couldn't lure me away even with lovely tits."

"Bet I could," she said, then left him to it.

Eve boosted up the heat in her vehicle so the warm blasted when Peabody got in.

356

"Oh, oh God! This feels good. I was seriously freezing my tits off."

"You did good, Dolly Darling."

"I made up a little background so I'd be more believable."

"As a licensed companion/stripper with a cheating boyfriend named Mickey."

"Yeah. A guy's going to figure his chances of getting laid are increased when it's an LC. I mean, it's my job to screw people. And the stripper deal? I figure guys are always fantasizing about women taking their clothes off, so it was a double tap. Oh, and Dolly Darling's my stage name. I'd have gotten to that if he needed more. Do I get a bonus for letting him grab my boob?"

"Your boob, like the rest of you, belongs to the NYPSD. Besides, McNab's going to ride you like a racehorse first chance. That's your bonus."

"You brought up sex and McNab!"

"This once, also your bonus."

"I've got this outfit at home Dolly would wear. I'm going to put it on tonight and —"

"You didn't earn that big a bonus. He's going to lawyer up. We surprised him, confused him, so he didn't start off yelling for one. But he'll go that route."

"We'll have enough on him, and plenty to work a deal."

"Yeah. I'd like to stall that for a bit. Why don't you let the PA know we've got him in custody, and we're going to start sweating him. I want that face match. We won't have to deal if we can ID the muscle."

"We're running short on time before we have to notify the feds."

"Tomorrow night, one way or the other. By tomorrow night we wrap it — or we bring them in."

And she wanted to wrap it, Eve thought as she headed for Milo and Interview B. She really wanted to wrap it in a goddamn bow.

She stepped inside with Peabody — back in her jacket, her shirt primly buttoned. "Dallas, Lieutenant Eve, and Peabody, Officer Delia, entering Interview with Easton, Milo. How's it going, Milo?"

"I've got nothing to say."

"Does that mean you've been read your rights and understand same?"

"I know my fricking rights. I want a lawyer. I don't say a word without a lawyer."

"That's fine, no problem. Just some free advice. Word's out that your . . . client, we'll call him, is still cleaning house. You're due to be swept up, Milo, so you're going to want to be careful which lawyer you call in. Any connection to that client, it could mean we wasted our time saving your bony ass today."

"Saving my ass? You think I'm stupid?"

"I'm told you're really smart, e-wise. I don't know how smart you are people-wise. You're the last thread he needs to snip. You might think about hiding in that electronic fortress of yours, but sooner or later, he'll get to you. We did, and it didn't take much."

Milo sat back, sneered. "Lawyer."

"All right. Peabody, contact the PA, let him know Milo's engaged his right to an attorney so there's no need to craft that deal. And let's get Milo his 'link call, then put him in protective lockdown, the full twenty-four/seven. We don't want anybody saying we didn't do everything we could to keep him alive while we have him."

Eve swore she could see the wheels turning — or in his case, the motherboard firing — as she got to her feet. "You can pull in a fleet of lawyers, Milo, but you won't walk out of this. We'll have enough to tuck you away — without electronic access — for a couple decades. And that's just with what we get out of your house. Add in the fraud charges, the tax evasion, the money laundering, book cooking, embezzlement, and you'll be a broken old man before you see daylight."

"You've got squat. You won't find anything on my equipment, and the fraud? All that shit? Bogus."

"Maybe you aren't as smart as they said. Won't find anything. Jesus, Milo, we found *you*, didn't we? And I'm betting half of the parts and equipment — more than — you've got in your geek haven was designed, made, and sold by Roarke Industries. And the man himself is even now taking all your toys apart."

It gave her some personal satisfaction to see his throat work at the mention of Roarke's name.

"You think you're the best? Please. You're not half as good as he is. So you call that lawyer, Milo, and if you live long enough to go to trial, which is pretty damn iffy at this point, you're going to go down, all by your lonesome, and spend the next, oh, I figure eighty years when you add it together, in a cell without so much as a PPC to play with.

"No deals for you."

She walked toward the door.

"Wait a minute."

"I've got places to go, people to see, Milo."

"I want to know what kind of deal before I decide."

"Oh, you want me to show you my cards, but you give me nothing? Forget it."

She reached for the door.

"How do I know you're not bullshitting?"

"Milo, Milo, we've got you cold. Why do I need to bullshit?"

"Why do you need to deal?"

"Me, I'd rather not, but the PA wants everything all tidy. Saves the taxpayers money. You're the least of it, so they're willing to give you a break in return for solid information. Alexander doesn't need you anymore, Milo, and you know too much. But you can take your chances."

"Look, look, the fraud, embezzlement, all that crap, that's not on me. He just brought me in to hack some files, for the audit deal. Hell, it's his company, right? If he wants to screw around with his own company, it's his deal."

"Lawyer or not, Milo?"

"Let's just straighten this part out first. I don't need a lawyer yet."

"Your choice. Screwing around with his own company — i.e., misappropriation of funds, skimming, laundering money, defrauding other parties and so on?

360

It's illegal, Milo. And since he hired you, paid you, and you did work for him, you're an accessory. You're on the hot seat."

"So I'll give you the solid on it."

"How?"

"My policy is copy and backup. I've got copies of all the files he had me destroy. And, you know, I like knowing the game through and through, so I hacked through his security. I've got names, contracts, deals. I've been working on his financials. It's coming along."

"And where do you have all this data?"

Milo shifted his skinny butt on the chair. "What's the deal? Tell me the deal first."

"You give me hard evidence that leads to the arrest and conviction of Sterling Alexander for murder and the state of New York will not pursue any charges of fraud, embezzlement or money laundering, or accessory thereto against you."

"What about the e-crimes, the charges for what you pull in from my place."

"Now you're getting greedy. I just gave you back about fifty years of your life."

"Come on. I can give you Alexander on a plate, and all his operatives. He's got operations all over the place. Dummy companies, Internet scams, land fraud. You'll put away a major case, right? How about I give you this, I testify against him, and then I just go away. Just —" He spread his hands, made a *poofing* sound.

"Can't do it." Eve gave a careless shrug. "Maybe I can talk the PA into lightening the load some."

"Alexander's the big fish," Peabody put in. "We might be able to work something, Dallas. Maybe house arrest, five to ten?"

"Jesus, Peabody." As if frustrated, Eve dragged her hand through her hair. "Might as well let him walk."

"Give us a good faith," Peabody told him. "You've got the hard on Alexander. Save us time, trouble, money. Give us some part of that. It'll go a long way toward softening up the PA. Dallas?"

"Yeah, yeah, it would. Hell." She sucked in a breath. "I'll push for the five to ten, house arrest," she told Milo. "On the hacking, on what we pull from your place outside of the Alexander issue. Give me something to push with."

"I've got a safe room. It's below ground level, fully secured and shielded. You can't get in without my palm print, voice print, retina scan. You have to take me back there so I can get you in."

Eve thought of Roarke, smiled. "We'll see about that. Peabody."

"I'm on it."

"Peabody exiting Interview," Eve said. "Okay, Milo. Now that we've got that tidied up, let's talk about murder."

"Huh?"

CHAPTER
TWENTY

Eve gave him a minute to assimilate, to sit, mouth agape so his narrow strip of chin hair looked like the stem on a wide glass bowl.

"Murder, Milo. You know, the unlawful killing of a human being. Like say, Marta Dickenson."

"I didn't kill her. I didn't kill anybody. I hacked into her files, okay? I told you that. We made a deal on that."

"That's right. Now we're talking about this." She drew out the crime scene photo, slid it toward him.

"I didn't do that." He shoved the photo away again. "I never *touched* her. If you're trying to throw that on me, I'm done talking."

"Your choice." She shrugged it off. "Same rules apply. I can't help you out if you don't talk. Or if you lie to me. If you try to tell me you weren't there, you don't know anything about it, we'll just stop right here. We can pick it up again after the lineup."

"What are you talking about? What lineup?"

"The one where we bring in the witness who saw you and your pal, and the van — *your* Cargo utility van — outside Whitestone's apartment on the night of Marta Dickenson's murder. Jesus, Milo, do you think we pulled your name out of a hat? We've got a witness."

He shifted again, swiped the back of his hand over his mouth. "I didn't kill anybody."

"You've admitted to working for Alexander, for corrupting and destroying files Marta Dickenson was working on. You and your van were seen at the scene of the crime at the time of the murder. You want to contact your lawyer, Milo, because I can promise you he or she will tell you that's some pretty hot water you're swimming in."

"I didn't kill *anybody*! Okay, yeah, it was my van, but all I did was drive."

"All you did was drive?" Eve repeated, pleasantly, and thought: *Gotcha, asshole.*

"That's right. I drove the van. I didn't know she was going to get killed. I drove the van, and I was supposed to get through the security if the codes didn't work."

"What codes?"

"The codes for the apartment, the codes Jake Ingersol gave us. Alexander hired me to use my van, to drive it and get us in if Ingersol pulled any crap, see? That's all."

"Okay, I'm getting it. But let's backtrack a minute. How did Alexander hire you? How did he contact you?"

"Through Ingersol. I've done some work for Ingersol before. I only work on referrals, you know? You have to be careful."

"I bet. So Ingersol brought Alexander to you?"

"Yeah. They had a good thing going, but Alexander wanted some tweaking, and a thicker slice. That's where I came in. You got a potential mark, or a group of

364

investors. I'd put together a file on them. Financials, other investments, what they spent money on — who they spent it on. If they had something going on the side, if they were into the kink."

Contradiction, Eve noted, as Milo had claimed earlier not to have been involved in the fraud. She'd give him more rope. "For blackmail purposes?"

"I didn't blackmail anybody either." Milo held up his hands. "I don't do that shit. I just provide the data to the client. What the client does with the data isn't on me."

"Got it. But being thorough, you'd have put together files on how Alexander used the data. You'd have that as a just-in-case buffer."

"Like I said, you've got to be careful. He put the screws to some of the marks, sure. Bled them a little harder that way if they started to make noise or tried to back out. Whatever. He's a greedy bastard. You know he even tried to get me to cut my rates?"

"Imagine that."

"Yeah, seriously. You get what you pay for, right? And my work made him a whole shitpot of money."

"I bet it did. How long have you worked for him?"

"Six months. Just doing those tweaks now and then."

"So you were involved in the fraud."

He blinked, shifted. "I didn't do any fraud. I just did the tweaks. We covered that."

"All right. So you did the tweaks, and helped Alexander make that shitpot of money. But then he was going to have some trouble. This audit he couldn't get out of."

"Shouldn't have been trouble, wouldn't have been if Parzarri hadn't gotten banged up, got put out of commission before he fixed the books. Now, see, here's what I'm saying." Comfortable now, Milo shifted forward conversationally. "He tells me he wants this new accountant picked up, to hack into her communications, get a line on her so she gets scooped when she leaves the office, before she can dig into the books. All I figure is they want the files, put some pressure on her to clam it up, go along. Maybe pay her a little, though, like I said, he's a greedy bastard. All I did was monitor her 'links, poke around in her comms."

"And drive the van."

"Right. Alexander doesn't like to pay, so he's got me multitasking. I'm okay with it because he's a steady revenue stream. I just drive his ass-kicker to the offices, then when he scoops the accountant, I take them to the apartment. No problem with the codes, so I just wait in the van. See? I never laid a hand on her. I was in the van."

"Okay, that makes sense. What happened? Take me through it."

"So, well, after she's scooped in the back, she's making some noise. The ass-kicker knocks her around a little. Look, I'm sorry about that, but it happens. It can be a rough business."

"Understood."

"Me, I just drive, then I check the security, the locks. We're go. I get back in the van to wait. He's not gone all that long. I don't know, I was working on my portable, so time passed. He comes back."

"And?" Eve said after a moment.

"That's it. Guy's not much of a talker. I just dropped him off back at Alexander and Pope like he told me, took the van back to the garage where I keep it, and caught a cab home."

"Who's the ass-kicker?"

"Don't know."

"Milo."

"Truth." He held up his right hand as if taking an oath. "Do. Not. Know. Don't want to know. He's a scary kind of guy, and I figured if I poked around there, things could get harsh. It's not like we hooked up for jobs regular. I'd only seen him a couple times before, and after all this, I don't want to see him again."

She leaned toward believing him, but she'd push on it later.

"He didn't say anything about Dickenson?"

"He didn't say anything about anything, except take him back to the offices. He had her briefcase, and weird, I thought, her coat. I just figured he was giving her the business, making her get home without the coat. Bitching cold that night. Then I saw how she'd been killed. They said a mugging, but . . ."

"You knew better."

"Well, it *could* have been a mugging, but I figured something went bad. I didn't ask any questions. When you start asking questions, you're asking for trouble."

"You didn't ask any questions when Alexander told you to break into the Brewer building, into the offices, into Dickenson's comp, the safe, take and/or destroy files?"

"That's a job." Milo set the edges of his hands on the table as if putting the matter into a box. "Now, sure, you have to ask some questions, but it was pretty straightforward. I tried to tell him I could take care of the files before, but he didn't want to pay the fee. He ended up paying it anyway, right? Cheap prick."

"Did you ask questions when he told you to hack into the hospital's communication and security?"

"Just standard ones, so I could program the job. Look, the same elements apply. I didn't know they were going to kill Parzarri. I mean, grab some reality, right? The guy was good at his work."

"What did you figure?"

"I figured Alexander wanted his guy to scare Parzarri, to make sure he hadn't blown it, talked to anyone. He was incommunicado for a few days, and Alexander started to sweat it. Especially after you got in his face. Man, he was steamed."

"Was he?"

"Maximum steam. Okay, full disclosure. Total cooperation. He wanted me to hack into your comms — at Central, portable, at home. Let me say you've got some major mag shielding. I didn't have time to get through it. So what I did, I got the other cop's — the one who was in here?"

"Detective Peabody."

"Yeah. NYPSD has some decent shielding, but it's doable. I ran the locator on her comm. That's how the ass-kicker knew where you'd be."

"But you didn't ask questions."

"I had to figure he wanted to mess you up some, scare you off. I figure that's stupid. He does that, you're just going to put it together, but he doesn't pay me for advice. Tossing that kid, that's cold, man. That was very unchill. Superior catch, by the way."

"Thanks. Let's go back to Parzarri for a minute, just to tie it up. You hacked in, got the data on the shuttle flight, the ambulance crew, generated the fake IDs, sent the fake communication."

"Yeah, that was the job."

"And drove the ambulance."

"That's a kick." He actually grinned. "Lights, sirens. A rush."

"But while you're driving, Milo, while you're getting that rush, Parzarri's in the back being smothered."

"I didn't know. Seriously, you have to pay attention when you're driving an ambulance."

"Tell me what you thought when you left it, and Parzarri at the underpass, switched cars?"

"Just like before." His eyes cut away. "Putting a little scare into him."

You're lying now, Eve thought. *Lying, weaselly little fucker.*

"Putting a scare in him by leaving him hurt, since you didn't know he was dead. Hurt and alone. Taking his suitcase, just driving off."

"I got paid for the hack, the driving. That's it, that's all. And I wasn't going to say anything. The ass-kicker looked . . . kind of pumped. Gave me a bad feeling. We're supposed to go to the WIN building, so the ass-kicker can talk to Ingersol."

369

"Just talk."

"That's all I knew. I tagged Ingersol, said how Alexander wanted to cover some new details. How it was important, and they should meet in the apartment there. But before that, the ass-kicker has me stop. Not on the schedule, but I do what I'm told. I don't argue with the guy. He goes into this crappy little hardware store. I've got to circle around, and it takes some time with traffic and all. He's waiting for me when I get back. He's got this bag from the store. I didn't know what was in it. As far as I know he needed some freaking hardware."

"Reasonable assumption."

"Sure."

Eve waited a beat. "And then?"

"Oh, well. Anyway, Whitestone changed the codes after what happened, but I had the pattern and the system, so I bypassed easy enough. Then I parked down the block, went for some coffee, sat and did some work until the tag to come back."

Milo stopped, moistened his lips. "This time I got spooked. The guy looked, I don't know, more than pumped. He looked a little crazy maybe. And I thought I smelled blood. I don't know for sure, but I do know for sure all I wanted was to take him back to the offices, dump the car in the company garage, and get home. I'm telling you I'd already decided to turn down any more jobs that involved that guy. Whatever Alexander offered to pay wasn't worth it."

"A little late, Milo."

"Look, I hack. I don't hurt anybody. I find information, and yeah, maybe funnel some money, but I don't do violence."

"You just sell information to people who do violence."

"It's not my responsibility what people do with the information."

"Well, actually, Milo, you're wrong about that. The law takes a different view. Which is why you're under arrest for accessory to murder, three counts."

"You can't *do* that. I just drove the van."

Eve expected that would be his war cry for the rest of his miserable life.

"That's why it's called accessory, Milo. You could look it up. You just drove the van on the night Marta Dickenson was abducted and murdered. You're also being charged with that abduction, by the way."

"But — what —" The words broke off, just crumbled.

"Now maybe, just maybe your lawyer can argue you didn't know about the intent to murder, that time. But by your own admission you knew she'd been murdered, that's accessory after the fact. Instead of coming in, you took the next job with the same people, then the next. Nobody's going to buy you were stupid enough not to know what you were part of. You kept going back to the well, Milo, knowing the water was poison. And three people are dead."

Eve saw tears start in the corners of his eyes.

"I cooperated. I laid it out for you."

"Yeah. Thanks." She got to her feet.

"You lied. You tricked me. You — you entrapped me."

"No, yes, no. I'm allowed to lie in Interview, but in this case, I didn't have to. If we hadn't dug you up, brought you in, Alexander would tell his man to do you next. There's no question there, Milo. In addition, the state of New York will not pursue charges of fraud against you. But I don't have any control over what the feds decide, and I'm pretty sure they'll come for you."

"I didn't hurt anybody."

"God, you actually believe that." Eve wondered if she should pity him, but couldn't find it in her.

"I'll also ask the PA to consider house arrest on the hacking. Of course, that house arrest will come after you've served your time in a cage for the murder counts, then in a fed cage for the fraud, should you live that long. But I'm going to bat for you there, Milo."

Tears swam freely in his eyes now, and his voice came thick with them. "You're a fucking bitch."

"Again yeah, and thanks." She opened the door, signaled to the uniforms. "Take him down, book him." She reeled off a string of charges while Milo shouted for his lawyer. "And let him contact this lawyer he's crying for. He's to be kept separate from the general population, and he's strictly denied access to any electronics. If and when the lawyer shows, it needs to be flagged in the file. No electronics allowed into his conference area.

"Peabody," she said when her partner stepped up.

"You had a rhythm going so I didn't come back in. I didn't want to distract him. I watched in Observation, in case. It didn't seem like you needed the information that I just got a minute ago. They got into his panic room. Working on the files and equipment in there now."

"Fast work," she said as the uniforms muscled Milo out.

"Yeah, apparently our team's better than he is." She smiled at Milo as he passed, then sobered again. "He really didn't get it, Dallas. He just drove the van, just accessed information, so he's not responsible."

"He liked the power and money too much to believe otherwise. Greed, that rush, and stupidity. That's the hat trick for this whole operation. I'd better talk to the PA's office."

"Reo came into Observation while you were leading Milo by the nose. She's talking to her boss now."

"Good. I'll touch base with her. I want that face match, goddamn it. We need Alexander's goon before we take down Alexander."

"He'd roll on him, wouldn't he? Alexander would hand us the goon for a deal."

"I don't want to deal, but even with that, once we pick up Alexander, the killer's in the wind. No way around it. We need to keep any media play of Milo's arrest down, even out if we can. We spook either of the other two, we could lose them. Let's put a couple of men on Alexander. If it looks like he's going to rabbit, we pick him up."

"I'll take care of it. Do you think Milo was telling it straight? He doesn't know the name of the goon?"

"I think the guy spooked him. And I think he didn't want to know so he could claim, and likely believe, just what he said in there. He didn't know, so he's not responsible."

"He'll have the rest of his life to think about how wrong he was." Reo stepped out, compact and blonde, with a hint of magnolia on her tongue. "You wrapped him up so pretty, with a big, fluffy bow."

"He knows electronics. He knows dick about people."

"You did some of my job in there. We get to negotiate deals."

"Just multitasking."

"Well, in this case, the boss agrees with you. We'll let the feds go after him on the fraud, if they want to add to his time. Most likely, they'll give him a pass on it for his testimony on Alexander. When are you picking him up?"

"Not yet. I need his hammer first. I'm working on it."

"Dallas, the feds may give the hacker a pass, but you can bet they'll go full throttle after a shark as big and toothy as Sterling Alexander. They won't quibble about trumping your three murders."

"I'm working on it," Eve repeated. "And if I don't have his VP in charge of murder by tomorrow, I have a contingency plan."

"I'm all ears."

"Let's take it in my office. I want to check on the face match."

"Are you ready for tomorrow?" Reo asked as they walked.

"I just told you I have a contingency."

"I meant the premiere. Even this job takes a break once in a while."

"Not exactly, and that's the contingency."

In her office Eve ran it through while Reo sat sipping water from a bottle she pulled out of a handbag the size of a baby elephant.

"You actually think he'll try for you at a red carpet event."

"I think he's assured I'll be there, and he'll believe I'm off my guard basking in the sparkle and attention."

"He doesn't know you, does he? You're never off your guard, and you don't bask. Not in sparkle anyway."

"His perception's his reality, and it's boosted by all that media on the flying baby, on Nadine's interview with me, on the media hype for the event. Mira's convinced he has to eliminate me in order to gain satisfaction for the job he's done, and because his level of violence and his enjoyment of it increases with each killing. I can't argue with it."

"There's room for slip ups here, Dallas."

"There always is, but he's going to be the one to slip. We take him, we take Alexander. We hand you conspiracy to murder, and a big, fat fraud and embezzlement bouquet you can pick through with the feds."

"His operatives will scramble, but I expect the feds will gather them up."

"Milo's data should help with that. It's a nice dish to offer the feds. They'll owe us."

"You'd think. It doesn't always work that way, but it's not only a good case, it's a nice lever we may be able to pull at some point."

She looked at Eve's monitor, the screen split between Yancy's sketch and a constant scroll of faces. "That's the guy?"

"It's what we've got. Yancy felt confident, but we've been searching for a match for hours without a solid hit."

"Good luck. I hope you get that hit soon because I'll have a much better time tomorrow without waiting for some hired killer with a grudge to take a shot at you."

"I don't know. It kind of adds a . . . sparkle."

"Only you," Reo said with a laugh and rose. "I'm going to check to see if Milo got his lawyer, then —"

She broke off when Eve's computer beeped.

Facial recognition match, ninety-five-point-eight probability.

"Holy shit! You must be like a lucky charm. If I go to Vegas, I'm taking you with me."

"That's him," Reo agreed, studying the ID photo over Eve's shoulder. "Clinton Rosco Frye."

"Age thirty-three, freelance personal security. Yeah, that's the name for it. He's not listing Alexander as employer." She scanned down. "I *knew* it. See? Semi-pro football. It's been about eight years, and it's bush-league, but I *knew* it. Two years regular army, four years paramilitary Montana Patriots."

"Straight out of high school into the army. Out of the army into the Montana Patriots, which — as I just looked them up," Reo said, tapping her PPC, "gets a three and a half on the four-star lunatic fringe scale. Play some ball . . . How do you go from that to personal security to killer?"

"You can't get into the bigs, can't make it out of semi-pro. Screw it, use your build, your moves for bodyguarding and make more money. Fall in with just the right client — pays good, makes you his go-to for head-knocking. It just escalates. See, he's got some dings on here, all involving violence. Assault, battery, destruction of property. He didn't do any time, just paid fines, anger management bullshit, community service. No illegals playing in, no alcohol. He stays clean, keeps in shape. And according to his official report makes a damn good living freelancing. There'll be more tucked away, but he doesn't mind reporting a hefty sum, and paying the freight on it. He needs the success."

"The address listed. It's not far from the first crime scene, is it?"

"No, it's not. Not far from Alexander and Pope. It's handy to live close to work." She rose, grabbed her coat.

"It looks like you'll have to settle for the sparkle on my shoes tomorrow night," Reo said. "They're fabulous. I'll get your warrant, and if I'm not here when you bring him in, just tag me. Work late tonight, party hard tomorrow."

"Maybe." She dragged on her coat as she strode into the bullpen. "Peabody, Uniform Carmichael, Franks, Baxter, Trueheart. Suit up. We got a hit on the UNSUB now ID'd as Clinton Frye. Let's go get his ass."

She set it up simply, pulling Callendar from EDD to run heat imaging, eyes, ears. She covered the exits on the eight-story building, considered the options of taking Frye from his top floor, corner apartment.

"Is he up there or not?" she asked Callendar.

"I'm scanning. I'm not finding any heat sources. No shields either. He's not home, Dallas."

"Damn it."

"I can patch into building security, give you eyes in the hallway outside his apartment, in the elevators and stairwells."

"Do it."

"Do we sit on it, Dallas?" Peabody wondered. "Wait for him to come back?"

It could come to that, Eve thought. "Let's see if we can get some information first. Is anyone in the apartment across the hall?"

"Give me a sec. Yeah," Callendar confirmed. "I've got two. One's either a kid or a midget."

"Good enough. Peabody, let's go talk to the neighbor. Everybody, just hold. If you spot him, don't spook him. The bastard can run."

She jogged across the street, scanning as she went. Nice neighborhood. A man could go out for a walk, drop down to the market, have a late lunch at the deli.

She didn't want Frye to wander toward home and spot her.

"He could be at work," Peabody suggested as Eve bypassed the door locks with her master.

"I don't think Alexander has him in all that much. He's the kind of guy who stands out. Why have somebody hanging around who people notice? Maybe he keeps a separate office somewhere. Or he's just out. Or he's killing somebody else either on his own or at Alexander's orders."

"Who's left?"

"Alexander would have a bigger slice of the pie, and remove a personal irritant if his half brother met an untimely demise."

"Have Pope killed *while* we're investigating three other murders with connections to him?"

"He may be that arrogant. My gut, and the probability I ran says he'll wait a few months. But, like Frye, killing's working for him. Why not use it again?"

They stepped off the elevator on eight, knocked on the door across from Frye's.

"Good security, but not good and paranoid from the looks," Eve commented as she studied Frye's door.

When the neighbor's door opened a woman in her middle thirties, hair tangled, clothes wrinkled, eyes exhausted stared out at Eve.

"Who are you?"

"Lieutenant Dallas, NYPSD." Eve held up her badge.

"You can't arrest me for thinking about buying shackles and chaining my son to his bed for a nap, can you?"

"It's probably not a smart thought to share with a cop."

"I'm past smart. I have no brain left. This is day three of the kid with the cold from hell. Why, why can't they fix a damn cold? I'd trade any technology for a cure."

She gestured behind her to a boy of about six who sat on the floor surrounded by a junkyard of toys. His nose was a bright red beacon in a heavy-eyed face that nonetheless clearly projected the devious.

"He's feeling better, and that's my hell."

"I want ice cream!" The boy shouted it and banged his heels on the floor. "I want ice cream!"

"You get nothing until after you take a nap."

His answer was an ear-splitting scream.

"Take me in." The woman held out her hands, wrists close. "Arrest me. Save me. They won't take him back in school until tomorrow, and that's only if I swear in my own blood, and I'm willing, that he's not contagious. His father's on a business trip, the lucky bastard."

"I'm sorry, but —"

"Ice cream!"

On the scream, the boy hurled the toy closest at hand. Eve dodged the toy truck that missed the mother by an inch.

"That's it!" The woman whirled. "I'm done. Sick or not sick, Bailey Andrew Landon, your butt's about to be as red as your nose."

Though Eve considered that a reasonable response, she put a hand on the woman's arm.

380

"Kid." She pushed back her coat so her weapon came clearly into view. "You've just violated Code Eighty-two-seventy-six-B. You've got two choices. Go take a nap, or go to jail. There's no ice cream in jail. No toys in jail, no cartoons on screen in jail. There's just *jail*."

The boy's sleep-deprived eyes went huge. "Mommy!"

"There's nothing I can do, honey. She's the police. Please, Officer." The mother turned to Eve, hands clasped as if in prayer, and with an almost insane grin on her face. "Please, give him another chance. He's a good boy. He's just tired and not feeling very well."

"The law's the law." Eve aimed a hard, cold look at the kid. "Nap or jail."

"I'll take a nap!" He scrambled up and ran as if pursued by demons. Eve heard a door slam.

"I'll be right in, baby," the woman called out, then turned back to Eve. "If you take off your boots, I'll kiss your feet. I'll give you a pedicure. I'll make you dinner."

"Just answer a couple questions and we're square."

"We'll never be square, but what do you want to know?"

"Clinton Frye." Eve gestured across the hall. "When did you last see him?"

"Yesterday, about five, I guess. I had some food delivered because I can't take Bailey out, and he was leaving."

"Did he say where?"

"He doesn't say anything. I haven't had a conversation with him in the five years we've lived here. He's not what you call neighborly."

"Any trouble with him?"

"No. But I'm not surprised to find the police at my door asking about him. He just gives off that . . . vibe. I've never seen anybody visit, never seen him with a single friend."

"And he hasn't been home, that you've seen, since yesterday?"

"That's right. He had a couple suitcases so I assumed he was taking a trip."

"Suitcases."

"Yeah. Anyone else, I'd have said something like, oh, you're taking a trip. Him? I just kept my mouth shut."

"Okay. Thanks."

"Are you sure I can't do anything else? Bake you a cake? I've never baked a cake, but I'd try it."

"No, thanks. We appreciate the time."

"He really is a good boy. He's just been so miserable the last few days. I think we'll both take a nap, and hopefully wake up human again."

"Good luck." Eve stepped back, looked across the hall.

"Do you think he went rabbit?" Peabody asked.

"I think he figured out we might come looking. The flying baby," she said again. "All those vids. He couldn't be sure somebody didn't get his face, and we wouldn't do just what we did with the sketch. So he took what he wanted, relocated. But he's not in the wind, not blown far."

She took out her comm, ordered a canvass, a check on cab pickups, and asked Callendar to come up to go through any electronics he'd left behind.

"Let's see what we've got," Eve said, and pulled out her master.

"That was good work with the kid, by the way," Peabody said. "Scaring him into thinking you'd throw him in jail."

"Who said I wouldn't have?" Eve countered and opened the door.

CHAPTER
TWENTY-ONE

The *absence* in the room struck Eve first. The living area seemed exactly the opposite — a nonliving area, lending the sensation the occupant had been gone weeks rather than a single day.

An oversized sofa, an oversized entertainment screen, a couple of tables, a single chair in the generous space made the room look lonely and lifeless. It lacked art, color, any softening or personal touches. Even the rug lay in a tired, listless gray.

Would he sit there, she wondered, the big man on the big couch watching the big screen? Would he sit, alone and silent while all those images of people and life and movement flashed by?

"This is taking minimalism to an extreme," Peabody commented.

Saying nothing, Eve moved through to the kitchen with all its shiny, glossy conveniences. She opened the refrigerator, found brew, a supply of bottled water, and sports drinks. She found energy bars and soy chips in a cabinet, and a set of four plates, four mugs, four bowls.

A lot of space for nothing, she thought, then moved to the wall of windows.

But he could stand here, look out, look down. Observe. Like watching a vid on his big screen.

She opened drawers at random. Four knives, four forks, four spoons, a couple of unused memo cubes.

"No junk," she said. "Nothing just tossed in a drawer or shoved in a cabinet to deal with later. No waste, except it's all waste. All this space, all this shine and he didn't know what to do with it."

With Peabody she moved off and into the bedroom.

The mattress sat on a frame, its brown spread tucked with military precision. She'd bet she could bounce a credit off it.

Again a single chair, and a large bureau, a computer station minus the computer.

"Check the dresser, the desk," she told Peabody and walked to the closet.

A generous space again, some built-in shelves and drawers. And empty.

"Not even a speck of dust left behind."

"Same here." Peabody shut a drawer.

She found the bathroom just as empty, including the laundry hamper. "Even took his dirty underwear, assuming he had any. Scrubbed out the sink. Took everything he wanted — and everything fit into two suitcases — and cleaned up after himself."

"Why?" Peabody wondered. "If we're here, we know who he is. We don't need his prints or DNA."

"I don't know. Let's check the other room."

And there, in the second bedroom they found pieces of Clinton Frye.

"Couldn't fit this in a suitcase," Eve stated.

He'd set up his own gym — machines, weights, a heavy bag, a speed bag, a glass-fronted cold box filled with more bottled water and sports drinks. A tidy stack of white towels.

Curious, she walked over to check his weight stack. "Set on three hundred pounds. Yeah, you're a strong bastard, Frye. He spent a lot of time in here, pumping, sweating — documenting, you bet your ass — his daily reps, times. Checking himself out in the mirrors, watching his form. This is what's important to him. This is where he lives."

Hands on hips, she circled. "We'll have a team do a search, but he didn't leave anything behind. He's precise in his way. This equipment isn't new, but we can still try to track it to the source. Let's find out where he got his food — his market, his take-out places, where he bought his clothes, had them cleaned. Let's get a sense of his routine."

"No electronics for EDD."

"The machines," Eve corrected. "There'll be records of his programs, his routine there. We take what we can get. It's not the money," she thought out loud. "Unless it's just the holding on to it. It's the doing, it's the having a job, a task. That's all he's got. And now he's found killing is doing."

"But with a purpose, right? Not killing just to do it, not bashing some guy on the street, at random. It's still a job."

Nodding, Eve gave Peabody an approving look. "That's just exactly right. Milo's goddamn lucky he's in lockup because whether or not Alexander ordered it, he'd be a target. A job. Cleaning up, just like he did here."

"He could go for Alexander."

"Yeah, he could, and very likely will. Dog bites master. It happens. But not yet," Eve calculated. "He's got us to deal with first. I'm going to work from home. I want you to have a couple of uniforms take you back to your place, and that means all the way in."

"Do you think he'd try to get to me like that?"

"I think he's gearing up for tomorrow night, but no point in taking chances."

She'd get more work done at home, Eve thought when she finally got into her car. And a little on the way, she decided, and contacted Mira.

She used the time it took Mira's admin to remind her of the doctor's busy schedule and the fact the doctor was about to leave for the day to set up the recording.

When Mira came on, Eve plowed right in.

"I'd like you to look at something, give me an opinion."

"Of course."

"This is Clinton Frye's apartment. You got the report we'd ID'd him?"

"Yes. And I've glanced over his data."

"Good. He left his apartment yesterday, early evening with two suitcases according to his neighbor."

"He's on the run?"

"I don't think so. I think he's just changed locations. Take a look."

She ran the recording, through the living room, the kitchen, and through to Frye's personal gym.

"Solitary," Mira said. "It's more than a lack of style or decor, but a lack of emotion, of connection. He may, of course, have packed up any personal items along with his clothes and electronics, but two suitcases wouldn't hold many."

"There's no sign there was any. No sun-fading on the walls where he might've hung art, for instance. And there's a sense in the place that this is how he lived. Alone and without connection."

"Except for the gym," Mira observed, "which is fully outfitted, well-stocked, and well-organized. This is, or has been, his interest. Which fits as he was both military and in professional sports."

"Semi-pro," Eve added.

"Yes, that's important, I think. He's never been quite good enough, or smart enough, or clever enough. He's never been, you could say, at the top of his game."

Until now, Eve thought. "The nightstands didn't have drawers or shelves or cabinets. Just two plain tables. No place for sex aides or protection. He could have kept that elsewhere, but according to the neighbor again, she's never seen anyone come to his place, anyone but him leave it. The canvass of the building indicated the same. People noticed him. He's a big guy, but they didn't know him."

"That lack of connection again, of companionship. Yet he played and worked with teams in the past. Sports and military."

"Yeah, I'm going to do some checking there, see why he left or if he was booted. The place was clean," Eve added. "Seriously clean. Even the drawers had been wiped out. His bed was made, right? A guy, living alone, a guy walking out and likely not planning to come back, but his bed was squared away like a bunk in boot camp."

"Yes. His training's important to him. Physical training, and maintaining his area. If you'd found clothes, they would have been tidy and organized. Plain, efficient, nothing flashy. Good quality. His dishes matched. Undoubtedly he bought them in a set, but he's kept them in that set. The fact that he took everything he could tells me he'd have been very unhappy to leave his fitness equipment behind. That means something to him. Replaceable, certainly. But it was his, something he used, enjoyed. Something that proved his strength and sense of self. He'll blame you."

"Only more reason to try for me, and it's going to be tomorrow. It's the only logical choice left. And going with his sense of self, his comfort zone, he'll go in as security. That's another logical choice."

"I agree. But, as he's shown, he's a scattershot planner. He may not take the logical choice. He may jump with impulse."

Eve considered that as she swung through the gates. "If he manages to get his hands on a ticket and come as a guest, or as one of the staff, we'll still spot him."

"He won't come at you directly. If he's able to infiltrate security, he'll know its weaknesses."

"Yeah. But so will I. Thanks. I'll see you tomorrow."

"Plan carefully," Mira warned. "When he comes, he'll be brutal."

"I'll be covered," she told Mira, and signed off.

She'd take an hour first, Eve decided. Get in a solid workout. Test and tune her body, clean out her head.

She sincerely hoped things didn't shake out with her going up physically against a guy who could bench-press three hundred pounds, but if it did, she wanted to be ready.

She had an insult waiting for Summerset, who she *knew* would comment about her being home early. She'd say it was Mortician's Day, and she'd taken off in his honor.

Quick and to the point.

But when she walked in, he wasn't on the lurk in the foyer. Out somewhere maybe, she assumed. Digging up mushrooms in some dank cellar or visiting a fellow ghoul.

Pleased at the idea of having the house to herself, she jogged up the stairs. And when she turned toward the bedroom very nearly squealed like a girl when he walked out of it.

Instead she said, "What the fuck!"

"Laundry must be put away," he said equably, "even the small collection of rags you call T-shirts."

The reminder he handled her clothes left her speechless. She lost any possible insult advantage when he just continued down the hall.

The best she managed was a muttered, "Damn it," as she walked in. Then nearly squealed again when the cat leaped out from under the sofa.

"That's two," she mumbled, letting out a breath. She was jumpier than she'd realized.

Definitely time to work out, sweat it out, tune it up.

A quick exam of her butt in the mirror reassured her. The sickly yellow bruises no longer resembled any land mass she could think of, but more a kind of blurry constellation.

Tits not too bad either, she decided, and gave her own sternum a poke. No thumping or twinging, not even when she tested her shoulder.

So she'd work those muscles, remind them they had a job to do.

She changed into a sports bra and workout shorts, and after a very short debate left the neatly folded and *not* ragged T-shirts in the drawer.

Inspired, she took the disc of the theater's layout, considering it as she rode the elevator down to the gym.

It took her some time — electronics always took her some time — but she managed to program three scenarios using the layout. She'd get in a good, hard run, she thought, and familiarize herself with the area.

She set a brisk pace. If she had to run, there wouldn't be time to warm up. Through the lobby, up stairs, down stairs, into the maintenance level, behind the screen, through the main audience area, up again, down again.

He was fast, she thought. She'd be faster.

He was strong. She'd be smart.

When Roarke came in she'd worked up a sweat.

He studied her view screen, raised his brows. "Did you program that yourself?"

"Yeah." She panted it out, not ready to quit. "I can do e-stuff."

"How long did it take you?"

"Shut up."

"Let's see if I can catch up."

"I've got . . . twenty-six minutes on you, and I'm taking it out to the street. You never know."

"You don't, no." He got on the machine beside hers, and in seconds had his synched with hers.

She wanted to ask him what he'd found at Milo's, what he knew, but realized she needed her breath to run.

She avoided people and street traffic, both of which she'd programmed the machine to throw in at random. By the time she'd circled around to run through the theater one last time she hadn't worked up a sweat. She was dripping with it.

"Okay. Okay." She slowed to a walk, sucked in air, guzzled down water. "Okay."

"Interesting scenarios," Roarke commented. "More so, I think, if you were in pursuit or being pursued. Mix it up, make a bit of a game out of it."

"Yeah, you do that."

She walked over, lay flat on her back, and told herself she'd stretch it out in just a second. For now she'd just lie there and watch him sweat.

God, he had the most excellent ass. She wouldn't mind taking just a little bite. Maybe a big one. And maybe she could stretch that hour into, oh, say, ninety minutes.

What better way to tune up?

She watched him while she stretched her hamstrings, her quads, so tight from the long run they all but pinged. And found another inspiration.

"I think I pulled something." She sat, head down, rubbing at her calf.

"What?"

"It's nothing. I just . . ." She let out a little hiss.

"Let me see." He shut off the machine, came over to kneel beside her. "What did you pull?"

"Your strings," she said, and yanked him down on top of her.

"Think you're clever, don't you?"

"Got you here, didn't I?" She hooked her legs around him, shifted weight, rolled him under her. "Just where I want you."

"Did you program this scenario as well?"

"No, this one I'm making up as I go. We're all sweaty." She leaned down to nip at his chin. "All worked up and wet. Why waste it?"

"I appreciate your sense of efficiency." He ran a hand over her butt, down the back of her thigh. "You're still tight."

"Why don't you stretch me?"

She started to lean down again, but this time he flipped her, pressing body to slick body and mouth to mouth in an explosion of heat that quaked down to the core.

Her system shuddered from it, then leaped toward it. Passion for passion, reckless and greedy.

She dragged at his shirt, short nails scraping along his skin, fingers digging into muscle. She craved his body, the weight, the shape, the glorious *feel* of it pressed into hers.

In moments she was breathless again, muscles quivering, heart slamming. Before she could catch that breath again, he drove her up and over with hands and mouth.

He felt her go, that shuddering release, the gasp and moan.

It wasn't enough, not yet, for either of them.

He yanked off her bra, knew his hands were rough. Didn't care. He wanted her wild, he wanted her desperate, wanted — needed — to drag her down into the madness with him.

She went. Her body alive and eager and reckless under his. Her hands, rough as well, grasping, taking.

No patience, no tenderness here. Not now. Only urgent, avid need gnawing to be quelled.

He set the animal in him free, and its mate met it as ferociously.

Crazed, careless, they stripped each other. He drove into her, hard and deep, shoved up her knees, wanting her to take more. To take all.

To take him.

She cried out, the pleasure tearing through her in keen, hot claws. Her hands gripped his hips as her own pistoned in response.

Fast. Faster, until her cry of release came in desperate sobs. Until her hands slid limply to the floor.

Until he choked out her name.

Her breath whistled out. She wondered her raging heart didn't jump out of her chest and dance around the room.

"Jesus!" she managed in a voice harsh with a sudden, impossible thirst. "Holy cartwheeling Jesus."

"Well, that's an image I didn't expect." He'd collapsed on her. He meant to roll off, give her air, and he would. In a day or two.

"I may really have pulled something that time."

"I won't be falling for that again. You've used me up."

"Good, because I don't think I can move."

With considerable effort, he rolled off her, lay on his back staring at the ceiling as she did. "We can stay here."

"Forever?"

"It's an option."

"Crime would overtake the city, and the financial world would collapse. We can't be responsible."

"I suppose not. I need water anyway. A gallon might do it."

"Just pour my share over me."

He gained his feet, realized he felt just slightly drunk. Pleasant enough, he decided as he retrieved two bottles of water. He gulped some down as he came back, then smiling down at her — her eyes closed, her face still flushed, tipped the bottle so cold water splashed on her belly.

"Hey!"

"As you requested." He sat beside her, offered her a bottle.

She drank half of it, sighed. "I figured on tuning up, clearing my head. Mission accomplished, with a big bonus." She laid a hand on his. "It's going to be tomorrow night."

"I suspect you're right."

"We'll be ready. Did you find anything at Milo's I can use?"

"Oh, we found quite a bit. More than enough already to put a number of people — including Alexander — in prison for considerable lengths of time. Milo keeps exceptional records, and has that insatiable curiosity of the hacker. Alexander opened his personal Pandora's box when he hired him."

"Anything on Frye? You got the memo on Frye?"

"I did, yes. Nothing by name. He called Frye the Ass-Kicker, or AK, but he did document the jobs by name. Marta Dickenson, time, location, fee. Parzarri, Ingersol, the same. Cocky little bastard, Milo. He made his own files on everything, secreted them away believing, obviously, no one would be smart enough or good enough to get to them and then past his shields."

"But you are, and you did."

"We were, and we did. And what about Frye, and hold that. It's a bit much, even for us, to sit here naked and sweaty talking murderers. Let's at least have a swim while you bring me up to date."

Because that wasn't a bit much, Eve thought, but welcomed the cool water, the time to run it all through for him.

"I need to make some contacts," she said when they'd dried off and changed. "I want to talk to Frye's commanding officer, get a sense of his military time, and talk to whoever his coach was when he played ball.

I should connect with Reo, just find out where they are with Milo. And figure out how to keep the feds out of this for another twenty-four."

"You could have Alexander tucked in a cage by then, but you want him there, at the premiere."

"I do. He thinks he's gotten away with it. He'll be all smug, puffing around in his tux, glad-handing with Hollywood. Those hands are bloody. Besides the petty satisfaction of arresting him in public, it'll give us time to coordinate, and have his operatives picked up. If the feds or the locals move on them too soon, somebody might alert Alexander. If we move on him too soon, it alerts them. I'd really like a clean sweep."

"Let's have a drink and some food. Mad sex has me hungry. And I think with Milo's data, and some I gathered myself, we may hand you a very big broom."

It was a damn big broom, Eve thought as she read over the files. It was the mother of all brooms. National, international, and global, between Milo the Mole and Roarke she had chapter and verse on Sterling Alexander's illegal operations. Names, locations, amounts. Add the audit files to it, and you had a bonanza.

The feds would wet themselves. But the trouble with feds was the bureaucracy. She didn't have time to waste untangling red tape.

But she had a respected judge, the NYPSD commander, and the chief of police to do that.

"Can you set up a holo-conference?"

"Yes, of course. What do you have in mind?"

"Judge Yung, Whitney, Tibble. They have connections and muscle. If the feds want Alexander, they not only have to play ball, they have to move on our timetable. I think the evidence we have, the scope of it's going to be enough of a lure to get the cooperation. It's a huge bust. They agree to that, and to prosecuting Alexander for the fraud and the rest *while* we prosecute for the murders? Everybody wins."

"And if they get greedy?"

"They can't move on Alexander until they have the data." Her ace in the hole, she thought. "They can't snatch the data from us until they go through the process. By that time, we'll have him. If they accept the terms, they get the glory. If they don't, they're afterthoughts."

"It could work."

"It could." Now she needed to make certain it would. "Let's add Reo in. And I need you."

"I think that was evident in the gym."

"Ha-ha. I also need your geek in case any of the data and the obtaining thereof needs to be spelled out. Shit, we should pull Feeney in, maybe McNab. Then if I leave Peabody out, she'll sulk."

"You make the contacts. I'll set it up."

She looked down at her T-shirt. "Is this a rag?"

"On what scale?"

"Come on."

"It's comfortable-at-home wear, and perfectly acceptable."

"That's right." She pointed at him. "Set it up."

398

It took more than two hours to report the details. She wished for coffee more than once, but didn't feel comfortable drinking it while briefing her superiors. She'd made the right call asking Roarke to participate. Feeney and McNab could explain the e-work, but Roarke cut through the ins and outs of the business quicker and more succinctly than she could have hoped to.

"I'm not second-guessing you, Lieutenant," Yung said. "I want to ask if you've thoroughly considered the bird in the hand. With everything you have, you could arrest Alexander tonight. It would be possible to have local authorities round up his operatives, or many of them."

"A bust of that size and scope, Judge Yung, information will leak. I don't want to give Frye any reason to postpone the plans he may be making. If he goes into the wind, I can't know when we'd find him, or when he may try to finish the job as he sees it. And I'm sorry to be blunt, Your Honor, but though Alexander ordered your sister-in-law's murder, and he needs to pay, Clinton Frye snapped her neck. Not only does he need to pay for that, and two other murders, but he needs to be stopped before he does it again."

"All right. If we're agreed, I do have some pull, and with the cooperation of the prosecutor's office can lay out a legal blueprint I believe the federal authorities will agree to."

"The prosecutor's office will assist in any way possible," Reo told her. "And we'll sweeten the pot with Milo Easton."

"We'll start the ball." Tibble nodded at Dallas. "This is good work, Lieutenant. Detective, all of you. It's good work. We'll start working on the politics."

"When we have it sealed, we'll let you know," Whitney told her. "Meanwhile, proceed as you've planned. And yes, good work."

When Roarke ended the conference, Eve hit the coffee. "God, I'm glad that part's over. Talk, talk, talk."

"Business is hell."

"And you love the front seat in hell. Okay. I'm going to fine-tune my op. Where the hell am I going to carry a weapon in that damn dress?"

"I thought of that. Actually, it's a little something I intended to give you for Christmas. You can have it now."

He went into his office, came back with a box.

"What is it?"

The look he shot her was a perfect mix of amusement and exasperation. "Why do you always ask when you've only to take off the lid?"

She didn't have a reasonable answer, so opened the box. "Oh, this is excellent." She drew out the sleek holster.

"It's worn on your thigh. Admittedly, not as easy a draw, but you'll have a weapon on you, and no one will know."

To test it, she stripped off her pants where she stood and strapped it on.

"Who knew I'd be giving myself a gift as well? That's quite a look, Lieutenant."

"My clutch piece will work. It'll work." She walked around the room to check the fit and feel. "Yeah, it'll work just fine. Thank you."

"Oh no, in this case, thank you."

"I used you up, remember?"

"Yet strangely, seeing my bare-assed wife walk around with a holster on her thigh re-energizes me. Your bruising in that area, by the way, is more like a faded map of Mexico tonight. *Olé*."

She laughed, unstrapped the holster, then pulled her pants back on. "It's a really good present."

"Merry Christmas."

"I'll test it out with my clutch piece tomorrow. I've got to be at Central by eighteen hundred."

"Understood. Trina's adjusted the schedule."

"No!" The simple horror slapped her silly. "No, no, no. I don't have time for that fuss."

"You'll be saved the time of fixing your hair and makeup, be able to talk the op through with Peabody, and be completely done before you go to Central. It's efficient."

"Fuck efficient," she complained.

"Be brave, darling," he said and patted her butt. "It'll be over before you know it."

It never was, she thought. But the bitch of it was suffering through it would give her more time to gear up.

The things she did for the job.

CHAPTER
TWENTY-TWO

She spent hours poring over the theater's blueprints, plugging holes where she found them, checking and rechecking possible routes, possible points of entry.

If he came in, he wouldn't get out again.

And if he didn't come in, she'd issued BOLOs and APBs, she'd sent his sketch, his ID, a written physical description to every transportation center, public and private, in the city. Despite the fact he didn't hold a valid driver's license, she did her best to cover vehicle rental agencies.

He could buy a vehicle, she considered. He could just take one of Alexander's company cars. But short of putting up roadblocks on every bridge and tunnel, she couldn't shut down New York in her pursuit of one man.

She weighed her options heavily on her own instincts and Mira's profile.

He'd come for her.

She looked forward to it. The idea of the confrontation, of taking down a killer took her mind off — mostly — a Trina session.

She told herself that personal torture was hours off, then spent so much time on 'link conferences, coordinating theater and NYPSD security, taking updates from her commander, she lost track.

When Peabody came into her home office, Eve didn't give it a thought. She'd asked her partner to come early to be briefed.

"Sorry I'm late."

Eve's head jerked up. "Late?" And her gaze shifted to the time. "You're late. Why are you late?"

"Traffic's insane. We figured since we had our fancy clothes to bring we'd take a cab instead of the subway. We hit jam after jam. We've still got time before Trina gets here to set up, and I've been monitoring all the memos going back and forth between you and the commander, you and the security head at the theater. You and everybody else. You've been at this all day."

"We've got civilians to think of, plus the freaking media. We have to be prepared to take him down when he comes because we don't want the civilians and media treated to a couple of dead or injured cops and the panic resulting therefrom."

"I vote against that."

"We also don't want civilians hurt, our suspect to escape, or the media blasting NYPSD screwups."

"Also vote nay."

"So the best possible outcome is we spot him, then take him down quick and quiet." Eve circled her neck, stiff from hours of work. "Which is very unlikely."

"Why? You've covered and recovered, you've got Plans A through Z. We're prepared."

"And he's big, he's fast, and not above hurling a toddler."

"I don't think there'll be any toddlers at the premiere."

"He can bench-press three hundred," Eve reminded her. "He could hurl both of us and barely break stride."

"Listen, Dallas, if you think it's going to go south, maybe we should cancel. Just not be there."

"I didn't say it's going to go south. We'll get him, but I'm not counting on the quick and quiet part. I'm holding for no civilian injuries and no panicked stampede."

"We can do this."

"We will do this," Eve corrected. "He's used to a chain of command. Army, paramilitary, organized sports. Probability is he'll go for me first. But that doesn't mean he won't take a run at you if he sees an opening. Where's your weapon?"

"With my stuff. We put everything in the guest room Summerset gave us. I was going to carry it in my clutch. I got a really nice bag with this fake ruby clasp on sale at —"

"Peabody."

"It looks good with the dress," Peabody said stubbornly, "and it's just big enough. But then I had a brainstorm."

"What kind of brainstorm?"

"Well, see, the dress has a kind of draping skirt, so I opened a side seam, and put in a kind of slit." She demonstrated with her hand low on her hip. "And I made a thigh holster."

"You *made* a holster?"

"It's sort of like a reinforced garter, but not very pretty. I didn't have time for pretty. I just made it last

404

night with what I had on hand. But it'll secure my weapon so I just have to slide my hand in the slit to get to it."

"You made a holster," Eve repeated, both puzzled and impressed. "The making stuff, that's Free-Ager roots. The holster? That's sort of anti-Free-Ager, but crafty cop."

"Crafty Cop." Peabody's eyes lit in appreciation. "I could make a whole line of them under that name, start up a police officer supply cottage industry. I saw the sketch of your dress. Where's *your* weapon?"

"Thigh holster, suited for my clutch piece. I didn't make it," she added. "I could use a damn slit."

"I don't think I could work that in your dress. I saw the sketch. It would ruin the line."

"Yeah, I'm real worried about that." But the important thing, Eve thought, was they'd both have quick access to their weapons. "Let's go over this again."

"Can I get coffee first? I figure since we're essentially on duty, wine's out, which is too bad because I'm still a little nervous about the whole red carpet thing."

"Be more worried about being attacked by a former semi-pro running back who outweighs you by over a hundred pounds."

"That's the other side of the nerves."

Fueled with coffee, they went over every inch of the operation, backtracked, rerouted, and then repeated.

Enough, Eve decided, and seconds later heard Mavis's signature laugh.

Maybe Trina hit Peabody's insane traffic. Maybe she was stuck in some hellacious traffic jam that would last for days and days. Maybe —

Then, beside the pink and gold pixie of Mavis came the doom.

"Hey! Are you ready to party?" Mavis asked and did two fast twirls. The twirls brought her close enough to see the screens, the blueprints, the operation outline on the computer. "You're working? Why are you working?"

"Crime never sleeps?" Eve ventured.

"Do *not* tell me you're not going." Mavis pointed index fingers at both Eve and Peabody. "This night is multimag. It's *your* vid, and Peabody and I have our total screen debut."

"We're going." Eve's gaze slid cautiously toward Trina who stood studying her as if she were smeared on a slide in Dickhead's lab. "We're going and working."

"And partying," Peabody added.

"You're going to look good doing all that when I get done with you." Trina, her hair piled in red and gold curls that made Eve think of a flaming tower, circled. Then she stunned Eve speechless by pinching Eve's cheek.

"Your skin's good. You've been taking care of it."

"I . . . Maybe." She slapped on the gunk Trina pushed on her. Not because she was afraid of Trina, very much, but because it felt pretty good. "Pinch me again and I'll flatten you."

"Relax. I'm going to give you both a hydro boost. It'll give you a nice dewy glow."

"I don't need a —"

"It's fast and relaxing." In her fearless way, Trina rolled over Eve's objections. "I prep and paint the canvas. Let's get started."

"I need to fill Mavis in on what's going on tonight."

"You can do that while your skin's hydrating. Mavis already had her boost. We're set up in the master suite."

"Already?"

"Do I paint you up like a slut? Make you look homely and haggard?" Trina demanded.

"You've painted tattoos on me without my knowledge or permission."

Trina just bared her teeth in a wide, wide smile. "Not tonight."

"Maybe I could get one. My dress has these rosebuds around the waist," Peabody explained. "A little rosebud tattoo would be cute."

"We'll take a look. Let's go," Trina insisted. "You changed the schedule so let's stick to it."

No arguing with that, Eve thought. Time to suck it up.

"Where's everybody else?" she asked as they trooped to the bedroom.

"McNab and Roarke are playing with the e-angle of the op," Peabody told her.

"Op? There's an op?"

Eve patted Mavis's shoulder. "I'll explain. Where's Leonardo?"

"He's still home with Bella. He's going to meet up with us at Central because you said we had to leave from there. We didn't want to leave her with the sitter so early. Carly's mag, she's the sitter. Completely on the sweet, and Bellamina likes her bunches, but it's a long time from now till after the after."

"They dote," Trina put in. "Belle brings out the dote in everybody."

"She's a dote magnet," Mavis agreed. "If there's an op that means there's a bad guy, and your bad guys kill people. We already had that on this vid, Dallas. No way to skip the replay?"

"Different killer, different play." Eve looked at the two portable salon chairs in her bedroom, wished she were anywhere else.

"You and Peabody first," Trina told Eve. "That way you can tell us what the hell's going on while you're boosting. Mavis, you can get us some of that bubbly Roarke told us about."

"On the job," Eve said.

"Me, too, but I get bubbly."

Trina opened one of her cases.

And so it began.

An hour later — or was it days — Eve had her face boosted, slathered, energized, and painted. Giving Mavis the basics helped a little, but when Trina got to her hair, she clutched.

"Don't do anything crazy."

"Define crazy."

"Look in the mirror."

"Ha-ha. I'm going to give it some shine, a little bit of lift. I was on set a few times, so I know how Marlo Durn had hers styled for the part, which is how I style yours anyway. I don't want to move too far away from that, but give it a little glam."

"I love mine!" Obviously enraptured, Peabody turned in front of the mirror.

She'd gone for a pileup, as Eve thought of it. Not a tower like Trina, but a kind of scoop and bounce, and a little rosebud blooming on the nape of her neck.

"I'm going to get my dress on so you guys can see the whole deal."

"Don't forget your weapon!" Eve called out as Peabody danced out of the room.

"Do you really think this asshole's going to try to kill you at the premiere?"

"Not only think," Eve said to Mavis, "hope. We're ready."

"Well, if he kills you, you're going to be a fine-looking corpse." Trina stepped back, eyed Eve critically, then nodded. "I am good." She gestured Eve up, pushed her to the mirror.

The hair didn't look that different, Eve decided. Fussier, and it seemed to go in more directions, but in a fancy way. Probably appropriate. There was a hell of a lot of gunk on her eyes, she knew because she'd watched Trina blending and mixing and smearing. But mostly they just looked bigger and a little dramatic. Probably appropriate again.

And no visible tattoos.

"Okay, it works."

"You look sexily uptown," Mavis decreed. "We'll go play with Peabody while you get dressed, then Trina can do me. We'll just hook up at Central."

"I thought you were already done."

With a rolling laugh, Mavis fluffed at her spiraling mop of pink-tipped blonde curls. "This is just regular. We're going out there for this."

Eve seriously couldn't stretch her imagination far enough for Mavis's definition of *out there*. She let herself take one long relieved breath when she had the room to herself again.

Op or not op, as far as she was concerned, the worst was over.

When Roarke walked in she was dressed, in a half crouch, one hand under the abbreviated hem of her dress. Smooth and quick she brought her arm up, weapon in hand, and shifted into cop stance.

"Do that again. I'd love a little personal vid."

"It's not as awkward as I thought, not after some practice."

"Holster it, do a turn. Let's have a look."

She hiked up the dress, rolled her eyes at his hum of approval, smoothed it down.

Would she see how she glowed against the deep, rich color of the dress? He doubted it. For a spookily observant woman, she missed much about Eve Dallas. It skimmed down her long, lean frame from its square neck where the teardrop diamond he'd given her lay above the subtle curve of her breasts, then floated ever so gently to mid-thigh.

"I needed to practice getting to it in these ankle-breakers." The shoes, the same deep color as the dress, sparkled like the diamond around her neck. "It's doable."

"I'm a very lucky man."

"Goes without saying."

"It can't be said often enough. You look stunning. Wear these." He took a box out of his pocket, flipped it open to a pair of long diamond and ruby earrings.

"Are they new?"

Her accusatory tone made him laugh. "They're not, no. I got them out as they work well with the dress. I'd another necklace in mind, but I think the Giant's Tear is exactly right, and a sentimental favorite. I'll be dressed in a minute."

"It's just wrong because you will be, and it took forever to make me up like this."

"Worth every moment. McNab and I — and Feeney — are set, by the way."

"Good." She turned back to the mirror, again drew her weapon.

So was she.

She dealt with Baxter's *hubba-hubba*, Trueheart's blush, Santiago's wiggled eyebrows by coolly ignoring them. Because she figured it helped tamp down nerves, she let Peabody do a couple exaggerated runway strides and turns to a chorus of wolf whistles.

Once the expected bullshit ran its course, she ran through the op, the positions, the codes.

"Any questions, problems, concerns, let me hear them now."

"Can we list popcorn as an expense?" Baxter wanted to know.

"No, and no corn. I don't want slippery fingers. Those of you on theater security or staff, head out now.

Those of you going in as guests, give it twenty. Checks every fifteen."

She scanned the room. "Let's go catch a vid."

Having Mavis along for the ride kept things light. Her *out there* took form in a cascade of shimmering blonde intersected with a multitude of thin purple braids that matched the color of her dress. Emerald green ribbon — the color of her shoes — twined around each braid. Beside her, Leonardo wore the emerald green in a long-jacketed tux with purple shirt and tie.

"I wish you could have some of this bubbly."

"After," Eve told her.

"You're not even afraid."

"Just that I might trip in these damn shoes."

"Those shoes are magalicious, Dallas. We all look magalicious."

"I might be sick." Peabody, in vivid gold, pressed a hand to her stomach.

Leonardo took out a little silver box, opened it. "Peppermints. They help. The first time I did a red carpet, I *was* sick. Remember, Mavis?"

"Poor babydoll." She cooed at him. "He barely made it to the john before he booted."

"You're not going to be sick." McNab rubbed her back. "You're going to have fun."

He wore what Eve supposed could be called a tux, except every time he moved or the light hit the material, colors shimmered. An instant of red, an instant of blue, an instant of gold.

It made her a little dizzy.

She looked away, checked in with her team.

"Everyone's in place. No sign of the suspect. Reineke reports the crowd at the barricades is bigger than expected." Nearly there, she thought. "Mavis, Leonardo, you're all right with getting out first?"

"No prob," Mavis assured her.

"I just want you out, and out of the way."

"Don't worry." Leonardo put his big arm around Mavis. "I'll take care of her."

"Oh, honey bear."

"No kissy-face, we're about to pull up. You mingle, and until this goes down I don't want you too close to me."

"We're all good. You stay that way," Mavis warned, and gave Eve a quick hug. "And you can follow my lead," she told Peabody. "Well, Dallas's for the op, but mine for the show. Remember?"

"Smile, but keep it easy and natural. Shoulders back, don't slouch. It's okay to wave. If I pose, oh God, shift my weight to my back foot. And looking-over-the-shoulder shots are usually flattering."

"Nailed it in one." Mavis patted Peabody's arm. "Here we go. Catch this bastard quick, okay, so we can have some fun."

The driver, one of Roarke's personal security team, opened the door. The sea of sound rolled in. Shouts, calls, flashes from cheap home cams and vids.

Leonardo stepped out first, offered Mavis his hand. And when she slid out, the sea of sound crested. Despite the circumstances, despite the tension, it gave Eve a boost to hear the crowds shout out Mavis's name.

"She's kind of a sensation," Eve observed. Then shifted modes. "Exiting vehicle now, Peabody to follow."

At her nod, Roarke got out, offered Eve his hand. Another crest of sound, and a stunning galaxy of lights greeted her. Faces and flashes and the bright red river of carpet.

Even as Eve's eyes tracked, searched out her man, the chants of her name, of Roarke's began.

She noted the route followed Peabody's intel, the river streaming straight, then spilling into an ocean of red. People in tuxedos and sharp suits, sparkling dresses, glittering jewels glided over it. Smiling, laughing, posing.

Clinton Frye wasn't among them.

Yet.

"Lieutenant Dallas is another sensation," Roarke commented.

"It's weird. And a little creepy. On the move," she added as they started up the red carpet.

It got weirder with the shouted questions, the mics stuck in her face, the effervescent enthusiasm of the media, and the half-wild energy of the people crowded against the barricades.

For what? she wondered. She walked these streets nearly every day, she'd probably — given the odds — busted at least one of the people out there cheering, calling, waving.

All this frantic excitement just to catch a glimpse of a cop? It made her embarrassed for New York.

When she whispered as much to Roarke, he laughed. Just laughed, then completed the embarrassment by kissing her.

414

And the crowd went wild.

"Cut that out!"

"I might resist," he said, lifting her hand to his lips, "if you'd stop delighting me."

"I'll work on it."

It was just part of the op, she told herself as reporters began to swarm. Just part of the trap.

Great night, looking forward to it, blah, blah, yeah, yeah, the dress is Leonardo. Whose shoes are they? They're my shoes.

For some reason this brought on a trilling laugh from some slicked-up fashion reporter.

She walked what she now thought of as a gauntlet, talking, smiling, searching, scanning, listening to reports in her ear — no sign yet — keeping both Mavis and Peabody on her radar. Then Nadine, in a liquid skin of silver, and Mira in deep and flowing coral. Dennis Mira, looking bemused and befuddled. God, he was so cute. The commander looking commanding beside his regal, slightly scary wife.

She heard her name called, glanced, and watched Marlo, her hand linked with Matthew's, hurry toward her.

"Dallas! You're here. I kept obsessing you'd be chasing down some murderer instead of making it. It's so good to see you both. We're really looking forward to tonight, and tomorrow."

"So are we." Roarke held out a hand. "It's good to see you, Matthew."

"It's great to be back in New York."

As requests pounded out for photo ops, Marlo smoothly shifted position, slipped an arm around Eve's waist.

Too close, Eve thought, then ordered herself to relax. With the sweep of blonde hair no one would mistake Marlo for her.

"We need to move inside," Marlo murmured in her ear even as she struck another pose. "Even with the heaters, it's cold out here, and they'll keep us as long as we'll stay."

"Sounds good. And right on schedule." Eve caught Peabody's eye, signaled.

Of course that generated more greetings, more photos, a round of you-look-amazings.

"You're getting cold," Roarke commented, and in his easy, unstoppable way, guided them all into the theater.

The carpet continued. The crowd was smaller here, more exclusive, and the noise more subdued.

And there, she thought, was Sterling Alexander, looking smug as he sipped a cocktail and cornered Mason Roundtree, the director.

She caught glimpses of Biden, of Young-Sachs. Continued to track.

Alva Moonie, her housekeeper beside her, stood off from the main group and held both of Whitestone's hands. Sympathy covered her face.

Across the lobby, Candida, in all but transparent white, held court with a gaggle of reporters.

"I wondered if they'd come," Eve murmured to Roarke. "Whitestone, Newton and his fiancée."

Roarke followed her direction. "It weighs on them. You can see it."

"Why come here, with all this hype and hoopla?"

"Some need people, distractions, noise in grief. Others need solitude and silence. But both can offer solace," he said as he watched Alva put her arms around Whitestone.

"I guess that's true."

Eve made her men, scattered throughout. Baxter, looking as though he'd been born in a tuxedo, chatted carelessly from all appearances with Carmichael who shined up very well.

But she saw the cop in their eyes, the alert in the set of their bodies.

She saw Feeney dragging at the knot of his tie. She wanted a quick word, but was intercepted by Julian Cross.

He caught her hands — looked at her with eyes not quite so blue, not quite so wicked as Roarke's — then lifted them to his lips. "I've been waiting for you."

He'd played the Irish accent well in the few outtakes she'd seen, but there was no trace of it now. "I wanted another chance to thank you for saving my life."

"Nadine saved your life."

"She did. She kept me from dying. And you figured out Joel killed K.T., tried to frame me, and would have killed me. More, doing that you gave me the courage to change my life. I'm sober, and I intend to stay sober."

"Good. I'm glad."

He bent to brush a kiss over her cheek, then looked at Roarke. "You're a lucky man."

"So I say myself. Sobriety looks good on you, Julian."

"And feels good on me. Thank you," he said again. "Both of you. I need to speak to Connie, and I know she'd like to see you both before tomorrow's . . . celebration," he said with a glint of his innate charm. "Mason's going to make a little speech before we go in, unless you can sneak in first and avoid the speech. We'll have more time to catch up at the after-party, and tomorrow."

"Sometimes you do more than save a life," Roarke said as Julian walked off. "You change them."

"He changed his own."

The noise level rose as drinks poured freely. Laughter rang out, kisses and air-kisses flowed.

She felt something, just a tingle at the base of her spine, started a casual turn. She heard the report in her ear seconds before she saw Frye. Deliberately she let her gaze pass over him, move off.

"I heard. I see." Roarke touched fingertips to her arm.

"He's wearing a security badge, so he may have access to those areas. Too many people in here. Better chance to take him quietly and without civilian injuries if we do it inside. I'm going in. He'll follow. I've got men in there," she reminded Roarke. "And I'm armed. That was the plan."

"Understood. And you understand I'll be coming in after him."

"Just don't rush it."

"Baxter, take Alexander — quietly — into custody as soon as I'm through the theater doors. McNab, send the green to the feds re the operatives. Clean Sweep starts now."

She gave Roarke a smile, strolled off toward the theater doors. Now when someone called her name, she ignored it or tossed a careless wave. She could feel his eyes on her, tracking her. Had to get closer, she knew. Couldn't risk another miss like before, so he had to get close.

A stunner, a knife. Maybe both.

Calculating, she slipped through the doors and into the gilded palace of the theater.

She'd never stepped foot in it before, but she knew every inch, every exit, every corner.

She drew her weapon as she eased away from the doors, moved carefully to the left. She needed him to come through, all the way, move beyond a chance to duck out again.

Two of her men would, as soon as possible, move over to those doors to block them. They'd have him in a box.

She walked a few more steps, deliberately turned her back to the doors.

Other eyes were on him now, eyes she trusted. And she'd hear him. She'd feel him.

She did both as the door quietly opened.

Closer, she thought, listening to the voices in her ear, listening to her own gut. Just a little closer.

She turned, weapon drawn. His face didn't change, but the hand holding the stunner jerked in shock.

"You may be able to get off a stream before I do, but believe me, if I miss, the other four cops in here won't.

You're going to want to lower that weapon, Frye, or you're going to get hit by multiple streams. It'll hurt like a bitch."

She saw his eyes dart left, right, saw his body shift, roll onto his toes.

"Nowhere to run," she began. "It's over."

Even as she spoke, the door swung open. "Eve Dallas!" Candida, obviously drunk, stumbled in. "I've got something to say to you, bitch."

Frye had fast hands to go with his fast feet. He grabbed Candida, swung her around, effectively blocking any shots, then launched her at Eve with the spin velocity.

A flailing fist slammed into her eye as the now screaming woman landed on her.

"You bitch!" Candida shrieked it, slapping, kicking. "You ripped my dress!"

Cursing, Eve shoved, pushed Candida into a heap then gained her feet. Streams blasted as Frye dodged and weaved through the theater. On another curse, Eve kicked off the damn shoes and sprinted after him.

Fast, she thought, but goddamn it, she'd be faster. Her right eye watered freely, blurring her vision and throbbing like a bad tooth.

He veered off from the exit as she or one of the others glanced a stream off his shoulder. He returned fire, wildly, leaped onto the stage like a receiver leaping for a long pass. She leaped right after him, set, fired.

This one hit him square in the back. He didn't stumble so much as sway, didn't jitter so much as shudder.

He swung around, weapon up, fear and fury on his face. Shouts of "Drop your weapon" rang out, her own joining them. But those angry eyes never left her face.

He couldn't miss at this range, she thought. Neither could she. She thought: *What the hell*, prepared to fire, braced for the return hit.

Roarke flew across the stage, a panther on the spring. He hit Frye low, at the knees, sent them both shooting through the air, across the floor.

"Restraints!" Eve shouted, dashed toward Roarke. Before she could get to him, he'd pulled back, plowed in, slamming a fist into Frye's face.

Twice.

"Okay, okay, okay. He's done. Suspect is down."

"LT." Jenkinson tossed her restraints, wincing as he climbed onto the stage.

"You hurt? You hit?"

"Nah, just burned me some. I'm wearing gear. It still gives you a jolt."

"I know. Sit down, get your breath. You, too," she said to Roarke, but he was already sitting beside the dazed Frye.

When Frye tried to rise, Eve stuck her stunner in his face. "You're done," she repeated. "On your face. Roll over on your face, hands behind your back."

When he groped at his pocket, Roarke jabbed him, not so lightly, in the side. "Looking for this, boy-o?" He held up a knife, let the light catch the blade. "I had it out of your pocket before you hit the bleeding ground. Put another hand on my wife, and it may find its way into you."

The best Eve could spare was a warning stare and shake of her head.

"Jenkinson, bag the knife, will you? The rest of you help me roll this big bastard over."

He bucked, drummed his feet, reminding Eve of the kid with the cold and his tantrum. "Jesus, you're *done!*" She had to expand the restraints to fit, and was fully, sincerely grateful she hadn't gone head-to-head with him. "Clinton Rosco Frye, you're under arrest for conspiracy to murder and murder for hire of Marta Dickenson, Chaz Parzarri, Jake Ingersol, human beings. Additional charges to come, including, you *dick*, assault with intent on police officers. Twice. Get him up, get him out — back door. Book him. I'll be in shortly."

She sat back on her heels, looked at Roarke while they dragged Frye to his feet. He'd yet to make a sound, but it took four cops to contain him and perp-walk him out the door.

Roarke nodded at her face. "Did he do that, bloody bastard?"

"Is it bad?" She touched her fingers to her cheek, her eye, sent them both throbbing madly. "Shit, shit. No, he didn't do it — directly. He threw that idiot Candida at me. Her fist hit me — I think her fist."

"First a baby, now a drunk idiot."

"Well, it's sort of consistent." She glanced back, saw the people crowded in the back of the theater with Peabody and Baxter and others trying to move them back. She gave Roarke a thin smile. "Sorry, but it looks like I'm going to miss the premiere. I need to deal with this."

"We'll miss it. I'm with you."

"You don't have to —" She broke off, shrugged. Of course he had to go with her. "Nice tackle, by the way."

"I spent some time on the pitch as a boy."

"On the — oh, right, Irish football. You've got a knack."

"I feel it in every bone," he said, and flexed his raw knuckles. "It was like hitting a wall of fucking concrete — tackle and punch."

She took his hand, studied the knuckles. "Looks like somebody else is going to need some ice."

"I'm after some in a glass, with whiskey over it."

"Who can blame you? Well, hell, I guess we put on a show anyway."

"We did indeed, and we'll make the after-party at some point." He rose, held out a hand to pull her up, then he laid the fingers of his bruised hand on her bruised cheek. They just smiled at each other.

"Dallas!" Peabody ran down, Eve's glittery shoes in her hand. "Ouch! You took a knock. Are you okay? Both of you okay?"

"Okay enough. We're going out the back. I'm going to finish with Frye."

"I'll go with you."

"I need you to stay here, handle this situation, calm it down, make sure that incredibly stupid Candida isn't hurt."

"But —"

"I can handle Frye, but I can't be here and there. I need you here. You're in charge here. I'll contact you when it's done. We'll hit the party if we can, otherwise, the rest can wait till Monday."

"All right."

"Alexander?"

"Baxter and Trueheart have him, and is he pissed."

"Sorry I missed that."

"Wow. Some night already."

"Some night," Eve agreed. She took Roarke's good hand, forced herself to put on her shoes. "It pretty much went as planned."

He laughed, gave her hand a squeeze. "Pretty much."

They went out the back, leaning on each other.

EPILOGUE

Eve sat across from Frye in interview. They'd put him in stronger restraints, and those restraints were attached to chains bolted to the floor.

He'd fought, according to Reineke, like a crazy, giant bastard every step of the way.

"Alexander rolled all over you," she told him. "He said you acted on your own, threatened him, coerced him. What do you say to that?"

What he said was nothing.

"Do you want him to walk?" Which was bullshit, as they had Alexander cold, as she'd just informed him and his four lawyers. He wouldn't walk outside of a prison for the rest of his life. "Don't you want to tell me your side of this?"

When he didn't respond, she settled back. "Okay, I'll tell you what I know, what I can prove, and what will put you in a concrete cage for the next three lifetimes. You abducted Marta Dickenson with the aid of Milo Easton, and on the orders of Sterling Alexander. You forced her into the empty apartment below the new WIN Group offices, questioned her, struck her, terrorized her, then you snapped her neck. Now

Alexander wants to claim the neck snapping was your idea, and Easton wants to say he didn't know what was going on. What do you say?"

Nothing.

"I can take you through the other two murders the same way, with Alexander claiming ignorance or coercion, with Milo claiming to be oblivious, and you acting on your own. If you don't tell me your side, you go down for everything, and they get a slap on the fraud. Are you that stupid?"

Fury leaped into his eyes. "Don't call me stupid."

And these, she thought, were the first words she'd heard him utter. With them, he'd shown her his weak spot.

"I'm asking if you are stupid. If you're just going to bend over and take it while Alexander screws you, question answered in the affirmative. I know he hired you. I know he paid you. I know he told you what to do. Show me you're not stupid. Show me you're not going to just sit there and let him hang everything on you."

She leaned in. "He doesn't have the right to make you the patsy. He's the one who thinks you're stupid, but we both know he gave the orders. You just did the job. You just followed those orders."

"He says take the woman, find out what she knows, what she did. Take what she's got, then shut her up for good. Get rid of her. *I* decide what to do and how."

"Okay." Face impassive, she sat back again. "You think for yourself, I get that. How much did he pay you to take her, to question her, to kill her?"

"Twenty-five thousand. I said cash. He tries to make it less, tries to string it out, like always. I said cash, now. I'm *not* stupid."

"That's right." Moron. "Like always? Had he hired you to get rid of somebody before?"

When he said nothing, she gave him a mild prod. "It goes to pattern, see? Alexander's pattern. Getting other people to do the work, trying to go cheap, thinking he's so much smarter than you are."

"He just pays for me to mess them up. Give them a pounding, break an arm maybe."

"Then Dickenson was the first time Alexander hired you to murder anyone."

"It cost more. Twice more. I told him. I took her stuff after, took her coat. Nice coat. So it's a mugging. You wouldn't know different if that asshole Milo hadn't told you."

"You made it look like a mugging, and that was good thinking. They were stupid, Frye, having you do it in that place, a place that connected to Alexander. That's not your fault. Then there's Parzarri. How was that arranged?"

"He —"

"Who?"

"Alexander, who you think? He says the accountant has to go. He screwed up, he's a . . . a liability. He says, 'Find out if he talked, then get rid of him.' I say it's more. It's a man, and it's not so easy as the woman, so it's more."

She nodded as if appreciating his business acumen. "You do the work; you set the price. How much?"

"Thirty thousand. He doesn't want to pay, but that's my price, so he pays. And I think how to get the ambulance, and the rest. So I tell him he has to get Milo, and that's more money. But he pays. He just says do this, but I figure how."

"The same with Ingersol?"

"He acts like I'm nothing, like he's better. Calls me Bubba. My name's not Bubba." Angry color streaked his wide cheekbones. "I don't work for him, but he acts like I do, like he can tell me what to do. Alexander says he's the liability, too, and get rid of him. I charge the thirty, but I'd have done it for less. I liked doing it. He made fun of me, treated me like I'm stupid. I'm not stupid."

"Sterling Alexander hired you, paying you twenty-five thousand dollars to kill Dickenson, thirty to kill Parzarri, and thirty to kill Ingersol."

"I told you already. He said get rid, I said pay me this much."

"All right. Why did you try for me and my partner?"

"Alexander doesn't like you coming around, asking questions. He said you were a couple of nosy bitches. You especially because you married money and now you think you're his equal. He says get rid of both of them, and do it fast. I said two cops, I get sixty thousand. He says two, you bargain the price. He says fifty. I think fifty's pretty good. You didn't fall down. You were supposed to fall down. But I'm fast. I've always been fast."

She didn't bring up the baby, no point in it at this time. "You missed."

"He wants his money back, but I say I'm not *finished*. I don't like how he looks at me. I think maybe he'll send somebody after me. Or maybe somebody saw me good enough and you'll come. I have to get another place. I liked my place, but I have to get another. And I have to finish. You start, you finish. That's that."

"Were you going to kill me and my partner tonight, Frye?"

"Should've. It's Milo's fault. He told you too much."

"Not really. I figured it out. I'm smarter than you. And I'm not a coward. You ambushed an unarmed woman, smothered an injured man after you strapped him down, beat a man to death after you stunned him. You tried to stun me in the back. You're a coward, you're a killer, and you're cooked."

He surged up, tried to grab for her, but the chains held him back. "I'll kill you. I'll get out and I'll kill you."

"You won't do either, but you can take some satisfaction in knowing Alexander's going to live out his life in a cage right along with you, and Milo makes three. And all the people he had out there defrauding, stealing, ruining people's lives? They're going to do some long, hard time, too. You won't be alone."

She rose. "Interview end," she said and walked to the door. "Take him back."

Four burly uniforms came in, and she walked away, toward her office. She stopped, surprised to see Pope sitting on a bench in the corridor. He got to his feet. "Lieutenant. I . . ."

"What are you doing here?"

"Sterling. I was told . . . His lawyer said he won't see me."

"Why do you want to see him?"

"He's my brother. Whatever he's done, he's my brother."

"You knew, at least some of it, didn't you?"

"I didn't know about the killings. I swear to you. I thought, after Jake . . . I wondered, but it didn't seem possible. I did know — think, suspect? I'm honestly not sure. About him, possibly, misappropriating funds. I would have helped him. I would've tried. He's always shut me out. I always try to open the door." Tears swam into his eyes. "But he always shuts me out."

"You can't help him, Mr. Pope. Your company is going to need help, and a lot of it. Your mother helped build that company. Maybe the thing you can do is look after it now, fix what's wrong."

"He didn't need the money. He didn't need it. He didn't need to do any of this."

"Sometimes it's not about need, and all about want. I'm sorry for your trouble, Mr. Pope. Go home. Go home to your family. It's the best thing you can do right now."

"Yes. You'll need to talk to me again."

"I will, and the feds will. But not tonight."

"All right. All right. I'll go home. But . . . if he changes his mind. If he asks for me . . ."

"We'll let you know."

Eve watched him go, weighed down by sorrow.

"It's a sad thing." Roarke stood just inside the bullpen. "He's loyal to something that doesn't exist. And he knows it, but he can't *not* be loyal."

"I hope he gets over it. His worthless, greedy, murderous half brother is going away, far and long."

"Did you get what you needed from Frye?"

"All of it, after he decided to talk. He's . . . a little off. Maybe too many hits on the field, or maybe he's just wired wrong. His ex-coach said he got so he couldn't follow the plays, couldn't or didn't listen to them. They cut him loose. But he knows right and wrong, he knows what he did, and he's proud he thought of how to do it in each case, how he negotiated the fee. He's not crazy, not mentally defective. He's just mostly empty."

He stepped to her, gently touched his lips to her injured eye. "Let's put some ice on that."

"It's not that bad."

"Let's see." He brought out his PPC, keyed in. "Here's something that's making the media and Internet rounds." He turned it around so on screen she saw herself, eye already going purple, smiling at Roarke as he smiled down at her, hand on her cheek, knuckles raw.

"Damn it. They took pictures? They're taking pictures when we're dragging a killer away?"

"I like it."

She started to sneer, took another look. "You know what? You're right. It's us. Absolutely us, and I like it, too. I want a copy. I want to put it in a frame for my desk."

"Do you now?"

"Home office," she qualified. "But yeah. It's us. It's who we are, and I like who we are."

"So do I. Ice for the eye."

"And the knuckles."

"And," he agreed. "We'll tend each other in the car. Is it for home then, or the party?"

She thought about her bruised eye, the lateness of the hour. Thought of the picture of the two of them. Who they were.

"Fuck it. Let's party."

Delusion in Death

J. D. Robb

The scene that greets Lieutenant Eve Dallas one terrible evening in New York is more shocking than anything she has ever witnessed. The downtown bar is strewn with bodies — office workers who have been sliced, bludgeoned or hacked to death with the nearest weapon available, turning on each other in a desperate blinding rage.

As Eve and her husband Roarke — who owns the bar among his many properties — investigate the city, they link the attacks back to the Urban Wars and the chemical warfare used all those years ago. With another slaughter imminent, Eve must turn to unexpected sources to stop a killer pursuing revenge by creating mass carnage . . .

ISBN 978-0-7531-9234-4 (hb)
ISBN 978-0-7531-9235-1 (pb)

Celebrity in Death

J. D. Robb

"We've got a corpse that looks like one of the investigators, a houseful of Hollywood and a media machine that's going to eat it like gooey chocolate."

Lieutenant Eve Dallas is panicking — but she's not at a crime scene. Forced to attend a celeb-packed party for a new movie based on her most famous case, she is surrounded by actors who look like everyone in her life. Then brutal reality crashes through the sparkly façade.

There's been a murder. The obnoxious actress playing Eve's partner, Peabody, has been found facedown in the roof-top pool. It's hard to find anyone who didn't have a motive for killing her, but Eve must fight to keep a clear head and stop a calculated killer.

ISBN 978-0-7531-9232-0 (hb)
ISBN 978-0-7531-9233-7 (pb)